The Essence of Fear

By Leigh Kenyon

The Essence of Fear

Copyright © 2015 by Leigh Nelson Kenyon

skenyon@tampabay.rr.com

ISBN-10: 0692398317 – ISBN-13: 978-0692398319

To my grandmother, Connie.

Chapter 1: Nightmare – Jessica

Thirteen-year-old Jessica Knight walked briskly down the hall of her school, her thick black hair pulled into a ponytail. She was enervated from all the studying going on for all the tests that were being taken. She had already pulled three all-nighters without meaning to, and had fallen asleep at lunch to make up for it. She had paid for that too, because she was left with a growling stomach for the rest of the day.

It was only a matter of time before she fell asleep in class as well.

Jessica didn't know that she was dreaming. Because, in her dream, she was still awake, in her same classroom. But, things suddenly began to change.

Her teacher turned from writing on the blackboard, and instead of a kind, smiling face, there was a twisted mask of evil. The corners of the insane smile stretched all the way to the huge eyes that were a spinning vortex of red and white. The skin on her teacher's face sagged, giving the impression of being dead.

The teacher's head jerked back so far that Jessica couldn't see her face anymore. But when it jerked forward again, Jessica let out a scream. Her teacher's face began to contort. The skin began to peel away, her hair began to fall out, and her mouth was still an insane smile but yet it was stitched closed. Her eyes seemed to grow even wider, the swirling red and white tumbling around in the teacher's widening eye sockets.

The teacher's head jerked back again, and blood burst out of her exposed throat. Jessica screamed again and again as rips appeared in her teacher's shirt and blood gushed out of those too. Blood spattered her classmates, the board, the floor, the wall, everywhere.

The teacher took a staggering step toward her, a hand that was not a normal hand outstretched...

Jessica suddenly realized she was the only one screaming. And then, terror filled her from head to toe as all of her

5

classmates twisted in their seats, wearing the same horrific expression the teacher had worn moments before. And the same gruesome transformation began.

The teacher now was as black as coal, with emerald green eyes and acid green hair that fell past her waist. She wore a cape of black, and holes were burned right through her body. Her smile was no longer insane, but a grim line of hatred.

The students began transforming into miniatures of her, only with blue bug eyes and short-cropped teal hair. Jessica let out a blood-curdling shriek as the hand of the creature that used to be her teacher landed on her shoulder...

"Jessica! Jessica! Wake up!"

Her teacher watched, a look of panicked worry on her face, as Jessica's eyes snapped open. The girl let out a strangled breath.

"I...saw...her."

"Who?" the teacher asked.

"The woman...demon...with acid green...hair."

Her teacher stiffened. "I need to get you to the hospital. Fast."

Jessica's classmates murmured anxiously. Why? Why was Jessica going to the hospital?

It was just a dream, right?

They didn't know that it wasn't just a dream, and that Jessica wasn't heading to a hospital. Nothing even close to that.

Chapter 2: Reminiscence – Jessica

I had seen her before. The woman with the acid green hair. I don't think it was a dream that time.

The memory is faint...I don't remember much. All I know is that I was in bed. I was little...I think. Yes, yes, I was about six or seven. Which is probably why, as I understand now, everyone thought it was a nightmare I had. A terrible one, sure, but nothing real.

I believed them, until today's nightmare.

When it all came rushing back, I knew that what I had seen seven years ago was not a dream, not a nightmare. It was too real.

I was under the quilts in my own bedroom. It was storming fiercely, and I couldn't sleep. Lightning illuminated the briefest of scary shadows, which were becoming more daunting with each strike. The thunder rumbled like a death march, the wind howled like the angriest wolf. The rain came in unrelenting sheets, hitting the windows with such force I was sure one more drop would cause them to crack.

Anyway, only my eyes peeked over the top of the sheets, as I sat there huddled in a quaking, scared little ball. I was too frightened to go wake my parents. Then, the shadows began to detach themselves from the walls. I'm sure my eyes were as wide as dinner plates when that began to happen, but I couldn't scream. For some reason, I wanted to see what was going to happen.

The shadows slowly began to swirl, forming a woman with a long black cloak, a cape of acid green hair, and a black body with gaping holes in it. Her eyes were also an acid green, and by looking at them I was sure she could burn a hole right through me.

She approached me slowly, almost as if she was wary of what was going to happen to her if she got too close to me. Would I start screaming, calling for my parents? I was a risk to her, but a necessary one. Whatever for, I had no idea.

I did start screaming, though, louder than all the thunder, lightning, wind, and rain in the world. I heard my parents' footsteps pounding down the hallway. They would be here soon, and they would catch her.

The woman let out a small hiss of frustration, and I saw she had two fangs and a forked red tongue like a snake. She cast me one last murderous glance and swirled back into shadows.

When my parents reached my room, I had stopped screaming, but was now crying uncontrollably. Once they got me calmed down and heard my story, they were convinced I had just experienced a very bad nightmare. I had insisted it was real for the first few minutes, but then succumbed to their comfort.

I put the woman with the acid green hair out of my mind and never thought about her again, until today. Only a fool would think that she would never come back.
What a fool I've been.

Chapter 3: Scaretale

"This fog is so spooky, Thomas! I can't see a thing!"

"Calm down, Aidrianna, I think we're almost there... "

Out of the concealing mist which appeared to be ever-present in this part of the forest, two kids, no older than thirteen, stepped into view, the bare trees on either side of them only serving to give this section of the wilderness a more mysterious allure. As the fog began to clear, the two kids finally saw their destination - a large stone building that resided in the center of the forest. No noise from inside resounded, no opening and shutting of doors. No distant echoes of the screams that had once inhabited the edifice in question in those centuries past when it was still in use.

"Ha, I knew we'd find it around here!" Thomas cheered.

The gazes of the two visitors rose to the top of the gate, where faded, engraved words were visible, enduring over the centuries since it had first been built:

Graystorm Asylum.

The brother and sister stared upward, the foreboding structure appearing to leer down at them, as if daring them to enter the decrepit halls at their own risk. Both members of the party carried small bags over their shoulders, packed with the provisions for the night ahead that they planned to spend in this forbidden sector of the forest. As they looked at the towering asylum, the kids wore opposing expressions - the girl with long brown hair bore a gaze that expressed she would rather be anywhere but there, while the boy, who had short brownish-red hair and plenty of freckles, was imagining that he was embarking on a grand adventure.

"W-Why did you bring me here again?" Aidrianna asked quietly, attempting to control her trembling. "You know I really, really don't like scary things."

"Because," her brother responded, as if stating the obvious, "remember that bet I made the other day?"

It was the day before All Hallows' Eve, and Thomas was partaking in one of his favorite activities - reading about the brave adventurer Bree Farnsworth. *So what if it was a girl—it was an awesome read. Currently, he was racing through* The House on Haunted Hill, *the cover adorned with an illustration of the titular character entering a large stone building, the surroundings dusty and decrepit with age. This was about the fifth time he had read it, though it was both for the sake of the upcoming holiday and the fact that the next book in the series was due to be out the following week.*

"Hey, you want to go to some place really *like that?"*

Thomas looked up from his book to see a tall kid with bright red hair and blue eyes, who was known as David. He wore an expression that seemed rather curious.

"I just saw the cover of the book you're reading and remembering the legends of an old cursed asylum that's said to be around here. I've seen drawings and it looks kind of like that."

"A cursed asylum?" Thomas suddenly started paying attention, David now having his full attention. That prospect sounded like an adventure waiting to happen.

"Yup," David turned his head in the direction of the Nightmare Forest, just on the outskirts of town. "It's called Graystorm Asylum. They say that a bunch of people used to be tormented there because they were insane, but that was centuries ago. I've even heard some kids say that the place was cursed."

"Cool!" Thomas placed his bookmark into the spot he had been reading and turned the cover upright. "So it really looks kind of like this?"

The redheaded boy nodded. "I thought that was Graystorm Asylum at first until I got a closer look at the cover..." He paused before a smile lit up his face. "Hey... how about you and I make a bet?"

"What kind of bet?"

David smirked. "Go to Graystorm Asylum on All Hallows' Eve, stay there all night, and come back the next morning and describe the experience in detail." David moved his head closer, knowing just how much Thomas liked a challenge. "And I mean a lot of detail. Enough to prove without a doubt that you were there."

Thomas was prepared to meet this challenge head on. "What do I get if I win?"

"Twenty dollars. And if you lose you have to give me twenty."

The eager thirteen-year-old let out a small but excited squeal. "That means if I win, I'll have just enough money to go get a signed copy of the next book!" Grinning widely, he accepted the challenge. "You're on!"

Before Thomas could take off, David held up a hand to stop him. "Hold it. There are a few rules for this.

"Rule number one, you can't leave the asylum for any reason, so if you plan to take anything, stock up. Rule number two, you have to take someone with you."

"Why?"

"So I can trust someone that you actually went there and didn't fake it."

Thomas stood up and crossed his arms in defiance. "Are you saying you don't trust me?"

The deadpan expression on David's face made it clear that the answer to that question was "no".

A sigh of exasperation. "Okay, okay, fine. I'll take someone with me."

"Oh, and one more rule I forgot - bring back a souvenir." David's narrowed eyes matched Thomas's in its challenging look. "Bring some relic back from the asylum as absolute proof."

The thought of bringing back some sort of object from the asylum was causing Thomas to feel more and more like an adventurer with each passing second. "What kind of souvenir?"

"Anything," said David. "A scythe, a list of tortures, living shadows, a map, a magic notebook that kills whoever's name you write in it, I don't know, just something as proof of your visit."

Thomas's blue eyes narrowed, and he extended his hand to meet David's in a high-five. "Challenge accepted."

"Wait, I forgot rule number four."

"What?"

The smile on David's face looked almost too cheerful, and Thomas had to admit that if he was going for a villain role in a play, he could be pretty darn good at it with his expression and voice.

"Don't die."

As Thomas completed his account of the Bet, Aidrianna only seemed more afraid than before. "But why'd you have to bring *me* here?"

Thomas tried not to look as exasperated as he felt. "You're my sister, and David knows that you wouldn't lie about our adventure when we come back."

Aidrianna squeaked in reply, attempting to focus her thoughts away from replacing "*when* we come back" to "*if* we come back".

"Wow, it really *is* like that one abandoned house in *The House on Haunted Hill*..." A grin spread across Thomas's face, his brown and red hair standing out in the sinister lighting. He nudged his companion. "Come on, Aidrianna, time for us to take a trip inside! Sounds like it could be fun, right?"

Aidrianna cringed and stepped back, wide blue eyes gazing upward at the imposing building. This definitely did not look like the kind of friendly place she was used to back in town, and she wanted nothing more than to get as far away from the creepy old asylum as possible. "Um...I'm not sure, Thomas. I've heard some grim stories about Graystorm Asylum."

The words got Thomas's attention. "Like what?" Though he recalled David mentioning the asylum was centuries old, he hadn't elaborated on any particular stories.

The girl whimpered slightly, averting her eyes from the asylum in question as her long brown hair hid her face. "When I mentioned I was going there with you tonight, Rose told me that the Demon King and Nightmare Princess used to run the asylum."

"Demon King? Nightmare Princess?" Blue eyes bright, Thomas took a step closer to his sister. "Who are they?"

Aidrianna gulped. "She told me that Demon King and the Nightmare Princess were people really involved in dark magic. The Demon King wanted nothing but power, and he became so consumed by the dark magic that he turned into a living shadow himself, and he used his dark magic to form a person from crystal, almost as shadow-like and evil as he was. They built the asylum and trapped the patients here and put them through terrible tortures until they tore each other apart." She swallowed hard. "And I also heard they'd morph the patients into crystal and shatter their bodies if they resisted long enough, and then they'd become part of the building and..." She closed her eyes and shuddered at the thought, stepping back and looking like she was going to run out of there any second.

If anything, that only seemed to make Thomas more eager to go in. "Wow, a place with a cursed history? Sounds awesome!"

Aidrianna stammered, eyes wide. "But Thomas... what if the stories are *true*?"

"Relax," Thomas assured his sister, appearing to harbor none of the fear Aidrianna possessed. "This place has been abandoned for centuries. We'll probably just see a few of the cells and a skeleton or two-"

Aidrianna squeaked.

"-But that doesn't mean that we'll run into anyone. Even if it is true, they're long gone."

"I hope you're right..." Aidrianna trailed off, her fears still not entirely eased by Thomas's attempt at consolation. It was clear that the story of this being a terrible legacy to the power of shadow magic was still nagging at her mind.

Unbeknownst to the pair, the old asylum wasn't completely abandoned after all. A lone figure watched them from a window in the asylum's higher towers, the windowpane dusty with age from the outside.

Their onlooker was a young woman with pallid skin and short white hair with ice blue eyes.

"Well, well, well..."

The expression on the woman's face brightened, her pale blue eyes appearing to house a rekindled spark. "Hmm, about time some others showed up. It was starting to get a little dull around here with the same old patients to torment..." She turned around, peering into the darkness behind her. It was clear that she wasn't the only being watching the new arrivals.

At first, it seemed that no one was there, only the darkness keeping the woman company. But soon enough, the shadows appeared to condense into a more solidified form. From out of the gloom, two bright red eyes materialized, gazing at the woman curiously.

"Doctor, I see we have some new guests arriving, I'll get everything ready for them." The grin on the woman's face grew, looking much more malicious than kind.

A shadow-like man stepped out of the darkness to stand beside her, letting out a slight huff of irritation. "Not right away. Come now, Roxy, they're our guests... Let us make their last moments *nice* for the time being..."

The woman bowed in respect, a smirk on her face that she was relieved her guests couldn't see. Though there were times where they wanted to see their "guests" on edge right away, they did like to have a little fun pretending every now and then. Her superior did have a satisfyingly sinister habit of tricking visitors with false placidity at first before their torment began.

"Yes, of course, Doctor Michael."

With a mixture of curiosity and fear, the two kids below stepped forward through the heavy iron gates of the asylum, all sound around them appearing to be muted. There was no blowing of the wind against their skin, no crinkle of dry leaves under their feet, no creaking branches reaching out to grab them. There was only the faint sound of their steps as their feet propelled them forward.

Reaching the door and pushing it open with a creak, the two of them stepped inside.

Neither noticed that in that same moment, the rusted gates of the asylum closed, and an ethereal shield briefly flashed above.

15

Roxy smiled from the upper floor. It was time to go greet the new visitors.

"And Aidrianna and Thomas were never seen again."

Chapter 4: Research – Kevin

"So no one knows what happened to them?" Kevin Smith asked his mom, Fleur, as she concluded the story of Graystorm Asylum.

She shook her head, her blonde hair shining in the pale candlelight. "No. No one ever ventured into the asylum to see if they were still there, or if there were bodies, or...anything at all."

"But it's just a legend, right?" asked Morgan, Kevin's twin sister. Her dark brown hair framed her face with a sharp edge, giving her unusual violet eyes a severe look.

"Of course," their mom said, now nodding. "It might have never happened at all."

"Was there ever a Graystorm Asylum to begin with?" Kevin asked, slightly tilting his head to one side, curious.

"Yes, actually, and it closed down about two centuries ago, just like in the story. But it wasn't evil."

"How do you know? It was before your time," Kevin challenged.

"Well...don't tell anyone, but..." Fleur leaned forward until she could whisper softly without anyone but her kids hearing what she was about to tell them, even though no one else was in the house.

"When I was your age, I was dared by some friends to go spend the night there, along with two or three other girls. We went, of course, and while it was spooky and creepy, there were no ghosts, no spells, and no tortures; there wasn't even a skeleton in sight. And we explored the entire place."

Morgan gave a small snort of laughter. "*You*, mom? *You* explored Graystorm Asylum? And what are you always telling us...

"'Never go dabbling in something that doesn't concern you, never climb the ruins, never stir up the ghosts of memories that are best left alone, never go against an adult's rules,'" Kevin and Morgan recited in perfect harmony while rolling their eyes.

"I couldn't have said it better. And yes, I did. And I tell you those things so you won't do what I did."

"But you said nothing dangerous was there—"

"I didn't say that. I said there was no *evil* there. But there were plenty of loose steps and floorboards, and all that dust would cause *anyone* to have an asthma attack. Just because there's no evil doesn't mean you aren't in danger.

"Now off to bed, go on!" their mom chided.

As Morgan and Kevin pushed themselves to their feet, Morgan said, "How do we know you were in Graystorm Asylum? Can you prove it?"

"Yes, I can, actually. Wait one second." Fleur disappeared into her room for a second, and then came back, holding a damaged photo. In the picture were three girls, all with silly-slash-scared expressions on their faces, standing in a dark hallway in front of a sign that said: Ward C, Up and Dining Hall, Down. Above the sign was a plaque that said: Graystorm Asylum, Level 3. One of the girls in the picture had long, curly black hair and brown eyes, the one in the middle had bright red hair and green eyes, and the final girl had short, straight blonde hair and unmistakable amethyst eyes. Their mom.

After the kids had finished staring at it, their mom tucked the photo into the back pocket of her jeans. "Believe me now?" Morgan nodded. "Well, then, good-night, you two." Kissing her kids on the top of the head, she turned and walked to her bedroom.

Morgan and Kevin looked at each other. "Tomorrow. Library," they said together.

The next day, they rode their bikes to the library. The old building sat on an empty lot with trampled, waist-high grass. The library itself was made out of stone that was 'as old as time,' as Morgan always said, the windows were grimy and the whole building just had an abandoned feel to it.

As they climbed up the steps and pushed open the old oak

doors, they were greeted by the smell of musty old books and a strong essence of rose perfume. An old woman with completely white hair sat behind the check-out desk, her nose buried in what looked to be the first edition copy of the first book ever written.

As the door swung shut behind them, the woman still didn't look up. Kevin and Morgan approached the desk cautiously.

"Um, excuse me, ma'am?" Morgan asked semi-loudly, clearing her throat before she spoke.

A wrinkled face looked up at them from behind the book. "Yes?" Her voice sounded ragged, like she hadn't spoken in years.

"I'm, uh, I mean, we, are, um, looking for books or articles on, uh, Graystorm Asylum."

The woman returned to her book. "Back row, top shelf. There are newspapers back there too."

Morgan let out a small sigh of relief that the woman hadn't gotten angry at her question. "OK, thank you."

Kevin turned to his sister. "I'll take the computer. You'll do the books?"

Morgan smiled. "Perfect."

As his sister walked to the back of the library, Kevin started toward the only computer, an ancient thing with a huge, bulky screen that looked like it hadn't been dusted in years. He sat down in the uncomfortable wooden chair, and waved the mouse.

To his surprise, the computer screen woke up. He was already on the Internet browser, so he clicked on the search bar and typed in: Graystorm Asylum History.

The computer was not slow at all, and the search results came back in less than a half-minute. There very few results, and none of them seemed helpful, until he came across one that said: Graystorm Asylum History.net.

Kevin clicked on it, and then watched as a news article appeared on the screen. The article was dated October 31, 20 years ago. Intrigued, Kevin began to read it.

Two Kids Vanish; Asylum in Question

Two kids by the names of Paige and Bailey, last name Harkrider, age thirteen, apparently visited the vacated Graystorm Asylum just yesterday on the bet of fellow high school freshman Matthew Kirby (in questioning).

"I woke up this morning and they were gone, their beds hadn't been slept in," their mother reported. "I knew something was wrong. So, I talked to all of their friends and Kirby admitted to betting Bailey twenty dollars if he spent the night at the Asylum. I guess he took Paige with him."

No one dared enter the asylum to search for the kids, though. "That place has a dark history," Sergeant Sean Porter said after Mrs. Harkrider called in that her kids were missing. "There is no way you'll get us in there. Those kids are gone anyway."

When questioned further, Porter admitted: "It's a scary place. When you think about all that's gone on in that building...you know in your heart that evil still resides in there."

"So you believe that Doctor Steele's and Doctor Cadenza's spirits still reside there?" reporter Hailey Sampson asked Sergeant Porter.

"Maybe not. Maybe they had nothing to do with it. But...there's something in that building. Something that time cannot erase." Sergeant Porter refused to say more after this.

Below that article, there was a link that said: Graystorm Asylum History. Kevin clicked it, and another article loaded before his eyes.

Chiefs of Staffs Jackson Steele (27) and Marietta Cadenza (24) opened and ran Graystorm two centuries ago, in the year of 2020. They were said to be quiet, quirky, but good people overall. They said they were helping people by taking them into Graystorm. But about a year after the asylum opened, a mass hanging was reported. Apparently, twelve of the patients had hung themselves in the dining hall. According to the records, Doctor Steele said: "It was tragic and terrible. How they broke out of their rooms, we don't know. Security will be upgraded. Nothing like this will ever happen again."

Also according to the records, one of the patients that had hung herself, by the name of Cadence Lorenzo (35), had been visited days earlier by her mother. "She was acting even stranger than usual," Mrs. Lorenzo (66) had said. "She kept talking about magic, about a Nightmare Princess and a Demon King. She kept talking about something called 'darkness falling' and a 'Tapestry of Decay.' I think once she mentioned a woman with acid green hair appearing in her room…"

Apparently, Doctor Cadenza was questioned about this mysterious woman with the acid green hair. "We believe it was just another of her scarier phantasmagorias. We have no such staff working here, for such hair color is prohibited, bright dye disturbs the patients…"

The case was dropped and life continued on as normal until two teenage boys reported screams of torture coming from the asylum about a month later.

"We were just walking, you know, and suddenly heard screams coming from the asylum walls. They were like nothing you've ever heard before…"

Doctors Steele and Cadenza were once again questioned, only to say that the patients do find themselves, at times, trapped in some terrible hallucination and start screaming, trying to escape it.

"It is nothing that can be controlled," said Doctor Cadenza sadly. "I talked to the builder and he said that we had the most sound-absorbent stone ever found. Screams will continue to echo around these halls, and possibly outside these walls. If anyone has a problem, I suggest they either stay away or find earplugs. It's what we do. It's an insane asylum, after all."

Once again, the case was dropped.

But over the years, more mysterious deaths and other stories began to pop up around the asylum. The case was discontinued each time, for there was no valid proof as that the doctors did anything wrong. "It's an insane asylum. It's not going to be peaceful," Doctor Steele reminded the people of the village calmly after a particularly gruesome death involving two patients cutting out their own hearts. "Our job is not enjoyable, but someone must take care of these people. And we were willing to do this—we cannot back out now."

Rumors had begun to circulate that the doctors themselves were starting to go crazy.

"It's a mad house. Something bad is happening inside those walls, I can guarantee it," says town-hall member Sasha Halls, 78.

But, as there was no good reason to search the asylum, a search warrant was not issued, so the building could not be explored.

"If they are truly doing nothing wrong, then they will open their doors for us!" Halls exclaimed upon hearing the news about no warrant.

Finally, Doctors Cadenza and Steele died at the asylum, Cadenza being strangled by a patient and Steele having his throat slit by another. The asylum closed, with no one willing to take over, and all the patients were sent far away to different asylums.

The building could finally be searched, and what the police found was horrifying. There were tables with straps and restraints that were hooked up to electrical machines that sent waves of electricity through you. Several other operating rooms were found, all containing various instruments and diagrams featuring the sort of horrible torture that went on inside the asylum. In the main office of Doctor Steele, in the file drawers, there were patients' information, as well as what kind of torture they had experienced and how it affected them. Some notes said "Resistant. Time to exterminate."

It also appeared that the Chief of Staffs dabbled in dark magic, practicing it on the patients.

"This is nasty stuff. The building must be destroyed!" exclaimed several people of the town once they heard about what had been going on within the asylum's walls.

Before any demolition could be approved, however, the experiments had to be proved true. "This could all be a bad prank," some police officers said. However, the next day, all the patients that had been shipped away from Graystorm were found dead in their rooms. With no witnesses, the building remained standing as a gruesome reminder of what horror braced the town.

Kevin went back to the first article and stared at it for a few minutes before it finally clicked in. Paige and Bailey...Aidrianna and Thomas...visited asylum on a bet...never returned.... Could the story of Aidrianna and Thomas really be the story of Paige and Bailey Harkrider?

Even more startling was the fact that their mom had lied.

She had to have known about this. It was too coincidental. He needed to let Morgan know.

"Hey, Kevin, what'd you find?" Morgan said, appearing behind him. Kevin started.

"Watch it! You nearly scared me to death," he hissed under his breath.

"Sorry," Morgan said, giving him a weird look. Her twin was like her—not scared when someone snuck up behind them or pulled a prank on them.

She set a stack of books down on the table. "Here are all of them. I didn't know which ones would be more useful, so I took them all. What'd you find on the computer?"

"Read it," Kevin said, his voice shaking. He got up, letting Morgan have his chair. He watched her face while she read it. It started slightly curious then slowly became more and more

23

scared.

When she reached the end, she breathed slightly: "Oh my gosh. Aidrianna and Thomas...Mom lied..."

"I know."

"But why? We need to confront her, talk to her. Somehow, I know, that after this," she motioned to the article, "she could not have spent the night there. We need to talk to her. ASAP."

"There's no need," a voice said behind them. Morgan stood up and spun around, Kevin wheeling around as well. Their mom stood behind them, a somber expression on her face.

Chapter 5: Hurdles – Cassidee

Time began to slow down as fifteen-year-old Cassidee Scott's left foot hit the black track, followed by her right. She took a step, then pushed off again, stretching her left leg in front of her and holding her right leg to the side at a 90-degree angle. Her left arm was extended behind her; her right arm flung out front, almost touching her left foot.

Time sped up again as she cleared the hurdle, feeling her left foot hit the track, followed by her right foot. She continued down the 110-meter stretch, running and jumping like she was being chased.

In her own mind, yes, she was being chased. Chased by the inevitable tiredness that threatened to overtake her...

Cassidee tripped over the next hurdle, and pitched forward. She hit the blacktop hard, tears of frustration threatening to leak out of her eyes. Her right knee throbbed, her left ankle felt like it had been yanked out of its socket, and she could taste the blood in her mouth from her bit lip. With a slight groan, she pushed herself up and forced her feet underneath her again. With shaky steps, she walked back to the start.

"Cassidee! Cassidee! What are you doing? You can't possibly do hurdles in the shape you're in! You need sleep!" a fourteen-year-old girl by the name of Corey Jefferson cried, running over from the chain link fence to her friend. She had short blonde hair and pure blue eyes like sapphires. Concern was written across her face as she gently grabbed her friend's shoulders.

Cassidee had a disgruntled look on her face. "It's just twisted. My lip and knee will stop bleeding. I'm fine, Corey, I really am."

Corey didn't let go of her friend's shoulders. "No, you are not." When Cassidee opened her mouth to complain, Corey interrupted her. "And don't go on about how you're a year older than me and how you're on the track team and I'm not and how I don't know what you're feeling right now---not that those things aren't true. But I've taken enough AP Health-Care classes to know that you're pushing yourself way too much." Corey looked at her watch. "And," she waved at the sky with one hand, "it's nearly eleven. At night. You've been out here running and hurdling for more than *six hours*. You must've set a record. You're exhausted. And don't deny it. I know it, and you know it."

Cassidee sighed, her shoulders drooping, admitting defeat. She still avoided meeting Corey's blue eyes that looked like they could see right to her soul.

"Finished with the monologue yet, Jefferson?" a fourteen-year-old boy asked as he sauntered over. He had vivid red hair, hazel eyes, and a face that was spattered with clusters of freckles.

Corey stuck her tongue out at him. "Why are you interested, Hill? Wanting to input a word or two?"

Kyle Hill rolled his eyes. "As if. I just wanted to ask if we were leaving yet. You *did* notice the time, right?"

"Of course! That's what we were talking about."

"Then let's go! I've been watching Cassidee doing hurdles for so long that *I'm* starting to feel sore!"

Cassidee sighed. She was tired of her two best friends mock-arguing. She was tired and wanted to leave before the night-man came around and spotted them.

"Cut it out you two, let's go before the night-man comes," Cassidee sighed, pushing between them as she headed for the fence to grab her bike.

"Does that mean you'll finally sleep?" Corey asked.

Cassidee froze. The dream from two days ago came flooding back...

She was standing at the track, alone, at night, about to take another run through the hurdles. But then, she noticed some shadows moving. She had called out, asking who was there, when the shadows swirled and seemed to solidify into a human shape.

26

By then, Cassidee was scared, she was considering running away, but the woman had quickly approached her. She was no regular woman. First off, no one can survive with at least seven holes burned right through their body. Secondly, her skin was blacker than night itself. She wore a long cloak of black that you could barely notice next to her skin, and her acid green hair and eyes stood out in the darkness.

Cassidee had then noticed the long, sharp scalpel in the woman's hand, dripping with blood. No, it wasn't exactly a scalpel...more like a jagged black horn or wand, or something along those lines. But whatever it was, it could kill, Cassidee was sure of it. She had turned and started to run, but the woman had caught up and tripped her and was about to stab her when she had woken up again.

She had known, as soon as she had woken up, that the woman would come back and finish what she had failed to do in the first dream. So, Cassidee had vowed not to fall asleep for as long as she could. And of course, the first people she had told had been her two best and only friends, super smart and kind Corey and that joker-slash-athlete Kyle. Of course, they had been worried, but Kyle seemed to know more than he had let on.

Are you going to sleep again?

"No...I don't think so, not if I can help it." Cassidee said slowly.

She could hear the disappointment in Corey's voice. "Cassidee! You need to sleep sometime!"

"No!" Cassidee whirled around to face them, her hands clenched into fists at her sides. She felt anger rising up inside of her. "You don't understand! If I sleep, she'll come back, and she'll kill me!"

"But it's in your sleep..." Corey began to say softly.

"But it feels so real! And I have a feeling that if she

accomplishes that, I'll never wake up again!" The panic and desperation rose in Cassidee's voice. Her voice dropped to a whisper, full of sadness and defeat. "I'm sorry, guys. This is just one hurdle I can't get over."

Chapter 6: Knowledge – Corey

As Corey rode her bike home, she dwelled over the fact that Cassidee was not alone in her nightmares. Sure, they weren't the same, no one was trying to kill her, but still…they were scary.

She thought of the scared look in her best friend's powder-blue eyes. Cassidee was truly scared that she would be killed if she fell asleep again, and Corey couldn't say she blamed her. For of all Corey's nightmares, they provided her with gruesome facts that wouldn't help her on any test, exam, paper or homework assignment.

Graystorm Asylum haunted her every sleeping moment, and had started creeping into her living ones. The place was always deserted in her dreams, but she felt like she was not alone. The Doctors were there, torturing the patients. She could hear their screams, and whenever she tried to reach them, she could never find them, but instead would be sucked into their pain, their lives, without seeing a thing, and wake up scared, screaming, and sweating. Sometimes she woke up with unexplained bruises or cuts, and she knew that she was slowly being 'drawn' into the tortures of Graystorm Asylum.

For once, this was some knowledge studious and intellectual Corey didn't want to have.

Chapter 7: The Empire – Jessica

Jessica's head throbbed with an un-yielding pain. The vision of the teacher transforming into that *demon* kept flashing before her eyes. White lights pulsed in front of her eyes, and she was slightly aware that she was being carried. Was she in the hospital already?

She stirred slightly, and everything became a bit more focused, but then blurred. She moaned, her body letting out a scream of pain, her ears ringing and her head hurting even more, like she had been hit over the head with a heavy iron skillet.

She heard a soft shushing sound, probably from the person carrying her. She could briefly see calm blue eyes and black hair against pale, almost ashen, skin. Then everything blurred into one light and her head hurt so much all she could do was fall into oblivion.

When she woke up, her head was stilling pounding, but her eyesight was no longer blurry. She tried to sit up, but everything began to spin and her head seemed to explode in pain.

"Whoa, there," a soft female voice said, and a hand reached over and gently pushed her shoulder back down onto the couch Jessica was lying on.

Jessica turned her head to see who had spoken, and saw a fourteen-year-old girl with wavy black hair and blue eyes sitting across from her in a chair.

"Glad to see you're awake again," the girl said. "My name's Waverly. I was…um…your teacher."

Jessica blinked at her. "My teacher?"

"The one that supposedly took you to the hospital." Jessica blinked again. "Sorry, it was the best excuse I could come up with. It's rather confusing. But, I'll explain it best I can.

"That woman you saw in your vision? Her name is Queen Desdemona. She is the ruler of the Okkultens, people who can change forms at will, usually for evil purposes of trickery and deception and spying. I am one," Waverly said. "But I left as soon as I could think properly. I came here, to the Empire's heart, and vowed to help Queen Sarissa and her army fight against the Nightmares. I've been a spy for them since I was five." Her voice had a hint of pride.

Jessica's head spun. "What's the Empire?" she asked groggily. "Who are the Nightmares? Who's Queen Sarissa?"

"The Empire," Waverly said patiently, "is the home of all 'misfits' and things magical, though not everyone possesses the skills of magic. We have no wand waving or unicorns here—our magic lies at our hearts and is very rarely used, but while you are here you will probably see more used than I ever have. I, since I am an Okkulten, have a 'magical ability', if you'll call it that. Shape shifting and all. Queen Sarissa possesses powerful magic skills, as do her sisters, Chandra and Hailey.

"Queen Sarissa is the queen of the Empire, except the Southern Region. The Exiled Queen, Justine, rules that part. The Nightmares are a dark group practiced in powerful black magic that plans to take over not only the Empire, but the Outside, or your world, as well. They are being led by Queen Sarissa's sister herself, Chandra, and co-commanded by Queen Desdemona and assisted by two shadowy spirits that dwell in your world, Doctors Steele and Cadenza, code names the Demon King and the Nightmare Princess. They ran Graystorm Asylum, where they tried numerous black spells, rituals, surgeries, and tortures on the already insane patients."

Waverly took a deep breath and twiddled her thumbs, giving Jessica time to digest this new information.

"But what does this have to do with me? Why did I see Queen Desdemona?"

Waverly shook her head sadly. "No one, not even all-seeing Hailey, Queen Sarissa's other sister, knows. We believe that you, along with five other kids, were prophesied long ago to have a special...connection with the Empire. We had no idea what this connection would be, but now we see it coming to light. For some reason, Queen Desdemona chose to watch you, along with another girl called Cassidee Scott and her friend Kyle Hill. I'm still trying to worm why out of her, but no success so far."

"So you're saying that I have been randomly dubbed a threat by the queen of people who can change forms at will and have been taken here to a magical place called the Empire that lies hidden from the real world, and I am being told that I, along with five other random kids, have been prophesied to do what exactly since before we were born? I must be dreaming. I have to be."

"You are not dreaming, I can assure you. And well, yes, that is what we're telling you, and you were not only said to have a special connection with the Empire, but you, along with the others, are supposed to save it."

Jessica let out a snort of disbelief. "I'm supposed to save a world that I've never even heard about? Yeah, right. So, can I wake up now?"

Waverly looked slightly flustered. "I told you, you're not dreaming. And yes, you are supposed to save us. I'm just telling you what I know."

Jessica emitted a laugh of doubt. "Yeah, right. There is no possible way that any of this is happening, it goes against the very laws of science."

"I can assure you, all of this is real."

Jessica gave Waverly the hairy eyeball. "You expect me to believe you?"

"No, but I expect you to believe me," a voice said from behind Jessica. Jessica's head snapped around, and she was staring at a woman with very long white hair and ice blue eyes. "I am Queen Sarissa. I believe Waverly told you about me?"

Chapter 8: Truth – Morgan

Fleur's strange amethyst eyes stared at Morgan and her brother, filled with regret and sadness. But what for? For lying to them? Or something else…?

Kevin was the first to speak after about three minutes of an uncomfortable silence. "Why'd you lie?"

"I didn't lie about spending the night at Graystorm. I lied about it not being dangerous," Fleur said, her voice shaking.

"We figured that last part. But why lie?" Morgan snapped.

"I didn't have a choice. I couldn't tell you why…why I was really there."

"Try us," Kevin and Morgan said simultaneously.

"This isn't simple."

"So why don't we get comfortable?" Morgan said, sitting on the floor. (The floor was much more comfortable than the chairs.)

Their mom sat down slowly and awkwardly. Her two kids stared at her expectantly. Finally, she took a deep breath and began.

"There…is this world…this community hiding inside our own. It's called the Empire—"

"Mom, I meant for you to tell us the truth," Morgan interrupted, fuming that their mother was feeding them lies again. "We're not going to listen to fairy tales."

"You read that article, didn't you?" Fleur suddenly snapped. Her whole body was visibly shaking with both anger and fear. "Did that sound like something realistic? It's no fairy tale, sure, and neither is what I'm trying to tell you. But it's all true. So can I continue?"

Silence answered her. Taking that as a 'yes' Fleur closed her eyes and breathed deeply again, trying to regain her composure. Then she opened her eyes and continued with the story.

"So, as I was saying, the Empire is a realm hiding from what they call the Outside, or your world. Queen Sarissa, who I work for, rules the Empire. To her, I am known as Fleur. This place is magical, though not everything or everyone in it is. Queen Sarissa and her sister Hailey are two of the most magically powerful people living in the Empire. There is another...group, if you will, trying to take over the Empire. They are called the Nightmares.

"The Nightmares are led by Queen Sarissa's own sister, Chandra. While the Nightmares are made up of all sorts of frightening people and creatures, about thirty percent of them are Okkultens, led by Queen Desdemona. That is the largest percent of one species in the Nightmares. Most others have been brainwashed, forced to work for Chandra, or are just the hating nonconformist. Most support the Empire."

"What does that have to do with us, or Graystorm Asylum?" Kevin asked. Morgan just stared at her mother in disbelief.

"I'm getting to that. As you know, two doctors, Doctors Steele and Cadenza, who supposedly practiced black magic on the patients, ran Graystorm Asylum. They really did practice the black magic, not only on the patients but the building and themselves. You remember in the story, where Aidrianna said that the 'Demon King' practiced so much black magic he turned himself into shadow, and that the 'Nightmare Princess' was made out of crystal? That is true also. And, Demon King and Nightmare Princess are Steele and Cadenza's code names.

"They are some of the top scientists working for Chandra. It is said that underneath Graystorm, there is a secret room that leads to the Empire. When I spent the night there, I looked for it, but never found it."

"So why did you spend the night at that creepy place?" Kevin asked.

"I was there on a mission for Queen Sarissa with two of her other informants, Asana and Crystal. Our cover was that we had been dared to go there by some friends. The picture I showed you was a fake. I made the sign and took an old photo of me and them, and then combined the two." Fleur gulped, then continued.

"So, we went to Graystorm with a pack of food, water, and sleeping bag each. We explored the whole building, as I told you, and even though we found plenty of horrible things," she shuddered, remembering, "we never found that room. In fact, we couldn't even get into the basement.

"It was horrible spending the night there. Nothing bad ever came to us, but I think the doctors were just playing with us, teasing us. We never saw them—no, let me rephrase that. *They* never *revealed* themselves to us. They were busy; we could hear the screams. But at times, we could feel a presence watching us. Almost as if they were making sure we didn't cause any trouble. I think, that to them, there was no need to take action against us. Just lock us in and keep us there for the night, letting us listen to screams of torture for ten hours." Fleur shook her head sadly. "It was more horrible than you could imagine. Once, they had us locked in a labyrinth hallway of sorts, where screams echoed from behind every closed door, and when you opened it, it would be completely dark, and with a flash of lightning you would see a person strapped to a table, hooked up to some machine, writhing and screaming and bleeding..."

"So how do we come in?" Morgan asked; Kevin was staring at their mom like he had never seen her before.

"You are two of the six 'Destined Ones', that's what Hailey dubbed you for the time being. There was a prophecy a long time ago that foretold that six teenagers, between the ages of thirteen and fifteen, would save the Empire. And they would have a special connection to it as well. Three of the kids, their names are Jessica, Cassidee, and Kyle, I think, have been targeted by Queen Desdemona, leader of the Okkultens. The other one, Corey and Kyle again, along with you two, have varying degrees of knowledge about Graystorm Asylum and what really happened in there, more than anyone else. Plus, I work for the Queen, Corey is being haunted by it in her dreams, and Kyle...just knows."

"So we're supposed to do what?"

"Save this Empire-place?"

"Yes."

"Is that what you think?"

The look of apprehension on Fleur's face at Kevin's question answered it for them.

"So you believe we can't do anything important?"

"No, I don't think that. I honestly have no idea what I think about this whole prophecy thing. I think you, with the other four, have the skills, guts, and brains to pull it off. But if we're acting too soon...I don't know."

There was a lengthy silence following this reply. Finally, Morgan asked the one question that had been weighing on her ever since her mom had told the real story of Graystorm.

"Mom...what happened to Asana and Crystal?"

"They...they couldn't stand the screams, the sights. The building affected them differently than it did me. They were not weak; they were in the top of our class for mental defense. But it was like the doctors found a slight crack in their defense and wormed their way inside their minds.

"Asana tried to escape. She ran crazily throughout the building. And finally...she went into one of the rooms. There was a horrible scream, a shattering sound, and we knew...she had been turned to crystal and shattered, become part of the building.

"And Crystal...I think she fared worse. She made it out alive, but she was never the same. It took about two years before she finally cracked and...hung herself."

For the first time, Morgan noticed the tears in her mother's eyes. "Well, that's the end of the story. We need to go...I'll take you to the Empire, you need to meet Queen Sarissa and the others..."

Chapter 9: The Night-Man – Kyle

The next night, Cassidee was practicing at the track like always. Kyle and Corey sat on the fence, watching their short friend's long dark blonde hair fly behind her like a cape as she ran the 1600.

Kyle suddenly felt a weight on his right shoulder and looked over. Corey, who had fallen asleep, had dropped her head unconsciously onto Kyle's shoulder. Kyle sighed, shook his head, and put his arm around her back so she didn't fall off the fence. He went back to watching Cassidee fly around the track.

Suddenly, he felt Corey shudder and groan slightly. He looked at her again and saw that her eyes were still shut, but her face was twisted into a look of great pain. Suddenly, two screams burst out around the track.

One scream belonged to Corey, whose face had turned from agony to horror, and the second one belonged to Cassidee, who was doubled over on the track, her eyes closed and seeing something that Kyle couldn't see.

He grabbed Corey's shoulders and shook her hard, trying to wake her up. "Wake up, Corey!" Finally, her screams stopped and her eyes snapped open. She looked around wildly before jumping off the fence and sprinting for Cassidee, whose screams were still echoing around the track. Kyle jumped off and quickly followed.

By the time he reached his friend, Cassidee had already woken up but was still doubled over, crying, while Corey hugged her friend.

"What happened?" Kyle asked, breathing hard.

Cassidee looked up and managed to say: "I didn't need to fall asleep...she came back...she almost killed me..."

"And I had fallen asleep, and well...I saw Graystorm Asylum again. I was in there...hearing the screams, feeling the patients' pain. Like every night. Only this time was different. This time...I could see," Corey murmured, still hugging Cassidee.

Shock raced through Kyle's body. For all this time, Corey, his best friend besides Cassidee, had been seeing Graystorm Asylum in her sleep? "Why didn't you tell me what you'd been seeing?" Kyle asked, who now had his hand on Cassidee's shoulder.

"I didn't want to trouble you."

"But I could have helped! I mean, you're not the only one—"

"You mean, you see it too?"

"More than that," an old voice said from behind them. Corey and Kyle whirled around, and Cassidee shakily turned her head.

An old man stood behind them, hobbling toward them on a cane. He had short white hair and dark chocolate brown eyes. The Night-Man. The man who patrolled the track every night.

"My name's Joseph. I am, as you know, the Night-Man. But I'm also one of Queen Sarissa's informants from the Empire. Yeah, yeah, I know what you're thinking, 'What the heck are you talking about, you delusional old man?'" he said in a high-pitched voice. "Well I can assure you that I am completely sane and would mind for you to shut your little yappers and listen."

Cassidee had stopped crying and was staring, along with Corey and Kyle, at the man in wonder.

"So, I work for the queen of the Empire, a place unknown to all you blind fools livin' here on what they call the Outside. Place for the oblivious. Anyway, magic can go on in the Empire, though not everyone possesses that mighty skill, in fact, I'm a one of 'em. Queen Sarissa is one of them most powerful, along with her all-seeing sister Hailey. Chandra has mighty powerful magic too, but she's over with the Nightmares, or the evil folk around there. They're trying to take over an' stuff, but that's where you come in.

"Ya' see, there was a prophecy a long time ago stating that six kids would save the Empire. They all get worked up about it and name you the Destined Ones, tacky but it'll do. So, you three are part of those Destined Ones 'cause you have a special connection to the Empire. You," he pointed to Corey, "see Graystorm Asylum in your dreams, and don' ask why, we don't know. And Graystorm is the lab of two notorious mad-scientists workin' for the Nightmares, named Doctors Steele and Cadenza. You," he pointed to Cassidee, "are seein' Queen Desdemona, leader of the Okkultens, in your sleep, and for some reason she wants ya' dead, don' know why, so don't ask. And you," he pointed to Kyle, "know a whole bunch o' stuff about this for no apparent reason.

"So, there, ya' have your explanation. Now come with me, and you can take all your questions to the Queen herself."

The three kids stared at Joseph in wonder. What had just happened? Was the guy going crazy? Or was it all three of them?

"Um...sir? Can you...um..." Corey began. Joseph turned around, annoyed.

"Guess ya' want me to explain it all again to your ignorant little ears? Not happenin'. Ask it all to the Queen, now let's go!"

They followed Joseph warily, their own curiosity egging them on. What was going on?

Chapter 10: Meeting – Jessica

"Oh!" Jessica exclaimed, seeing the woman standing behind her. She was definitely not a dream. And if she really was the queen of this...Empire...she, Jessica, had better pay her respects.

"I'm sorry, Queen, uh..."

"Sarissa. Queen Sarissa," the woman in white said calmly. "And you have no reason to be sorry. It is I, since I dumped all of this on you in the blink of an eye. No wonder you had doubts. In fact, when I was first told about the Outside, I was as skeptical as you were." The queen smiled. Jessica felt a rush of relief fill her.

"So I won't be going to the gallows after all?"

The queen laughed. "Of course not! We need you, as Waverly just explained."

"Where are the others?" Jessica asked, some of Waverly's monologue coming back to her.

"The other Destined Ones? Oh, they will be here soon. I've sent my assistants to round them up." At the startled look on Jessica's face, she said, "Oh, no, they won't be passing out and being carried to a so-called 'hospital' like you were. We didn't cause that nightmare of yours."

Something in her voice made Jessica believe Sarissa wasn't lying to her.

She looked around the room. The ceiling was about twenty feet high, arched into a dome with glass panels. The walls were a warm crème color, decorated by mahogany bookshelves and portraits, adorned with crown molding in fancy patterns. Though the floor was really a dark hardwood, a plush red and gold tasseled carpet covered most of the room's base. Sunlight streamed in through windows on the wall to Jessica's right. She could see that they opened onto a balcony. There was a set of dark brown doors on the far wall, and behind Jessica's couch there was another set of dark brown doors. There was a red, gold, and silver tapestry on the wall.

Suddenly, the door opened and a small old man hobbling on a cane was leading in three kids.

"Joseph, I see you got them."

"Yes, Sarissa, I got 'em. Kept tryin' to ask me what I was talkin' 'bout, but o' 'course they weren't listenin' so—"

"We did listen," the girl in the middle said quietly. "We just don't understand what's going on."

"An explanation will be provided to you as best possible when the other two get here," Queen Sarissa said, dipping her head.

As if on cue, the door opened again and the three kids shuffled out of the way. A woman with blonde hair and strange amethyst colored eyes came striding in, followed by two thirteen year-olds. They looked like twins, with the same dark brown hair and deep violet eyes. They stared at the room in awe.

"I think introductions are in order," Queen Sarissa began, motioning for Jessica to stand. "I am Queen Sarissa, ruler of the Empire." She pointed to Waverly, who gave everyone a small smile. "That's Waverly. She's an Okkulten, but she is one of our best spies and no harm will come to you from her. She's very smart and a strong girl."

Sarissa pointed to the old guy. "That is Joseph, as you three know. And the woman next to him is Fleur, or Fleur, their mother," she said, pointing to the twins.

"These are the twins, Morgan and Kevin Smith. They have varying degrees of knowledge about Graystorm Asylum, a place the rest of you will, unfortunately, come to know a lot about." She turned to the group of three. "The short dark blonde is Cassidee Scott, who has been visited by Queen Desdemona on two occasions. The girl with blonde hair is Corey Jefferson, who visits Graystorm Asylum in her sleep, and the tall boy is Kyle Hill. He knows about both things."

Finally, Sarissa turned to Jessica. All eyes were on her. She felt her stomach swoop. "This is Jessica Knight. She, like

Cassidee, has been visited by the Okkulten queen."

Corey walked over to Jessica and held out her hand. "It's nice to meet you," she said softly as Jessica took her hand and shook it. Jessica just nodded, a bit too overwhelmed of what had just been dumped on her to speak.

Get over it, Knight! Yeesh, were you named after the grand people of old just to swerve out on them like some chicken? Get a grip! Jessica yelled at herself silently. This was a test—yes, she was already starting to feel a bit calmer. A test of her own sanity, sure, but it was also to prove how much she could show on her face, how much she could control her own raging emotions, and handle those of the others. It was a test unlike any she had taken before, but yet she felt like she had studied for it.

Maybe this won't be so bad after all.

Chapter 11: The All-Seeing Hailey – Cassidee

Cassidee looked at the other 'Destined Ones' curiously, besides Corey and Kyle, of course. She knew them. But the others...they were interesting.

The twins she immediately liked. They looked bookish (not that there was anything wrong with that, Cassidee loved to read) but not athletic or fit at all. They looked tough, though. Like you could sneak up on them and not scare them. Not mean. Just...resilient. Withstanding. Unflappable.

The kind of people she liked.

The lone girl, Jessica, she wasn't sure about. She looked like she was trying to be tough, to live up to everyone else, and not crack under pressure. Cassidee liked people who weren't afraid to be themselves, and Jessica looked like she could be the opposite.

Cassidee sighed. *Don't judge a book by its cover,* she recited silently.

Suddenly, the door behind her opened again and a woman with a fair complexion and long golden hair swept in, wearing a golden gown that was finely stitched. She had violet eyes like the twins, and her face was beaming, her smile one that was ecstatic and possibly bordering on psychotic. The look in her eyes was far away and distant, but elated, as if she was seeing something grand that no one else could see. Who was it Joseph had said she was? Ah, yes, Queen Sarissa's all-seeing sister, Hailey.

Sarissa turned to her sister and smiled warmly. "Hello, Hailey, I was wondering when you might be joining us."

Hailey stared around the room. "There you all are. You're all here," she said in a tone of awe. She let out an excited squeal and grabbed Sarissa's shoulders, jumping up and down. "Don't you see what this means, sister? The Nightmares can finally be defeated!"

"Calm down, Hailey, I believe you are starting to freak them out," Sarissa said softly.

Hailey stopped bouncing and let go of her sister's shoulders, looking around the room with a huge smile on her face, seeming to remember that they were there. "Oh! Hi! I'm Hailey!" she exclaimed excitedly as she raced around shaking the six kids' hands. "It's nice to meet all of you! Such a huge honor!"

"Hold up on the congratulations, we haven't done anything yet," Kyle said, smiling as Hailey shook his hand so hard that his arm jumped around.

"But you will! The stars have said so!" Hailey exclaimed as she shook Cassidee's hand. Cassidee noticed that she smelled faintly of roses and lilac.

Jessica, who had grimaced when Hailey shook her hand, rolled her eyes. "How can the stars tell you anything? Divination is a whole bunch of guess-work and superstitions, if you ask me."

Cassidee quickly used all the self-control she had to restrain herself from marching over and slapping the prep right out of that know-it-all girl. They were in a world of *magic*, for crying out loud! What didn't the girl understand about that?

Hailey's enthusiasm showed no signs of slowing at this obstacle. She turned to Jessica. "I understand your skepticism. I possessed it too, at first. But it is more than guesswork—it is a feeling. When the stars tell you something, you just know," the woman said with a dream-like voice. Suddenly, her face fell into a grimace, and her tone became flat. "And it's the creepiest feeling in the world, trust me," Hailey muttered, shuddering. "How would you like to spend your nights plagued with the feeling of being dropped into a pit of mud slugs and vipers? And the visions that come with it..." She shuddered again and let out a sound of disgust, her eyes squeezed shut.

Hailey suddenly opened her eyes and her exuberant aura returned. "So, shall we proceed to dinner?"

Chapter 12: The Assignment – Morgan

Morgan scanned the faces of the other 'Destined Ones' as they proceeded across a sunlit atrium filled with green plants sprouting flowers of neon colors that looked like they had been picked in the old city of Seattle. Before it was wrecked, anyway.

Morgan considered herself a good judge of personalities. Like with Hailey, she seemed loopy but yet Morgan sensed honesty and consideration.

Cassidee looked like she was up for any challenge thrown at her, but not like a bully. She wouldn't push anyone out of the way to get her own victory. And was it her imagination, or did her eyes look a little puffy?

Morgan looked at Cassidee's friend, Corey Jefferson. She seemed quiet and kind, not socially withdrawn but shy. Cautious. But, once you earned her trust, she would become someone who would die to defend you. She had a sharp glint in her equally sharp blue eyes that showed intellect and determination.

Next was Corey and Cassidee's other friend, Kyle. He seemed loose and liked to enjoy himself. But if they ended up going into Graystorm, how long would that personality last?

And finally, there was the lone girl, Jessica. Morgan wasn't sure what to think of her. She seemed like she was trying to put on a brave face. But yet, Morgan could understand why she doubted everything. She wasn't trying to be mean—she just didn't understand. To her, magic isn't real and science is. And to have all this dumped on you so suddenly...Morgan could give her a chance.

They reached the dining hall—a long room with large windows on all the walls, and a twenty foot oak table stretched the length of the room, with elegant matching chairs seated around. On the table there were platters of food, from roasted turkey and chicken to mashed potatoes and gravy; grilled cheese sandwiches and peanut butter and jelly. About ten different baskets of rolls with different kinds of butter sat on the table; one basket held wheat rolls and real butter, another held raisin and cherry bread with grape spread.

There were fine china plates in front of eleven chairs that were toward the middle. There were also placards in front of the eleven chairs, each with a name written on them in calligraphy.

Morgan scanned the cards for her name, and spotted it between Cassidee's and Kevin's. Across from her were Corey, Jessica, and Kyle. Waverly sat on Cassidee's left, and Joseph on Kevin's right. Her mom sat on Kyle's right, and, to Morgan's surprise, Queen Sarissa was on Corey's left. Hailey sat on Sarissa's left.

There was a squeaking of chairs as everyone sat down in a some-what awkward silence. Well, it was awkward for the, what was it? Oh yeah, the six 'Destined Ones', which she, Morgan Smith, was now a part of. They just met and they all understood that they'd be doing dangerous stuff together, trusting each other with their lives. Not your everyday predicament.

After they were all seated, a butler in a black suit came by and picked up the placards, then filled their crystal glasses with ice water. The butler left, and Queen Sarissa cleared her throat.

"Before we begin enjoying the delicious food the cooks have generously prepared for us, let me tell you your…assignment, as it were.

"You will spend two months here before embarking on your mission. While we have little time, we do value your lives, and do not plan on throwing you out into the great unknown without a little knowledge on how to survive. Note that none of this will prepare for what is really out there, but it will give you an edge. Hopefully, you will only need that, each other, and your wits.

"Your parents, except for Morgan and Kevin's, will have their memories modified. It will be like you were never gone.

"The six of you will be split into threes; three of you will be trying to find a pathway in Graystorm Asylum that is supposed to lead back here, to the castle. I want you to find it and *shut it down.* Waverly has only managed to get a small bit of information out about it, confirming that the Nightmares plan to use it to attack the castle in a siege. We have already searched the castle and have found no secret entrance or exit; therefore we can assume it is a one-way path. So, when you find it, do not use it to come back. Blow it up, or bring the whole building down if you have to. Just make sure that they can't get through.

"For the other three, you will be going to the abandoned Southern Empire and finding my other sister and brother, Alex and Jonathan. They have had their memory washed away and are supposed to live somewhere out there. The only reason I do not search for them myself is that I am staying here, trying to keep the castle and surrounding villages secure while I also try to get Chandra, my sister, to see reason and come back to our side.

"You will not be traveling alone—Fleur will be going with you to Graystorm. Joseph and Waverly will be accompanying whoever goes south. They all have been where you are going before and will act as your guides. You will all find out where you are going tomorrow.

"So, dig in!"

Chapter 13: Training

Kyle

The food was delicious, unlike anything he had expected from royalty. Weren't they all about eating swan and black licorice, washing it down with centuries old wine? And the fact that the queen herself wasn't sitting at the end seat was a rarity in itself. How often did the queen eat like a commoner? She was probably doing it to make them feel welcome. If he were king, he'd do that too. And rent a jester for entertainment, instead of sitting here with the knowledge that in two months they'd be going to the scariest places in the Empire?

Not exactly pretty thoughts during dinner.

So he struck up a conversation with Kevin, who sat across from them. They were the only guys—birds of a feather flock together.

Corey

Corey watched as Kyle conversed with Kevin. The two seemed to hit it off pretty well. Turning back to the grilled cheese on her plate, she took a bite and felt the warmth and flavor of the pepper jack cheese on toasted blueberry bread. She had never tasted anything like it.

She thought about the 'missions'. They sounded almost…cheesy. Unreal. But, hadn't she just thought an hour ago that magic wasn't real?

After swallowing, she figured she might as well talk to the others. So she chose Morgan, who was cutting some turkey into chunks and dipping them into mashed potatoes and gravy.

"Hey, Morgan?"

The girl looked up, and in one fluid motion, swept her long brown hair over her shoulder, tying it back with a rubber band so it wouldn't get in her food. "Yes?"

"Did you, uh…want to talk?"

Morgan took the hint. "Sure." She took a bite of turkey,

gravy, and mashed potatoes. "So, do you play any sports?"

"Yeah, I do. Volleyball. What about you?"

"Basketball and soccer. Should give me a little endurance, you think? I have the feeling we'll be doing a lot of running. Hey, is the grilled cheese good?"

"It is, actually," Corey said, taking another bite of the succulent sandwich.

"I've never heard of blueberry bread before," Morgan said, taking a blueberry roll from the breadbasket closest to her and buttering it with cream cheese. She took a bite. "Mmm, it tastes like a blueberry muffin with whipped cream inside! Delicious."

Corey took a raspberry roll and spread grape jam on it while she continued to talk to Morgan.

Kevin

Joseph led him and Kyle up to their room after dinner. Their room was circular and held four four-poster beds with green drapes and white bed sheets. There was a small furnace in the middle, and bookshelves lined the walls between the beds. A lamp hung in the center, and at the foot of each bed was a small trunk holding clothes.

"Here ya' are. Sleep well, you got a big day headed for ya'. Be down at breakfast by seven."

As Joseph turned and started awkwardly down the hallway again, Kevin called out: "Where are the showers?"

"Look at the bookcase next to bed on the east side of the furnace." The old man rounded a corner and his lamplight vanished.

Kevin and Kyle looked at each other and shrugged, and then both went over to the bookcase on the eastern side of the furnace and ran their fingers over the spines of the books, pulling on them to see if they triggered a mechanism. Only one book wouldn't budge.

"Maybe it's locked. Maybe we share a bathroom with the

girls and they're already in there," Kyle suggested.

"Don't know. Let's check again in the morning," Kevin said, yawning.

They searched their trunks and came up with a pair of pajamas each. After changing, they climbed into their beds and fell asleep.

Cassidee

Cassidee finally succumbed to sleep after Waverly, who had led them to their room, had assured her that Queen Desdemona wouldn't be able to enter her dream world tonight. Sleep felt wonderful, even if she didn't dream. It ended too soon. Soon Waverly was shaking her shoulders, telling her to get dressed and go down to the hall for breakfast.

In her trunk she found a gray t-shirt, black gym shorts, white ankle socks, electric blue and yellow running shoes, a hairbrush and a hair tie. Cassidee changed from her night shirt into the clothes provided, brushed her hair, and tied it back loosely. Everyone's outfit was the same, only with different color shirts. Morgan's was a light violet, Jessica's was lime green, Corey's was a sky blue, and Waverly's was a bright red.

They walked down the hallway to breakfast and were surprised to see that, except for Queen Sarissa, Hailey, and Fleur, they were the first ones there. They grinned at each other. Now the boys couldn't blame them for taking their time.

The table held platters of pancakes, ranging from buttermilk to a blueberry-chocolate chip-M&M mix, plates of waffles and scrambled eggs, French toast, regular toast, bagels, cinnamon rolls, muffins and assorted fruits. At each place setting there was a glass of milk.

Early morning sunlight came pouring through the grand windows, illuminating the hall with a warm glow. Cassidee saw Jessica lazily yawning and squinting as the dawn-light fell upon her.

As they sat down, the two boys came tramping down into

the dining hall, their hair wet as if they had just taken a shower, which the girls had done last night. Both of them were wearing black gym shorts like the girls and electric blue running shoes. Kyle had on a red shirt that matched Waverly's, and Kevin wore a royal blue one.

They plopped down into their chairs, yawning and muttering good-mornings under their breath, grabbing muffins and sliding pancakes onto their plates.

"I think, if you're awake enough to see, you will find that you already have something on your plate," Queen Sarissa said politely, a small, teasing glint in her eye that was directed at the boys.

Kyle stopped half-yawn, and Kevin accidentally dropped the blueberry muffin he'd been holding. Everyone looked down at their plates and saw a piece of paper lying there. A schedule.

Queen Sarissa spoke again, both her face and voice suddenly somber. "But before you go over it, you might want to know what your assignment is. Take a slip of paper, so it's random."

Waverly got up, clutching six pieces of paper. Her face, which had been cheerful moments before, was now white. She stopped at Kyle's shoulder and opened her fist, letting him take a piece of paper. He opened it and sighed, but not out of relief. "I'm finding your brainwashed siblings."

Waverly walked over to Kevin's shoulder and opened her fist again. He took a slip of paper carefully and slowly as if it might detonate, holding it a safe distance away. He opened it. "Graystorm Asylum."

Next was Jessica. "The siblings."

Corey. "Graystorm."

Morgan. "Graystorm."

Even though Cassidee knew which one was left for her, she still opened it with shaking fingers. On her paper were four words in scribbled handwriting:

Find the queen's siblings.

"The siblings," she said in a shaky breath. Her body seemed to shake with both excitement and fear. Two months from now, she'd be heading out with Kyle and Jessica—wait, Jessica?!

I have to travel with that prep?! Cassidee groaned inwardly. At least she would be with Kyle, who might give her some sanity.

She looked at the paper in her hand, which basically spelled out, in four words, her entire future, if she never returned.

But you will *return! You have to.*

Right?

Morgan

Graystorm Asylum.

The place she had just discovered the horrific truth of.

The place her mother was connected to.

And, it was curious, for her at least, to see that the three people who actually had a connection with Graystorm were going there.

You had her and Kevin, whose mother went there as a kid.

And then you had Corey, who had been visiting it in her sleep.

At least they had some idea of what they were up against. Right?

She hastily put the slip of paper under her plate and looked at her schedule. It was a chart, laying out their day.

She looked at Corey's schedule. It looked just like hers. She could see her brother's across the table. It was the same, too.

After breakfast, they all headed outside onto a grassy lawn next to a run-down track. There was a forest nearby, wrapping around them and the castle. Waverly and Fleur stood at the front, demonstrating the stretches as the six kids followed suit.

Queen Sarissa spoke to them as she walked around the

group as they did pushups, sit-ups, lunges, jumping-jacks, backbends, and all other kinds of stretches imaginable: "Remember, we are only doing this to get you in shape. This will not be what your days are like once these two months have ended. Those days will not be organized; they will be arbitrary. Be on your guard, even when asleep. It is easy to fall prey to sleep, comfort, and safety, leaving your defenses down. Also remember, your enemies might not attack you physically—there must be a mental shield as well."

Next, they had to run through the woods for a mile. They ran in a line: Fleur, Waverly, Kyle, Corey, Cassidee, Morgan, and Kevin. Morgan kept herself at a steady pace, running directly behind Cassidee, watching her long dark blonde hair fly behind her as they leapt over logs, turned sharp corners, trampled through briar thickets, dodged hanging branches, and hurdled over pools of water and muck, wading through those that were too wide to jump.

By the end, Morgan's already pale skin was flushed and sweaty, her face a brilliant shade of red, her long brown hair stuck to her neck and violet shirt, which stuck to her skin. Her legs were shaking, there were leaves in her hair, and from her waist-down there was dried mud from wading through a particularly deep and wide mud pool.

Sarissa passed out water bottles while Hailey and Joseph set up an obstacle course. Morgan took hers with hands that were shaking from fatigue and unscrewed the cap. Her trembling hands shook the bottle, sloshing water all over her legs, rinsing the mud off. Morgan took a long swig of water and poured the rest over her head, letting it fall down her body like a brief, but cold, rain shower. She took the end of her shirt and wiped her face with it, breathing in the pungent smell of her own sweat.

"This way!" Sarissa called, waving them out of the woods and toward the obstacle course. Everyone groaned when they saw it. It was shorter than a mile, it was only two turns around the track, or ½ a mile, but it looked grueling. There were hurdles of various sizes, fake tree trunks to swerve around at the last minute, and a dense cloud of fog that could hide anything in there. There was also a pool, that covered about half of the track that held fake snapping alligators and rolling logs that they had to hop across half way through, then the logs ended and you had to swim the rest of the way. There was an open stretch with a cage on the sidelines, holding a growling dog.

"Waverly, will you show them how it's done?" Sarissa asked, pointing to the start line.

Waverly nodded and walked to the line. Sarissa whistled, and Waverly sprinted down a stretch before flying over some three-foot to four-foot hurdles for 200 meters. Then she dodged trees that sent branches flying out at you at sudden moments, dashed through the fog, and leaped onto the rolling logs. She bounded from log to log, never stopping, not even when the alligators jumped out of the water and snapped at her. She dove into the clear water after reaching the last log and swam free-style, speeding through the water like a bullet. She reached the end, and wasting no time to stop, grabbed the edge and used her momentum to pull herself out and kept running. She flew past the cage onto the open stretch, triggering the release of the dog. She was far in front of it for most of the run, but at times it snapped at her heels. Finally, she burst across the line again and the dog stopped, still snarling, but headed back to its cage.

Sarissa handed a panting Waverly a bottle of water and sent her to the back of the line. "Great run! Who wants to go next?"

Morgan found herself going next. She tripped over several of the hurdles, and ran right into a branch a tree had thrown out in front of her. In the fog there was actually a cliff edge they had to try and stick to as wind howled inside the cloud. Morgan almost fell to her supposed death but reached the end and started log hopping. She tripped over the third log and missed the alligator's jaws by centimeters; she hit the water with a splash and forgot the logs entirely, swimming all the way to the end until she struggled out of the pool, her arms feeling like spaghetti and water dripping into her eyes. She gave her last ounce of strength in darting past the dog's cage. She felt its hot breath on her ankles and was pretty sure she heard its jaws snap close millimeters from her flesh.

After crossing the finish line and gulping down a bottle of water, she and Waverly watched Kevin clear all the hurdles, trees, and fog, but fall victim to the fake alligators twice. Cassidee cleared the hurdles easily but scrambled to get back on the logs after she fell off. Kyle practically ran through the hurdles and was tackled by the dog; Corey was one of the few who made it through the logs without falling into the water but had fallen off the 'cliff' just before that. And Jessica, who went last, got hit in the head by an appearing branch, and, by the scream that emanated from the fog, she had fallen off the imaginary cliff, too.

Their clothes and hair practically drenched with sweat, they ate lunch (sandwiches and salad with water to drink) outside on benches. Morgan sat next to Corey and Cassidee, not daring to talk for it used up too much of their precious energy.

Jessica

As the group trudged inside like mindless zombies, Jessica was pretty much asleep on her feet. She had never been through that much physical exertion in a four hour span of time before. However, when she heard they would be in classrooms next, she brightened right up.

They studied maps of the Empire and learned about what kinds of things would be waiting out there for her, Kyle, and Cassidee when they went to the Southern Empire.

"Werewolves are not uncommon, especially in this area," Sarissa said, her hand circling a rather large island on the map. "This island is called *Île de la Pleine Lune*, or 'Island of the Full Moon' in French. And this large island next to it is called *Pays de épouvantail;* Country of the Scarecrow. It is a dark place—

hopefully you will not have to cross it, for far more things worse than Okkultens live here.

"Now for the more difficult task: putting up a mind shield. As I said earlier, not all creatures may attack physically—some, like Doppelgangers, Sirens, Wendigo, and Will-o'-the-wisps confuse you or hypnotize you. This will leave your mind open to all those who wish to look inside it, the worst being mind-invading demons. They will automatically enter your mind and dig up all your secrets, your sanity—they will overtake you."

Jessica scribbled this all down in a notebook she had found in her desk.

"Mind shields can only happen by great will and determination. There is no magic involved. It takes only the greatest strength of the soul to accomplish. So go on, try it. Hailey and I will be walking around, trying to see if your defenses are strong enough."

They made it sound so simple—as if this was a test and they were checking the answers. It almost resounded as wrong in Jessica's brain, almost too forced, as if they were hiding something. *You're probably just imagining things*, she thought. There was nothing 'right' about any of this—so why were they following along? It wasn't because they had to, right? Almost too late, she noticed Sarissa coming toward her desk.

Jessica closed her eyes and focused on protecting her sanity, every thought in her mind. She grunted; this was harder than she thought. Suddenly, she felt something probe gently at her mind, like a cold finger of steel. Jessica panicked suddenly, her brain screaming: *No! My sanity! My brain! MINE!* She felt the prober disappear, and she heard a crash. She opened her eyes and saw Sarissa on top of two knocked over desks right next to her.

"Wow, Jessica, that was good!" she complimented, standing up again and resetting the desks. She brushed off her jeans. "Your defense was so strong it literally forced me and out and away from you."

Jessica smiled as she always did when being complimented by a teacher, forgetting completely about the doubt she had just housed in her mind.

The practice continued for a few more minutes until Sarissa had finished trying to probe everyone in the room. "Alright, then! Aerobics, now!"

Jessica groaned inwardly. *More* athletics? This was like gym class set on repeat.

So for the next hour and a half, they stretched, walked, ran, rode bikes around the track and climbed rock walls and chain-link fences. Afterwards, though, it was time for a two-mile run around the track.

Jessica wasn't the only one to walk. Corey slowed after a mile, looking like she might collapse any second. Kyle also stopped after a mile, looking green. Only Morgan, Waverly, Kevin, and Cassidee managed to run a full two miles, even though they were practically tripping over their own feet at the end.

Afterwards was dinner (steak, chicken pot pie, and a vegetable mix), which was eaten in silence, and then a shower. Jessica felt the hot water run over her sore muscles, threatening to do in her tired legs. Only when the mirror was covered with a thick fog did she finally come out of the shower, her curiosity about the Empire back in her mind. She didn't sleep well that night.

Chapter 14: Leaving Safety – Kyle

It had been two weeks since their arduous training regime had begun. Now the run through the woods had progressed to 1.5 miles, and the regular two miles had turned to 2.5. The obstacle course became longer and new challenges were added on. Everyone could clear the hurdles and jump across the logs with ease. The run through the forest no longer vanquished all energy. Sore muscles were everyday pains. Their mind shield became stronger; their knowledge of what lay outside the castle grew with each passing lesson.

And now, something finally happened.

Kyle felt himself being shaken awake and when he blinked open his eyes he found himself staring into the strange violet eyes of Kevin Smith. Worry was written across the thirteen-year-old's face, and his face was flushed. Something was very wrong to have Kevin, who was actually a pretty tough kid, scared like that. Kyle felt a surge of panic as he struggled to sit upright with Kevin straddling his chest. "What's going on?" Kyle asked, sitting up now, his face now reflecting Kevin's.

Kevin swung his legs over the side of the bed so that he was standing. It was still dark outside. "We're under attack! The Nightmares have sent Cynocephali."

Kyle scrambled out of bed and to his feet, now fully awake. Cynocephali were an ancient race of dog-headed men, who could understand any language but could not speak. Though people on the Outside depicted them in legends and artwork as being civilized, they were really savage beasts who lived to hunt and kill. If the Nightmares had sent them, they really were in trouble.

"Here!" Kevin showed a handful of clothes at Kyle. "Get dressed! We're supposed to meet the girls downstairs!"

Kyle took off his nightshirt and pulled on a red shirt and black jeans. He slid his socked feet into black running shoes. He pulled on a black jacket and zipped it up so that he was entirely covered in the color.

The two boys raced out of their room and flew down the hall—accidentally running into the girls, which led to all seven of them, including Waverly, tumbling down the stairs.

The girls were also dressed in black, wearing the same thing as the boys. Kyle helped Cassidee stand again, her long dark blonde hair falling down her back like a wave. "What do we do?" she asked, looking around wildly as everyone struggled to his or her feet.

"Here!" A voice called from the entrance to the atrium. They turned their heads, and, to their surprise, spotted Hailey standing at the threshold, beckoning them to come to her. She looked frazzled, her long golden hair tangled and her eyes were still clouded with sleep.

The seven kids ran over and saw that Fleur and Joseph had joined Hailey at the doorway. "You guys need to leave! Now!" Hailey exclaimed. "It isn't safe for you here anymore."

"Wha' abou' us?" Joseph asked, stamping his cane on the ground. "Who's supposed ta' go with 'em?" He pointed at the seven kids.

"You are, of course, and Fleur too."

"But you need us here!" Fleur exclaimed, stepping forward.

"No, we don't. It is more important that these kids are protected as much as possible during their mission."

"But we haven't completed our training!" Jessica exclaimed.

Hailey gave her a despairing look. "And I wish you could. Now, take these," she picked nine brown bags up off the ground and handed them out to the kids, Joseph, and Fleur. "I have a back exit that Fleur and Joseph know about. They'll take you there. Now *go!*" Hailey shoved them forward, then turned and ran across the dining hall, picking up the folds of her nightgown to run.

Kyle watched the strands of her vibrant golden hair disappear into the darkness, then turned and ran after the others, biting his lip.

As Waverly and Fleur led the way through the shadow-filled castle, the sounds of battle slowly became louder. Suddenly, a window burst open and two Cynocephali leaped into the castle, causing the group to let out a collective scream and fall over, covering their heads as the shattered glass rained down over them.

Moonlight flooded into the corridor, illuminating the two figures of the dog-headed men. They had ruffled, short gray fur and long snouts, like those of a wolf. They wore black robes, covering their pale skin, and wore black boots that disappeared under the robes. They had gloved hands that gripped the handles of sheathed swords. But their eyes...their eyes were the most disturbing things of all. They were human, and empty of all emotion.

As the group scrambled back to their feet, with Waverly and Fleur helping Joseph to his feet, the Cynocephali drew their swords, the sharp steel blades practically glowing in the moonlight.

Jessica let out a frightened squeak as one sword missed slicing open her chest by inches.

"Run!" Waverly screamed. The group took off, following Waverly and Fleur down the corridors, descending further into the ground, steadily becoming swathed in shadows. The dog-headed men followed, hot on the group's heels, as Joseph's cane turned into what looked like a rocket skateboard and he passed all of them.

Kyle had never felt so scared before. It was getting darker and darker until he couldn't even see Corey's blonde hair anymore. Suddenly, he felt his foot go down a step. Stairs. He ran down them as fast as he could without running the others over and tumbling down the stairs.

Kyle felt somebody grab his sleeve and yank him around a corner. He dove to the ground as the Cynocephali raced past them down the corridor. The group waited silently until they heard a howl of frustration come from the creatures a long way away.

Kyle felt a tug at his sleeve again, and he pushed himself to his feet, keeping hold of the person's sleeve that was in front of him.

They walked through the passageways underneath the castle, with no light to guide them. Occasionally he heard Waverly murmur something unintelligible, but it didn't matter, because it obviously wasn't for his ears. It was becoming colder, damper, and, if even possible, darker. The blackness began to weigh on them like a cloak in the height of summer—heavy and smothering.

Suddenly, the group rounded the corner and saw torchlight flickering down at the end of a passageway. They all sighed in relief. Kyle saw Cassidee let go of his sleeve. "Pull up your hoods," Fleur instructed softly, and the group did so. Joseph stepped off his transformed skateboard and it automatically turned back into his cane. Kyle shook his head to make sure he wasn't hallucinating.

They walked down the hall, and soon saw a door at the end. "Is that the back exit Hailey wanted you to take us out of?" Kevin asked.

"Yes," Waverly said. She stopped at the door and opened it. They all emerged, blinking, into the bright sunlight.

Chapter 15: Parting – Corey

They had emerged about five miles away from the castle. The sunlight was almost blinding, but the hoods helped shield their eyes somewhat. They were in a field, with rolling hills for miles. Fluffy white clouds blew by overhead, a soft breeze barely stirring the grass.

The group turned to one another. "Well, I guess this is where we leave each other," Cassidee said firmly.

"But not forever, right?" Corey argued, hope straining in her voice. "I mean, we'll see each other again?"

"Hopefully, yes," Waverly said quietly. "Good luck with Graystorm, you three," she said.

"And good luck with the queen's siblings," Morgan whispered back, her voice catching.

"We won't need luck with them, it's crossing the territory that we'll need help with."

"But we still might need help," Kyle argued, his voice and smile shaking slightly. "What if they go all royal on us and refuse our help? Like, 'Why would we need the help of you lowly lives? Humph!'" he said in a rich voice, tossing his pretend long hair over a shoulder and sticking his nose in the air, doing a great impression of a stereo-typical queen.

Everyone laughed weakly. It might be hard to admit, but they had grown to appreciate each other over the past two weeks of practically living together. And now they were supposed to say goodbye?

"We always knew this was going to happen, guys," Cassidee murmured, breaking the silence, her eyes on the ground.

Everyone dropped their eyes to the ground, as if in a silent prayer. The wind gently blew through the grass, tugging at their pant-legs.

Fleur coughed gently to break the silence. "So...um...goodbye, Waverly, Joseph. Good-bye Kyle, Cassidee, Jessica. It was nice knowing you." Her voice cracked.

"And it was nice knowing you," Jessica returned.

Goodbyes were exchanged shakily, carefully. Corey felt tears swimming in front of her eyes. *Do* not *cry,* she told herself forcefully. She wiped her face with the back of her sleeve and hugged Waverly, Cassidee and then Kyle tightly. She squeezed Jessica's hand in goodbye and nodded to Joseph. He nodded back, giving them a wobbly smile.

Finally, the group broke away from each other. Corey stood with Fleur, who laid a hand on her shoulder, and Morgan and Kevin. Jessica, Cassidee, Kyle, Joseph, and Waverly stood on the other side of an invisible barrier, sending the other side sad smiles.

"Good luck, guys. We'll see you soon," Fleur said, speaking for the three teenagers.

"Take care," Joseph said, giving a small salute.

And the groups turned away from each other and walked away into the sunlight.

Chapter 16: The Outside – Kevin

Fleur led the group to the Outside safely, where they waited in a patch of woods, going through their bags.

Inside each bag's front pouch was two packs of dried fruit, dried beef jerky, and warmed hamburger meat. There were also two frozen water bottles and a small cup of vegetables.

Inside the bag itself was a two-days change of clothes, each exactly the same. There was also twenty dollars in fives. A black sleeping bag and flashlight with extra batteries lay inside as well.

Kevin saw his sister and Corey sling the bags over their backs again and stand up. He followed suit, watching his mother examine the items in her bag one last time before standing up, too. "Come on," she said, taking the lead. "Let's go."

They walked on for hours in silence. There was nothing to say. Glances were cast at each other as they walked on, the sun, which had reached its peak, finally starting to sink. Their stomachs started to growl loudly with hunger; they hadn't had anything to eat all day.

Pretty soon, they stumbled upon the town of Hovington. It was small and partially abandoned; cars no longer traveled along the cracked black pavement, causing grass and weeds to grow inside the tiny divides. The buildings were falling apart, like at home, and everything had a shabby look to it. The windows were covered with grime, shutters were drawn tight on the occupied houses, and the curtains flapped lazily in the abandoned ones. Some doors were locked tight; others were falling off their hinges. Sometimes Kevin could faintly hear static from a TV set blaring through a closed window.

After a mile, they reached the edge of town. There sat a diner from what looked like the 1950s, electric blue with white neon lines running around the walls. The black door hung open, and cold air blasted outside onto a cracked sidewalk. A filthy, scruffy pink floor mat was outside. The neon OPEN sign flickered on and off, the E out completely.

The group walked inside, meeting a blast of air conditioning. The floor was a checkered black and white, there were bright red booths that were torn with the stuffing and springs sticking out, the tables were dusty and holding old dinner trays still loaded with trash. The bar stools were wobbly, some were completely out of the floor, and a burning smell came from the kitchen. The old and probably broken jukebox blared an old song Kevin had never heard of, constantly skipping. They were the only ones inside, besides the waitress.

The waitress was a short, plump woman with piled blonde curls in the shape of a beehive with too much red lipstick. She wore a pale pink shirt that looked faded from sunlight and had ketchup and grease stains on it. She wore a black apron and a knee-length white-and-pink checkered skirt and black roller skates. She held a black tray up by her head, and her white nametag read: MACY.

"What can I do for you?" she asked, wobbling slightly on her roller-skates.

"Just some food, please," Kevin's mom said politely, holding out ten dollars.

"It's free. Don't worry. I stopped charging long ago," Macy said, refusing the money and skating away into the kitchen.

About ten minutes later the foursome sat in a torn-up booth as they hungrily devoured hamburgers, French fries, thick malts, and (on Fleur's orders) a glass of water.

After using the restroom, they thanked Macy and asked for directions to the nearest hotel.

"Well, the nearest place with an open bed is Graystorm Asylum, but you don't want to go there. They say it's haunted, plus its been abandoned for so many years. Bed bugs and termites, you know."

This caught Fleur off guard. "Where is Graystorm?"

Macy eyed her suspiciously. "Why do you want to know?"

"Just curious?" Kevin's mom said.

Macy nodded after a moment. "I see. Only natural you'd want to know...but I don't know anyone who hasn't heard about Graystorm...heck, this town was practically famous for being so near it... Well, then, it's about five miles from here, just down that road through the woods."

They all looked out at the darkening sky.

"Is there anywhere closer we can stay?" Fleur asked hopefully.

"There is the Burnsons' place, they usually let passer byes sleep at their place. It's about five buildings down," Macy said, jerking her thumb down the street. "In fact, let me go get them for you."

She skated out of the diner and down the street, the group following warily. Macy pounded on the door of a building and yelled: "Hey! Loretta! I've got people who need somewhere to stay for the night!"

The door opened and a woman wearing a gray tank top and black gym shorts stepped outside. Her black hair was pulled into a tight ponytail, and her gray eyes looked tired. Her face was stretched, her thin lips stuck in a hard line. "Yes, Macy? Where are they?"

Fleur stepped forward, Kevin, Morgan, and Corey following her. "Hi, I'm Fleur Smith, and these are my kids," she said, including Corey as one of her own.

Loretta Burnson eyed the group warily, then waved them in. "Come on. I have a bedroom open."

Needless to say, the inside of the building was crumbling as well. White paint peeled off the walls, the carpet stank, and the air inside was stuffy and warm. Loretta took them through a narrow hallway and opened the last door. Inside was a queen-sized bed with white sheets and a pullout couch. "Here you go. I want you out of this house by six o'clock tomorrow morning," Loretta snapped, shoving them into the room and slamming the door in their faces before Fleur could even open her mouth to say 'thank you.'

They stared, blinking, at the closed door for a few minutes before Kevin's mom sighed and walked over to the bed, setting down her bag. "At least she's letting us stay here."

The teenagers set down their bags while Fleur pulled out the worn couch. "Alright. Corey, you can share the bed with me. Kevin, Morgan, you're brother and sister so don't look at me like that. You two divide up the couch. Put up a pillow barrier; I don't care. Just find someway to sleep."

Within a few minutes, shoes had been kicked off and jackets were being used as blankets. Kevin curled up on one end of the couch, Morgan on the other, the bottom of their feet touching. Soon the excitement of the day began to weigh on him, and he closed his eyes, letting sleep overtake him.

Chapter 17: Over the Hills and Far Away – Cassidee

The wind howled, rain came pouring down in sheets, and thunder shook the ground. Heading south, Cassidee and the others were soaked to the skin. They'd hiked their backpacks up over their heads to try and keep their vision clear.

Cassidee felt her foot sink into a mud puddle, letting out a small snort of disgust as the filthy muck and water filled her shoe, soaking her already numb foot.

They had been slowly advancing south for two days. So far they had made about thirty miles, doing all of this on foot. Joseph was on his rocket skateboard most of the time, for he couldn't walk as fast or for as long as they could.

Now they were out on a hilly landscape, in the middle of nowhere, with no shelter in the fifty mile radius that Jessica could see from the top of the highest hill.

They were quickly burning through their food rations, no matter how little they ate. Only one bottled water, dried fruit pack, and two strips of beef jerky were left per person. It was getting darker by the minute, and the weather was not helping.

"We need to find somewhere to stop!" Cassidee yelled to Waverly over the wind. Waverly turned her head and nodded, acknowledging Cassidee's request.

"There's a valley about a mile from here, I could see it about half an hour ago. We can stop there," Waverly yelled back.

So on they walked, trudging through the rain as sleep weighed them down. Cassidee's thoughts drifted to Morgan, Corey, Kevin, and Fleur. Where were they? Were they safe? She hoped so.

Soon, the hills started to slope downwards. Cassidee let out a sigh of relief. Maybe they could finally find someplace to sleep.

The hill continued down, down, beginning to slope at an almost precarious angle. Cassidee felt her feet slip occasionally if she ran across a particularly slippery mud puddle.

Suddenly, there was a scream behind Cassidee and Waverly, who were leading. They stopped, whipping their heads around, and saw Jessica tumbling down the hill, being chased by a mud slide. So Cassidee, Waverly, Kyle, and a gliding Joseph ran down the hill as fast as they could without tripping but without being caught by the mud slide. Jessica had already rolled past them, so Cassidee dove for the ground, landing in a slick mud bank, and tumbled down after her, her eyes squeezed shut as she rolled into the air and hit the ground with painful thuds.

She heard two more 'thuds' behind her, and knew that Waverly and Kyle had decided to tumble rather than run. It felt like ages, but finally, she felt herself roll to a stop at the bottom of the hill, the mudslide still chasing after them. Cassidee scrambled to her feet, helping Kyle up while Jessica dragged Waverly to her feet. As soon as they were standing, they took off again, Joseph still gliding after them.

Finally, though, the mudslide had run out of momentum and stopped just before a river. Cassidee dove in, swimming to the other side, checking behind her to see that Waverly, Jessica, and Kyle were managing okay.

Dragging herself onto the other muddy bank, Cassidee flopped to the ground, panting, but forced herself to crawl over to the edge and help drag Waverly out of the river.

Once everyone was safely on the bank, they were still covered with mud, waterlogged, and unbelievably cold. Hands and legs shaking, Waverly showed them toward a small cave in the now-upward-sloping hill. They crawled inside and shoved their sleeping bags together for body heat. Cassidee crawled inside hers and scrunched her four-foot-ten-inch tall body into a small ball, and, ignoring her wet clothes, fell asleep.

Chapter 18: Legacy of Darkness – Morgan

Her mother shaking her shoulders jolted Morgan awake. "Get up!" she hissed as Morgan blinked open her eyes sleepily. "We said we'd be out of here by six, so let's go!" As Morgan sat up, yawning and gathering her stuff, Fleur repeated the process with Kevin. Corey stood at the door, nibbling on a small strip of beef jerky, eyes still filled with sleep.

Morgan grabbed her bag and walked to the door, Kevin following, still yawning. Fleur opened the door quietly and the four walked stealthily down the hall. There was no one around, not so much as a glance of a shadow.

They disappeared out the front door and walked down the abandoned street, the sun barely grazing the horizon. They stopped at the diner from the night before, and saw Macy opening shop again. "Mornin'," she said sleepily, yawning. "You want some bacon 'n biscuits for the road? I got plenty."

Fleur nodded. "Sure. Thank you."

"No problem," Macy said, skating back to the front holding a large paper bag. "Here you go."

Macy then disappeared back into the diner, closing the door behind her.

After walking on a while, they began looking for a building. They had no idea what Graystorm looked like—they had actually never seen a picture of it before. Soon though, they reached the only building in the woods.

Towering behind a black stone wall, visible between the bars of the wrought-iron gate that was loosely padlocked with a rusty chain, was a four-story-tall building. It looked like a grand mansion that had been turned into something sinister. There were two 'peaks' on either side of the bell tower, which led all the way down to the front doors. The windows were covered in grime. An eerie mist rolled just beyond the gates. The black oak doors stood waiting, beckoning to be opened. Silent whispers filled the group's heads, buzzing around inside like flies.

Graystorm Asylum.

After a few moments of silence, Fleur swallowed hard, then said: "Well, let's go."

Morgan walked forward, suddenly seized by a strong fear of this building...this *entity*. The building seemed to almost breathe. It seemed like the place that would fit in a lightning storm, with flashes illuminating the scary sanitarium.

Fleur took the padlock in the hands and roughly yanked on the chains. It crumbled in her hand.

The gates swung open, slowly. The creaking sound filled the early morning, casting shadows among the trees. A slight breeze whispered through, the curious fog looked as if it was restraining itself from catching the foursome in its opaque fingers.

Fleur and the others gulped. "Be strong," Fleur murmured, whether to the teenagers or to herself, Morgan didn't know. She felt Kevin's hand unconsciously grip her own. It was cold and sweaty. She squeezed it, holding onto it like a lifeline. She reached her hand out to Corey, and felt the fourteen-year-old take it, almost cutting off the circulation in her fingers and grinding her bones together.

They stepped through the gates, and the fog swirled around them, almost trapping them. They walked up the drive, their hands intertwined like lifelines, as if they could cling to each other's sanity. They were not aware of the gates creaking closed behind them, or the fact that they were being watched.

A woman stood at the last tower at the window, glaring down at the new guests through the outside grime. Her mouth was twisted into a look of disgust. "Those Empire brats are back. And they've sent the soul survivor with them. I told you we should have exterminated her first," the woman said to apparently no one. She had blonde hair that was wavy and danced in loose ringlets all the way down her back to her waist. Her eyes were an acid green. She wore a white lab coat and carried a clipboard.

A figure seemed to solidify out of the shadows. A thin man, probably about six feet tall, who also wore a lab coat, strode forward. His hair was black and wavy, curled on his head like a sleeping black mamba. His eyes were like the woman's, a glowing acid green. "Now, now, Cadenza, we can have fun with this. She thinks she knows all of our secrets."

A sinister smile replaced the scowl on the woman's face. Her voice was now a sickly sweet kind. "You're right, Doctor Steele, she thinks she does. So why don't we surprise them? I'll get everything ready."

As Cadenza turned to walk away, Steele grabbed her arm. "No, not yet. Let's welcome them to our home first. I'd hate to be rude," he said, his voice mimicking hers. Cadenza smiled back, her acid green eyes glowing.

Slowly, Fleur reached out a shaking hand and pulled open the black doors.

Chapter 19: Ghosts of the Midway – Kyle

The rain had stopped, and had been replaced by a thick mist that hung outside of the cave. It was eerily quiet and still.

Kyle blinked open his eyes and crawled out of his sleeping bag, trying not to wake the others. It failed, however, because Cassidee woke up, eyes wide and panting as she took in her surroundings and remembered where she was. She groaned and flopped her head back onto the sleeping bag, her jacket still damp.

Her groan stirred Jessica, who woke up the same way as Cassidee, and Waverly slowly blinked, sitting up and yawning. Joseph blinked his eyes open and brandished his cane, but when he realized that enemies didn't surround him, only kids, he set down his cane, mumbling about poor vision as he packed up his bag.

Everyone ate a strip of beef jerky and downed it with two gulps of water. "That's all we can allow," Waverly said quietly. "I know your stomachs are growling, mine is too, but we can't blow all our rations this quickly. Maybe a nearby town will have some more food."

"Speaking of that, Waverly," Jessica said, stumbling over to her, still half-asleep, "where are we going?"

Waverly stood up. "Well, I say we continue over the hill and continue south. We have to reach a town sometime, right?"

"Alright, then. Lead the way," Joseph grumbled.

They climbed out of the small cave and started up the hill into the mist. To Kyle, it still felt like nighttime. The sun was behind clouds, not that they could see the sky through the thick fog.

They hiked on for about two miles before finally reaching the crest of a hill that sloped into flat land below. There was the shape of a town beckoning below the mist.

"Yes!" Waverly exclaimed softly. "This way!"

She led the way down the steep incline, staying on her toes and going this-way and that, so as not to provoke another mudslide. The rest of the group followed as best they could, trying to copy Waverly's movements.

As they reached the bottom of the hill, though, the fog seemed to only thicken. They could not see any lights that indicated a town was there. "Maybe they're still asleep," Waverly murmured, mostly to herself.

They walked forward, the wetness from the dew-laden grass seeping into their running shoes. Even though his jacket was damp, Kyle was glad to have it. The air was still, but it had gotten colder.

Suddenly, Kyle felt his foot land on top of a board. "Huh?" he muttered, looking down at it. In fact, the board spread to other boards, which created a boardwalk. Like you would find at a circus, long ago.

He stepped onto the boardwalk and walked forward lightly, in case the boards weren't stable. They seemed to hold his weight just fine. "Hey, guys! I think I've found your town, Waverly!"

He heard the creaking of boards and knew that Waverly and the others were joining him, cautiously, on the boardwalk. "It's alright, it'll hold our weight," he reassured them.

He heard the thumping of footsteps then sensed that the others were beside him. Waverly walked forward. "This is so strange," she whispered in awe. "I thought all the circuses were torn down a long time ago."

They continued down the boardwalk, and the fog began to thin. They saw the remains of the old circus booths that held games and prizes, hot dogs and cotton candy. Just peaking over the top of the mist was a lightning rod on the tip of a huge red-and-white striped tent. The Big Top.

Suddenly, a voice boomed out of the loud speakers: *"Welcome ladies and gentlemen to the circus of the strange, the sideshow of the sinister and the theatre of the bizarre... If you dare, explore the shadows of your most diabolical nightmares...Cast your eyes upon the cruel oddities of nature and behold monstrous creatures from the depths of the abyss. Marvel with awe and dismay at unbelievable death-defying acts that teeter on the very brink of doom. Leave the mundane world behind, for those who visit this festival of specters are never the same again... Step this way... There is no turning back!"*

Jessica squeaked softly.

"Well... Okay," Waverly said softly. "This must be someone's idea of a joke. Come on, let's go."

They walked back toward where they came from. At least, they thought they did. But the boardwalk never ended. The mist never cleared. And even though time must have been passing, the sun never rose.

"Come on!" Waverly said, sweat running down her forehead as she doubled back for the third time and dashed down another un-ending walk. "There has to be a way out!"

Jessica and the others stood in the center, watching Waverly dash madly around them. "Alright!" she announced, her face red. "I'm going to change forms and fly above the tents to find a way out. Be right back."

Kyle and the others watched as Waverly turned away from them, arching her back as her skin stretched and crumbled away from her, not leaving a skeleton, but a raven. She flapped her oil-black wings, lifting into the foggy sky, disappearing into the cloud.

They waited. And waited. It seemed like forever. Kyle was starting to get worried, the others fidgety. Where was Waverly?

Suddenly, there was a painful and frightening squawk, and Waverly the Raven hit the ground. She changed back into human form, and came unsteadily to her feet, looking worse for wear. "There is no way out," she panted. "There's a dome. It's surrounding the entire place. This place wants something from us...and if we don't pay, we'll never get out."

Chapter 20: Graystorm Asylum – Kevin

The oak doors swung open silently. There was no creaking, no groaning. Just silence. And that is very weird for an old building whose doors have not been opened in quite a few years.

But of course…this was no ordinary building.

Inside the building it was dark. A long hallway stretched before them. Candles flickered in their iron sconces. Fleur stared at one of them. "They were here when I first came, too. Has anything really changed?"

The floor under their feet was a dark hardwood. To their left, there was an iron grate, and behind that, spiraling stairs. A sign said: "Level 2 – Up | Cellar Ward – Down" Fleur walked forward unsteadily down the hallway, the kids following. They rounded the corner and saw what must have been the lunch hall. The tables still held the remains of food that sat on small plates. The grimy windows had rusted steel bars.

Fleur cautiously walked through, the kids following. The silence was making Kevin uneasy. In back, in the kitchen, a green light flickered. They carefully walked forward, the three teenagers cowering behind Fleur.

They walked into the kitchen. Knives were still in the sink, unwashed and rusted. Plates were stacked high, and there was a red spatter on the wall. Tomato sauce? Or blood? Kevin couldn't be sure, and didn't know if he wanted to find out.

They continued walking toward the light. They rounded another corner, the one that led to the pantry, and saw an overhead light with two wires cut, one still hanging on to the ceiling. The green light it emitted zapped and buzzed, flickering, casting strange shadows over the walls.

Fleur pushed them past the strange light. "Come on," she whispered quietly, and then continued through the iron grate that led to the pantry.

The place looked like it had been ransacked. Bags of food were tipped over, spilled, scattering rice and dried beans across the floor. No mice scuttled about, though, eating the spilled food.

Dust and cobwebs clung to corners as the foursome carefully advanced through the dark asylum.

They had just made it out of the kitchen when a scream erupted from a level up. The group froze and stared at the ceiling as they heard the overhead floorboards creak, and a dragging, shuffling sound.

"I t-t-thought only the d-d-doctors haunted t-t-this p-p-place," Corey stammered.

"I think every soul lost to Steele's and Cadenza's tortures inhabits this cursed building," Fleur murmured as they continued on.

Morgan looked down at her feet. "How sad. Imagine being a person who can't really control their condition, and you come to this place and end up being tortured." She shook her head. "They deserved some other place where they had a chance, even if it was slim, of getting better. And look at what these doctors gave them!"

Kevin's mother just nodded to Morgan's lament. "Graystorm's history is really more sad than it is scary."

Now they had reached the gym. It was very large, probably taking up the rest of the first floor. The basketball hoops were lowered and padded on all sides, even the rims. The nets were hanging by threads, the floorboards were torn up. Kevin wondered how many fouls you would get if you tripped over one while playing basketball.

They found another set of stairs locked behind an iron grate. One led to the second-story ward, and the other led down into the boiler room. Fleur pulled the grate to one side easily, breaking the lock. "Let's go upstairs. We don't need to visit the cellar ward yet, I think."

"But that doesn't speak for the building itself," Kevin reminded them, going back to their original conversation. His voice was shaking slightly. "There is *evil* inside these walls, and believe me, I think we shouldn't be feeling sorry for that."

They continued up the rotting spiral stairs. They passed a window, and it looked like dawn was finally beginning to break. But it could barely penetrate the grime on the windows—they weren't going to get much light, even at noon.

Corey nodded. "The doctors did what they did. There's no going back. But maybe we can put these souls to rest, and close down whatever entrance is supposed to be here."

They walked down the second-story hallway in silence. The walls were padded; gouge marks present and blood streaks on the dirty hardwood floor. The doors were made of steel and locked with a small window looking out into the hallway. As they walked past one, Kevin peered into it. Inside the room, the walls were also padded. Dust motes swirled above a twin bed, where a rumpled and stained pillow sat against the padded walls. The room was not much bigger than the bed itself, and besides that bed, nothing else occupied the room.

Nothing visible, at least.

They continued down the hallway until they reached the next set of iron stairs. "The next two floors are just more rooms," Fleur informed them as they went down the stairs to what was supposed to be the activity room.

As the walked into the inky blackness again after descending the stairs, Kevin almost tripped over a fallen wheelchair. Blood stained the seat and back. He shuddered and kept walking.

Even though the place was old and falling apart, he kept thinking back to the flickering green light and the fact that the mice were non-existent. The building wasn't exactly being lived in, but it wasn't abandoned either.

Chapter 21: Madame Nirvana – Cassidee

"Pay? What do you mean? How do we pay?" Jessica asked Waverly, her voice shaking.

"I don't know. I just know that this place wants something from us, and we won't do it by standing around. Come on, let's explore," Waverly said, waving the group down a boardwalk to their left.

The place was certainly creepy. They seemed to be the only ones there. But then again, they couldn't be alone, for someone had spoken to them over the intercom. For whatever reason, Cassidee felt like she was in danger.

They walked along the boards carefully until they heard a humming sound coming from a tent around the next corner. They stopped and stiffened. Waverly turned to them and held a finger to her lips, then tiptoed toward the humming sound.

The rest of the group followed, as silently as possible, Joseph still gliding in the air, rolling his eyes.

They rounded the corner and were surprised at what they saw. A woman with long, curly red hair sat inside the tent, shuffling a deck of cards. She wore a violet medieval dress, and her face seemed full, her eyes small.

She looked up at them, and they stumbled backward. Her eyes were black, with no pupil. Her mouth was twisted into a bizarre smile.

"Welcome children, I have been waiting for you," she said, disregarding Joseph completely, who looked like he wanted to spit. Her voice was soft and melodic, and Cassidee felt almost entranced by it.

"How did you know we were here?" Waverly asked cautiously.

"I heard the announcement. It's been so long since we've had visitors," the woman simpered.

"'We've?' You mean, there are more people here?" Kyle asked, disbelief in his voice, ignoring the woman's sneer.

She ignored his question. "My name is Madame Nirvana. Step closer, allow me to show you the path of your destiny."

"No thank you," Waverly said, about to start away, but Cassidee saw her stop and turn around, as if pulled by an invisible force.

"Your future is in the cards," Madame Nirvana continued, holding the deck out before them. She fanned them out and motioned for Kyle to take a card. He chose one around the middle and flipped it over. "The Moon. Danger and fear lurk in the shadows."

She motioned for Waverly to take one. She shakily took a card and turned it over. Waverly flinched when she saw it. "The Hanged Man. Sacrifice will not avoid you."

Next was Jessica. "The Tower. Distress and deception are clouding your future, stopping your progress." Jessica whimpered.

Finally, it was Cassidee's turn. She carefully took a card and turned it over. Everyone, except Madame Nirvana, gasped and winced when they saw it. When she read the card, her melodic voice echoed around the ghostly circus like a bell of tolling doom. "The Devil. Evil follows your every move."

She raised her head and stared at them with her black, pupil-less eyes. "A storm is coming… Beware… Beware…"

She tossed her head back and let out an evil, bellowing laugh that ricocheted off every object in the circus. The kids and Joseph watched, fearful of what would happen next, as the mist swirled in around Madame Nirvana, and, when it cleared moments later, she was gone, but her evil laugh still echoed around the deserted boardwalk.

Chapter 22: The Doctors' Welcome – Corey

As they entered the activity room, everything was dark. Nothing, not even an outline, could be seen. Corey felt her heart pound in her chest. What if something was there, in the dark, waiting for them?

Suddenly, a light buzzed and flickered on and off in the center of the room, an eerie green like the one in the kitchen. When it buzzed on, illuminating what lay beneath it, the foursome stiffened.

A table had been set up as if for some kind of party. A festive cloth, faded blue with white-faced, almost evil grinning clowns, covered the table. Someone had arranged white paper plates for a gathering that had never occurred. A cake, which looked like it had solidified under its faded violet sugar coating, perched in the center on a small silver stand, right under the flickering green light. Several conical party hats ranging in different faded colors littered the floor. A ragged white banner had half-fallen from the ceiling, and it's original blue letters, which they guessed had read 'Happy Birthday' had been crossed out in what looked like blood and new words were printed over it in small, careful lettering.

'Welcome, newbies. Welcome back, Fleur.'

Fleur stared at the sign, stuttering meaningless words. Finally, she seemed to manage the ability to speak again. "What a horrible place," she whispered.

"You say 'horrible' like it's a bad thing," a sickly-sweet male voice said from the darkness. It sounded like a tone that would be used with a child when they were in trouble. Corey's heart thudded painfully against her ribcage, swelling with fear of this man that lurked in the shadows.

"Doctor Steele," Fleur whispered, her voice barely audible. In the flickering light, Corey could see that the woman's face had gone white, and sweat was running down her face.

"I'm so glad you remember me, Fleur," the doctor continued, still not revealing himself from the shadows. "Perhaps you remember my other fellow doctor as well?"

"Hi again, Fleur," a soft voice purred from the darkness.

"Cadenza," Fleur murmured, her voice shaking.

"Ooh!" Doctor Cadenza squealed from the shadows like a little girl. "She remembers my name! What an honor!" In a flash of light, Corey saw some acid green eyes roll comically with the last word.

"Well, we decided to throw a welcome party for you," Doctor Steele continued from the shadows, in his fake-sweet voice. "Do you like it? Cadenza spent *so* much time decorating. I'd hate for all her hard work to go to waste." At the last sentence, Corey could detect a sinister smile curling the corners of his lips upwards.

"Ugh, it wasted so much good torture time!" Cadenza groaned, all of her fake-happiness gone.

"Now Cadenza, be polite. I still don't think they're impressed with all the hard work we went to, doing this for them," Doctor Steele said patiently, consoling Doctor Cadenza.

"I'm sorry to say that none of this is new," Steele said, his attention back to them. "Our last party...got cut short. Perhaps you remember, Fleur? I decided to leave it be. It could still work for a welcome party. We always knew that you'd come back. When we heard whispers of the six 'Destined Ones' we decided to edit the banner a little bit. Do you like it? I think Cadenza did a great job with the writing. Of course, it wouldn't be hard finding some more blood, since we're all, well, not dead but not living...but...we wanted to give you a proper greeting, so Queen Chandra generously supplied us with one of her own worthless minions."

The voice was moving toward them now, still sticking to the shadows. "And what have we here? The three newbies? I hear the other three of you 'Destined Ones' went searching for Queen

Sarissa's missing brother and sister. Too bad Queen Sarissa doesn't realize it's a lost cause, otherwise they could have come here—I think they would have enjoyed this party. After all, the more the merrier!"

"For you maybe," Corey found herself saying, suddenly angry that the doctor was taunting her and her friends. Even though her voice shook slightly, it was strong. She tried to glare at where she thought he was.

"Oh, we have a brave one!" Cadenza squealed. Corey and the group stumbled backward, for the voice was only feet away. "Now, now, don't go anywhere! The brave ones are so much fun! What's your name?"

A cold and almost slimy hand grabbed Corey's wrist. She felt herself yanked forward until she was staring into bright acerbic green eyes that mimicked the flickering lights. In a short flash, she caught sight of a long blonde curl, pale skin, a white lab coat, and a cruel smile. Corey struggled to back away again, but Cadenza tightened her hold, her long fingernails sinking into Corey's skin. Corey whimpered.

"Sorry, I didn't catch that," the doctor whispered, her soft and sweet voice sending chills up and down Corey's spine.

"Her name's Corey," Fleur said, grabbed Corey's other wrist and yanking her from Cadenza's hold. Cadenza let her go, and in a flicker of light, she saw a snarl full of disgust.

"And would you mind telling me who the lovely brother and sister are?" Cadenza murmured, and Corey heard the click of a heel as she stepped forward.

"Stop that, Cadenza, you're scaring them. And we don't want that...yet anyway. We want them to feel welcome," Doctor Steele said, his voice now next to where Cadenza would be. Corey guessed that he was holding her back. "I'm sorry about Cadenza," he said to the trembling foursome. "She can get a little...impatient. But don't worry, her work is some of the best. She really calms down nicely. Like a dog after you give it a satisfying treat for a trick it has yet to perform. She is eager to

83

show you her skills, like that dog. And I would like to know your names, you two. Makes it easier to talk to someone."

"M-m-morgan," Morgan stammered, her face white as she gripped her twin's hand tightly.

"Well, it's nice to meet you, Morgan," Steele said, and Corey could see his tall outline bow mockingly. "And Corey, it's nice to meet you too." Another bow. "And who are you, Morgan's brother?"

"I'm her twin, actually," Kevin said, his voice starting to crack. "I'm Kevin."

"Well, Kevin, now that we're all on a first name basis, why don't we get down to business? And don't look so scared—we're not going to kill you, not even going to touch you until you become a threat. So stay away from what doesn't concern you, and we'll gladly let you go. Consider my offer, now, take your time."

Corey desperately wanted to leave. But a small part of her knew she couldn't, no matter how scared she was. She knew, deep down, that the doctors would never let them go, not now. They had already damaged them, mentally. She felt her mental shield pop up, forcing something back, out of her mind. Yes...that was better. She felt braver already.

She felt Morgan squeeze her hand, and she knew that her friend and Kevin were thinking the same thing.

Together, they sent a mental message to Doctor Steele: "*We're not leaving. But you can't take our sanity, our minds. We won't let you. We stand together.*"

He spoke next, clearly having gotten their message. "For now. It's only a matter of time. That's your decision though, so very well." In a flash of light, Corey saw a long, red scar across the doctor's pale throat.

"Welcome to Graystorm, and let the horror begin."

Chapter 23: Doubts – Hailey

Hailey scrambled up the steps leading to the tallest tower in the castle, clutching the hem of her golden dress, her blonde hair matted with sweat. She had to find Sarissa and tell her what she had just seen...

She ran up the spiraling steps, her legs beginning to shake. The recent battle against the Cynocephali had left them all struggling to get back on their feet. Chandra had sent more and more reinforcements, only drawing back when two of her dog-headed men came scampering back with none of the Destined Ones.

Chandra was worried, Hailey had realized. She had gotten wind of the prophecy, and knew that if these kids really were that powerful, then she was in trouble. She wanted to put them out of the game. Hailey really had no idea what Chandra would have done with them. Would she have killed them...or worse?

Clutching a stitch in her side, Hailey was at the top of the tower. Sure enough, Sarissa stood at the widow, her long silver gown sweeping the floor, her white hair straight and smooth, like the battle had never happened. Without turning, she said: "You've gotten a change in prophecy, Hailey?"

"Not a change, my sister, no. But it looks worse than it did before. Our horizons are darkening. Should we have kept the Destined Ones here, even after the attack, until their two months were up?" Hailey asked, coming to stand by her sister.

"No. The attack would not have stopped until she had them. They were no longer safe here."

"But they're not safe out there either!"

"True, but they have Fleur, Joseph, and Waverly, who all know what they're doing."

"But still, they can't guarantee the kids' safety—"

"Listen to me, Hailey!" Sarissa snapped, the anger in her voice rising. "Those kids have never been safe. And they never will be, not until this is all over. We can't lock them in the castle every time something bad happens—we'd never get anywhere, we'd never let them fulfill their destiny." Her tone softened. "When a destiny is fulfilled, as you should know, sacrifice is required. It was not easy, letting them go without finishing their preparations. But as I said, they have three of my most skilled informants who have been watching them for years. I could not have placed them in safer hands."

"But Sarissa, what if we were wrong? Should we have told them where they were really going and what their real objectives were? The horizons are darkening."

"They always do before the worst, Hailey. We've seen enough battles to know that is true. As for the truth..." She sighed, looking out the window, "...it would be too dangerous to tell them. But they'll figure it out. They're smart."

"Sarissa, I've also had a feeling that the group headed south are trapped in the Circus of Lost Souls."

Sarissa's head snapped toward Hailey, her eyes suddenly housing a fierce fear and anger. "What?"

"They've gotten stranded in the Circus of Lost Souls," Hailey repeated. "Sarissa, you know what happens to those who go in there...some of our strongest, most well trained, and they never come out. Even if they do, they are...different. Like Crystal, Fleur's friend, when she came from Graystorm. That place holds such a strong aura of black magic, I can't even begin to imagine who's behind it."

"We need to get them out."

"But we can't, I've had some of my dove messengers try, but they can't break through the shield that surrounds the place."

"They need something inside, then. Something powerful enough to get them out... Hailey, didn't you mention something a few days ago about Pandora's Box?"

"Yeah, but Pandora opened the box, and it can't suck the evil back in...what are you saying?"

"I'm saying that maybe Pandora planted something there, in the box, that helps a person get out of the Circus."

"Like a talisman?"

"Yes, of a sort."

"So, you think that if that thing really does exist, then they can get out of the Circus unharmed?"

"That depends on how fast they find it, and how fast we can get word to them."

"But...their destiny hasn't changed, I think. That means we can get word to them, right? That means the Empire will still be saved?"

"Hailey, you are the one who had this prophecy, not me. I am sorry, but I cannot help you when it comes to the mysteries of divination. You will have to either delve deeper or trust your gut. But do not lose hope. If the stars have not changed, then all will be well when this storm passes."

Chapter 24: Nightmare Parade – Kyle

Waverly turned and ran away from the place where Madame Nirvana had sat. The others followed her as she blindly charged through the mist, trying to escape the woman's evil laugh that echoed around the Circus.

"Waverly? Are the cards right?" Jessica asked, breathing hard.

"I don't know. You can never tell with the cards. Hailey doesn't mess with them because if she sees something bad, she doesn't want to send everyone into an uproar for nothing."

They rounded a corner and saw a sign hanging above a tent. "'Circus of Lost Souls Merchandise?'" Kyle read, confused. What was the Circus of Lost Souls?

Waverly obviously knew, though, for she stiffened and her already-pallid skin turned even whiter, like she had seen—no, *was*—a ghost. "The Circus? Why didn't I see the signs? Oh, no, this is bad. Very, *very* bad," she mumbled, backing away.

"What's wrong, Waverly?" Cassidee asked, cocking her head slightly in question.

"We're in the Circus of Lost Souls, one of the most haunted and evil entities in the Empire. Black magic was practiced here; this is where Pandora opened her box to let all the evil loose in the world. This place is considered almost worse than Graystorm Asylum. Because here, they have the Circus *Diabolique*. The Circus *Diabolique* came from the very heart of Pandora's box, only after the devil himself. He likes to...torture people here until they go mad, and he makes them part of the Circus. Very few people ever come out. And if they do...they're never the same. All of them have either ended up killing themselves or getting sentenced to mental institutions. And the worst part is...the Circus never stays in one place. It will disappear and reappear at random, usually popping up wherever lost travelers are. Then it locks you inside, no time passes...and...that's the end for you."

"How did those people ever get out to begin with?" Cassidee asked.

"They weren't fit to tell us, were they? And neither Sarissa nor Hailey could figure out what had gotten people out of that immense evil. As you should probably know, very few ever escape the devil's clutches after wandering in."

Suddenly, a bell rang. It was like a church bell, a mourning sound, but also sounded demented and dark. It was ominous.

Waverly turned her head away from the store. The boardwalk began to creak. "Look," she whispered, pointing to the center of the midway.

Kyle turned his head and nearly screamed. He felt his heart thump painfully against his ribcage while his face paled.

People wearing costumes, dressed as fairies, princesses, jesters, kings, queens, and knights walked in a two-by-two march, parading down the boardwalk, heading straight toward the kids and Joseph. A man wearing a black top hat, like a magician, and a long black cape, was leading them. They could not see his body, only his glowing red eyes as he led the Nightmare Parade.

As the parade grew closer, Kyle could see more and more detail on the people in the parade. The closer they got, he could see that their clothes were stained with blood, and that they were actually corpses with bony faces and rotting flesh. Knives protruded from the jesters' chests. The queen held a bloody knife in one hand, and there was a dark bloodstain over her heart. The king carried his own head, and the knight behind him carried an ax, riding a bony phantom steed, his own sword stuck through his chest.

He felt someone grab his sleeve and yank hard, and his gaze broke away from the Nightmare Parade, and turned to see Cassidee pulling him along the boardwalk, running. He followed, glad that she had broken him out of the trance.

They continued running, but it was as useless as running on a treadmill. The ghostly parade, led by its demon magician, continued to gain on them. When they were only about two yards away, the whole Circus disappeared from around Kyle and he found himself hurtling through blackness while he watched all of his nightmares take place. His family getting murdered viciously. Himself, being beheaded. Old, but still frightful, monsters that used to lurk under his bed and in his closet, like Cujo or whatever demon possessed that car, Christine. They continued, growing more and more gory by the second, until all he could see was corpses, blood, and heard awful screams of pain, terror, and sadness...

And then, the visions faded. He found himself lying on the boardwalk, everyone else slowly stirring, rubbing their heads as if trying to forget what they had seen. The Nightmare Parade was gone.

Chapter 25: Insane Humor – Morgan

The light went out.

Morgan stumbled backward and heard Doctor Steele let out an ominous laugh that tried to penetrate the shield of her mind. *Don't let it in!* she urged herself as she felt her mother grab her hand and turn toward the stairs. Morgan groped in the darkness for her brother's hand and found it, and Corey grabbed her sleeve. They followed Fleur blindly through the darkness, up the stairs and down hallways until she finally let them stand still. She let go of Morgan's wrist, sighing.

"Sorry, but I had to get us out of there after the light vanished. I didn't know if the doctors would make their first move then, or..," her voice trailed off.

"It's fine. So, what do we do?" Kevin asked, only the slight trembling in his voice giving away how scared he was.

"I don't know. I can't see far in this darkness. That's why I always told you two to eat your carrots," Fleur sighed, only bothering to let out a weak chuckle.

"Then you would have done the doctors' job for them, mom," Morgan said teasingly. It seemed morbid to try and joke around while they were locked in a haunted insane asylum with doctors who were out to torture them, but they might as well try and cling to their sanity and happiness for as long as they could.

"Yeah, they wouldn't like that," Kevin agreed, and Morgan could see him shaking his head in mock disapproval.

"Come on, let's look around and see if we can finish this job before the doctors finish us," Corey said, trying to sound as cheerful as possible.

"Agreed," Fleur said. "We should look for Doctor Steele's office, it might hold some important documents. I know this sounds lame and everything to you kids, but I think we better hold wrists, sleeves, or something, that way no one gets lost in this blanket of black."

The kids didn't vocalize it, but the idea of forming a human chain somewhat comforted them.

"Oh, well," Kevin sighed, taking hold of Morgan's wrist. "If one of us must get sucked into the vacuum of doom, then why don't we all go? As Doctor Steele said, the more the merrier."

Morgan elbowed her twin in the ribs. She didn't need a reminder of the doctors'...um...*insane* cheeriness.

They continued down the hallway, twisting this way and that as Fleur led them around toppled over gurneys, wheelchairs, and other objects that Morgan couldn't and didn't want to see.

It was probably only one or two minutes, but walking in the darkness made it feel like one or two hours. Suddenly, Morgan's mother tripped and fell to the left, dragging Morgan and the others with her. They crashed through a steel door, and Morgan heard it thump against a wall, then rebound, hitting her arm.

She groaned and clambered to her feet, then helped the others stand. A light, white this time, flickered on in the center of the room, and the foursome sucked in a breath as they saw what lay before them.

What looked like an operating gurney lay in the center of the small room, directly under the beam of white light. There were restraints, not padded, on the metal table. White sheets that were spattered with dried blood lay across the table, across a lump that formed a body shape. The table was hooked up the several different, large machines that had different dials. Morgan didn't want to ever find out what they did. A tool tray was next to said operating table, holding bloodstained scalpels, knives, tweezers, and the like. The corners were shrouded with shadows.

They had found one of Graystorm's Torture rooms.

The door slammed closed behind them, causing everyone to jump. Corey turned the knob, but the door didn't open. "Locked," she whispered, her eyes wide, her voice shaking.

Simultaneously, they looked toward the covered body. The head was covered, too.

Morgan stepped forward, her legs shaking. She reached out with a trembling arm and hand, grasped the sheet, and pulled it back.

Chapter 26: The Story of Pandora – Cassidee

Once again, Waverly helped everyone stand up and took off through the midway, running from things they couldn't see. Cassidee was truly scared of what she had seen of the Nightmare Parade—the magician in front, especially. She caught up with Waverly and asked her a question: "Was that man...in front of the parade...the Circus...*Diabolique?*" Cassidee panted.

Waverly shook her head as they ran. "No," her voice was full of fatigue and fear. "He was...the...Ring Master." Cassidee shot her a questioning look. Waverly skidded to halt and turned to face Kyle, Jessica, and Joseph.

"Joseph, you know this story better than I, so why don't you tell it?" Waverly said, motioning for Joseph to step forward as she sat down, chest heaving.

"Well, alright," he grunted, looking at the four kids as they sat in a circle around them, like first graders assembling for story time.

"Perhaps I better start at the beginning. The legend is sketchy, but here is the short version that's details never change, through any version.

"In Greek mythology, Pandora was the first woman on earth. Zeus ordered Hephaestus, the god of craftsmanship, to create her and he did, using water and earth. The gods endowed her with many talents; Aphrodite gave her beauty, Apollo music, Hermes persuasion, and so forth. Hence her name: Pandora, "all-gifted".

"Pandora was sent to Earth, and the reason is one of those details no one can decide on. With her, Pandora had a jar, box, crate, something of that nature, that she was not to open under *any* circumstance. Impelled by her natural curiosity, Pandora opened the container, and all evil contained within escaped and spread over the earth. She hastened to close the lid, but the whole contents of the jar had escaped, except for one thing, which lay at the bottom, and that, was Hope.

"No one is sure what happened to Pandora—another one of the details that remains unclear. And this is the part that is known only to the Empire: that she opened the box at an abandoned Circus, of sorts, and this is where most of the evil stayed, including the Circus *Diabolique*. She supposedly hid the box after letting Hope free out into the world outside of the place she had turned into an entity. But not before she made Hope leave something in her box that would help someone get out of the Circus. No one, not even Queen Sarissa or the All-Seeing Hailey, knows what this talisman is. Nor where Pandora hid the box, leaving this information completely useless.

"But anyway, there's another part to this story, the one that deals with the man you saw leading the Nightmare Parade.

"After Pandora, died, left, whatever, the Circus *Diabolique* created his own right-hand man, a dark magician named the Ring Master. The Circus *Diabolique* rarely shows himself, only for the most gruesome tortures and scares. The rest he leaves for the Ring Master. I believe it was he who announced our arrival and set up the Nightmare Parade for us.

"As for Madame Nirvana, she is supposed to be the Ring Master's sister, who supposedly turned against him but is stuck here anyway. I don't know if she was helping you tonight or not, but I still wouldn't trust her if she ever shows her face again."

Chapter 27 – Blood that Stains These Walls – Corey

Nothing was there. The sheet seemed to deflate, the human shape beneath them vanishing. Corey and the others sighed in relief.

"It was just another trick of the doctors'," Corey breathed, her hand over her heart.

"Yeah, but it isn't going to stay this way," Fleur whispered, looking around the torture room with sadness. "All those poor souls... Corey, is the door unlocked?"

Corey jiggled the handle of the locked door. The steel door wouldn't budge.

"No luck. If that was what they wanted to show us, then why are we still here?" she inquired.

Kevin suddenly turned and kicked the door hard, slamming his right foot into the unyielding metal. The resounding blow of sneakered-foot-to-metal impact turned into a thud of Kevin falling back and hitting the floor, clutching his right foot and letting out a howl of pain, his face contorted into one of apparent agony.

Morgan turned around and dropped to her knees by her twin, the look on her face a cross between concern and anger. "That was incredibly stupid. Are you okay?"

Kevin moaned, beads of sweat running down his pale face. "I don't know. It *really* hurts, Morgan."

"Of course it hurts, you just slammed it into a steel door!" Morgan exclaimed, only her tear-filled eyes showing how upset she was at her brother's pain. "Why did you do that, anyway?"

Kevin shrugged as best he could while still holding his foot. "I don't know, sis. Something just came over me. Anger. The feeling of being trapped. The feeling of being a sick, wounded animal who wanted *out*."

"That's the doctors' doing. You need to keep your mental

shield up," Fleur said, her watery eyes mirroring Morgan's.

"But the strongest of yours couldn't do it—why should we be able to?"

"You have to," Fleur said quietly. "Come on; can you stand?"

Corey walked over and grabbed Kevin's right wrist, Morgan taking his left, and the two girls hauled him to his feet. With the two still supporting him, he tried putting weight on his right foot, but winced and let out another moan.

Fleur bent down and eased her son's shoe off his foot and touched it lightly, feeling him flinch. Concern and concentration were scrawled across her face as she examined his injury.

A minute later, she looked up. "Several of your toes are broken. The metatarsal bones—at least three are more than likely fractured. Your ankle is pretty much busted."

Kevin groaned. Corey and Morgan sighed. "So, are we supposed to carry him the entire time? 'Cause, that's not going to work out very well," Corey said, ducking under Kevin's arm so that her shoulders supported his right side.

Before Fleur could answer, a voice whispered from the shadows, "Bring him here."

The speaker was a young woman with bleach-blonde hair that was cropped short around her shoulders. Her blue, bloodshot eyes resembled ones that Corey knew very well, though she couldn't place where she had seen them. A gray patient gown hung off the woman's shoulders, the wearer being no more than twenty years old. The hem hung just past her thigh, her feet were dirty and bare. Her ribs were prominent through the gown, and her face was boney, her lips dry and cracked. Her arms and legs were thin like toothpicks, as if no muscle ever existed. The blue eyes were hollow, full of fear and sadness.

"Who are you?" Corey asked, her voice shaking, her eyes dilated in fear. What if it was Doctor Cadenza in disguise?

She felt something probe her mental shield, almost

cautiously. It wasn't like Cadenza's metal claw, but something more...*human*. Corey immediately understood that this was not Doctor Cadenza. The probe withdrew, vanished, and Corey also understood that this woman wasn't trying to break into her mind—she was showing Corey that she could be trusted.

"I am Trixie," the woman answered, her voice raspy. "I was—*am*—a patient here at Graystorm. Doctors Steele and Cadenza did this to me, along with the others."

"The others?" Corey asked cautiously.

Trixie let out a low, long whistle. The shadows seemed to shift, and two more shapes appeared. Fleur's jaw dropped as two girls appeared.

"Asana! Crystal! What are you doing here?"

The red-haired girl, Asana, wore the same gown as Trixie—hers was torn and hung around her knees. Both of the girls had hollow cheeks and equally vacant, bloodshot eyes, their fingers scarred and lash marks visible through their skimpy garments. Crystal was hunched over, her spine jutting out oddly, and it was clear that her right arm was dislocated, and her right wrist bone was sticking out of her mutilated flesh. Corey tried hard not to throw up.

Neither Asana nor Crystal answered Fleur's question; they turned their heads simultaneously, and Asana said in a voice as ragged as Trixie's: "The other two—they are not here. They did not answer your summons."

Trixie gazed sadly at the two tortured teenagers. "I did not think so. We will find them, however. They will help."

Fleur cleared her throat, and the three girls turned their heads back to the foursome.

Trixie stepped forward cautiously, a shaking, thin arm outstretched, and bent over to touch Kevin's injured foot. He whimpered as she ran her bone-thin fingers over it, and Corey felt an icy chill wash over her, like someone had dumped ice on her.

Trixie withdrew, and Kevin's face relaxed a little bit.

Corey felt her shoulders sag temporarily under his weight.

The dangerously thin girl stood up again, her shoulders rounded. Her blue eyes met Corey, and Corey was sure she had seen those eyes before—but where?

"I have done what I can. Only time can heal the rest. He will no longer need your support; a crutch will do.

"I am not human, not anymore. We are three of the five remaining tortured souls that died here in Graystorm. Our blood still stains these walls." Trixie gestured to the operating table, the bloodstained sheets and appliances. "This was my welcoming gift—where they first committed me to shock treatment, wrapping me in the horrible hallucinations of Dementia 13, the very soul of mental torture.

"And we are here to help you."

Asana and Crystal joined in on the last sentence of Trixie's short speech, their hollow voices empty of hope and courage—they were done for. There was no going back for them, Corey realized. But they were here to help them—did that mean they could still fight?

As Trixie gazed at them with her bloodshot blue eyes, Corey suddenly recognized those eyes. Those blue eyes that she was sure used to sparkle like water in the sunlight...

Those were her own eyes.

Chapter 28: Hall of Mirrors – Kyle

"So...where do we go?" Kyle asked Waverly as they walked along the boardwalk.

"I don't know," Waverly replied, shaking her head sadly. "There's no one here that we can trust—we're on our own. And one false step can lead to the end of our lives. We need to be careful in choosing where we go."

The silence was crushing. The mist still hung in the air, eerie. The small tents and shops that crowded the boardwalk were empty, open, ominous. As far as they could tell, they were alone, but not entirely.

Suddenly, Kyle noticed a familiar-looking building in the distance. "Hey!" he called. "Isn't that a Hall of Mirrors?"

He felt drawn to it, for some reason. He took a step in the building's direction, but only to be snapped out of the trance by Cassidee grabbing his wrist, her fingernails digging into his skin. He gave a small yelp as she tightened her hold. "Snap out of it!" she growled.

As soon as he looked away from the building, he was out of its trance. Cassidee must have seen a change in his eyes, for she let go of his wrist. He rubbed it. "Sorry," she said. "But we couldn't have you dashing off."

Kyle just nodded. As the group walked away, he got a feeling that someone from the Hall of Mirrors was watching him.

An hour later, everyone's stomachs were grumbling and they had been walking around the endless Circus for hours.

Kyle lightly clutched his stomach as he heard it grumble, feeling the juices in his stomach gurgle with displeasure.

"Hey, Waverly? Can we have something to eat?"

Waverly didn't say anything, just took out her two strips of beef jerky and dried fruit pack. "Here," she said, tossing it at the group. "Divide it amongst yourselves. I'm OK." As she turned away from the group and sat down, Kyle heard her stomach growl.

While Jessica, Cassidee, and Joseph divvied up Waverly's food, Kyle took out his own strip of beef jerky, half of the dried fruit, and took it over to their black-haired Okkulten guide.

He touched her shoulder. "Here," he said, holding out the food to her.

She looked up at him. "No, don't waste your food. I've been trained to withstand things like this." She went back to watching the boardwalk.

"Eat it."

"No."

"Eat it."

"No."

"Eat it!"

Waverly didn't reply, just kept staring out into the mist.

"Do I have to shove it down your throat?"

Waverly grinned reluctantly and sighed, then took the small amount of food. "Thanks," she mumbled through a mouthful of beef jerky. "Why'd you give me your food?"

"You're our guide. You need to show us through this."

"Well, thanks," Waverly said, standing up and brushing herself off. "What will you eat?"

As if in reply, Cassidee tossed him half a strip of jerky and three prunes. He caught it and ate it quickly. "That."

Waverly grinned again, then waved at the others. "Come on!"

Despite having some food in his stomach, hunger gnawed at him. They needed some more food. They couldn't live on dried fruit and beef jerky forever.

Suddenly, Jessica pointed to the House of Mirrors. "Let's go there."

Waverly turned and glared at the black-haired girl. "No. That place is more than likely dangerous."

"But what if Pandora's box is in there?"

Waverly hesitated. Before she could reply, Cassidee butted

in. "Yeah, let's go look."

Kyle spoke up. "Sure."

Joseph shrugged. "Even if Ah was with you, Waverly, which Ah'm not, you'd be outnumbered."

"OK. But mental shields up!" she barked, sounding like a general. Kyle half-jokingly saluted. Waverly directed her glare at him.

They trudged toward the Hall of Mirrors, preparing their mental shields for what they might encounter. Joseph, who had finally stepped off his rocket skateboard, followed on his cane.

The building was dark, looming, menacing. Evil, manically smiling clown faces stared out at them, leering. The two mirrors at the front of the building reflected their scared faces. A sign hung above the entrance, the letters looking as if they had been written in blood:

Enter for a horror-ful scary time

Jessica gulped. Kyle felt sweat start to break out on the inside of his wrists. Cassidee was hugging herself. Joseph wouldn't look at the sign. Waverly stared in the dark abyss of black that lay beyond the threshold of the silent, scary building.

They stepped inside, and they were all swallowed by black.

They kept walking into the darkness, forming a human chain so as not to lose anyone. Suddenly, though, some lights flickered on, creating a dim glow, and an evil laugh emanated from down the hall and around a corner.

Waverly, legs visibly shaking, waved them on.

Kyle looked at the mirrors. They portrayed him as normal Fun House mirrors would, distorted and twisted. At least until he looked closer.

His face had begun to twist strangely in the mirror, his mouth growing into a maniacal grin that was beginning to stretch past his cheekbones and off his face. His eyes were slowly becoming wider and wider, turning green and beginning to swirl with white.

He forced himself to look away, and suddenly saw Jessica turn and look at him.

Her black hair was in tatters, and her face looked just like the one he had seen in the mirror. He screamed and jumped back as she reached for him, and suddenly felt something grab his shoulders. He whipped his head from side to side and caught a glimpse of his evil self trying to drag him into the mirror—

"Kyle!"

The evil him was gone. Joseph stood in his place, holding Kyle's shoulders. The man looked at him gruffly, but his eyes understood what he had just seen.

Jessica was back to normal, standing a few feet away. "Sorry," she mumbled. "I just wanted to see if you were okay."

Waverly and Cassidee were staring at him, alarm on their faces.

"I'm okay, guys. Sorry."

No one said anything, but Kyle knew that his apology had been accepted.

The longer they walked, the more unnerved he became. The shadows seemed to loom and follow them in clusters, evil faces stared out at them from mirrors, and Kyle was sure they were being followed, no matter how many times he saw no one behind them.

Suddenly, Jessica and Cassidee screamed, staring behind him.

Kyle whipped around, along with Waverly and Joseph, and saw the demon versions of themselves climbing out of the mirrors. They were not like zombies; they ran right at the group of kids.

Joseph swung his cane at the demonic version of himself, but it jumped back easily and stuck its tongue out at the real Joseph.

Kyle felt something grab his left arm, but he whirled around and sucker-punched the mirror version of himself in the jaw. Blood flew out of the demon's mouth, but Kyle felt his own blow rebound on his jaw, felt his own blood fly out of his mouth. He rubbed his jaw. The mirror version of himself hadn't punched him…so had he done that to himself?

The demon saw his opportunity and lunged, baring sharp white teeth and aiming for Kyle's throat. Kyle knew that whatever the demon did to him would hurt itself as well, but he also understood that this was a suicide mission. Kill your copy, kill yourself.

Kyle blocked the attack with his arm, and howled in pain as the razor sharp teeth sank into his forearm. He saw blood spurt out of the demon's arm, and the other version of him gave the same howl of agony.

Kyle looked around him and saw the others fighting their mirror copies valiantly, but not inflicting enough wounds to hurt themselves. Suddenly, Jessica gave a loud screech as she kicked herself in the gut, and her fist hit a mirror, making it shatter. Her fist came out, bleeding, but the demon version of her had vanished, sucked back into the broken mirror.

This was to no avail, though, for another one of her climbed out of another mirror. Jessica slammed her fist into another mirror, and that demon got sucked back in.

"Break them!" she shouted gleefully. "Smash the mirrors!"

Feet and hands went flying, along with shards of glass. They had nothing else to break the mirrors with, and Kyle could feel blood running down his wrist and leg, pooling in his shoe.

The last mirror shattered. No more demons appeared. The sound of shattering glass stopped. Everyone sank to the floor, exhausted by their efforts, bleeding from minor cuts.

They sat in the broken glass, hunched against the wall, ears ringing, hands and wrists oozing blood.

Suddenly, though, the shadows stirred.

A man wearing a long black magician's cloak stepped out, twirling a black and white wand, wearing a black top hat. He wore a white shirt and crisp black pants. His hat was pulled low over his eyes.

The Ring Master.

He slowly removed his hat, revealing his red eyes, and gave the group a somber expression. His next two words were sad, yet happy at the same time. Almost pitying, but teasing.

"You lose."

Chapter 29: The Connection – Corey

Trixie has my eyes, Corey thought, her mind reeling at what she had just realized. *This ghost, this spirit, this...whatever she is has* my *eyes. My eyes. How did she get them?*

She didn't say anything, though, as Trixie shuffled past her to the unyielding steel door. The young woman ran her bone-thin fingers over it, then slowly turned the handle and opened the door, where it glided above the dusty floorboards with ease.

"There," Trixie whispered, her voice ragged. "Now, let's go. The doctors will begin their 'performance' soon, and we need to find the other two before that happens."

Asana and Crystal shuffled out the door after Trixie, then Fleur, Kevin, Morgan, and Corey followed. Corey closed the door behind her, making sure it closed properly.

Fleur turned to Trixie. "Thank you for getting us out. How do you know the doctors won't bother us until later?"

"Oh, they like giving people a one hour grace period. Just to watch them squirm."

"So people have been in here before, and you've seen them?"

"Yes. The two we're going to find are two of them. Perhaps you've heard? Paige and Bailey Harkrider?"

Corey, Morgan, and Kevin exchanged a bewildered glance. Paige and Bailey, the two kids who vanished in here on a bet, were still in Graystorm?

Fleur nodded stiffly. "Yes, we've heard of them." She turned to her two former comrades. "How did you two obtain those injuries? You never suffered them while you were here."

Asana spoke up. "Cadenza and Steele would have gotten mighty bored if they had no one to torture. And they couldn't rely on kids coming here on bets every other week. So...they summoned us. Some spirits that had died here, or been affected here. And then...they made us partially mortal. Meaning we could be tortured and beaten, but couldn't die again."

Fleur sighed sadly. "How long has this been happening to

you?"

Asana shrugged her thin shoulders. "Ten years, for me and Crystal, maybe."

Corey felt her eyes grow wide. Ten years of unrelenting torture?

Trixie spoke up. "I was here for fifty, in death. Alive...seventeen. I don't know how I made it that long. Then finally...it was time for me to meet my end. It was right before the doctors died. They strapped me to a table, not unlike that one," she gestured to the closed torture room, "and sent wave after wave after wave of harnessed lightning through me while they sat by and watched my body be seized by powerful shocks, which steadily grew past anything they had given me as torture...then, there was an immense pain in my chest, like something was exploding, and then...peace. My heart had just burst. Then everything faded to black."

Corey tasted salt, and realized that she was crying. How could anyone be that cruel to another human being?

Morgan voiced Corey's question, tears of her own running down her cheeks. Trixie gave Morgan a hard, yet kind look. "Those two..." she sighed. "They stopped being humans the moment they opened this asylum."

The original foursome, now increased to a group of six, walked down the halls as silently as they could, looking in rooms and down dark corridors for Paige and Bailey Harkrider, the two kids whose misadventure had become a legend in the eyes of two other kids, Aidrianna and Thomas.

Every shadow seemed to mock the group, and light was very scarce, only appearing through the slightest cracks in windows, or flickering light bulbs, which were obviously short-circuited.

It had been forty minutes into their one-hour 'grace period', as Trixie called it, before they finally found the brother and sister. They were in room sixteen, shoulders hunched, sitting on the bed and facing the wall. Paige's long red hair ran down her rounded back, seeming dark and wet in the near-blackness. The group could hear her sniffling, and her brother simply stared at the wall, his eyes vacant.

Trixie didn't even knock, just swung open the door and stood in the threshold. "You two. I called. You didn't come. What gives?"

Bailey Harkrider turned and gave Trixie a watery glare. Whatever his sister was crying about upset him, too. "What do you think? Your call equals new people that have come to be tortured. And every time, you say that you're going to get them out, but you don't. You don't, Trixie Jefferson!" His voice rose to a wail.

"Wait—Jefferson?" Corey said, recognizing her own last name. "Your last name is Jefferson?"

"Yes," Trixie said, giving Corey a quizzical look. "What of it?"

"That's my last name," Corey answered, her voice shaking slightly.

Trixie and Fleur raised their eyebrows and looked at each other. Fleur started counting on her fingers.

She looked up. "Corey, do you know the name of your great-great-great grandmother?"

"Yes, her name was Lillian."

"Did you know she had a sister?"

It all fell into place. She gazed at Trixie with her wide blue eyes. "Oh my gosh. So this is all the pain I've been feeling. I've been you."

Trixie gave a watery smile. "It's nice to meet you, Corey Jefferson, my great-great-great niece."

Chapter 30: The Circus *Diabolique* - Jessica

The Ring Master led the group, with wrists, hands, and ankles bleeding, from the Hall of Mirrors. Waverly had no energy to change forms. So, they had no choice but to follow willingly.

As they left, however, Jessica picked up a shard of broken glass and kept it hidden in her fist. It cut into her palm, but she was already injured and bleeding, so it didn't matter.

The Ring Master led them through the Circus, heading toward the Big Top. As they walked, the group could begin to hear sounds of a regular Circus; people chatting, children laughing, the carousel music. Soon, the smells began to drift through the air as well; popcorn, cotton candy, still-hot hotdogs. Ripped posters on the booths fluttered in a wind that was non-existent. It felt like people in an actual Circus surrounded them, only they were all invisible.

The red-and-white striped Big Top loomed before them. The tent flaps were open under a traditional circus awning, and the Ring Master led them through. Inside, there were the cheerful yellow benches all around a large sand ring, but all were empty. Still, Jessica could feel the presence of others; hear their excited voices; smell the popcorn they were eating.

The Ring Master led them to a front row of bleachers, where he motioned for them to sit. He then turned and strode to the center of the ring, where the kids heard thunderous applause coming from all around them as he swept his hat off in a bow.

As he straightened, he began to speak, his voice magically louder, and the audience's applause died down. "Welcome! Welcome, souls. Thank you for coming." Jessica realized that his voice was the one they had heard over the intercom when they first entered the Circus of Lost Souls.

Something else he had said grabbed her attention. He had said, 'Welcome, *souls*.' Not 'Welcome, ladies and gentlemen, boys and girls.' Souls. Jessica swallowed nervously.

"As you might have noticed," the Ring Master continued, "I have brought some mortals here tonight. They were unfortunate enough to stumble upon this Circus, and now I've brought them here to give them a warm welcome. Now, what did you all think of my Nightmare Parade? Scary, right?" The crowd cheered, and the Ring Master grinned maliciously.

"What did you all think?" he asked, turning to Jessica and the others. "Was it a good enough welcome?"

"It was scary," Cassidee blurted. Jessica saw her clap a hand over her mouth, as if she had been somehow forced to say it.

"Well, I should hope it was," he said, his voice dripping with malice.

"Now, why don't we get right to the program?" The Ring Master cleared his throat. "Ladies and gentlemen," he boomed, "allow me to direct your attention to the center stage, where you will bear witness to terrifying sights that will haunt you forever. Behold the Circus *Diabolique*, and let the nightmare begin..."

The Ring Master vanished with a bow, and the invisible audience went wild. A violet and yellow stage had appeared in the center of the large ring, and standing on it was something that looked like a human from the pits of a fire.

Tall, thin and muscular, stretching about seven-and-a-half feet, it stood on the stage. Long, unruly black curls fell down the creature's back, his skin a burnt red, like he had been toasted over an open flame. The creature had two eyes, which glowed like hellfire and had no pupil. His mouth was a jagged, thin line stretching from the corners of his eyes, dipping low to his chin. His chest was bare, and he wore black pants that seemed molded to his skin. The muscles in his arms were thick, and it looked like he could break someone's neck with a simple twist of his arm. Smoke seemed to pour from his nose when he gave a snort, like a horse, as he looked around the Big Top. A black whip that was slick with blood was curled in his right hand.

Everything was silent.

The demon breathed deeply, and smoke poured out of his nostrils again. Jessica recoiled slightly.

The Circus *Diabolique* turned to Jessica, Waverly, Joseph, Cassidee, and Kyle. His long mouth twisted into a smirk. His eyes seemed to glow even more, and Jessica could feel the burn of them from her seat.

The creature—for he was certainly not a human—addressed the crowd. "Thank you, thank you, for coming," he boomed, his voice magically amplified like the Ringmaster's had been. "Not that you had a choice." His mouth twisted into an evil smile. No one dared laugh. No one even breathed.

"Today, my assistant brought you some mortals. They are here on Queen Sarissa's orders."

To her own surprise, Jessica raised her hand and the demon glared at her. "What?" he hissed.

Lowering her arm shakily, Jessica answered. "Well, we weren't here on Q-q-q-queen Sariss-s-s-sa's orders..." she stammered as he strode closer to her, his black boots crunching and slightly burning the sand. He towered over her, and she shrunk back. "W-w-w-we were j-j-j-just p-p-passing through..."

The *Diabolique* snorted again, smoke rising in curls from his nose, then turned and strode back to the stage. The sand smoldered where he had stepped. Jessica whimpered slightly. How had she been able to do that? This creature terrified her!

He turned to face the invisible crowd. "Likely story. Yet, I believe you. You are searching for something of greater importance, something that is not here. Is that right?" He glared at Jessica, who quickly nodded. He went back to the crowd. "Yes, yes, and we would *hate* to hold you back," he cracked his whip, and his voice dripped with sarcasm and malice. "But unfortunately, we need something from you. Something that you're searching for, in here, I believe?"

He didn't wait for their answer. Jessica's mind was reeling. He knew they were searching for Pandora's box? How did he

111

know?

"You are wondering how I know. Yes, I have been searching for it too. But not to leave. No, not to leave. I need that box. I need it so that I can destroy it. And you five," he cracked his whip at the group, causing them to flinch, "will find it for me. Yes, I know I said my true motives, when a villain rarely does that. But why lie? You will find it for me...no matter what. And in case you have doubts, let me show you why you will do what I say..."

He snapped his fingers, and two men dragged a large wheel to the stage. They grunted, setting it up, then retreated, bowing. The demon snapped his fingers again, and the Ring Master appeared. He swept his hat off in a bow again to the cheering, invisible, crowd.

"Now, why don't we have a volunteer?" The Circus *Diabolique* said, turning around in a circle, as if searching the audience. The invisible souls held their breath. Who would he pick?

He rotated a full 360 degrees, then his gaze landed on Jessica. "Why don't we have this pretty little lady be our volunteer?"

Jessica felt her blood turn to ice. She was frozen, her mouth opening and closing. *No! He can't mean me! What is he going to do to me? What?! No! They can't take me! I have this glass shard...* But as soon as she thought it, she knew the glass would be futile. These monsters weren't human. Things that could hurt people like her couldn't hurt things like *them*.

An assistant strode up to her and grabbed her arm, forcing her to stand. Her legs shaking, Jessica could only follow, sure her arm was bruising under the assistant's iron grip. Cassidee let out a screech when she saw Jessica stand up and tried to grab her, but failed. Instead, the small fifteen-year-old swung her fist and uppercut the assistant in the jaw. "Cassidee! No!" Waverly shrieked, grabbing the girl by the waist and hauling her back as the man turned and snarled at her. Tears ran down the girl's face. Jessica didn't know why Cassidee was doing this for her, a girl she didn't like, but it didn't matter.

She was up on the stage, next to the Ring Master and the Circus *Diabolique*, feeling the demon's heat that radiated off of him, just shy of a blazing inferno. He gave her a sinister smile. "What's your name, girl?"

Jessica managed to choke out her name. The demon grinned malevolently. "Well, Jessica, today's your lucky day. You are going to be a participant in one of the favorite attractions: The Flaming Daggers." The invisible crowd roared their approval. "Now, do not worry, you will not be harmed. This time. It will hurt, but I will make sure you do not die. But first, why don't we heal those injuries you already obtain?"

Jessica felt all the cuts and gashes on her body heal. She was filled with a short sense of relief—he wasn't going to kill her. Yet. She gulped. What was the Flaming Daggers?

"Now that that's been taken care of, why don't we get down to the act. And no need to worry about her, the four of you, the Ring Master is an excellent marksman." Jessica swallowed hard as he addressed her friends.

She felt one assistant grip her right wrist, and another take her left wrist. With ease, they lifted her up and grabbed her ankles with their other hands. They took her to the wheel and inserted her ankles into two black metal shackles, they put her arms out on either side of her head, like a Y, and chained her wrists to the wheel. She was now vertical, and unable to move.

The assistants walked away, and the Circus *Diabolique* stepped off the stage...or where the stage had been. It was gone now, and the wheel and its stand were on the flat, thin sprinkling of sand. The Ring Master stood about thirty feet away from her, his back to her friends. She could see the terror on their faces. She felt a tear leak out of her eye and roll down her cheek, with no hand to wipe it away.

The Ring Master opened his cape to reveal ten flaming daggers. Jessica moaned and struggled in vain against her shackles. She could not move. Could not twist her body to avoid the daggers.

The Ring Master took the first one and showed it the crowd. They roared their approval. He turned toward Jessica, held the knife behind his back, over his shoulder...and threw it.

It whirled through the air, flaming, before finding its spot in her neck. Jessica screeched with pain, closing her eyes, feeling like she might vomit. Pain slashed through her, as sharp as the flaming knife, so intense she felt like she might black out and die. But the Circus *Diabolique* said she could not die. The pain subsided, but only a touch. Jessica could feel the flames lick at her skin, but felt only their heat.

Slowly, the wheel began to spin in place.

Jessica could hear her friends scream. *No...please no.* Jessica whimpered as the wheel picked up speed. Another tear rolled down her face, which quickly evaporated in the heat of the flames. She closed her eyes. Her neck seared, the knife still stuck in her jugular vein. But oddly enough, she felt no blood pour down her neck. *Of course not, dummy, he said you wouldn't die.*

She felt another knife strike her chest, right where her heart would be. She couldn't summon the energy to scream, but heard her friends wail. The flames started to spread over her body, consuming her. The pain, though it was subsiding, was intense and unlike anything Jessica had ever felt before. No tears leaked out of her eyes--the heat of the flames was too great.

The Ring Master threw the remaining knives, hitting her lungs, her legs, her forehead, her arms, her stomach. Each time, her friends' screams lessened to whimpers. Jessica kept her eyes closed the entire time, unable to look. Fear raced through her veins, and her stomach tumbled with sickness as the wheel spun faster and faster and faster, until she was sure everything was a blur. The flames from each dagger consumed her entire body, and she felt her skin melt away. She opened her mouth to scream, but the fire raced down her throat and she gagged, choking on the searing heat. Pain took over. Blackness crept to the edge of her mind. She was sure, had she not been protected by whatever spell the Circus *Diabolique* had put over her, she would have been dead at the first knife strike.

She felt the wheel slow, the flames vanish. The crowd roared. She heard her friends scream. Of course, she was probably a walking skeleton.

Two assistants came over and freed her from the shackles. They picked her up and set her on her feet. She dared to slowly open her eyes.

She was not a skeleton. She was normal. There were no burn marks, no cuts from the daggers. The daggers themselves were gone. When had they disappeared? With the flames? She swallowed hard, her legs shaking violently. The Ring Master took her arm and led her back to her seat while the two assistants took the wheel away.

The Circus Diabolique grinned at them, his eyes narrow slits, his mouth twisted into an evil smile. "Scared you, didn't I? But I told you, you would be fine. And you see…that is what will happen to you, if you do not find me Pandora's box. And this time, you will feel every dagger impale you, feel the heat burn your skin away…But you will not die, not until you've felt all the agony every single dagger brings to your miserable soul. Not until you've turned to a charred skeleton and have bowed to the crowd will you die. Your lives were wretched, and that is how you will go out. Now, get busy!"

He cracked his whip at them and turned to stride away, but then turned and smiled maliciously at them. "Oh, and do not think that you are safe from the Circus's horrors. You can still die, or go crazy…I do not really care. I can always find someone else to find the box." He then turned and vanished in a puff of smoke.

Chapter 31: Race for the Office – Kevin

"You better eat, and rest a little bit," Paige Harkrider advised Kevin, Morgan, Corey, and Fleur. "Once your grace period is up, you won't have a lot of time to do those things." The thirteen-year-old ghost grimaced, remembering her own grace period and how she hadn't used it wisely.

Kevin and the others opened their bags and took out half of the dried fruit, the warmed hamburger patty, which was now cold, and a water bottle. They ate the food, drank half of the water, and then curled up either on the small bed or on the floor, trying to save up precious minutes of rest.

He drifted in and out of a dreary haze, not really sleeping but not really awake. He felt Paige shaking his shoulders soon, though, and he quickly stood. His right foot ached, and he didn't have a crutch, so he had to limp pretty drastically.

"Your grace period is over," Bailey whispered, his voice low for whatever reason. "It will not be long before the horror of the asylum is unleashed onto you."

Kevin swallowed hard and tried to contain his fear. What were the horrors, exactly? He didn't want to find out.

"We will be there to help you," Asana said. "But we cannot go with you. The doctors forbid us."

"But you will get out," Trixie said, placing her bony hand on Corey's shoulder. "We'll make sure that you will."

Crystal gave the foursome a slight shove, and they unwillingly stepped out of room sixteen.

"Where do we go?" Morgan whispered as the door closed behind them.

"Let's try Doctor Steele's office," Fleur murmured, before setting off down the hallway. The three kids followed, trying hard not to be the one in the back of the line.

"Do you know where the office is, mom?" Kevin asked, shooting a glance behind him at a shadow he was sure had moved.

Fleur shook her head. "No, I don't."

Suddenly, Kevin thought he heard a footstep behind him. He tossed a glance over his shoulder. No one was there. But yet, as he continued to walk, so did the footsteps.

"Hey, guys? Can you stop for a second?"

The foursome halted. The footsteps continued, slowly approaching them. Kevin felt his eyes grow wide in fear. There was nothing behind them...right?

"Run," Fleur said quietly.

"No need to tell me twice," Kevin muttered before limping-slash-running off after his sister and Corey, going as fast as they could down the hall.

Only, the hall seemed to stretch in front of them. It was like they were running on a treadmill...

Kevin, Morgan, and Corey almost ran into the door at the end of the hallway, but were able to brace themselves in time. Corey looked up at a dusty and spider web-covered plate on the door. It read: **Steele's Office**.

"Open it!" Corey exclaimed. Kevin frantically pushed on the door, turned the handle, but to no avail. His hands were sweating and slipped on the handle of the door, and his foot was killing him.

Suddenly, Morgan kicked the door, doing some kind of karate kick, hitting the nameplate. The lock broke and the door swung open.

Cadenza tried not to giggle. While they were fussing with the door, they hadn't noticed her silent approach behind them. The door was swinging open—she didn't have much time. She raised the syringe, which was full of a clear liquid.

Morgan whirled around suddenly and screamed just as Kevin felt something prick his arm. He whirled around too, only to see Cadenza's bright acid green eyes smiling back at him as she injected the clear liquid into his arm. The room started to

117

spin, and Kevin toppled backward, hitting the floor with a thud.

Chapter 32: Cries in the Night – Cassidee

Cassidee, Waverly, Joseph, Jessica, and Kyle walked out of the Big Top in a scared silence. Cassidee could hear her own heart pounding in her chest, breaking the silence that filled the Circus. The whisper of invisible spirits had faded; everything was still, silent, and shrouded by mist.

The boards creaked under every footstep. Cassidee felt tears running down her face, and felt the cool mist touch her cheeks. She shivered, and drew her jacket closer to her body, hugging her rib cage.

Every step was slow. They walked in an uncertain group— walking together, but yet apart. Waverly had not taken the lead; instead, she was hugging herself, like Cassidee, as she kept her blue eyes on the ground, staring at her wet shoes.

Suddenly, Cassidee heard a sound. Not quite a wail, not precisely a scream. It was a cry. Something sad, sorrowful, mourning. It seemed far away, emanating from the mist.

The group stopped and stared in that direction. Cassidee could hear her own scared breathing. What was making that sound?

The Circus was silent once again, but the group was now heading toward the alley where the cry had come from.

As they walked toward the sound, it started again. This time, it sounded like a sad woman vocalizing, her voice clear and pure like a brook bubbling over rocks, like high bells. Cassidee found herself to be mesmerized by the sound; it drew her in, and at the same time, pushed her away.

Whatever it was doesn't want us to come near it, Cassidee thought. Her hands, which now hung limply by her sides, shook slightly, and her breath caught in her throat. They were getting very close to the source.

They rounded a corner and saw a huddled figure cowering

by a booth. Cassidee couldn't see the figure clearly, but it was most certainly a girl. She could see the long hair draped over the girl's face, falling past her knees, which were against her chest, held there by skinny, pale arms. A long, stained white, plain dress was what the girl wore.

She stepped toward the girl, extending a shaking arm. "Cassidee," Waverly hissed. "Be careful."

Cassidee touched the girl's shoulder gently, and the head snapped up. Cassidee got a glimpse of an angry, tear-stained face with black eyes and a cruel smile before the girl vanished into thin air, her poignant wail echoing around the Circus.

Chapter 33: Sanitarium Gates – Jenika

Storm clouds hung overhead, covering the already dark night sky. No stars dared to penetrate the clouds and shine their light upon the building that sat just yards away from the woods, feet away from the three people standing just in front of those dark gates...

Graystorm Asylum stood, waiting, hiding in the dark. It was waiting...for me, Jenika Albritton.

The windows held no grime; ivy had not taken over the stone wall. The plants were neatly trimmed, but yet, the building was just as scary as it would have been if abandoned.

I was strapped to a wheel chair. There is an iron muzzle over my mouth, strapped tightly around my head, so I could not scream or bite. Really, I don't like biting people, it tastes disgusting, but still, when you are about to be sent to your doom, you might do anything.

My wrists, arms, and legs are secured to the chair by iron clasps. I wore a gray, thin, hospital gown that only hung an inch above my knee. My long dark hair, which used to be so sleek and shiny, long and graceful, was now a stinking, snarled mess. There were circles under my eyes from lack of sleep, and my muscles could barely stay tense, they were so worn out from fighting the demons that plague me everywhere.

Yes, I can see you at the edge of my mind. You are a person from the future. No, I will not tell you my story or why I am here. That is for you to figure out when you wake up again, Kevin.

How did I know your name? Well, I have a peculiar sense of...knowing. There's no other explanation. I think it's one reason why they're locking me up here, but it's most certainly not the only one.

And you are wondering how I can speak to you, but not vice versa. And how should I know? You're from the future—don't people from your time have a brain, maybe one that is smarter than the 'insane' one inhabiting my skull? I said I had a sense of knowing, and that doesn't mean I'm some stuck-up smarty-pants groveling at her teacher's feet, begging for more homework and gladly blurting out useless, complicated facts at all the wrong times, like that other girl, Corey. Yes, that made your thoughts still.

They roll me toward the gates, which swing open, assisted by a man dressed in a white lab coat and black slacks, who moves like a robot. He stands as still and stiff as a statue, not moving, not blinking, just staring past us into the dark night. I can't turn my head to watch him move, so I keep staring straight ahead as they roll me toward the asylum. I hear the gates swing shut, but I don't see a man join us as we walk-slash-roll toward the doors. Where did he go?

The oak doors swung open, and I was pushed into Graystorm Asylum. Suddenly, I had a sense of knowing, and what I knew terrified me.

I would be here for twenty more years, and I would not leave as myself. Who I would leave as, I had no idea. Would my name change? What about my appearance? Would I still be human?

These thoughts rack my tired, confused, and demon-filled brain as they roll me down the hallway, toward the next twenty years of my life.

Chapter 34: Haunted Carousel – Jessica

The silence was deafening. The crying girl's face was etched into Jessica's mind, and she could not get it out. Jessica wished for anything to take that face away.

The black-haired thirteen-year-old sat up in her sleeping bag, looking around her. The Circus was very eerie, especially when you were the only one awake.

Waverly had decided to let them sleep while they could, for which they were all grateful. They had been running around the Circus for what seemed like days, but was really only hours. And after the whole scare with the Flaming Daggers, everyone, Jessica especially, was ready to sleep, and try to dream of normal things.

Jessica, however, could not dream of 'normal'. The Flaming Daggers clouded her visions, only this time it wasn't her at the wheel, but Cassidee, Waverly, Kyle and Joseph, and she had to watch them all be turned to ash-built skeletons, before they crumpled to the ground...and the Circus *Diabolique* and the Ring Master ignored her screams...and then the ghostly girl appeared, vocalizing that sad tune as her face contorted into the one from the Hall of Mirrors...

As she sat, watching the night for signs of trouble, she heard Cassidee whimper and stir in her sleeping bag. Jessica turned her head and saw the small fifteen-year-old's brow wrinkle, her mouth frozen in a frown, her eyes squeezed shut. She appeared to be locked in an unpleasant dream.

Jessica reached over and touched her shoulder, then shook it when Cassidee didn't respond to the touch. The girl flinched in her sleep and tried to scrabble backward, out of the sleeping bag, but couldn't. Instead, her eyes flew open as she scrambled into a sitting position, propped up on her elbows, turning her head from side to side as she tried to assure herself the coast was clear from whatever haunted her dreams.

She then turned to look at Jessica, her pale blue eyes wide.

"Thanks."

Jessica just shrugged. "I couldn't sleep either."

Cassidee shuddered and hugged herself. "Do you think they'll ever go away?"

Jessica turned to look at the girl. "What will go away?"

"The nightmares."

Jessica stared out into the darkness. "I don't know," she said slowly. "They've been with me since almost the beginning. Maybe they never will go away." Cassidee did not reply.

Suddenly, a calliope began to play, its cheerful tune ringing through the night. Jessica and Cassidee turned their heads toward the noise. They were drawn to it, just as they were the Hall of Mirrors. The two girls turned to the others, but they were sound asleep. The haunting carousel music could not penetrate their dream world.

As if in a trance, the two teenagers stood up and began to stiffly walk toward the noise. Jessica's mind had gone foggy—she couldn't really think straight; it was like her brain had gone to autopilot.

The two walked on into the mist, until, if they bothered to turn their heads, they would no longer see their sleeping companions that they had left behind.

Jessica's mind cleared as soon as she saw the carousel. It leered out at them from behind its veil of mist; big and black, silent and still. Well, silent except for the calliope that still played the ethereal tune.

Even though her senses had cleared, and every muscle and nerve in her body was screaming for her to turn tail and run away, she couldn't. The carousel mesmerized her, and she knew that even if she tried to leave, something wouldn't let her.

She looked at Cassidee, who looked at her. The pint-sized fifteen-year-old's face was a mirror of Jessica's; it held the same fear, worry, and small excitement.

"Pandora's box could be there...right?" Cassidee said, her voice straining.

Jessica did not reply, since she could tell Cassidee was not looking for one. They stepped toward the carousel.

Waverly bolted up in her sleeping bag. Something had woken her; she didn't know what. Her head whipped from side to side, and she noticed that two sleeping bags, whose occupants had been Jessica Knight and Cassidee Scott, were empty.

The Okkulten scrambled out of her sleeping bag and shook Kyle and Joseph awake. The old man grumbled in complaint while Kyle blinked the sleepiness out of his eyes and yawned.

"Quick! Cassidee and Jessica are missing!" Waverly shouted-slash-whispered. Kyle and Joseph snapped to attention.

"Where could they have gone?" Kyle asked, staring out into the mist.

Jessica and Cassidee climbed the steps to the carousel. Intricately, almost unearthly, carved horses were two-by-two, surrounding the middle of the carousel, which was decorated with mirrors and paintings that depicted clowns juggling human skulls, the Flaming Daggers, a man charming three deadly-looking serpents, and so forth. Jessica tried hard not to look at them.

"Maybe we can find the box underneath the carousel?" Cassidee asked, glancing nervously at Jessica.

Jessica nodded mutely, but after one circle of the carousel, it was clear that this attraction was like the rest: *fantomatique*. There was no 'under' the carousel. There was no operating booth. How silly she was to have imagined there would be such a thing in this unnatural place.

Suddenly, a voice, belonging to the Ring Master, blared over the carousel intercom. "Ladies and gentlemen, we are about to start the ride. Please find your steed and do not get off until the carousel comes to a complete stop. Thank you, and have a nice ride."

Jessica ran to a black horse whose eyes glowed as red as

the Circus *Diabolique*'s. She grabbed the pole and swung herself into the high leather saddle. There were no stirrups. She turned to look at Cassidee, who was right behind her on a skeletal gray horse, whose eyes were white and vacant of all sights, memories, and emotions.

The calliope started up again, and the carousel began to turn. The horses began to rise and fall. It seemed normal...until Jessica felt a buck.

She gripped the golden, paint-chipped pole and turned to look over her shoulder. Her black steed's powerful hindquarters rose above the ground and hit Cassidee's horse right in the chest!

A shrill whinny rose above the calliope, and Jessica watched Cassidee cling to the pole as her horse reared, pawing the air, his ears flat against his head.

Jessica felt the horse beneath her move. He was no longer a painted model, but a real, live horse, with a golden pole sticking through his neck.

Smoke curled from her steed's nostrils, and his eyes glowed lava red. He turned his head to look at her, his mouth twisted into a snarl of sorts, before the carousel started to spin faster and faster.

Everything on the outside world became a blur. Jessica clung desperately to the pole as her horse bucked and reared beneath her, trying to unseat her while battling the horse behind it.

Then the ride slammed to a halt.

Jessica slumped against the golden pole; her muscles weary from hanging on for dear life. The horse beneath her was no longer moving—he was a statue, like before.

The calliope music had stopped. Jessica turned her head to look at Cassidee. "You OK?"

But there was no answer. The fifteen-year-old was gone.

Chapter 35: A Dose of Insanity – Jenika

I was wheeled past rooms that were all identical—the same small bed, the same rumpled pillow, the same window, and the same padded walls. Some rooms had patients in them, others did not. Some doors were closed, others hung open. Some of the patients were crying, wailing, or just lying there, sleeping, or staring at the wall with the blankest expression on their face.

Nurses and doctors patrolled the halls, checking in on patients and wheeling other patients down the hall in wheelchairs, restrained and muzzled, like me. Some fought their restraints, others simply went limp, like they had either realized the effort was futile, or, like me, they were not in the mood for a fight.

You have not left yet, Kevin. Why? Why do you want to watch what happens to me? Or do you have no choice? Do you have to watch this? There's no need to try and answer—you can't, remember?

Still your thoughts. I want to take in my surroundings.

Instead of wheeling me to a sleeping room, however, I am taken to one where a tall man with dark hair waits. He wears a white uniform like the rest of the doctors, but he seems...*different*. I don't know why I think this, but I do, and it turns out I'm right. He's Doctor Steele, the Chief of Staff at Graystorm.

The door closes behind me after someone takes off my muzzle and loosens my restraints. I do not move, only stare at the man who sits feet away from me under a green light.

"Well, Jenika," Doctor Steele says. "Welcome to Graystorm. I am Doctor Steele, owner, founder, and Chief of Staff of this place. Do you know why you are here?"

"I know things," I say, my voice raspy from not being used in a while. "And demons plague me day and night."

"Demons?" The doctor asked, cocking his head in question.

I could tell he already knew about my 'demons', but wanted

to hear my account of it anyway.

"Both you and I know what I mean. But I'll go ahead and humor you.

"They are shadows, darkness, fear, loss, sadness, regret, horror and death. They stalk me through my brain, never allowing me a happy moment. They have threatened to do me in, but not of my own will. I would never take my own life, so when I die, it will be because these demons finally met me with a battle I could not fight. I will have met my match. So if you're locking me up for my own protection, I don't need it."

Doctor Steele raised an eyebrow. "No, you are not here for your own protection. You were right, of course—I knew about the demons. But that is not why you are here, no, you are here for something much more important."

As soon as he finished his sentence, a light flickered on in the center of the room. Underneath it was an operating table.

I realized what this meant—they were going to experiment on me. I didn't want any part of that! For the first time, I fought against my restraints, but they tightened, cutting into my body, and causing me to cry out in pain. Doctor Steele gave me a grin dripping with malice.

"You cannot escape, Jenika. You should feel proud that you are part of such a huge movement in science."

"But I'm not," I growled, sweat now beginning to run down my forehead, my jaw clenched.

"I think," Doctor Steele said thoughtfully, "you will come to appreciate what we are doing to you. You will have abilities very few others have. We will free you from the binds of being human. You will leave your worthless, sorrowful life and live one with greater purpose."

"Why would I want to be part of a great purpose?"

Doctor Steele shook his head. "I see you are not going to yield." He snapped his fingers, and suddenly I felt a needle sink into my arm. I twisted my arm and fought as hard as I could against the manacles, but I was already beginning to lose consciousness. My brain grew foggy, and blackness descended on me.

When I came to, powerful, skull-splitting pain raced through my body. I wailed out loud, hearing my scream echo around the room. Tears sprung into my eyes. My muscles burned. My head felt like it would split open. And there was something burrowing into my arm...

Although I was strapped down, I managed to turn my head a little bit and saw something that made me almost faint: a syringe and two scalpels digging into my left arm. Two doctors stood there, wearing their surgical blue caps, gowns, facemasks and slippers instead of shoes. I could only see their black, vacant, pupil-less eyes, which held no emotion whatsoever of what they were doing to me...

And there was blood, racing down my arm. My heart hammered in my chest like a drum, and I felt like it was going to break my rib cage. A thick tidal wave of dark red blood streamed down my arm, and I screamed again, feeling them dig in deeper.

And then I noticed they were injecting something that looked like green and black blood. My brain was so confused by this, so transfixed, that it blocked out the pain. However, another needle sunk into my right arm, and the blackness descended on me again.

When I woke up, I was in a gray hospital gown, lying on a small bed in a room similar to the ones I had passed earlier, when I had first arrived. I sat up, propping myself up on my elbows, and looked around the room. I blinked my eyes wearily. I was so tired! And my left arm felt fine. I couldn't even see the stitch—

And then I saw him.

Doctor Steele was sitting in the corner of my room, smiling at me. I automatically scrambled backward, feeling an immediate fear of this man, and drew my blanket over my knees and to the point where it almost covered my face. Only my hairline and eyes remained.

"What do you want from me?" I whimpered.

He smiled at me, his smile pitying and sarcastic. "I need nothing more from you. We have completed the first stage of many, but now, we only need your body."

I huddled closer to the wall. "I won't give it to you!"

"My dear, I am afraid that's not possible. Are you familiar with the creatures known as Okkultens?"

I knew a little bit about them. We had studied them in school. Creatures of myth, shape-shifters, they looked very gruesome, with blue bug eyes, coal black skin, and teal hair that was buzzed. I also knew they had a forked tongue like a viper and matching fangs, which were the only teeth they had.

"I know a little, yes."

"Well, then, look at your left arm." I did. I couldn't see anything out of the ordinary. "Try again, look closer."

Then, upon closer inspection, I noticed it. My hand was a pale, ashy-colored black. And in my veins, I could see black and green blood racing up and down, replacing the red blood that used to be there.

I looked up at the doctor, my voice shaking. "What have you done to me?"

"You see, Jenika, the Okkultens...they are real. And they need a leader. A queen."

I was able to put the rest together.

"So you chose...me?"

"Yes. And all we had to do was inject Okkulten DNA into your arm. It will begin to take over you...but I am afraid we will still have to make some more...modifications."

"Like what?"

"Like remove your memory, for instance."

"Why would you do that?"

"You are no longer Jenika. Her memories do not belong to you. You are someone, something else completely different from that troubled girl. Within the next few months, you will have become an Okkulten. You will have become their leader. You will be Queen Desdemona."

"When I entered this building I had a feeling of knowing that I would be here for twenty years. You said this would only take a few months."

"Just because you are still here does not mean you are still a patient."

Everything he said sunk in. And instead of feeling scared, I felt curious and excited.

"What is my new name again?" I asked, letting my body relax.

"Desdemona," Doctor Steele said.

I turned it over again and again through my brain. Desdemona. Desdemona. Jenika was gone for good.

I looked Doctor Steele in the eye. "It works."

Chapter 36: Living Dolls – Kyle

Kyle, Jessica, Waverly, and Joseph raced through the Circus, trying to see if they could spot Cassidee. Kyle went back to when they found Jessica, remembering the panic in the thirteen-year-old's eyes...

She was dazedly stepping off the carousel, her head whipping from side to side, looking for someone. We ran up to her, shouting her name, and she fixed her eyes on us. Tears were running down her face, and she looked very spooked and scared.

"What's wrong?" Waverly asked hurriedly, skidding to a halt just before Jessica. "Where is Cassidee?"

"I don't know!" Jessica cried, still turning her head from side to side. "I looked behind me when the ride stopped—and she wasn't right behind me! I circled the ride once, twice, five times and she wasn't there. Then I heard you four approaching."

"Why'd you go off anyway?" I had asked.

"We were both awake at the same time. We couldn't sleep, and then this calliope started to play, and we couldn't snap out of it."

"How many times have I told you all to close your minds?" Waverly sighed, exasperated. Jessica looked at the ground as she was lectured, and I could see the tears hitting the boardwalk. She had been given quite a scare. All of us, really. But still, this might not have happened if they had blocked out the music.

"Come on, we need to look for her," I said, turning away and walking in the opposite direction of the carousel.

Kyle shook himself out of his memories. And now, here they were on the boardwalk, no closer to finding Cassidee than when they had first found a terrified Jessica thirty minutes ago.

Finally, though, Waverly stopped, forcing the rest of them to slam to a halt as well. Joseph clattered faster on his cane until he reached them, clutching a stitch in his side, wheezing.

Waverly looked around, and fear was written across her face. Kyle heard himself speak up. "Can't you change into something that will help us find her, Waverly?"

The Okkulten turned her head and pierced him with sad, but almost frighteningly angry, blue eyes. He automatically took a step back, holding his hands up. "I'm sorry, I didn't mean to say anything wrong—"

Waverly's glare softened. "It's okay." She sighed and turned to face the front. After a moments silence, she continued, "I wish there was something I could change into that would help us find her."

She then led them on in a silent march, as their eyes swept every inch of the boardwalk and surrounding tents.

It had been about five more minutes when they came across an unusual trailer. It stood well away from the other tents and shops, and was a plain metal gray. A small set of three foldable steps led to a narrow steel door that was about four feet off the ground. They could not see inside it.

The group stopped and stared at it. "Should we go in?" Kyle asked, then bit his tongue, wishing he hadn't. They had been to so many dangerous places now that he realized what the answer would be this time.

But to his surprise, after a moment's silence, Waverly answered in a shaky voice: "Yes."

Three sets of bewildered eyes went to the Okkulten's face, looking for the reason she had said 'yes'.

"We have to see if Cassidee's in there."

Waverly then walked up the steps and put her hand on the door's handle. "Well?" she asked, turning to face her frozen companions. "Are you coming?"

At her words, Kyle felt his body work again. Jessica and Joseph slowly joined Waverly, standing just behind the steps, and Kyle joined them. Waverly turned the knob, the door swung open, and they stepped inside.

Though nothing jumped out at them, Kyle was suddenly overcome with a chill of foreboding, and he knew they were not alone in that trailer.

"Cassidee?" he asked, his voice shaking. There was silence. No one answered. The door to the trailer creaked closed.

"Maybe she's tied up, gagged," Waverly whispered. Every nervous breath they took seemed to echo in the trailer.

"Maybe," Jessica echoed, her pallid skin standing out in the darkness.

"One o' you kids light ah match 'er something," Joseph grumbled, not as unnerved by the darkness as the others. "There ain't nuttin' wrong with the dark. Quit bein' scaredy cats."

Suddenly, undistinguishable whispers filled the air around them. "Cassidee? Is that you?" Jessica asked, her small voice raised a notch above the whispers.

The whispers joined together into a single word, blowing like a fierce wind. "*NO.*"

Waverly dug deep inside her bag and pulled out a flashlight. She switched it on, and swung it around the room. They gasped at what the flashlight illuminated.

Shelves and cabinets that filled the trailer were full of porcelain dolls. Normally, this would have made Kevin sigh with relief and maybe even laugh. Normal dolls couldn't hurt anyone. Then he would call Cassidee's bluff and tell her that the joke was over, and she could come out.

But this was no normal Circus. These were not normal dolls. And none of this was a prank.

Waverly stepped forward carefully. Kyle noticed the dolls' black eyes move with her body, and that no doll was the same. Cracked porcelain faces painted with harlequin designs peered out from amidst more innocent looking dolls with somber gazes. An antique desk held a large book that contained occult symbols and strange diagrams on its ancient yellowed pages.

"Cassidee?" Jessica asked again, her voice wavering. No reply. The fifteen-year-old is nowhere in sight.

The whispers begin again. Kyle saw Waverly reach to pick up one of the dolls--a sad-looking little girl in a blue satin dress-- but before she could touch her, a tear forms in the doll's painted black eye and her lips curled up into a sinister smile, exposing a row of pointed teeth. Waverly quickly drew her hand away, and Kyle noticed that sinister grins were forming on the faces of the other dolls as well. The whispers begin to form faint words; "*Stay with us...*"

"We need to get out of here," Waverly whispered.

"But what's in the book?" Jessica asked, not noticing the dolls' murmurs or ominous smiles.

Before he could change his mind, Kyle darted to the desk and grabbed the book. Waverly turned the flashlight to him, and he looked over the pages in confusion, before switching items with Waverly.

The Okkulten studied it closely, turning the yellowed pages. "I can't make sense of it. I think we should take it, just in case."

Suddenly, the whispers intensified, creating a relatively strong breeze as the dolls spoke as one.

"*TAKE THE BOOK, AND YOU DO NOT LEAVE US,*" their small, childish voices said.

"You can't stop us from leaving!" Waverly insisted.

"*BUT WE CAN, AND WE WILL.*"

The flashlight died.

"Get to the door!" Waverly shrieked, and Kyle blindly followed her orders, and felt Waverly and Jessica almost knock him over as they barreled the short distance to the door.

Kyle could hear Waverly furiously pumping the handle of the door, but it wouldn't budge. Kyle banged his fists on the door again and again, even though there was no one outside that could hear him.

Kyle was distantly aware of smaller, smoother bodies pressing around his ankles. The dolls' chanting had resumed its normal 'Stay with us', but this time much louder, sounding like a death march. Which, Kyle thought vaguely, it was.

Suddenly, something razor sharp and similar to a knife sank into his left calf. A doll had bitten him! He let out a bloodcurdling shriek that sounded something similar to a girl's scream, and kicked out with his leg. He heard the sound of shattering porcelain and the doll released its hold on his calf. He felt his own, warm blood run down his leg and begin to pool in his shoe, but he didn't care. As the dolls were shattered, the others broke their chants and their child voices raised into a single wail of despair and loathing.

Waverly still could not get the door open.

Kyle could feel the dolls coming back to avenge the ones they had destroyed.

"Waverly! Can't you magically open the door or something?!" he cried, trying to kick another doll, only for his foot to strike air—the dolls had jumped out of the way, grinning at him abysmally.

"No! I've tried, but this place is different! I can't open it!"

Meanwhile, the dolls closed in.

"*STAY WITH US...*

"*STAY WITH US...!*

"*STAY WITH US!*"

The dolls' roar erupted through the air, and just as they were about to strike, Kyle saw the door open, and Waverly, Jessica, Joseph, and himself (still clutching the book), toppled out of the trailer on to the ground.

As Kyle looked up to see who had saved them, he groaned inwardly. Seeing the face above him, he wished he was still inside the trailer with the macabre dolls. And judging from some moans around him, his companions were thinking along the same lines.

"Ah, well, there you four troublemakers are," the Ring Master said, grinning. "The Circus *Diabolique* wants to deliver your punishment now."

Chapter 37: The Office of Doctor Steele – Morgan

As Morgan hauled her unconscious brother into the office, she saw Corey slam the door shut and lock it, then grab the nearest chair and prop it under the lock. It didn't matter. Cadenza had somehow vanished right before the door closed. She had achieved her mission: injecting something into Kevin's arm.

What did that liquid do, anyway? She knelt beside her brother and looked him over. He looked like he was sleeping somewhat peacefully, and didn't look to be in any immediate danger or pain, so she guessed she would have to wait and see.

Standing up, Morgan wiped some sweat from her brow. Her heart rate was slowly returning to normal, and her lungs didn't need as much air. She turned to Corey, who was leaning against the closed door, eyes closed, fingers on her temples.

Morgan let herself look around the office. It was cluttered, with an old wooden desk holding both paper files and a computer, which no doubt held tons of information on the patients. It looked as though Doctor Steele had been converting the paper documents to the computer when he died. Why was he doing it so late? Even two centuries ago, almost everything was computerized, especially on Apple computers, which eventually went out of style.

There were filing cabinets (locked or empty) that were covered with dust until Morgan touched the handles. There were no keys anywhere that she could see, so the contents of the locked cabinets would remain unknown. Diagrams lay scattered across small tables and the main desk, and looked to be a lot older than two centuries. They depicted gruesome experiments and grisly delineations of monsters created by the experiments.

Morgan picked up a diagram, and saw that it was a drawing of an Okkulten. This Okkulten looked even more gruesome then in real life, and it also showed the various stages of changing. Scribbled in the margins were different ideas on how to make a person become an Okkulten. On a piece of old notebook paper was the final solution.

Okkulten DNA Experiment – SOLUTION

Subject: Jenika Albritton
Status: Complete Okkulten – still functioning properly but now resides in new form. Looks different from other Okkultens. Is taller. Okkulten hair color has changed from blue to (the next words were blurred, so Morgan couldn't see what they said) and her eyes are now similar in color, and human, not bug-resembling, like all the others. Experiment considered success.
Procedure: Inject patient with anesthesia. Strap to table. Insert Okkulten DNA mixed with Visdelues into Median cubital vein. Stitch close arm. Return patient to room and let them sleep off sleeping drug.
Follow up: Patient should wake up and have body return to function with minimal side effects (mild headache, coughing, possible but light rash) within three to four hours following procedure. Should not experience any changes until the following day. Takes a few months for transformations to be completed. Minimal discomfort. Side effects vanish within one to two days of waking up.

Morgan still had the paper clutched in her hand when she heard her brother stir on the floor. "Kevin!" She and Corey ran over to him and watched as he slowly blinked open his eyes.

As he slowly woke up, blinking and propping himself onto his elbows, he looked around the room. "We're in the office, then?" he asked groggily.

"Yes. How are you feeling?" Morgan asked, helping her brother to his feet.

"Tired. And I had the worst nightmare—"

He suddenly broke off when he caught the name on the

paper Morgan was holding. "Not a nightmare," he whispered. Kevin quickly snatched it out of her hands, and while reading, stumbled backward and into a chair, which he sank down into gratefully. His eyeballs seemed to get wider as he read the procedure report. Finally, with shaking hands, he lowered the paper and stared at his sister with wide eyes.

"Morgan. Morgan! I saw her—I was her—I know who this girl is!" he sputtered, getting to his feet and almost stumbling into his twin. He held the paper to her face and shook it. "This Jenika, I was her in my nightmare. Only it wasn't a nightmare."

Morgan just shook her head. Why was her brother making this up? He knew things like that weren't funny now that they were actually in an insane asylum.

"It was just a bad dream," Corey said before Morgan could console her brother. "And a coincidence."

"No, no, you don't understand. You weren't there, you weren't her. I was part of her brain, and she could see me, she knew all about me, but I couldn't talk to her or ask her questions, but she could read my mind, talk to me without speaking a word."

"Kevin, this is ridiculous!" Morgan exclaimed, tearing the paper from his grasp. "Are you saying Doctor Cadenza took you back through time? Well, she didn't, because you were here the entire time! Corey was watching you. He was there, wasn't he Corey?"

Corey nodded in mute agreement.

"But I'm not making this up! And no, it wasn't time travel, but I think I was in a memory. I think Cadenza wanted me to see it."

"And why do you think it's a memory? And why would Cadenza show it to you?"

"I can't answer the second one, but I know why it's a memory.

"Doctor Steele mentioned, after this operation—" he pointed at the paper—"that he was going to take her memories. I think that was one of them."

"What'd you see?"

"I saw her first arriving at Graystorm, and I saw her operation. He said she was going to change into an Okkulten---no, no, not just an Okkulten. The Okkulten queen. Desdemona." Morgan and Corey's faces were still blank. "The lady with the acid green hair!" he exclaimed.

The light bulb flickered on in Morgan's brain. Her jaw dropped. "So you're saying that this Jenika person is Queen Desdemona, leader of the Okkultens, the very woman Cassidee and Jessica see in their dreams?"

"Yes," her twin said quietly.

Morgan's brain couldn't think of a response. Her mouth kept opening and closing in astonishment.

Corey spoke up, voicing what Morgan couldn't. "So Queen Desdemona went...here?"

"Do we know of any other Graystorm Asylums run by a Doctor Steele, that happened to look exactly like this one? No. So yes, she. Was. Here."

They looked around uneasily. "So what do we do now?"

"Look at the computer, I guess," Morgan suggested, her brain now over the shock.

Morgan walked over and shook the mouse. Nothing changed, except the 'dock' appeared at the bottom, holding the trash can, Finder, and an outdated Microsoft Word.

Morgan double clicked on Finder, and within ten seconds, the menu had popped up. One of the most recent files (dated over two centuries ago) listed a 'Jefferson, Trixie.'

"Hey, I found Trixie's file," Morgan called out, clicking on it. Corey rushed over to see the screen, and Kevin followed.

The Word document popped up, and Morgan read the entire, ten-page-long summary.

"It says she was here for severe depression...here for her own protection..." Corey snorted in disbelief behind Morgan. "It also says that she wouldn't 'succumb', whatever that means.

'Unresponsive. If not succumbing within the next three days, revert to disposal means.'" Morgan scrolled down. "Oh, and here it says, 'Medication and torture increased, still unresponsive. Crystal heart will not cooperate. Use shock therapy.' And...that's it."

Suddenly, Corey pointed at the screen. "No...there's something down there."

Morgan squinted, then enlarged the font. "'Revive soul...make a balance between mortal and immortality...experiment complete...see Procedure Document 236.'"

When Morgan clicked the link, another document popped up, showing the procedure on how to revive the souls. As Kevin read it over his sister's shoulder, he commented: "This isn't your regular séance and ghost-summoning bile. This seems pretty serious."

Unexpectedly, there was a knock at the door. The three teenagers stared at the door with reserved expressions. Morgan carefully walked to the door and pressed her ear against it.

"Mom...? Is that you?"

"Yes, Morgan."

Morgan swallowed. "What was the toughest object on the obstacle course for me to get through, back at the castle, when we were training?"

Her mom replied in a heartbeat. "The hurdles. I remember all your track meets...you never did do them."

Morgan felt a smile creep across her face, then opened the door. Her mom rushed inside the office, and Morgan closed the door again and locked it.

Chapter 38: Storm – Jessica

As the group trudged along in a line toward the Big Top, Jessica was surprised to feel no tears come to her eyes. They had failed to find Pandora's box, and had failed to rescue Cassidee, meaning they had (altogether) failed Queen Sarissa. But something, Jessica wasn't sure what, kept her head looking up and forward.

The Ring Master had locked the dolls in their trailer, after promising that 'he might give them the leftovers'. Jessica shuddered, as she automatically knew what 'leftovers' meant.

The pressure of invisible bodies arrived once again; the almost overwhelming aroma of popcorn and cotton candy filled the air; and Jessica could faintly hear calliope music in the background, which she tried not to hear at all.

As they entered the Big Top, an invisible audience cheered. The Ring Master bowed as he led them to center stage, before booming in a loud voice: "Sorry to prolong the performance, but this group must go backstage. They have questions; we have answers."

With the crowd booing their dissent, the Ring Master lead them through an opening in the tent to a separate, small room which had five chairs. Jessica swallowed a lump of discontent in her throat, knowing that one chair would remain empty...

"Sit," the Ring Master commanded as he turned around to return to the tent. "And stay."

When the flap swung closed behind him, Jessica saw Kyle hand Waverly the book. "Maybe you should try reading this again," he prompted. "Maybe from a different perspective."

Waverly flipped through the pages again, lost in thought. "Hmm...this seems to be written in...really? Arabic? No...no...the symbols don't match. It's not a human language..."

"You mean humans aren't the only things that have a written language?" Jessica asked, astounded by the news.

"Of course not! Why would you think that? But...what

language is this? Um…stand back. I want to change forms."

Waverly changed from human to raven. "Caw!" the raven responded, which Jessica took for a 'no', because Waverly then changed into a snake. Then, a rat. A horse. A lion. Then, several strange looking creatures Jessica had never seen before, and couldn't exactly name.

Waverly changed forms again, from a curious-looking creature which had dragon wings, a unicorn's horn, one eye, and snake hair like Medusa, to a creature that looked so like herself, Jessica was sure it was the real Waverly until she took in the slight wavering form, the black eyes, the wet hair…she looked like the sad girl who had been crying only a mere few hours ago.

Waverly seemed to be able to read the book, whatever form she was in. As she turned through the book, her expression became more and more crestfallen. The different Waverly shut the book sadly and turned back into her human form. "I have been such a fool," she whispered.

"What form was that, Waverly?" Jessica asked.

"A young banshee."

"You mean that girl's cries we heard earlier…that was a banshee?"

"Yes and no. She wasn't fully grown…her cry can't kill you…"

"So what'd the book say?"

"In short, it told me where Pandora's box is."

"Which is…where?"

"Right under our noses."

"…Can you elaborate?"

"'Within the deepest flames lies a heart of stone, possessing all of which you need. Heed not the instructions; the lure of safety. It is within the devil's clutch.'"

"Speak English."

"That was English."

"What'd it mean?"

Waverly took a deep breath, but just as she was about to

explain, a figure appeared in the tent where they sat. The Circus *Diabolique*.

He spoke no words of greeting; instead he waited for Waverly to speak the answer. She stood, shaking with what appeared to be fury. "You are a monster," she whispered, the anger clear in her voice.

"Many people have said that, and it is true. I am a monster. I came from Pandora's box—what did you expect? A fairytale princess?"

Ignoring his comment, she continued. "You sent us on a wild goose chase. You didn't need us to find the box. You just wanted to watch us scramble around, losing our minds in the process."

"It was rather interesting. Each group is different."

"Waverly, what do you mean, he didn't need us to find the box?" Jessica asked, confused at how this conversation was going. "It's not in the Circus?"

"It's in the Circus," Waverly said, the anger still pulsing in her voice. Jessica was expecting smoke to start coming out her ears any minute.

"Then where?"

"Here."

It slowly dawned on Jessica. "You mean...?"

"Yes. You—" Waverly turned to the Circus *Diabolique* again, "—had it the entire time."

He gave them a simpering, sarcastic, malevolent grin. "Correct."

"And you destroyed it eons ago."

"Ages and ages past."

"And you've been playing this sick game ever since."

The demon shrugged. "I need to keep my spirits entertained."

"What'd you do with Cassidee?" Jessica and Kyle snapped.

"I do not know."

The two kids turned to Waverly, who shook her head sadly.

"He's telling the truth."

"Then where is she?" Kyle whispered, looking at the ground. Joseph mumbled what sounded like a prayer as the Circus *Diabolique* lead them back into the Big Top.

The stage from the Flaming Daggers was still there. The demon urged them onto the stage, where they bowed their heads, not listening to the Ring Master's announcement, not even hearing the crowd's wild cheers as they learned of what was to happen to the four mortals on the stage—

Suddenly, the lights (wherever they were) went out, plunging the tent into blackness. The crowd murmured apprehensively. This obviously wasn't routine. Jessica could hear the Ring Master pacing around, trying to see in the dark. "Let them go," a calm female voice said. It sounded familiar, making Jessica's heart lift a little bit.

Lightning flashed, illuminating two figures, one short and one somewhat taller, which Jessica had never thought she'd see again.

Cassidee and Madame Nirvana stood in the entrance to the backstage tent, a strong gust of wind blowing the fortuneteller's violet cloak around her ankles. Jessica was sure she could have cried with relief.

Jessica heard the wind blow ferociously outside. Lightning cracked through the sky again, this time right outside the Big Top. She heard the invisible spirits murmur among themselves anxiously.

She remembered Madame Nirvana's words to them earlier... 'A storm is coming...beware...beware...'

The Ring Master appeared next to the Circus *Diabolique*'s side. "We have to get their souls, now! If the storm ends before we are able to do so, they will run free."

"They will run free." Madame Nirvana, followed by Cassidee, strode up to the Ring Master and the Circus *Diabolique*. She met their steely gaze with one just as hard and cold.

"No."

"Yes, brother, they will," Madame Nirvana said indifferently to the Ring Master. It was only then that Jessica remembered that the Ring Master was Madame Nirvana's brother. "Only...you are not my brother. Not really. I am the Circus *Diabolique*'s brother, more than anything."

Jessica shot the woman a confused look in between the lightning strikes. Her returning glance said, "I'll explain after."

"I am tired of being held here against my will. It's time for something to be done."

"It's a shame I'll finally have to do you in, Nirvana. But you put on this silly act almost every year," the Ring Master sneered.

"Only this year, it is not an act. This time, you will no longer get away with all the soul stealing."

"Finish her," the Circus *Diabolique* snapped at the Ring Master. Thunder rumbled outside. "Finish them all, now!"

Before the Ring Master could do a single thing, however, Madame Nirvana withdrew a card from her cloak's sleeve. She turned it over and simply showed it to the Ring Master, whose expression became one of utter fear. She then handed it to Cassidee, who held it up to the sky.

There was a large crack of lightning, and violet fire started to consume the Big Top. The ethereal lightning had struck the top of the tent.

Jessica felt the scrambling of spirits around her as they tried to flee the burning tent. No smoke filled the air, there was no heat. And despite the rain that was falling heavily, the fire continued to devour the large tent.

The rain hit Jessica's head, soon drenching her and all the others surrounding her. The wind blew like a fierce gale.

In another flash of lightning, Jessica saw the tarot card Cassidee still held high. Death.

Madame Nirvana withdrew another card and showed it to the Circus *Diabolique*, who took a step back. Madame Nirvana then handed the card to Cassidee, and Jessica saw the image. It was Madame Nirvana herself. Jessica couldn't see the words that told what the image was.

As Cassidee held both cards high, Madame Nirvana said to the Circus *Diabolique*, "Pandora said I would always be your downfall. What was that she told you?"

Lightning struck the two tarot cards. Jessica screamed, afraid her friend was about to be electrocuted, but no such thing happened. A great flash of light erupted from the cards, and there was silence as the whiteness illuminated everything.

"You never could kill me, could you? No matter how hard you tried..." Madame Nirvana said.

The world returned to normal. It was still storming, but the circus was slowly disappearing, being consumed by violet flames. Madame Nirvana stared down at two figures, the two creatures that had terrified Jessica the most, but now looked particularly gruesome.

Violet fire slowly began to consume the Circus *Diabolique* and the Ring Master, leaving no trace of them behind. Madame Nirvana also began to disappear, being eaten alive by the same violet flames. She turned her face to them and uttered one last direction: "Run."

Everything exploded in a blinding flash of real fire and light. Cassidee, holding the tattered remains of a card, ran alongside Jessica, Waverly, Kyle, and Joseph (who was on his skateboard again).

There was another explosion, and the force of it tossed them all into the air. Jessica felt the soft, wet, muddy grass connect with her face, and then struggled to her feet. She turned around and gaped at the scene behind her.

The Circus of Lost Souls was gone. Instead, there was an empty plateau of land. Rain was still falling, but the wind and lightning had stopped.

They all staggered to their feet, shaken and still taking in all that had happened.

Jessica hugged Cassidee, glad that her friend was still

alive. "What happened to you?"

"I got thrown off the carousel. Madame Nirvana picked me up and took me back to her booth. She instructed me on what to do." Cassidee stepped back and held out the tattered remains of the tarot card that Madame Nirvana had shown the Circus *Diabolique*. Faint words read, beneath Madame Nirvana's picture, *Talisman*.

Chapter 39: Sanctuary – Chandra

"They managed to escape the Circus," one of my spies informed me. Even though I was disappointed by their escape, I didn't show it. Rule one to being evil: Never show your emotions. My sister could learn something about that.

"Pity. Where are they headed next?" I asked. There was still plenty of time for those so-called important 'Destined Ones' to be caught. I snorted inwardly. What a bunch of brats they were.

"We don't know. They are currently on their way to *Île de la Pleine Lune*," he told me.

I smiled inwardly. "Good. Maybe a werewolf would finish them off."

I then turned my back to him, and he bowed, scuttling backward out of the room, for he had been clearly dismissed.

As I sat there in my chair, staring out the black and blue stained window, my thoughts began to drift to where I never wanted them. My reason for becoming what I was. I sighed. Being evil was my sanctuary from my bad past. I had always been rather ready to explode and fight.

I took a deep breath as the memories started to flood me. I had been...how old? Fourteen? Yes, fourteen seemed to be right. Anyway, that was the day our mother died...

"Where has she gone?" I asked Sarissa. She looked down at me with sad eyes. My sister hadn't slept for days—her tear stained face was also sweaty, and her long, usually well-groomed and pretty silver hair had turned off-white, and was matted and tangled.

I wasn't much better off, but I had, at least, tried to conceal my emotions and my current psychological state. Even in times of death, it was important not to be weak. My sister, my older sister, could not see this.

"I don't know where she has gone, Little Chandra," Sarissa

answered, more tears pooling in her eyes. I let her hug me, but I didn't hold her back.

"I'm ruler of the Empire now," Sarissa whispered into my ear. I shrunk back a little bit. I should have been the ruler of the Empire. I was more aware of everything. I wasn't nearly as emotional and could deal with things much better than my sister. I should have become Queen.

And so I told my sister those exact words. I was not expecting a fight. A fight—from my older, yellow-bellied, goody-two-shoes sister?! She wouldn't dare do such a thing.

Of course, it wasn't a physical fight, but one of words. My sister didn't even have enough strength to pick up our twenty-two-pound dog, she could never beat me in hand-to-hand combat.

"How dare you say that when mother's death is still fresh in the air! It is an insult to her memory to proclaim such a thing," Sarissa fiercely whispered.

"No, it is not. She is dead, gone. Her memory cannot be affected by whatever we do now."

"Who was just asking where she had gone? How do you know her memory can't be affected?"

"Because if you are dead, I believe you have no knowledge of current events. Time has no meaning for you, so why do you check?" I protested. To me, the logic was clear. My sister wasn't even that smart!

"So you, a tiny girl of fourteen, wants to rule the Empire?" my sister (who was only fifteen herself) snorted.

"Yes, I do. And I figure I could do a whole lot better than you!"

That was when my other three siblings arrived. Hailey, who I thought needed to be locked up in a mental ward, all the so called 'prophecies' she received were ridiculous. She was a year younger. Then, you had my brother and sister, Alex and Jonathan, who were both eleven. Complete fools. They needed to join Hailey at the psychiatric hospital (Graystorm, I think it was) on the Outside.

"Chandra, you could be nicer to her," Alex consoled me. She was normally a dare-devil and didn't care much about rules or looking nice, but if you offended someone in our family (other than her; she didn't care) you'd have her to answer to. She was definitely a pint-sized brawler, and thought Hailey was deeply weird herself. She also would fight anyone who said so.

"Why?"

"Well, she's about to become Queen, she's only fourteen, and she just lost her mother—"

It was that comment that made me explode, almost literally. Blue and black magic pumped through my veins and caused my hair to crackle and stand on end like electricity was running through them. My blue eyes became as sharp as a knife. I was aware of myself rising slightly into the air, but didn't care much. Alex—and Hailey, Jonathan, and Sarissa, oh, definitely Sarissa—had just crossed an un-crossable line. And they were going to pay.

"SHE JUST LOST HER MOTHER?! WAS SHE THE ONLY ONE TO LOSE HER? NO, IT WAS ME, ME, AND THE REST OF YOU! LIKE I'M NOT SUFFERING TOO!"

"I'm not saying that Sarissa was the only one to lose a family member, Chandra, we all did."

"YOU DON'T UNDERSTAND! ALL MY LIFE I'VE BEEN OVERSHADOWED BY MY OLDER SISTER, WHO'S ONLY, LIKE, A YEAR OLDER THAN ME. SARISSA THIS, SARISSA THAT! AND WHAT DO I GET? 'OH, NICE TRY CHANDRA. YOU'LL NEVER BE AS GOOD AS YOUR OLDER SISTER!'"

Alex was back to her pint-sized brawler mood. "Chandra! Calm down right now, or I swear I'm going to hurt you."

I knew better than to mess around with Alex. If she said she was going to hurt someone, she was going to. I came back to the ground, my magic surge faded, but I'd had enough.

I then left the castle, and started my own uprising against the queen. It was long and tedious work, and it nearly failed several times, but I had finally succeeded.

As I snapped out of my memory, I was surprised to feel something wet run down my face. I lifted a finger and touched it. The pearly drop of salt and water bobbed on my finger, then slid down it and disappeared.

A tear.

Was this tear evidence that after all these years of hating, my brashness was finally coming to an end?

I wiped the thought away as quickly as the tear. I had been listening to Hailey too much for all those years. Still, something nagged at my conscience.

I was determined to ignore it.

Chapter 40: Unbalanced– Kevin

"Well, we have to look for the passageway anyway!" Morgan persisted five minutes later. "We can't just stay locked up in the office!"

"The doctors are out there waiting for us," Fleur insisted quietly.

"They can break down a locked door, can't they?" Morgan argued, pacing the floor of the office in agitation. "Kevin, back me up!"

Kevin stared at the floor, slumped over in the chair. His head was aching. For the last five minutes they had been arguing about when and how to get out of Doctor Steele's office. And when it came to an argument between his sister and his mother, he'd rather not take sides. If he did, he usually ended up getting hurt.

"You know my views on choosing sides," he muttered as he felt her gaze of fury land on the back of his neck.

"Fine!" she huffed, before turning to Corey. "What do you think?"

Corey didn't quail under Morgan's flaming tone. "I think we should know where to go before we leave."

"But how will we know that cooped up in the office?"

"We can ask your mother, she's been here before."

The three kids' gazes turned to Fleur, and she looked up, for her head had previously been in her hands. "I'm not sure. I think we should explore some more."

"How about we find the cellar ward and check anyway?" Kevin asked.

"Why not?" Corey and Morgan agreed at the same time. Only Kevin's mother looked skeptical.

"I don't know. It's not pretty, down there."

"Mom, it's not pretty anywhere in this building."

"It's worse."

"We should go anyway!"

"Agreed. Mom, you coming?"

Fleur shrugged and got to her feet. "Have I got a choice?" she retorted to Kevin. "I can't leave you three wandering throughout this building."

"You can, but you choose not to," Corey responded. "You always have a choice."

Kevin shot Corey a look of exasperation and curiosity. "Was that really needed?" he muttered, and she only glared in return.

"*We're not getting anywhere stuck up in this office!*" Morgan exploded, when she stopped pacing and waved her arms around her head like a madman.

Corey shook her head and Kevin heard her whisper. "Someone's bored..."

"She just wants to get out of this place," Kevin retorted, sticking up for his twin. "As do I."

"I do too, don't get me wrong. But something just seems...odd...about her reaction. All of this built up energy, all of a sudden? You'd think something was..." Corey suddenly froze, and her eyes widened. "...wrong."

"What do you mean?" Kevin asked, looking at the fourteen-year-old in confusion.

"We need to get out of this office," Corey hissed. "And Morgan can't come."

"What do you mean?! She's my sister—she's coming!"

"Kevin, listen to me, in a minute or two something really bad is going to happen. Something involving Morgan."

"Like what?"

"I don't know, but it's not good."

"So why don't we take her?"

"There is something wrong inside her brain. I think the doctors are taking over. They might use her against us."

Fury swelled inside Kevin's chest. Using an old twin stand-by, her tried his best to communicate silently with his sister.

Are you OK?

...

154

Mentally. Are you OK mentally?

Yes. Why wouldn't I be?

Corey seems to think the doctors are taking over your brain.

Understandable. But...I really want to get out of here, especially since we have new information.

I know... Are you sure it's only...well...you, inside your head?

Kevin! Good grief! For this entire time of using the old twin stand-by, have you once experienced interference?

...No.

You wanted to believe her, didn't you?

No, Morgan. How could you think that?

How could you think the doctors were inside my brain?

Kevin could detect a slight smile on her face. He returned it.

Sorry.

Apology accepted.

Chapter 41: Night of the Wolf – Cassidee

As the rain-dampened, wary-looking group wandered away from what used to be a haunted circus, Cassidee felt her spirits lift slightly. They had gotten away, and they hadn't failed Queen Sarissa at all.

They wandered about the hillside for another two days, becoming increasingly hungry, impatient, short-tempered, and tired as the minutes drove into hours and hours drove into days; or at least, that's what it felt like.

Joseph couldn't walk nearly as much as before, and was becoming impatient with everyone; Waverly was short-tempered and quick to snap when a single word was uttered; Kyle's cheerful mood seemed to be crushed and his stomach was always heard rumbling (it was driving Cassidee crazy); and Jessica hummed 'Tiptoe Through the Tulips" (which was an ancient song) very quietly and jumped at small noises.

As for Cassidee herself, well, it was all she could do to remain composed.

Waverly swore lightly under her breath when a strong gust of wind nearly knocked her over. Lightning cracked across the sky; thunder shook the ground; and rain began to dump on them in torrents. "*Why* another storm? *Why*?! Someone tell me why!"

Of course, no one replied, for fear of being slapped or glared down. Cassidee remembered it perfectly...

It had been storming. Again. On their first day away from the circus. Waverly was complaining. And Kyle had commented, half-heartedly, "Why don't you turn into an umbrella?" Waverly had suddenly whirled around and seemed to be restraining herself with great force not to slap him. Kyle had gotten the message, but it hadn't stopped Cassidee from making a short question about shelter ("Do you think we'll be able to find some soon?"). Well, she wouldn't say that again, for Waverly had lost all self-control for a brief second and had slapped Cassidee so hard she had seen stars. Cassidee rubbed her cheek in the present storm, thinking back to the pain.

After a few minutes, however, it appeared that this storm would be worse than others. It was almost...unnatural. "Waverly!" Cassidee heard Kyle shout above the gale. "Why is this so bad?"

Instead of swearing and losing her temper again, Waverly shouted back, "We're nearing an island. Storms are always bad around them."

That was news to Cassidee, and it appeared to be the same for the others. Casting curious glances at one another, they followed Waverly through a particularly strong band of rain and wind, only to come out on the other side to a gleaming full moon over rippling water and still, calm, skies without a cloud in sight.

"What?" Cassidee and Jessica whispered at the same time.

The island was not the least bit tropical; indeed, it looked small and not a single palm tree was in sight. Oak trees crowded all the space on the island, and a fallen tree trunk bridged the passage of water between the island's shore and the mainland.

"Waverly?" Kyle asked after a minute of silence. "What are we doing?"

"We're crossing," she answered shakily after a minute. A glazed look came over her face as she stared at the full moon. Suddenly, a sharpness appeared in her blue eyes and she whirled around, running straight to where the storm band used to be, and seemed to run into an invisible brick wall.

Pounding her fists on the transparent barrier, she cursed loudly. "Stupid, stupid, stupid!" she exclaimed, finishing her rant. "How could I not have seen it?"

"Um...seen what?" Cassidee asked nervously.

"*Île de la Pleine Lune*," Waverly muttered. "'Island of the Full Moon.' Home of werewolves."

Cassidee was sure her stomach dropped at least three feet down into her feet.

"I really need to pick up the pace on noticing these things!" Waverly exclaimed. "Now we have to cross the island."

"Then let's go. We aren't safe standing here on the shore, right?" Jessica commented. Waverly just nodded, a look of grim defeat on her face.

The group then proceeded down to the fallen tree trunk in what looked like a funeral march. "I don't know how big this island is," Waverly announced, "but I think, if we try, we should be able to run all the way across. *Do not slow down*. If you think you have to stop, remember there's probably a werewolf chasing you. That should give you enough motivation to run some more. Oh, and try to run as silently as you can."

Jessica, Cassidee, and Kyle exchanged looks.

"Alright. Let's go."

They had reached the tree bridge.

Waverly walked across, followed by Joseph (who was on his skateboard), then Jessica, Cassidee, and finally, Kyle.

Her heart hammering in her chest, Cassidee followed the others in a strong sprint as the first howl split the still night air.

Cassidee was sure that if this scene were being shown in a movie theater, it would be one of those scenes with no background music. The audience would be able to hear her pounding heart, hear her ragged breaths, and hear every footfall as they sped across the island.

There was a thud of a large, probably four-legged animal landing about ten feet behind her, only five feet behind Kyle. There was a loud snarling and a frustrated howl as Kyle sped past Cassidee, running as fast as he could. Cassidee felt hot breath on her ankles as jaws snapped closed just inches from her flesh. She sped up, and now realized that they were all basically running in a horizontal line.

The forest scenery kept flashing by, around them, underneath them. A log. A puddle of mud. Low-hanging branches. Spider webs. A brief glimpse of a squirrel. And trees, lots of trees, popping up in their path and causing them to weave around the thick trunks at the last second.

They seemed to run forever. All that Cassidee was aware of

was the fact that she could not stop, despite her burning lungs and her burning legs...

A scream and a furious howl caused Cassidee to turn her head. She skidded to a stop at what she saw.

Kyle was back against a tree, kicking at a werewolf that had him cornered. The others were just catching up. The werewolf that had cornered Kyle was just about to strike, when suddenly; a cougar jumped past Cassidee and tackled the werewolf.

Cassidee shook her head in disbelief. A cougar? Where'd it come from? Only when it spoke ("Go! Run! Now!") did Cassidee understand.

Waverly. Okkulten. Of course.

As much as it pained her to leave their guide, Cassidee grabbed Kyle's wrist and yanked him after her. She didn't pause to see if the other werewolves were following. As she fled with Kyle, Jessica, and Joseph she didn't think once of Waverly.

Time slowed down as they neared the shore again. This time, there was no log. The water couldn't be that wide or deep, right?

Cassidee launched herself across the water like she was competing in long jump (which she had never been too good at), and landed on the other side, nearly slipping back into it when she lost her footing on the slick, wet grass.

As she and the others scrambled up the bank to the top of the hill, where the storm band was, a long, plaintive howl came from the heart of the island. A name snapped back into Cassidee's mind.

"Waverly!" she shouted. A vicious snarl came from the edge of the forest, followed by a whimper and the unmistakable wail of an injured cougar. "Waverly!" Cassidee and Jessica yelled again, and started to stumble down to the bank, only to have Joseph and Kyle hold them back weakly.

There were several seconds of what seemed to be everlasting silence, then a mangled, bloody body of a werewolf stumbled into the water and died. Its muzzle was wet with blood.

The next creature to limp out of the woods into the full moon's light was Waverly, still a black cougar, limping, basically dragging her left hind leg. There were slashes and bite marks all across her body, and she was spattered with blood. Whose, Cassidee couldn't tell.

"Waverly?" Cassidee asked quietly, her voice basically a whimper. Slowly, the cougar drug itself through the water in a kind of half-swim and proceeded to drag itself up the bank. Only when it collapsed halfway and turned into a human did Cassidee regain her senses.

This time, no one held her and Jessica back as all four of them ran to the fallen, injured Okkulten.

Waverly was a mess. Her black hair was soaked with blood, and her jacket and jeans were slashes. Blood seeped out of the cuts. In her hands, there were tufts of wolf fur.

"Thank you, Waverly," Kyle said. "You saved my life."

"You saved all of our lives," Jessica said next.

"Don't die." It was all Cassidee could say.

Waverly didn't respond. Jessica checked for a pulse. Cassidee saw her close her eyes with concentration. It was a long minute before she said, "It's there, but barely."

Cassidee felt hot tears of relief slip down her face.

Chapter 42: Abandoned – Corey

"What's this?" Corey asked the others as they were about to open the door to the office. As she looked at it, she realized it was a letter and newspaper clipping that looked as old as the building itself. The text in the letter was faded and in fancy cursive, but the writer had pressed hard enough to make it legible, even after two centuries. Corey wondered if the writer had been worrying when the letter was written—why else would you press that hard?

"It must have blown off the desk," Kevin said dismissively. "Come on—we need to leave."

Corey ignored him and began to read the newspaper. It was titled: "Graystorm's Chief of Staff Dies". Intrigued, Corey read on.

Yesterday evening, at 5:10 PM, Chief of Staff Brandon Emerson was found dead in his bedroom, having apparently hung himself. His successor, Doctor Jackson Steele, was the one who found him.

"I noticed his absence from the dinner table," Doctor Steele said. "And the good doctor was never late for dinner. He considered it a crime. But why he would hang himself, I haven't the slightest idea."

When asked why Doctor Steele was over for dinner at the Emerson's place, he replied: "It was a business discussion. Since I am, as some would put it, his 'Deputy Doctor', I share a good amount of his work and responsibilities. Of course, we need to share information, but at the asylum the time is hardly appropriate. We cannot afford to leave our patients unattended. So we schedule time when we are not currently at Graystorm to swap our findings.

"Should any of the doctors working the nightshift at Graystorm need us, Doctor Emerson's house is just over in the woods in front of the asylum. It was very convenient, but also very disturbing. It's almost like living with the patients."

"The doctor will be missed," Steele's half-sister, co-founder, and Vice Chief of Staff Marietta Cadenza said on inquiry. "I'm sure that my half-brother and I will do a great job. We both have degrees in psychology, health, and science. We founded Graystorm, now we get a chance to run it as well."

Doctor Emerson is survived by his wife, his son, Abraham, and his daughter, Justine. The doctors who worked with him at Graystorm as well will remember him.

The funeral will be held on the grounds of Emerson's estate at 10:00 AM next week.

"That's interesting," Corey said. "Cadenza and Steele may have founded Graystorm, but they didn't run it as Chief of Staffs until about two years after it opened," she commented, reading the date on top of the paper.

"Really?" Morgan said, raising an eyebrow. "I wonder why that wasn't mentioned in the article Kevin and I read."

"He hung himself just like the other patients," Kevin muttered, sidling over to where both Corey and Morgan now stood.

When Corey shot him a confused glance, he explained: "In the article Morgan and I read, there was a mass hanging of twelve patients in the dining hall. That was twelve years after Doctor Emerson died. Both had to do with dinner, both were hangings, and the number twelve was involved with both as well. Was it some sort of a pattern?"

"Maybe," Corey said vaguely, turning to the letter that was stapled behind the news article.

"I bet you it wasn't a coincidence. If the Doctor Steele or Cadenza didn't have anything to do with both hangings, I'll eat my shoes," Morgan stated, giving a snort of disgust as she looked at the article.

Corey, no longer paying attention, began to read the letter.

It appeared to be for Doctor Steele from his Goddaughter, Doctor Emerson's daughter, Justine.

Dear Doctor Steele,

It is I, your not-so-beloved goddaughter, Justine. Yes, I know I'm being blunt, but I must admit you never much cared for me. You more or less abandoned my brother and me when we needed it most, right after dad died.

But complaining is not why I have written to you. I must admit that I am worried about how things are going at Graystorm. I heard about the mass hangings, and it seems that you are up to trouble again. I will never forget what you did to my father, not to mention the rest of my family. You wanted him gone so you and your simpering half-sister could finally claim that you founded and ran Graystorm. I know what you're really up to—and it isn't about the money, or the claims.

I live in a world of magic. Please, trust me for once when I say this: "Your experiments will NOT work." They won't, it's impossible that they will. And what you're doing to those patients is cruel and unjust. You're taking advantage of defenseless people, and even sucking in people who are perfectly healthy and then, once they don't succumb to madness, turning to crystal and making them part of the building. I heard about that girl Jenika. Even you have her fooled. I am quite sorry to say that you do your job very well, Doctor.

One day, the truth will be released about you, your half-sister, and Graystorm. One day, I will get my father's revenge. Everyone— on the Outside and in the Empire—will see what monsters you are, and they will torture you and treat you as you did those poor patients.

This is where we say farewell, Doctor. I have disappeared into my sanction of the Empire, and you'll never find me. Not that it matters. What are the threats of a silly, nineteen-year-old queen anyway?

Sincerely,
Queen Justine Emerson

"Corey! Come on, let's go. I thought we agreed we were leaving the office an hour ago!" Morgan whined, standing at the door to Doctor Steele's office.

"Okay, coming," Corey replied, detaching the letter from the article and stuffing the letter into her jacket pocket. She didn't know why, but this felt important.

"So where are we going once we leave here?" Corey asked Fleur as she approached the door.

"The basement," Fleur answered. "I don't know what the doctors will do once we leave—maybe they'll sit back and watch, or possibly they'll attack. Which is why I think it's best to travel at a fast walk."

Fleur then opened the door and they stepped out into the dark corridor that seemed to stretch before them.

Taking off a brisk pace, they started down the hallway. Faces seemed to leer out at them from open doorways, missing eyes and mouths with blood pouring out of every scratch, skin as ashen as a gossamer mist.

As they descended the stairs to the basement, the darkness seemed to press in on them, choking them, blocking their senses. It spun around them, making Corey extremely dizzy. Was it all a trick of the doctors'? Or was it really happening?

The steel steps clanged beneath each footfall as the broad, firm steps turned into spirals barely a shoulder-width-and-a-half wide wrapped around a rusty metal pole with no handle, and the edges of the steps dipped under any weight other than air and dust. Corey was afraid to step too far away from the pole for fear of falling into nothingness.

"Mom?" Morgan asked her mother, "Is all this real? Or is this stairwell just happening inside our head? Mom? Mom? MOM?!"

Fleur had not answered, but instead had suddenly stopped on the steps and was shaking violently. Her violet eyes rolled into the back of her head, her blonde hair seemed to twist through the air like coils of ropes with minds of their own. She rose into the air, still jerking and twitching, her bare throat exposed. Corey knew what was going to happen before it did.

A blade whished through the dark air above Fleur, leaving a clean cut at her jugular vein. But instead of blood, a thin, mist-like vapor poured out of the cut like it was a fog machine, making it even scarier than the blood that wasn't there.

"Mom?" Kevin whimpered. Tears were running down Morgan's face, and her twin looked close to tears himself. Both of their skin was as pale as the unknown, scary faces in the doorways upstairs.

Fleur's body faded, the mist still hanging in the air.

Morgan began sobbing. "What happened to her?! Where is she?!"

Kevin just shook his head.

Corey reached out and felt the mist. Her fingers only touched air. She stepped to her left, toward the outside of the step. Her foot seemed to touch air, but then the 'air' solidified into a step. Corey was scared by what she realized.

"I don't know where she is. But she isn't dead. And I'm pretty sure she's here in Graystorm. But here's the catch. I think, ever since she came back into the office, she's been a figment of our imaginations. Fleur wasn't real, just like that mist and the faces and these stairs. They aren't real. Not at all."

Morgan's tears dried up lightning-fast. Her voice didn't waver once when she spoke again. "You mean we're going crazy?" she asked harshly.

Kevin had rejoined his sister in her strong demeanor. "Yeah, are we going insane? Maybe we need to lock ourselves up."

"This isn't a time for jokes!" Morgan insisted, punching her brother on the arm. "Become a little more your age, won't you? This is serious. The doctors confused us, they made the line between reality and phantasmagoria almost invisible. So how are we going to do this if we can't trust what we see?"

"I don't know. But we need to get down to the basement—it's the only way to solve this mission as soon as possible," Corey answered. But Kevin seemed unable to take what was going on seriously. He was laughing; crazy, loud laughter that ricocheted off the walls of the empty stairwell. His eyes looked misty and distant, and they were starting to roll back into his head.

"Kevin!" Morgan screeched, and was able to catch her twin before he fell over. "What's wrong with him?" she asked Corey, the panic rising in his voice. "I can't get through to him using the old twin-stand-by. Something's wrong, Corey, something's really wrong—"

Only Corey screamed as Kevin's body evaporated into the same mist, followed by Morgan. Tears began to stream down Corey's face as she took it all in. They hadn't been real, Kevin and Morgan hadn't been real. Fleur hadn't been real. Question was, where were the real ones? Where were they? The tears poured fast and thick down Corey's face, and her chest began to heave in sobs. She was all alone and slipping toward madness. She had been abandoned by her sanity.

Chapter 43: Rock Climbing, part 1 – Kyle

To the girls' obvious dislike, Kyle carried Waverly, who was still unconscious, to their next campsite.

"It's so…so…" Cassidee sputtered, looking for the right word.

"Stereotypical," Jessica suggested.

"Yeah! It's so stereotypical for the guy to carry the injured girl. If I wasn't so small, I'd carry her myself!" Cassidee argued.

Kyle sighed. This had been going on for an hour. He hadn't wanted to carry Waverly, but Cassidee was too small, and Jessica and Joseph were too weak. So, he had to carry Waverly and was currently paying the price for something that wasn't his decision.

"Can you two jus' shut your yappers for once?!" Joseph exclaimed. He, too, had had enough of the girls' complaints. "He didn' choose to be the body-bearer, so just be quiet!"

"But she's not dead, right?" Jessica corrected. "So how is he the body-bearer?"

"Oh, here we go again…" Cassidee muttered, loud enough for Jessica to hear.

Jessica snarled at the smaller girl, then looked back to Waverly, her body still limp. "Is her pulse still there?"

Kyle nodded. The injured Okkulten's heartbeat was steadily getting stronger.

"Do you think she'll now be a werewolf?" Cassidee asked bitterly.

"Nah, she ain't human. Werewolf bites only work on a human. Since she's an Okkulten, she's just really injured," Joseph said.

"We need medicine for her, don't we?" Kyle asked.

"Yeah, and we can on'y find it at *Pays de épouvantail*," Joseph informed them.

"Pays de what?" Kyle asked, dumbfounded.

"It's French, dummy!" Cassidee burst out, punching Kyle's arm. "If you were paying attention in our lessons that weren't even a month ago, you'd know that means 'Countries of the Scarecrow'."

"Why can we only find it there?" Jessica asked.

"There's a special plant that grows on that island, and it's only harvested on a blue moon," Cassidee said.

"You studied that?" Jessica asked, surprised.

"Yeah, it sounded interesting…"

"Anyway, how are we going to wait for a blue moon? She could die before then!"

"Well, a blue moon's scheduled for tonight…" Cassidee muttered, avoiding Jessica's gaze.

"Ya studied the star charts?" Joseph grumbled. When Cassidee nodded, he exclaimed: "I though' not a one person did that no more!"

"What made you do that?" Kyle asked. Cassidee was a jock, and while she liked to read, she'd rather be out on the track or playing basketball than studying star charts.

"I just got the feeling that it would be helpful."

"So, what's this plant we're looking for? Is it wolfsbane?" Jessica asked.

"No, those things are poisonous and can't be found here," Cassidee corrected. Kyle could see that Jessica was not happy about being the student and not the lecturer.

"So, what's this plant?"

"It doesn't have a name."

"Why? I thought all plants had names."

"If you give something a name, that means it exists, either in the imagination or real life. This plant wasn't supposed to ever be found again, so it wasn't given a name."

"How do you know about it, then?"

Cassidee looked uncomfortable and annoyed. "It's a long story. But I'm not as ignorant as you think I am."

The group continued on in silence.

Pretty soon, they reached a larger island, where the sun was shining over it. Kyle was sure he could see blue cat-like eyes peering out at them from a line of shrubbery.

"Is that it?" Jessica asked, looking down at the island from a high, craggy bluff.

Kyle, Cassidee, and Joseph climbed up a steep hill of grass to join her. As soon as they joined Jessica on the cliff, a gust of salty wind hit them. Water crashed onto the jagged rocks that were more than twenty feet below them. The sun, which used to be shining, was now hidden behind dark storm clouds, which hadn't been there moments before.

They had entered the island's territory. It's aura. Whatever. Kyle turned around and stepped back down the hill. He stepped out of the storm clouds and saw sunshine again.

"We can leave," he said, returning to the group.

"Why?" Cassidee asked.

"What, you didn't study this, too?" Jessica sneered.

"No, I didn't, and let me remind you that you didn't either, did you, Miss Know-it-all?"

"Stop!" Joseph wheezed. "This is the last thing we be a' needin'. Together, we stronger. Apart, destiny cannot be fulfilled."

"I think we can leave," Kyle said loudly, directing the conversation away from the fight, "because the island knows we need something from here. We're here for a purpose, and it knows we can't leave until we get it."

"How can an island know what we're thinking?" Jessica complained. "It's not a thing that thinks, and even then, mind-reading is impossible."

As if the retort, thunder shook the ground and lightning cracked off in the distance. A strong sweep of wind came up the cliff and blew her jacket up, leaving Jessica to stumble backward, sneezing the salt in the air out of her nose. Cassidee chuckled.

"It's a world of magic, Jess. Anything's possible. And this thing is alive, it's an entity," the fifteen-year-old said, shaking her head.

"Don't call me Jess," Jessica growled, straightening her jacket and blowing the rest of the salt out of her nose. "My cousins, Corrine and Aiden, always called me that to tease me."

"Well," Joseph said loudly, cutting into the argument yet again, "why don't we get movin'?"

"How?" Jessica asked, looking around the cliff for a path, or lack thereof. It was the latter.

Cassidee dug into her backpack, and pulled out a rope. "You ever been rock climbing, Jess?"

"If you call me that one more time, I swear I might slug you," the thirteen year-old growled.

Cassidee just shrugged. Kyle could tell that she wasn't scared by Jessica's threat.

Cassidee found a sturdy tree branch sticking out of the cliff that was only a foot away from the top. She tied three knots around the root, then slipped the rope through the belt loops in her jeans. She gave the end to Jessica and Joseph, then turned to Kyle. "Give me Waverly."

"Why?" Kyle asked, almost forgetting the limp body he held.

"I can carry her down."

"How?"

"I have enough rope to tie her to my back." Cassidee took an extra length of rope from her bag that could easily tie a fourteen-year-old to her back.

Kyle looked at his friend skeptically. Joseph wheezed from behind him, "Give her the Okkulten. Cassidee knows what she's doin'. Waverly safe with 'er."

"I swear, Joseph, your speech is getting more and more slurred," Cassidee commented lightly. "But thanks for sticking up for me." She turned back to Kyle. "Give her here. You know I wouldn't dare drop her.

He turned over Waverly. He did it somewhat begrudgingly, but knew he needn't be worried. His friend was hardy, surprisingly strong, and always kept her promises. Plus, she would never risk something as serious as this.

Cassidee bent over so that her back was horizontal, and had Kyle place the Okkulten on her back, upside down, so that Waverly's feet were on her shoulders and her face was hanging between Cassidee's legs at around the backs of her knees. She had Kyle also loop the extra rope around her middle and Waverly's back, cinching it tight so that Cassidee's stomach was sucked in.

He stepped back, and she stood up. Waverly remained on the small dark blonde's back, even though she was upside down, her black hair brushing Cassidee's ankles. Cassidee cut a small length of rope and tied Waverly's ankles around her neck, so that they were locked there and the Okkulten's legs wouldn't fall over her head.

"Won't all the blood rush to her head?" Jessica asked, staring at the two girls in confusion.

"No, I looked up this special carry. I forgot what it's called, but we had a race in school, where we had to carry our partner through an obstacle course like this." Cassidee sniffed. "I carried Corey, since she wasn't strong enough to carry me. Usually, the person who's being carried props their heads up with their arms."

"But she's unconscious, she can't do that!"

"She'll be fine." Cassidee tied a knot in the rope that went through her belt loops. "I'll climb on down, and then untie myself. Then you can come down one at a time. Just pull the rope back up once you see me land."

Before anyone could object, she backed off the cliff edge and climbed down, finding a suitable foothold after a few seconds of searching. Slowly, she lowered herself and her cargo down the cliff face and to a small spot on the beach that was clear of jagged rocks.

Suddenly, about halfway down, it appeared that Cassidee lost her foothold. The wind caught her and blew her out, then slammed her into the cliff face. Jessica screamed. Kyle, his breath caught in his throat, saw Cassidee struggle to regain a foothold as rain began to fall in torrents.

Her face full of blood, Cassidee skidded down the cliff face as she lost her grip on the slick rock once more, and went tumbling to the ground.

Chapter 44: Rock Climbing, part 2 – Cassidee

Cassidee was halfway down the cliff when she felt a thump on her back. Gripping her rope tightly, she turned her head and saw Waverly staring up at her with scared and angry blue eyes. An acidic green flashed in them as lightning cracked through the sky.

"Waverly! You're awake!"

"You shouldn't have brought us here," Waverly hissed, her blue eyes slowly turning an acid green as they narrowed into cat-like slits. "You shouldn't have brought *me* here."

A strong gust of wind made Cassidee dig her nails into the slippery shale. "What do you mean? We had to get you your medicine!"

"Then you should have left me in a cave or something, so I couldn't endanger you! But now I've brought all of your lives into peril because you brought me into the place of my entire existence!" Waverly's voice was a harsh hissing sound.

Cassidee felt her back strain under the Okkulten's weight. She was beginning to get scared. "W-waverly?"

Waverly's pallid skin crumbled away to reveal coal-black skin with holes burned through. Her eyes turned from cat-like to bug-like. Her black hair seemed to retreat into her skull, turning teal as it shrunk into a buzz-cut. Waverly hissed, a forked tongue showing between the two fangs she had.

Waverly cut the rope between her and Cassidee, and was suspended in air, before slowly rotating eerily on the spot until she was upright. Cassidee felt her jaw drop open. Fear coursed through her. This was not the human Waverly they were used to—this was Okkulten Waverly, and she seemed to have lost all sense of who she was. As long as she was like this, she was a danger to Cassidee and the others.

The rain began to pour. Cassidee tried to scrabble up the

shale and shimmy up the rope, but she couldn't secure a grip. Waverly seized her shoulders and yanked Cassidee off the face of the cliff. As Cassidee opened her mouth to shriek, her mouth was suddenly flooded with water and she choked and sputtered. Waverly pushed her, hard, and suddenly, there was an intense pain as her face and body connected with the cliff face.

As her nose smashed into the rock, her face pressed against the shale, Cassidee thought it was a miracle that her nose wasn't broken. It gushed blood from both nostrils. Her face was cut and stinging. Her jacket was ripped and blood ran in streaks down her arm through several deep cuts. She tried to spit out the metallic taste of her own blood as it gushed from her nose into her mouth.

Above her, she heard a scream, probably Jessica's, cut through the air.

Her thoughts seemed muddy, and she couldn't think straight. She tried to secure her hold again, but Waverly bit her hand and sliced the rope holding her to the cliff.

Cassidee shrieked with pain again, and Waverly lunged for her throat. Cassidee kicked the Okkulten and her fingernails and jeans ripped as she skidded down the cliff face, digging her nails into the rock to try and maintain a hold. Blood was all over her body, and there was not a part of her that wasn't in pain.

Something—Waverly, probably—shoved her chest and sent her to the ground. Cassidee felt her left shoulder pop out of its socket as she landed, and her tailbone was bruised, if not broken. Screaming in pain, Cassidee saw a dark shape looming over her as she fought to remain conscious.

Chapter 45: When Darkness Falls – Morgan

Tick, tock
Tick, tock
Tick, tock
Goes the clock
In the silence that speaks so loudly.
It echoes through your mind
The only sound in the silence of the night.
A death march to your deepest fears
Sleep is not a refuge

Tick, tock
Tick, tock
Tick, tock
Goes the clock
Condemning you to the abysmal dreams
Or the frightening silence, if you are lucky

Darkness swallows all you know
Even in insanity, sleep is not a refuge
Swallowing all that steps in its way
No man is safe from the demons that lurk within its depths
Darkness covers Graystorm, which is the world, all you know
Unleashing a new kind of terror that captivates every mind

The doctors are immune
They have this all planned
My end is coming
Darkness shall bring it forth

Tick, tock
Tick, tock

Tick, tock
Goes the clock
You are not safe
When the blanket of darkness smothers all

Tick, tock

Trixie Jefferson

It was Corey's screaming, her absence from the group, that made them turn around on the stairs leading down to the cellar ward.

Morgan spun around, gripping Kevin's arm as he teetered on the edge of the steps, her eyes locked on a screaming, crying Corey, curled up on a step, her eyes squeezed shut.

Fleur stepped up to the fourteen-year-old and shook her shoulders. "Corey! Corey!" The girl finally stopped screaming and crying, only to look past Fleur, not seeing anything except what was in her mind.

"Alone," she whispered, her voice shaking, her blue eyes wide. "I'm all alone."

Kevin and Morgan stared at Corey with wide, startled eyes. "She's gone mad," Kevin muttered.

"The doctors got inside her mind," Fleur whispered, fear lacing her voice like a delicate poison.

"Bring her to me," a voice called from up the stairs, belonging to a small, thin, hunched over silhouette, with eyes as blue as Corey's that pierced the darkness.

Trixie.

"You followed us?" Morgan asked, her voice dry like a creek bed in Old Nevada.

"You would need me, and you do. Give her to me, darkness is about to fall."

Fleur, Morgan, and Kevin advanced warily up the steps. "What do you mean?" Fleur asked cautiously.

"You spent the night here. Didn't you feel the darkness's wrath?"

Fleur's stunned silence answered.

"It's when everything gets worse. The darkness condemns you to the darkest, deepest corners of what seems like Tartarus itself. If you get submitted to the torture, you're lucky. It's the silence, except for the ticking of the clock, which drives everyone—even perfectly sane people—into a dark, primal state of hysteria and paranoia.

"Here at Graystorm, the night can last for what seems like forever. Shadows no longer lurk in the corners. They are everywhere, which means the doctors are everywhere. Doctor Steele, he's the Demon King, made of shadow, he sees your every move. He can be at your door...

"In the corner of your room, slinking along the wall...

"Right by your bed, waiting to call in Doctor Cadenza, the Nightmare Princess, made of black crystal, for her to touch your forehead and launch you into an inescapable labyrinth of nightmares, phantasmagorias, and dementia.

"You thought you could survive the day, and that the night would be no problem.

"You have never been so wrong."

Morgan, Kevin, and Fleur stared at Trixie, startled by her frightening monologue.

Trixie motioned to Corey, who was shaking, eyes open, looking possessed, on the stairs at her feet. "She's already succumbing. And if you don't achieve your mission by night's end, you'll never escape. Your mind will never be right again. And the Destined Ones will fail..." A flash of green leapt into Trixie's eyes. Morgan cocked her head.

Trixie, not noticing Morgan's head inclination, picked up Corey in her twisted, broken arms, and carried her up the stairs and down the hallway, headed far away from the cellar ward.

The others had no choice but to follow.

As they walked up the stairs to the third floor and down

the hall, Morgan looked out the windows and through the grime; she could see the blood red of the setting sun. It stained the sky scarlet like blood, like the blood that spattered the walls of Graystorm Asylum. Like the blood that, even though the asylum had been closed for centuries, still flowed through the building, at the hands of the two insane doctors.

Ironically, Morgan stepped into a pool of crimson light that poured in from a crack in the window, staining her leg and shoe like she had been dipped into a vat of gore.

The shadows stretched, and the scarlet light swept over everything, darkening to crimson, to a dark red that bordered on black. For the first time since entering Graystorm, Morgan suppressed a whimper.

Chapter 46: *Pays de épouvantail* – Jessica

Jessica's mind was blank as she descended the rope down the cliff face. She was blocking out her fear of heights, and all feelings about seeing Cassidee fall ten feet after crashing into the cliff. She had read about this happening when you experience great shock; it's like the brain goes into overdrive, protecting you from feelings until you can get your grip on them.

As she passed the place where Cassidee smashed into the cliff, she saw the fifteen-year-old's dark blood on the rocks, dripping down into the sun-bleached sand.

There was a scream down from the beach, and Jessica twisted her head and saw something that horrified her, so much more than all else she had seen in the Empire.

Cassidee was standing on her feet, clutching her left shoulder as she leaned precariously to that side. Her shoulder looked dislocated. Blood was running, thick and fast, out of her nose and down to her chin. Her lips were stained like she had smeared on too much lipstick. Her eyes seemed haunted, and dark circles of dirt were smeared under eyes, making them look sunken into her skull, and zombie-like. Her jacket was torn and a hole was ripped on the knees on her jeans. Blood dripped heavily from her torn fingernails to the sand, staining it. She staggered toward a black being with holes burned through its body, teal hair buzz cut and green bug eyes, hissing and spitting, sporting two fangs and a forked red tongue.

It took Jessica three seconds to realize it was an Okkulten, and five more to realize something even more harrowing: that particular Okkulten was Waverly.

"Kyle! Joseph!" Jessica screeched, her voice high and shrill as she tried to be heard up on the bluff over the howling of the stormy wind.

Kyle grabbed the rope hanging down and quickly

descended, peering over his shoulder the entire time. His jaw dropped as he saw Cassidee charge at Okkulten-Waverly, stumbling over herself. "Joseph!" He called, and the old man, grumbling, hooked his cane around the rope and glided down.

Jessica stared at him in awe. "I'll tell yah later, if we survive," he grunted, before limping as fast as he could toward Cassidee and Okkulten-Waverly, the latter currently being tossed toward the cliff by the enraged fifteen-year-old, who had charged at her, driving her head into the Okkulten's stomach, launching her into the air.

The Okkulten hit the cliff, crumpling to the ground before scrambling onto all fours, hissing and spitting, infuriated. Cassidee growled back, blood dripping out of her mouth. The Okkulten charged, running like a large dog or cat would.

The small dark blonde met her head on, kicking and punching the Okkulten with one good arm and two badly bruised legs. Within the next five seconds, Okkulten-Waverly had Cassidee pinned, a thin, bone-like black hand wrapped like a vice around her throat. Cassidee choked, her right hand on the Okkulten's shoulders, trying to push her away.

Jessica grabbed Waverly around the waist and yanked her off the dark blonde, who sat up, gasping, as the Okkulten, hissing with rage, fell backward onto her attacker and crushed the air out of her chest. Waverly twisted in Jessica's grip until they were face to face. Waverly hissed and snapped at Jessica's face, who felt the spit hit her. Jessica shoved her knee into the Okkulten's stomach, which caused her to loosen the grip on her shoulders.

Something slashed at Jessica's arm, and she felt blood run down it. A knife, black and jagged and horrible looking whipped through the air, ready to strike again. The attacked girl didn't know where Waverly had gotten it.

Joseph whacked Waverly again and again with his cane, and the Okkulten backed off Jessica, hissing, spitting, and swiping at the old man's weapon. While she was distracted, Kyle took the extra rope from Cassidee's climb and tied the Okkulten's wrists together and bound them to her back in a fluid motion.

Jessica grabbed the longer rope and tied Waverly's ankles as Cassidee, dead as she looked, managed to hold the Okkulten down. Joseph took the knife and Kyle (once again) picked up the Okkulten.

However, Waverly turned into a snake and slithered out of the bonds. She turned back into Okkulten form and scampered off toward the island like a particularly large dog before any of them could react.

Kyle and Jessica exchanged puzzled looks. Jessica picked up the ropes and stuffed them into her bag. Cassidee, who looked like she might drop from sheer exhaustion and extreme pain, insisted that she wouldn't be carried. So Jessica slipped her arm around the dirty blonde's shoulders, who reluctantly agreed to the support.

The tired and injured foursome managed to swim through the water, including Joseph, dog-paddling, and Cassidee who was too exhausted and too mangled to swim. Despite her protests ("Put me down! I still have both legs and can swim with one arm! I don't need to be carried!"), Kyle insisted on transporting her to shore. So Cassidee went in reluctant silence, nursing her bruised ego. "Stereotypical," she muttered sulkily. Kyle rolled his eyes but remained silent.

The water was cold and swirled around and past them strongly, feeling like a rushing river. Sometimes waves would come up and slap them in the face or wash over their heads. Jessica gave up on trying to keep her head above water and swam underneath the surface until she needed air again.

Despite the storm clouds overhead (the rain had stopped) the water surrounding the island was clear and beautiful. There were no fish or plants, but it still reminded Jessica of when she used to go to the beach with her parents and would swim through what seemed to be an entirely different world.

They climbed onto the shore of *Pays de épouvantail* sopping wet, thoroughly drained of energy, increasingly hungry, and shivering; all of which put them in bad moods. Cassidee, especially, was being a cow, but no one blamed her.

"Now what? Why do we even need that plant now? Waverly changed and ran off. With all those holes in her body you wouldn't notice the werewolves' injuries anyway," Cassidee grumbled, her knees almost giving out as Kyle set her down. She turned her bad mood on him. "I don't know how Waverly survived you carrying her all that way," she complained, taking off her jacket and wringing it out—or at least, was trying to with one hand. She looked at her limp and dislocated left shoulder. Her face calmed. "Sorry, Kyle. It just hurts so much, I have to lash out."

Her friend shrugged. "What does it matter? I can't believe you're still standing and not crying or something."

"I can't believe it either. I really thought I'd have crumpled by now."

"I'd relocate your shoulder, but I don't know how."

"I know how," Jessica said as she finished dumping the water out of her shoes. "We really need some boots," she mumbled before coming over to Cassidee. She picked up a stick and handed it to her. "Sit down and bite on this."

Cassidee looked at the stick doubtfully. "I have to bite this?"

"Yes, it helps, trust me," Jessica replied smoothly.

Cassidee sat down, folding her legs beneath her. "Are you sure you know how to do this?"

"I had to it to my younger sister and older brother before. It went fine."

"I'm sure you had your parents around."

"Actually, I didn't. Me, my sister and brother had gotten lost on a camping trip looking for wood and they fell from a pretty high tree."

"How'd you know what to do?"

"Just be quiet and bite on the stick."

182

Cassidee, feeling foolish, put the stick in her mouth while Jessica placed her hands on her left shoulder. Jessica pushed Cassidee's shoulder back into place with a strong push, and the pain intensified. Cassidee felt the stick splinter between her teeth and she spit it out, along with a wail of pain. Jessica got up and stepped back, grinning sheepishly, as Cassidee clutched her shoulder and winced from the pain, tears of agony running down her face.

As Jessica looked the fifteen-year-old over, she noticed the dirt was washed from around her eyes, making them look normal instead of sunken in and dead. The blood was mostly washed from her chin and mouth, but a little trickle still oozed from her nose and out the corner of her mouth. The scratches that were all over her looked clean and well-defined. Her jacket was ripped, soiled, and water logged. It would be pointless to keep it.

"Cassidee, you can get rid of your jacket. And once we're off this island, I say we find a town or something and get some fresh clothes," Jessica proposed.

"I'm all for that," Kyle agreed as he helped Cassidee to her feet.

"I'm there," the dirty blonde approved, all of her bad mood gone.

"Of course you're there!" Joseph grumbled, limping over and waving his cane. "Where'd ya be if ya weren't? Kids. It sounds nice," he finished, referring to Jessica's proposition.

"So, where do we go from here?" Kyle asked, looking around at the greenery that inhabited the island.

"We need to go get Waverly back. She is our guide, after all, and our friend," Jessica directed.

"Then let's go. I don't want to be on this island any longer than I have to," Cassidee mumbled, walking toward the woods.

The island forest was full of lush greenery as well as dead wood. There were clearly animals about, as branches and bushes rustled constantly, but one was never seen.

A light flickered in the distance over a peat bog. "What's

that?" Cassidee asked, staring at the light.

Jessica stared at it, mesmerized. "It looks like a firefly."

The light pulsed and started to move away from them.

"Where's it going?" Kyle said, confused.

"Should we follow it?"

"Nah," Joseph said, coming to the front of the group and waving his cane. "That ain't no dumb-bunny firefly. That's a will-o'-the-wisp, an' you get lost if ya follow it. Right to the clutches of the Wendigo, some say."

"Wendigo?" Cassidee asked, cocking her head to the right.

"Cannibalistic giants. They bite ya, and ya turn cannibal as well," Joseph muttered. "Not pleasant subjects, no, not a tiny bit. Let's get a-goin'. I think I know where Waverly be a hidin'."

"Where?" Jessica asked.

"It'd be best if I was to start from the beginnin', but it'd be a might long story. So I'll just a say that she's with her others, the other Okkultens."

"Why?"

"Yah just wanna know everythin', don' ya? Who, what, when, where, why and how. Save it for the paper."

Joseph led them away from the bog and the will-o'-the-wisp, and deeper into the forest. Soon they came across what seemed to be a pretty girl sitting on some rocks, her hair and clothes wet. Her figure wavered slightly. Jessica recognized the girl as a banshee, and led them away before her scream could split the air.

"Where are we going?" Kyle asked after he got whacked in the face by a branch. Jessica wasn't sure, but she thought the tree giggled.

"To the Okkulten camp."

"Where is it?"

"Somewhere in here."

"Why are we going there?"

"Didn' ya hear what I said to Jessica? Save it."

Suddenly, several Okkultens burst out of the woods,

snarling and hissing, as they surrounded the group. "Don' move, don' fight. We could' beat one, but Okkultens together are impossible to beat."

The Okkultens took them even deeper into the woods, if that was possible, and took them through an archway of trees to the main camp, which looked nothing like the rest of the island. Okkultens sat around in groups, feasting on fresh meat, blood spattered over their faces. Some Okkultens lounging in trees saw the group entering first. They let out a loud, strangled trumpeting sound, to alert the Okkultens on the ground that newcomers had arrived.

Jessica wilted slightly under their similar, bug-like stares.

There was a bang as doors Jessica hadn't even noticed swung open from the base of a tall tree at the opposite side of the camp. Several Okkultens strode out like guards, then stopped and separated into two lines on either side of the door, standing erect and motionless.

Two Okkultens let out the loud, strangled trumpeting sound they had heard earlier, and a single Okkulten strode out, wearing a dark gray vest like a scholar would, and black pants. The hair was still buzz cut and teal, but something looked different. Suddenly, realization hit Jessica and the others. They had seen this Okkulten before. She was wearing clothes now, and wasn't as ugly as when they had first seen her changed. She glared down at them, fixing them with a bug-eyed stare.

"Waverly?"

Chapter 47: Tapestry of Decay – Kevin

A bell, deep and low, chimed once. An organ piano began to play somewhere deep in the night. Silence fell over Graystorm Asylum as the chords ended, ringing low and deep but fading.

The clock started ticking.

As Trixie carried Corey, who was now limp, down the hallway, time slowed. The hallway spun around Kevin, slowly revolving. The food that he had consumed only a few hours ago churned in his stomach. He closed his eyes and concentrated at putting one foot in front of the other. *It's just the doctors. Don't let the night get to you.*

They continued to walk down the hallway, past rooms, past torture chambers, until they reached a set of stairs leading up. On the sign, it said: Bell Tower – Up. "Come on," Trixie said, sliding open the metal grate that blocked the stairs. "We're going to the Tapestry of Decay, where Paige will meet us."

"The what?" Morgan asked, starting up the stairs after Trixie.

"The Tapestry of Decay."

"What's that?"

"You'll see."

The stairs were thin and spiral, but sturdy and firm. No one said a word. The clock tick faded, but Kevin could still hear it resounding in his head. *Tick, tock, tick, tock, tick, tock.*

The stairs seemed to take forever. Lightning crashed outside, and even though there were no windows, shadows flickered on the walls, not showing their silhouettes, but other people and glimmers of gruesome moments. One was the outline of a young girl, sitting on the stairs and weeping silently. Another showed a man standing before a head that hung from the top of the tower. An additional shadow depicted a woman holding a long, slender butcher knife that dripped with blood over the body of another woman. Though they were just images, brief moments of time, unrest clawed at Kevin, reminding him of what horrors had happened here.

"We're almost there," Trixie said as lightning cracked again, what seemed like hours later. She stopped, even though the stairs continued on up to the bell tower. Or nothingness. Kevin couldn't see the top.

"Aren't we going to the bell tower?" Fleur asked as Trixie handed Corey to her and began pressing her fingers against some bricks on the wall.

"No. The bell tower can't hold the Tapestry of Decay. The doctors didn't want anyone to find this, but I learned all their secrets."

A face made of shadow appeared on the bricks after Trixie tapped a sequence. "Password, Miss Jefferson?" the face said. No details were prominent on the face, but it sounded like Doctor Steele's voice.

Trixie said a string of Latin words: "*In aeternum*".

"Very good," the shadow face said, and his face morphed into a shadow door. Kevin waited for the real door to appear, but Corey reached for the knob on the shadow door, and the shadows curled around her hand like smoke as she grabbed the knob and pulled open the door.

The door—the shadows, more than likely—seemed to sigh as blackness lured them across the threshold and swallowed them.

A light flickered in the inky darkness. A candle was lit, sitting in its holder. Trixie muttered more Latin words, standing away from the candle.

A whole candelabra full of candles flickered to life, their flames battling the darkness, which crept back into the corners.

In the brief light, as Trixie led them into the room, Kevin could glimpse a large tapestry hanging on the stone wall. The table holding the candelabra sat in front of it. And in front of the table stood a taller figure wearing a midnight blue cloak. From under the hood, red hair spilled down the front of the cloak. Sympathetic brown eyes gleamed in the darkness.

"Paige, thanks for coming," Trixie said. Paige nodded.

"I don't like doing this, Trixie, you know that. But anyway, bring her here."

Trixie led them to the table and had Fleur set Corey down on it. Paige turned to her and the others. "I am revealing the Tapestry of Decay, and replenishing Corey's sanity. The doctors needed it sometimes when the patients insanity wore on them too much."

"Well, it didn't work, they were already insane," Kevin scoffed.

"True," Paige said. "But I'm certain it will work for Corey."

Turning around, Paige spoke directly to the moth-eaten tapestry on the wall, her Latin words sounding like a spell, even though Kevin couldn't tell what they meant.

The tapestry on the wall glowed an ethereal green, and the lines became detailed, glowing an acidic green. Paige chanted the same thing in Latin again, and then a third time. The tapestry glowed so brightly that Kevin was sure he'd need sunglasses.

A picture jumped out at him from the tapestry. It was gruesome. A man held a heart in his hand, a knife in his other hand, and a hole in his chest where he had just hacked out his own heart. As more pictures began to swirl, Paige announced loudly: "Behold! The Tapestry of Decay!"

The tapestry seemed to show the descent of the patients' sanity at Graystorm Asylum. With each picture it grew steadily more gruesome and insane: patients twisted and bent in gymnastic feats that no Olympic gymnast could do; spiders crawling into the forced open mouths of a handful of patients; people being given horrible doses of shock treatment and gruesome lobotomies. And almost every other image showed lightning striking the bell tower. Kevin could almost hear the screams resonating from the patients depicted in the tapestry; he could hear the clanging of a bell as the tower was struck; and the ticking of the clock never stopped, never stopped. Tick, tock, tick tock tick tock ticktockticktockticktock...

And suddenly, a picture appeared on the tapestry that he could not ignore. It was less gruesome, much less, than the other pictures, but it was still disturbing, and it clawed at his heart. Corey was curled up on the ground in an empty stairwell, crying relentlessly and pitifully. Shadows leered at her and her tears were creating a big puddle on the floor, which she was in the middle of. Her wails carried all the way out of the tapestry and nailed itself right in his heart. He felt Morgan grip his wrist and knew that his twin felt the same pain he did.

They stared at the scene for a second longer, before Paige shouted one more Latin phrase, her voice ringing through the air.

A smoke-like substance oozed from the Tapestry, bright green and glowing. It swirled through the air toward Corey, who lay still on the table, and it gently probed her forehead, her chest, before splitting and being sucked into her heart and her brain. Her body suddenly started to shake, her eyes open and completely white. Her body glowed green, rising an inch off the table, before dropping next to the candelabra.

Kevin saw her go still as wind whooshed into the room and blew out the candles, plunging them into darkness.

Chapter 48: Queen Desdemona – Kyle

"Waverly?"

The question did not come from one person—it came from the entire group, Joseph included.

"My name issss Waverly, yesss," she said, hissing.

"You-you don't remember us?" Jessica asked mournfully.

"I know who you are," Waverly said with a rattling intake of breath. "You are Jessssssica Knight, from the Desssstined Onesss. The boy issss Kyle Hill, the other girl issss Cassssssidee Sssscott. The old man I do not recognize."

"His name is Joseph—" Cassidee began, but Waverly cut her off, holding up a hand.

"I do not need to be on a firsssst name basssisss. I have come to take you to our home, to ssssee the Queen."

At the word 'queen', all the Okkultens in the camp fell into a genuflect. "Rissse," Waverly hissed quietly after she herself stooped into a bow.

"Let ussss go, now. Three guardssss will accompany ussss. If you try any trickery, you will pay dearly."

Three guards stepped from the line leading from the oak tree to the center of the camp. Standing tall and proud, moving in even, short steps, they walked to Waverly. They wore red martial jackets with a white sash and black pants that seemed to be molded against their skin. Their black boots went over their pants and up to their knees. A sword, similar to the one Waverly had attacked them with earlier, was clutched in their fists.

"Perfect," Waverly said scathingly. She waved her bone-thin black hand toward the exit to the camp, motioning for them to follow.

It turned out that the Queen's place was not on *Pays de épouvantail*, but a region just over the border of the Southern Empire. To their surprise, it was only a day's trek away.

"So, um, Waverly?" Kyle asked cautiously. "Why are you escorting us?"

"I am not exactly a transsslator for the Queen assss much assss in charge of the island camp," she hissed bitterly.

"And that bothers you?" Cassidee asked, noticing the discontent in her voice.

"I could have been a good transsslator, but the Queen can ssspeak any language."

"So she doesn't need you at her camp? Because you don't serve a greater purpose?" Kyle asked.

Waverly whirled around and slapped him. She grabbed the front of his jacket and lifted him off the ground with one hand. "Inssssolent child!" she hissed, before throwing him to the ground. "I sssserve a greater purpose than all thossse othersss ssstuck at the island camp."

Cassidee helped him stand after Waverly turned back around and marched off, Jessica and Joseph following close behind. The guards spat at them angrily, and threatened to jab them with their knives until Cassidee and Kyle caught up with Waverly.

"That was inane," Cassidee muttered to Kyle. "Absolutely stupid!"

"I know, I know. I wish I hadn't asked that," he grumbled back, his face glowing red from both embarrassment and the slap.

They walked for an entire day, and rested close to midnight. Kyle's legs were burning, and he was short of breath. Cassidee, Jessica, and poor Joseph weren't any better off. The hills were steep, much steeper than anything that they had ever scaled. They rested out in the open, under a literal blue moon. It started off as a powder blue, like Cassidee's eyes, and ended up being a brilliant glow of dark blue.

"When you said 'blue moon' earlier, I thought that meant we were having two full moons in one month," Jessica said, staring up at the clear sky.

"It's different here. A blue moon means when the moon is blue. It is said to give incredibly strong powers to the Queen of the Night, which would be Chandra if she was a queen right now..." Cassidee explained.

"So does she still get the powers?"

"Yeah, since she is the Princess of the Night. Its whoever holds the power of the moon and stars that gets the power of the blue moon."

"We don't need her to be crazy-strong right now," Kyle commented.

"Well, from what I read, it says that if the night should be used for dark purposes, the powers of the blue moon are cut off from the current ruler of the night."

"So Chandra isn't any stronger tonight than any other night?"

"Right, except that, despite the absence of the blue moon's powers, she could still be immensely strong tonight, or any other night, because it's her birthright."

There was a pause from both Jessica and Kyle. "What?" they finally asked.

"The night. The night is her birthright. She controls it. She is weak during the daytime. And, blue moon or not, her powers are magnified several times over when day turns into night."

"So, she could still destroy us?"

"Anyone can destroy us, we're just human beings," Cassidee said.

Jessica gulped. The idea didn't appeal much to Kyle, either.

"Well, goodnight," Cassidee muttered, and she rolled over in her sleeping bag, her breathing quickly slowing.

Jessica did the same, and Kyle followed suit. But before he fell asleep, he couldn't help thinking about how six kids could defeat an entire league of creatures that were so much stronger than them and could defeat them with a single flick of their hand.

At six in the morning the next day, they were roused from sleep and told to eat whatever food they had left. Too hungry to care that this was the end of their rations and that the only dried fruit left were apricots, the four prisoners gobbled down their food.

As they went over the crest of a green hill, they looked down into what looked like rotting land. It was a deep valley with craggy mountains looming in the background. The sky seemed to be filled with dark greenish-gray smog. As the kids and their escorts descended the hill, they noticed the lush green grass turn to something that looked like swamp muck but was actually solid. A putrid odor filled Kyle's nose, making his eyes water. He didn't know what it smelled of, and he didn't really want to know. Tendrils of some unknown plant rose out of the ground, lined with sharp, tiny prickles that looked like microscopic knives. A few lone trees rose out of the dried swamp ground, but the wood was rotting and thick, and there were no leaves. There were no animals (or anything edible) in sight.

As they walked across the barren land, Kyle began to wonder how anything could ever live out here. There was no food in sight, and no shelter. But Waverly kept walking, so the four prisoners had no choice but to follow farther into the wasteland. After trudging on for about a mile, Kyle saw the first sign of life.

A shadow person with buzz-cut hair stood in the distance, and a trumpeting call echoed from them. The person turned and ran off into the distance, scampering like a dog. "What was that?" Jessica asked Waverly in an undertone.

"The lookout. Ssshe'll alert the Queen that we have arrived."

"Okay...I guess," Jessica murmured under her breath.

"How could she tell it was you?" Cassidee asked.

"We Okkultenssss have very good eye-ssssight."

"But you all look alike."

"All Okkultenssss are able to tell each other apart."

After thirty more minutes of trekking into the seemingly-endless Okkulten territory, they finally reached what seemed to be a camp. They couldn't really tell, but most of the Okkultens seemed to be there, in the center of the territory, heads peeking out of the mucky ground, peering at the arrivals with loathing in their bug-eyes.

"Call the Queen," Waverly hissed to a Okkulten whose head was poking out of the ground.

The Okkulten nodded and disappeared into its hole in the ground. In a minute, a loud rattling intake of breath seemed to echo around the camp. Then a drum sounded, deep and loud. It continued, the rattling breath sound turning into a loud and steady buzzing. A figure, flanked by two guards, walked toward the camp.

Between the two guards stood a tall, thin woman with acidic green hair and matching human eyes. Her skin was still as black as coal and had holes burnt through it, like the typical Okkulten. She wore a black cape and black boots that Kyle could barely see. If she hadn't been an Okkulten, Kyle would have called her beautiful. And scary. That went without saying, Okkulten or not.

About fifty feet away from them, a mound of a sticky, gooey yellow substance rose up out of the ground, looking like a throne. Queen Desdemona sat down, her back straight and rigid, her eyes looking over all of them—even her own Okkultens—with malice.

"Are these the ones, Waverly?" Queen Desdemona asked, after the Okkultens had come out of their bow. Kyle noticed that she did not hiss, her voice sounding almost human.

"Yesss, my queen," Waverly said, bowing again.

"Rise, foolish girl, you have already bowed. Go pay respects to your elders now; I'll deal with these four," Queen Desdemona said, her voice cold and cruel.

Kyle was sure that if Waverly could have turned crimson with embarrassment, she would have. The dismissed Okkulten straightened up and walked swiftly away, out into the barren lands.

Queen Desdemona beckoned to Kyle, Jessica, Cassidee, and

Joseph with a long black finger. "Come with me, you three. Guards, get rid of the old man."

Chapter 49: Hidden Horrors – Corey

Black and white flashed in front of my eyes. But then it stopped flashing and started spiraling...I was falling...falling into myself.

How had this all happened? How had I managed to lose my grip on my sanity?

Faces flashed above me. Some, I recognized, like Trixie and Morgan, Fleur and Kevin. But others I did not recognize, and those faces were gruesome. I saw horrible things coming from them. Spiders were being forced into mouths; hearts and other vital organs were being hacked out. And somewhere, in the background, I could hear someone chanting in Latin.

I was scared. I was shaking. I wanted this to be over. *Either let me die or let me wake up, I just don't want to be stuck in insanity!* I pleaded silently.

Something raced through my body like an electrical current. Panic joined it. I felt tingly all over, like when my foot falls asleep, only that feeling had spread to every other part of my body.

A scream, shrill and high, entered my brain and echoed around in there, making me want to join in, to make it stop. But yet I couldn't even move, let alone make a sound.

Then a bell started tolling. A clock started ticking. Light flashed in front of my eyes like lightning. And screams, wails, of torment and despair, merciless, cruel laughter joined in to a crescendo of invisible torture. Everything was spinning. I couldn't think straight; I couldn't even register what was happening. I wanted this all to be over. I couldn't handle it.

I swore, that despite my immobility, I felt a tear run down my face.

All of a sudden, I was standing in a hallway that was free of grime and loose floorboards. But yet, I recognized it immediately. I was inside a younger, newer, not-yet-abandoned Graystorm Asylum.

I looked down at myself. I was wearing a gray gown, not unlike the one I saw on Trixie. It fell to just an inch above my knees. Scars riddled my body in various places, and fresh cuts that still oozed small trickles of blood also covered my arms, legs, and even a few spots on my face. Bruises bloomed over my body like gray, blue, and violet flowers.

I looked bone-thin, and I felt starved. I felt my hair, and not only did it feel gross, grimy, and oily, but it was much longer than my own. It was a dark brunette, and fell just over my shoulders. The ends were split and it felt like a rat's nest. Then again, the patients at Graystorm were never viewed by the public, so why clean up?

"Hey!" a curt female voice yelled at me. "Get moving, Genesis!"

My name was Genesis? How strange. That used to be a really old name...

Someone shoved me, forcing me to step forward. "Hey!" I shouted in a hoarse voice that didn't belong to me. "Watch it!"

"Xanthe! Escort Genesis to her appointment!" the female voice yelled again.

A woman with straight golden hair placed her hands roughly on my shoulders and steered me down the hall, all the while shouting back over her shoulder, "Yes, Doctor Cadenza."

I started at hearing the name, and turned around. Doctor Cadenza was very beautiful, but by the scowl on her face and the hate in her eyes, I could tell she was rotting away on the inside. She had sharp green eyes that glowed with malice and looked like they could burn a hole through you. Her skin was pale and porcelain-like, almost like what you would see on a china doll. Her blonde hair was perfectly curled—not tight ringlets, not loose waves—and it fell in a stylish curtain to half-past her shoulder blades. She wore a black jacket and carried a straight jacket over one arm. Instead of wearing a traditional nurse's skirt and high heels, she wore black pants and gray tennis shoes.

I looked up at the woman steering me. She had a flat, thin

face with the skin stretched tight. Her lips were pale and thin, almost non-existent. Her eyes were cat-like and matched her perfectly, had-to-be-flat-ironed straight gold hair.

Xanthe, I thought wearily. *It means gold, or yellow. Greek origin.*

I had no idea what my 'appointment' was, but I was certainly nervous. Was I going to be stuck here until Genesis died? How much torture would I have to live through?

I was already beginning to hyperventilate, my breath quickening and shortening, my heart climbing up my throat and threating to burst.

I twisted in Xanthe's grip, trying to free myself and run away. Her grip tightened so much on my arms that I thought she'd cut off circulation. Her incredibly sharp fingernails (were they fixed with something lethal?) dug through the skimpy gown I was wearing and into my skin. I felt my body relax a tiny bit. Was there a sedative leaking into my body through her nails? I fought harder, and finally stomped my bare foot onto hers, and smashed my head back into her face.

Her grip vanished as her hands whipped up to her face to stop the bloody nose. I darted, and Doctor Cadenza immediately noticed my flight.

Her acidic green eyes locked with my brown ones and her face twisted into a disgusted snarl. "Security!" Cadenza barked automatically, like she had done it several times before.

I only had seconds to find an escape route. People tried to grab me, but I eluded their hands, thanks to Genesis's skinny frame and the fact that she was quick on her feet. I yanked open a stairwell door and ran down, down, down. I didn't stop at the other levels. Only when I reached the basement did I fling open the door and step inside to unforeseen horrors:

Grimy white walls that looked nothing like upstairs.

A cracked linoleum floor with water trickling through the cracks.

Rows of cells with several patients clinging to the rusted

bars, all of them either half-naked or fully nude, their bodies so twisted, scarred, and damaged beyond medical help that it didn't matter if they wore anything at all.

Some of them snapped at me, their teeth sharp like a dog's. Thin, corpse-like hands crept out of the cells and clawed hungrily at the hem of my dress. I stepped in puddles of mixed blood and water, to my disgust.

One patient began to bark madly like a dog, his head cocked sideways with a distant look in his eyes. "No! Shh! Shh!" I whispered loudly and hurriedly to the barking patient, tears welling up in my eyes. "They'll find me!"

Someone tugged at my dress, and I spun, stifling a yelp. A young woman who looked in slightly better shape than the others sat on the ground of a cell, her legs twisted and bruised. Her right shoulder looked dislocated, and I was sure I saw a bit of bone sticking out of her gray, torn gown in the back. I gagged, feeling the contents of my stomach race up my throat. I clapped a hand over my mouth.

The woman had soiled, short blonde hair. Her face was tear-stained and covered with dirt. Her eyes were hollow, but they shined a bright blue. I gagged again, this time from recognition.

"Trixie?" I whispered, a tear spilling from my eye.

The woman didn't answer my question, but she looked up and gazed at me. "You said 'they'll find me,'" she whispered, her voice cracked and hoarse. "They already have, Corey."

Chapter 50: The Tale of Genesis – Corey

Once upon a time,
There was a sad tale
Of a young girl whose mind
Was not in its right state.

So off to Graystorm Asylum she went,
Prayers from her family being the only thing she had
But, once upon a time
They would slip away…
Into the shadows
Under the watch of the Demon King and Nightmare Princess

Graystorm was a cruel place
A place of misery for 'bad' people who were like Genesis
'Not quite right'
Genesis knew that a storm was coming
But who listens to the insane?

An appointment one day she had
Frightened, she was.
She fought her captor and fled the scene,
Under the eye of Miss Cadenza, the Nightmare Princess.

Down, down the stairwell
She didn't pause until the stairs ended
And she was left at the door to something terrible
With doom nipping at her heels.

She opened the door to the cellar ward,
Not knowing what she would find.
But all of her previous horrors,
Could not justify this kind.

She wanted to help,
She really did.
But what could she do?
For those in the cellar ward are beyond all need.

A woman sat in a cell, and looked up at Genesis
She said something that would make the girl seal her fate
Those words unknown, people could only guess
At what could prompt what happened next.

When security found Genesis only moments later,
The girl was curled up on the ground
Sitting in a puddle of her own tears.

Cadenza did not show pity.
She ordered, 'Take her away!'
Genesis slept soundly, thanks to a sedative
But her mind had slipped into that irretrievable place.

The next day, Genesis was taken to the heart of Graystorm
And all its evil that lay there
She was turned to crystal,
And shattered.

And just like that,
The last prayer given to Genesis
Slipped away
Forgotten
Never to be heard.

This concludes the sad tale of Genesis.
So kids, beware.
When doom comes knocking on the door,
Don't go into the cellar ward.

A fairytale told to Empire children. Date of origin unknown.

"Trixie?" I whispered, clutching at the bars of the cell. "How'd you know my name?"

But Trixie had dropped her head again and had fallen silent. I dwelled over the words she had just spoken: "You said 'they'll find me.' They already have, Corey."

They already have? The question echoed around in my head, but only for a second. I heard security running down the stairs. I only had seconds. I spun on my heel, trying to escape. But at that moment, the shadows in a far corner stirred.

"Who's there?" I asked. The shadows separated from the wall and formed the shape of a tall man, before curling atop Doctor Steele's head like a snake.

He smiled at me, his gray-green eyes glinting. "Hello, Genesis. Or should I say, hello, Corey."

"How'd you and Trixie know who I really was?" I asked, backing up as he stepped forward.

"Things will be explained in due course, my dear. Do you remember those fateful words told to you?"

"'They already have. They already have found me.'"

"And who are they?"

"Security. Cadenza. The other doctors. You. Insanity…" My voice trailed off, breaking. Because in truth, Trixie had been right. They'd found me. There was no point in running, because there was no escape.

"Ah, I see you know the truth. Insanity is a huge, intricate maze with only one way out: death. No one ever leaves. Not truly."

"But that's not true! There have been people out there who have healed, who have gotten better…"

"But they weren't here, were they? The Threshold of Madness isn't a physical thing, Corey. It's a bridge, in your mind. To that irretrievable place everyone is afraid to search. And the journey begins here." Doctor Steele gestured to the cellar ward.

"Don't be scared, Corey. You are lucky. Genesis's end will not be very painful."

Doctor Steele then melted back into the shadows with one last malicious smile. I was shaking. I sank to my knees and cried.

A few minutes later, something pricked my upper arm. Security had found me. But I was too broken to care.

I slept soundly, with no nightmares. Sometimes, I caught glimpses of a door. It looked welcoming, but yet it loomed, tall and menacing. I wanted to open it, but I was too scared of what would happen if I did.

The next day, I was sedated and taken along an intricate maze of hallways I couldn't remember to a large, dark room. I was seated in a leather chair, with straps binding my wrists and ankles to it.

As the sedation wore off, I heard Doctor Steele's voice in my head again: "You are lucky. Genesis's end will not be very painful."

I was alone in the room. I couldn't see. What were they going to do to me? I twisted in the seat, trying to see around me. Why hadn't they bound me with metal? They obviously weren't worried about me getting away.

The shadows shifted, and I saw familiar gray-green eyes staring at me in the total darkness. "What do you want, Doctor Steele?" I asked, my voice shaking with hatred and fear.

"I have come to tell you a story, my dear. Have you been told the tale of the crystal heart?"

"The what?"

"You know how I formed Doctor Cadenza, right?"

"Yes, she was formed out of black crystal."

"You are smart, my dear. Do you know how?"

"No."

"Of course you don't. Present the Crystal Heart!" Doctor Steele shouted. I felt the floor shift. In the darkness, a large heart made of clear crystal rose out of the ground. It glimmered

203

and shone in the darkness.

"The Crystal Heart is also the heart of Graystorm. It is the heart of my power. Do you know what happened to the twins' mother's friend, Miss Asana?"

"She was turned to crystal and shattered," I said vaguely, still taking in the beauty of the crystal.

"Exactly! Which is what we're doing to you."

"What?!" I shrieked. I started fighting my restraints, surprised that the leather held. Doctor Steele smiled at me and retreated back into the shadows.

In the background, I heard him say: "Begin."

Blackness swelled inside the Crystal Heart, before expanding and shooting out of its core straight at me. I screamed as what felt like ice-cold water washed over me and covered me from head to toe. My scream was cut off. I was frozen, captured, inside crystal.

Another jet of blackness sped out of the heart and sent fissures all over the crystal encasing me. As it did that, I felt what seemed like a knife dig into my spine and chest. I moved my eyes what little I could and saw cracks spread along my body, cutting all the way through me. The pain was minimal, like the small pain of getting a paper cut, only prolonged sixty seconds.

I saw jagged lines cross my vision. I couldn't close my eyes. Then, there was no need. I was floating in blackness, being sucked into the building. There was nothing left in that room except the chair. The Crystal Heart had sunken back into the ground, and there were no crystal shards left.

As I was sucked into Graystorm, I saw Genesis's spirit leave. Or...wait, she was being sucked into Graystorm, her mouth still open in an unfinished scream. I, however, was floating away, back through time, back to my own body.

The clock started ticking. The bell started tolling. Lightning flashed. All those harrowing images floated before my eyes. But I wasn't bothered. I now knew what we had to do. We could get rid of Graystorm and the passageway in one shot. The doctors would never torment anyone ever again.

Soon I would realize my idea had as many cracks in it as the shattering crystal Genesis had become.

Chapter 51: The Hive – Cassidee

"The territory of the Okkultens was unlike anything I, or anyone else, had ever seen...decaying land...flat except for the sharp, jagged mountains in the far distance...there were few trees, but they were all dying...tendrils rose out of the ground, as thorny as a rose bush and as creepy as kudzu.

The worst was The Hive, where the Queen lives and her minions serve her...it is unlike anything, unlike even the rest of the territory...it is almost indescribable. Full of sticky green lumps that rise out the ground...inside are her kids...the Queen has no mate...something about Okkultens makes them unable to reproduce...but the Queen somehow has an ability to literally grow her own young...out of the ground...nightmarish.... If the Queen was to die, the entire Okkulten population would die out, for no one, not even one of her own young, is quite like the Queen...."

-- Excerpts from the travel diary of adventurer J. Alan Elphinstone

Two Okkulten guards came up and grabbed Joseph's arms, starting to drag him away. Cassidee started forward, but Joseph shook his head and Kyle grabbed her arm, making her stay still.

"Follow me," Queen Desdemona hissed, beckoning to the three children with a claw-like hand. Guards surrounded them again, forcing them to march after the Okkulten queen.

"He'll be okay, right?" Jessica asked Cassidee nervously as they watched Joseph be led away. "I mean, I bet he's been in worse situations, right? And he's still here..."

"Well, he's not getting any younger," Cassidee said abruptly. "We need to find a way to rescue him."

"I'm not sure if you're aware, Miss Scott," Queen Desdemona called over her shoulder, "but we Okkultens have excellent eye-sight *and* hearing."

Cassidee felt her face burn and looked down at her feet as she walked.

As they walked, the land began to change. Not in a good way, but it wasn't the dull land that was behind them. Instead, lumps of a ghastly green color were sticking out of the ground. Cassidee peered into one in passing, and immediately wished she hadn't.

Inside was a twisted, skinny figure with a large skull that had large, empty eye sockets. At least, they looked like eye sockets, until Cassidee saw the eye roll and look directly at her. She squeaked and jumped away from the thing, utterly unnerved.

"I see you have seen one of my children," Queen Desdemona said, looking at the lumps sticking out of the ground with pride in her acidic green eyes. "Beautiful, aren't they?"

Cassidee gagged.

Soon, a mouth of a cave rose out of the ground. Desdemona led them inside, into the darkness. A loud buzzing filled their ears. Cassidee clapped her hands over her ears, trying to block out the noise.

"Welcome," Queen Desdemona called to them, "to The Hive!"

It was like someone had turned on a floodlight. The entire cave lit up, and Cassidee almost fell over.

Green cocoons hung from the ceiling, and inside were creatures similar to the ones Cassidee had seen in the lumps outside. Okkultens walked around, carrying bugs and bark from the decaying trees. A throne of sticky substance rose out of the ground, and the stickiness on the front jutted out in the shape of a dying woman, her hand clapped over her heart, mouth open in a scream, with large, empty eye-sockets.

Queen Desdemona walked to her throne and climbed up as the Okkultens bent over so she could step on their backs to get up. The queen turned and surveyed the kids with her green eyes.

"Hmm... Bring me the old man!" Desdemona barked.

Within a minute, three guards dragged Joseph into The Hive. In the few minutes he had been separated from them, he had suffered a black eye and a near concussion.

"Joseph," Queen Desdemona said as the guards forced him to his knees. "What are you doing on my land?"

Joseph glared at her for a moment before answering. "I was not meanin' ta cross your land, you incompetent ninny. We're only 'ere because your little family on the island captured us and dragged us 'ere!"

Queen Desdemona narrowed her eyes at him. "And why were you on *Pays de épouvantail?*"

"Well, it started out as Waverly gettin' bit by a werewolf, an' the medicine is on that island, an' then she changes into Okkulten form an' goes off to the camp and we 'ave to go get 'er—
"

"Alright! I've heard enough of your babbling! What did I tell you last time you were here?"

"Ya told me too many things, Desdemona—"

"Fool! What did I tell you about coming back!" she snapped, her tongue flicking out in anger.

"Ya told me that you'd imprison me in one o' those freaky green globes and leave me there to rot."

"I'll have to go back on that, since you have returned with company. I'll still leave you to rot, but this time, you have a show: watching those brats be slaughtered!"

"Wait!" Cassidee shouted. Queen Desdemona turned her green gaze on the dark blonde. "What do you mean, Joseph's been here before? We didn't know that."

Jessica and Kyle both nodded.

"You mean, you don't know who your guide is?" Queen Desdemona said, interest sparking in her eyes. "Sarissa never told you?" At the shaking of heads, she announced: "He is Joseph Alan Elphinstone."

"Who?" the three kids asked at once. Queen Desdemona

face-palmed, shaking her head. *Kids*!

"He is Joseph Alan Elphinstone! Great adventurer! He mapped out more than seventy-five percent of the Empire!"

"Really?" Jessica asked, curiosity rising in her voice. "That's why she sent him with us?"

"Yes, idiots."

Jessica frowned. "Since when do queens go as low as to speak petty insults?"

Queen Desdemona disregarded the question. "This is not some silly trivia game! Quit asking things that don't matter!"

"Quit telling us what to do!"

"Did you just talk back to me? I am a queen, you little—"

"You're not *our* queen."

Queen Desdemona narrowed her eyes in dislike. "You are really starting to tick me off."

"I think you're already ticked off. And not because I'm arguing with you."

"Then, if you're so smart, tell me why."

"I think you're agitated because you're scared."

"Insolent child! Why would I be—"

"Your hands are sweating," Jessica cut her off, "you've never left your throne—if you weren't scared, you'd probably have come over and slapped me—"

"How dare you speak to me that way!"

"And," Jessica added, smiling, "we are prophesized to save the Empire. We are destined to be your downfall. What evil wouldn't be scared?"

"Shut up!" the queen hissed through clenched teeth. "Guards!" she barked a moment later, "take them away!"

"Where to, my queen?" a guard asked as they marched up to the three kids and grabbed their arms.

"Just away! Anywhere!" Desdemona shouted. "And tell the others to leave me alone."

Cassidee smiled to Jessica as they were marched away. The diversion had worked. Cassidee had slipped the knives out of the guards' belts while they watched the fight. Those guards taking them away were at their mercy.

Chapter 52: The Real Reason – Chandra

There was a sharp knock on the doors that led to my private wing of the dark castle. I looked up from my book and barked: "What does thou need now, Victoria?"

"Chandra!" my sister barked, throwing open the doors and striding in, her silvery hair flowing behind her like a flag in the wind. "We need to talk," she said more calmly, halting in the center of my room.

I rolled my eyes at my bratty sister and went back to my book. "What, Sarissa? Have you finally given up on those silly Destined Ones? Queen Desdemona has them, you know, and they won't escape this time," I said mildly, like it didn't matter to me at all whether they lived or died.

"They'll get out. Joseph is there," Sarissa said, plopping down in the chair next to me, somehow still managing to remain queenly.

"Why are you here? I'm sure you didn't come to discuss the Okkultens," I muttered, still not looking at her. I turned a page in my book.

"Look at me, Chandra," my sister growled. I ignored her. "Look at me. Look me in the eye and tell me why you became this way. What did I do to you to make you this way?"

I kept 'reading' my book, even though the words meant nothing to me now. I didn't want to talk about this because being in my sister's presence brought up horrible memories—including the real reason mom had died and the real reason I was here.

"How can someone as evil as you be shaken by such a question?" Sarissa said. I could feel her eyes roll. With the next sentence she became much more serious. "Chandra, I'm not kidding. Put down your book and talk to me."

"I don't have to answer to you anymore," I hissed, slamming my book shut and throwing it across the room.

"Then why did you close the book? Chandra, really, when you turned evil you should have left the temper tantrums behind."

I bit back calling her a name. Instead, I spat out my explanation: "You bring bad memories."

"You mean, I remind you of the bad things you've done?"

I shake my head, seething with rage, unable to talk. No, it's not what I've done that haunts me. Something about my sister is burned into my heart, and it hurts so much to be around her. It isn't her 'purity', that's for sure.

"You act like you've done nothing wrong!" I exclaimed, jumping to my feet. My heart was hammering in my chest. For some reason, I was frightened. But of what? I could overpower my sister, especially since she had so willingly walked into my castle.

Sarissa stood as well, curiosity scrawled across her face. "What do you mean, Chandra? What have I done?"

Suddenly, the fragments of memories came rushing back...

I was standing by my mother's bed, looking down at her sadly. She was very sick, with something that had no known cure. I looked around the room, anywhere but at her or my dear older sister.

Then I spotted it. Out of the corner of my eye I saw a trickle of foamy substance dripping from the ceiling. I didn't ask my sister what it was, for whatever reason, and stood on my toes to look at it in closer detail.

The closer I looked at the substance, the more I recognized it as a lethal poison. And what was that, curled up in the foam like a color-changing gecko? Using my magic, I gently eased the evidence out of the foam. It was a strand of Sarissa's hair. I looked down at my mom, and saw the foam-like substance eating away at her heart. She had touched it, and this is what it had done.

I then looked at my sister. Her eyes no longer looked sad— behind that mask there was undeniable happiness at being the next in line for queen. But how had she planted the foam without dying from it herself, and how'd her hair get caught? Whatever the reason, I knew the truth...Sarissa had killed our mom.

No wonder I was scared. If my sister could kill someone as powerful as our mother, then I was barely a threat to her.

"Why haven't you killed me already?" I asked, the fear now coursing through my veins. Forget evil. I was the good person in this fight.

Sarissa's eyes widened, but then she quickly tilted her head to one side and asked, "What do you mean, Chandra? I was hoping we could work something out. You're my sister, and I don't want to kill you."

Right. That couldn't be true. "It was never about power for me. It was about taking you down. That way you couldn't kill people for power like you did mother."

Sarissa glared at me, but beneath the glare was fear. I was onto her. "Why do you accuse me of killing to gain power? I never did anything to hurt our mom!"

I ignored her. "The roles were always reversed, Sarissa. You wanted to gain power, and I wanted to overtake you, but you always had me believe the opposite. You always had me think that I was the one who had done something wrong! You planted the false memory of my leaving in my mind, that way I could blame only one person: myself. You made a mistake in coming here."

Sarissa the Mighty took a step back, looking shocked. "You are delusional, Chandra! I did nothing to Mom, nothing! Nothing...on purpose..."

"So you did it? You did kill her?!"

Sarissa spun on her heel and almost ran toward the doors. "I have to go now."

I debated letting her go. In the end I did, but I yelled after her, "Everyone pays for their betrayal, Sarissa!"

Hopefully that would leave a thorn in her heart.

Chapter 53: Shock Therapy – Morgan

"Corey! Oh my god, are you okay?" Corey was sitting upright, panting and looking around the dark room with scared eyes.

"Where am I?" she hissed, looked around frantically. She spotted Morgan and gripped the girl's wrist with a vice-like hold. "Morgan! I know what to do!"

The group descended the stairs back down to the third floor. The ticking of the clock had resumed, and it seemed ominous. They didn't talk—Corey had told them everything up by the Tapestry of Decay. Morgan thought the idea seemed sketchy. Why had Corey's soul gone into a memory that was in the Tapestry? Was it the doctors trying to give them a false lead? Trixie agreed, saying that the doctors were impeccable actors and that it was impossible to tell if they were lying or telling the truth. She also said she wondered why the doctors would give away information that could take them out? It didn't make sense.

So now, tension was all around them as the kids chose their sides. Kevin sided with Corey; Paige, Fleur, and Trixie were on the other, and Morgan was stuck, quite depressingly, in the middle. She wanted to believe Corey (that whole thing couldn't have been for nothing, right?) but yet, Trixie's argument seemed logical. Morgan hated being in the middle when it came to arguments, or just about anything.

While they debated about what to do next, the three kids and Fleur decided to eat. It had only been one day since they'd entered Graystorm—but it seemed so much longer.

"Trixie?" Kevin asked the spirit as he gobbled down some beef jerky. She raised her head. "Is it just me, or is this day longer than usual?"

"It's not just you. In Graystorm, people are literally behind times. The doctors slow down time so that they can make the

214

torture last longer. But really, I'd say you've been in here for about a week and a half, maybe two."

Kevin's jaw dropped. "So…why aren't we so tired?"

"You don't feel the extra time. When you get outside, however…that's different. I remember when you came—" Trixie said, pointing to Fleur, "—and when you left, you dropped to the ground with sleepiness and hunger. It was quite funny."

Fleur ignored Trixie's jab and remained silent. Discontent filled her mother's eyes. Morgan looked at Kevin, nodded at Fleur, and her brother nodded back. "Hey, mom? Can we talk to you?"

After a warning from Trixie to keep their conversation short, Fleur, Morgan, and Kevin were standing down the hallway, some distance away from the curious ears that were certainly pressed up against the door.

"What? Why did you want us to leave the room?" Fleur said shortly, running her fingers through her long blonde hair.

"We wanted to ask you what's wrong," Morgan began. "Something obviously isn't right."

Fleur let out a weak, unconvincing laugh. "We're in a mental institution. That isn't right, to begin with."

"Mom! But whenever you look at Trixie, you look…I don't know, like you're not happy with her or something. Like something about her troubles you," Morgan explained.

Fleur sighed and sagged against the wall, her fingers cutting a clean path through her hair. "Something about her *does* trouble me."

"What?"

Fleur sighed again, hanging her head. "I don't know. Something just isn't right with her."

"Well, she's been in this place for…how long? Long enough, I'm pretty sure. Of course she's a little off—you stay with the insane, you become insane," Kevin said, shrugging.

"It's not that!" their mom exclaimed, and started pacing anxiously. "Did you see that glint in her eye when Corey slipped into madness? She's not the angel we think she is, I know that."

"Mom...we know that Trixie's not completely innocent. No one is. But aren't you taking this a bit far?"

Fleur didn't seem to have heard Morgan's query. "No...no...she's not just insane, she's evil!"

The twins' jaws dropped. "Mom...?" Kevin asked uncertainly.

Fleur grabbed their shoulders. "We need to get Corey and get out of here! Before she hurts us."

Morgan stumbled backward. "What have you got against her?! She's not insane, and she's definitely not evil! She's the only one who's helped us since we arrived!"

"Please...trust me on this," Fleur pleaded, tears pricking her eyes. Morgan just shook her head.

"I'm going back to the room, the others will be starting to worry." Turning on her heel, Morgan ran down the hall, looking for the door that Trixie and Corey were behind.

But before she reached the door, however, she was yanked sideways into another dark hallway. Before she could scream, a hand clapped over her mouth and a needle sank into her arm. And before she blacked out, she found herself staring into the acid green eyes of Doctor Cadenza.

The electricity was already running through her when she swam back to consciousness. Letting out a howl of pain, Morgan felt the machine switch off as Doctor Cadenza whirled around to face her, a scowl set on her pretty face.

"Finally!" she hissed, before marching over and slapping Morgan. The girl tried to shrink back, further against the table, but to no avail. Cadenza sneered at her, and did not strike again.

"We have been waiting forever for you to wake up! And I just wasted lots of volts on you, Sleeping Beauty. She will *not* be happy, not at all!" Cadenza punched the button to turn the machine back on, and Morgan felt another excruciating wave of agonizing pain wash over her. Her limbs jerked and twitched under the restraints. She felt herself seize up…and then it was over again. She lay panting on the table, all fight gone.

"Why?" Morgan croaked, her throat dry.

Cadenza's head snapped around. Her green eyes blazed. "Why what?!" she snapped.

"Why'd you do this?"

"Hmph. I didn't do it because I felt like it, no. I did because A, you deserve it, B, Doctor Steele told me to, C, you didn't listen to your mother, and D, you deserve it."

"You said that already."

Cadenza slapped her again. Morgan felt the side of her face hit the table, but she didn't feel the cold hit of the doctor's hand.

"Insolent child. I can say what I please as many times as I want to." Cadenza's voice sounded distorted, like it was coming through a badly tuned radio.

As the insane doctor turned the machine on again, Morgan no longer felt. It wasn't the no feeling sort of thing when you die—she just couldn't feel, couldn't hear well. She could still see, still move (as best she could), but all feeling had evaded her. Was it the extreme pain? She ruled that out. She would have blacked out, and her vision wasn't even slightly fuzzy.

Could Trixie have slipped her something? But how would the spirit girl know that this would have happened? Had it been a precaution? But it didn't seem likely. As knowledgeable and cautious as Trixie was, she wouldn't have given Morgan a drug without her consent. And the timing was too perfect…

A voice broke through, sounding rough and jagged. "Cadenza, stop." The machine stopped. Doctor Steele solidified, stepping out of the shadows. His mouth was set in a grim line. "Cadenza, you know the rules."

The female doctor dipped her head, acknowledging her superior. "Yes, I know."

"Let the girl go."

Morgan blinked rapidly. What? Did she hear that right? Did Doctor Steele say to just let her go?

"Deposit her on the second floor, third corridor. Her companions are one corridor away from there."

Cadenza, back to scowling, undid the restraints and picked up Morgan, who lay limp, still unable to move or feel.

When they reached the drop-off point and the doctor set her down, feeling rushed back. Her body was riddled with spasms left over from the voltage that had passed through her. Every part of her body burned and shook. Hot tears slipped down her face. It had finally been too much for her. She hoped her brother and mom would find her soon, for she was sure she wouldn't survive much longer on her own like this.

Blackness had almost swallowed her when she heard Corey's shriek as her companions turned the corner and found her on the ground, barely hanging on, tears still burning her eyes.

Chapter 54: The Madness of a Queen – Jessica

Jessica felt the sharp blade of the knife she was carrying in her pocket poke her leg. It would be easy to escape the guards—just catch them unawares and stab them. Joseph was seventy-five percent sure this wouldn't kill them, only grievously injure them, since Okkultens were hard to kill. And the next part of the plan was to find Waverly, hog-tie her, and get out of Okkulten territory. They didn't know if she'd change back to human on her own, or if they had to do something for that to work. But they did know that they needed their guide back.

As soon as they were a good distance from the Hive, Jessica felt Cassidee step lightly on her foot. Jessica nudged Kyle in the ribs with her elbow, who in turn tapped Joseph on the back. The old man nodded in understanding, then stumbled over Kyle's foot, who gripped Jessica's arm, and made Cassidee trip so that they were all on the ground.

The guards turned and hissed at them with disgust. "Get up," one said.

"Filth," another muttered, glaring down at the four.

Jessica saw a guard start to reach for his knife, which wouldn't be there because she had it. "Hey, aren't you going to help us up?" she said, shouting the first thing that came to mind. The guard stopped reaching for the knife and bent down so close that Jessica could smell its breath.

Before it could speak, however, Jessica gripped the handle of her knife, whipped it out of her pocket, and put it through the Okkulten's chest. Black blood flowed out, spattering her clothes. The guards reached for their knives, but found their belts to be empty. Jessica rolled out from under the guard, drawing her knife out of its chest as the others attacked.

It was a pretty gory battle; by the end, black blood stained the kids' shirts and pants, spattered their faces, and was smeared on their hands. The Okkultens lay, out cold, on the ground, the knives withdrawn and tossed far away.

Jessica clutched at a stitch in her chest as she regained her composure. The Okkulten blood was heavy and plastered her shirt to her body. On her hands, it felt like sticky tar.

"Are you sure they aren't dead? That's a lot of blood," Cassidee asked Joseph, looking over the nearly-destroyed bodies of the shape-shifters.

"Oh, they're alive all right. Takes a lot to kill 'em. We better hurry up and find Waverly—these guards will be up and at 'em in a minute or two, and they won't be happy."

"Do we know where Waverly is?" Kyle asked as they ran away from what looked like a brutal massacre.

"Desdemona sent her away to pay tribute to her elders," Jessica remembered. "But where would that be?"

"The *Uctivost* Arc."

"Ucti-what now?" Kyle sputtered.

"*Uctivost*," Jessica replied happily. "It means 'deference' in Czech."

Kyle blinked.

"Deference! Respect!" Jessica said, exasperated.

Kyle shrugged and looked at Joseph. "Where is this Uctivone place?"

"*Uctivost*," Jessica corrected under her breath.

"Hmmm....good question," Joseph wheezed. "I know where, but I don't know *where*..."

Jessica rolled her eyes.

Cassidee, her face contorted with pain, was holding her previously dislocated shoulder. "Ugh...can we hurry up and find this Uctivosi ("*Uctivost*," muttered Jessica) place? I'm tired, hungry, and my shoulder would rather be chopped off than healed."

"That would mean more pain, and more healing," Jessica said smartly.

"I didn't mean I *wanted* it chopped off!" Cassidee exclaimed, annoyed. "Do you take everything seriously, Jess?"

"No, I don't," Jessica snapped back. "And if you call me Jess one more time..."

"You will slug me, yeah I know," Cassidee said placidly. "And even though I'm a half-pint, I don't really care."

"You're a real laugh, you know that?" Jessica snarled.

"The only *real* laugh is Kyle, and by the look on his face I'd say he doesn't want in on this conversation."

"*Conversation?*" Kyle asked disbelievingly. "You call this a *conversation*, as in, civilized talk?"

"Hmm, good point," Cassidee said. She looked over and grinned at Jessica. "Come on, Jess, let's go."

Jessica scowled at hearing the despised nickname, and set off after the others.

As they ran, Joseph led them even farther away from The Hive, until the only thing in sight was a decrepit chapel. The *Uctivost* Arc was made of gray stone, with ivy and kudzu wrapping itself around the crumbling building. And in front of the arc, a small figure stood between two guards.

Waverly, back in human form, looked horrible. Her long black hair was tangled, matted with sweat, and stuck to her neck, where a knife was to her throat. Her jacket was gone, revealing her blood-red t-shirt underneath. Jessica noticed that Waverly was about an inch off the ground, the guards restraining her with such force.

And, she was shaking her head, as if saying 'no', as discreetly as possible.

Joseph and Kyle both stopped suddenly, causing the girls to slam into them. The foursome crumpled to the ground, but Kyle hissed: "Stay down."

"Why'd you stop?" Cassidee muttered, yanking her long hair out from under Jessica.

"Waverly didn't want us to come closer."

"Why not?"

"She's held captive."

"We can beat the guards."

"But we're too close to the camp, it'll get us caught for sure."

"Okay, but we can't leave her here..."

"Wait, hold on a second... I think she's talking to them..."

"Hold...on..." Waverly croaked, struggling against the guard's iron grip. It was hard to draw in air with his arm so tight around her throat. Her feet scrabbled at the empty air, still not used to being only a few inches above the ground. She felt a knife poke her in the back. Despite herself, she winced.

"Don't like that, huh?" the guard holding her snarled. "Stay still, then, and I won't do it."

"Just...listen..."

Waverly got poked in the back again.

With no other options before her, she kicked the guard in the shin. Hard.

The Okkulten jumped, swearing in pain, letting her fall to the ground. Waverly let herself crumple, not trying to get back up and flee. The other guard ran to her and snatched her up, his knife now to her throat.

"No...put it down for a second," the other guard muttered, and the one currently holding Waverly lowered the knife hesitantly. Drawing back a fist, the injured guard punched her.

Waverly's face turned to the side, feeling the hard, painful hit of the shape shifter's fist. She chuckled weakly, and the guard hit her again, until her mouth and lips were bleeding. Choking briefly on her own blood, Waverly stopped laughing and looked the guard right in the eye.

"I am one of your own," she said placidly.

"You work for Queen Sarissa," he snarled.

"No, I don't."

"Oh, yeah? Queen Desdemona's told me all about you, little brat."

"Has she? Does she not know that I'm spying for her?"

"Prove it."

Waverly tried her hardest not to show regret. "There are three of the Destined Ones and their old-man guide behind those rocks over there," Waverly said, lifting an arm to point to where she had seen her friends only moments ago.

"Hmph," the other guard snorted. "She's right, actually," he said after a moment of careful observation of the rocks in question. "Queen Desdemona will be happy about this."

"Well, we'll need the troops to go handle this. But we still need someone to guard her."

"Get one of the other brats to do it, I'm not missing out on this kind of glory…"

"Should we alert the queen now?"

"Yes, yes, I'll do it."

The guard not holding her put two fingers in his mouth and whistled, long, loud, and clearly. It echoed across the plain, and the air seemed to go still.

After a moment of complete silence, shrieks burst across the open area as Okkultens raced toward the rocks where the four people were hiding, and at their lead was Desdemona, a look of pure desperation on her face.

Jessica nearly screamed when she saw Desdemona—followed by hundreds of Okkultens—running right for them.

"Let's go! Run!" Cassidee shouted, turning around.

Kyle, Jessica, and Joseph gave no objection.

Joseph clicked an unseen button on his cane, which turn into something that looked like a levitating skateboard with rockets attached. As soon as he stepped on it, it took off, keeping pace with the three kids.

Jessica thought vaguely that if they got out of this place alive, she'd say how cool it was.

Knives whistled through the air past them as the

Okkultens failed to overtake them physically. Jessica felt one rip open the back of her jacket, but not touch her skin, making her run faster.

One thought was in her mind: *Why?* Why had Waverly betrayed them? Had she done it to get them to run, and leave her? But why did she want them to leave her? Jessica didn't know.

"Get them!" Desdemona shrieked, rage making her voice about ten times louder. "Get them, get them all!"

Jessica knew they had her beat.

Chapter 55: Nightwatcher

The rain fell in torrents, soaking the traveler to the bone. A cold, clammy hand still dutifully clasped the front of her black robes together at the base of the throat, ever still tempted to snake back beneath the cloak. But, no, that couldn't happen. The traveler couldn't reveal her identity.

Graystorm Asylum stood in the darkness, no warmth emanating from a friendly hearth, like a lot of the places she had been. The traveler had never liked those places, however, so maybe Graystorm was what she had been looking for.

The traveler pushed open the gates and walked up the path to the asylum. She knocked on the large doors, waiting for someone to come open it. And who should open it, but the very person she'd been looking for.

"Doctor Steele," the traveler said, dipping her head, not removing her dripping wet cloak as she stepped inside.

"Yes, yes, you are finally here..." the doctor said impatiently, waiting for a name.

"Just call me Nightwatcher," the traveler said.

Steele looked her up and down. "You aren't very tall, and your voice sounds young."

"I am young, yes, but not a child. And height has nothing to do with why I have come."

"Fine, Nightwatcher, why don't we take this to my office?"

"Only if Cadenza comes, too."

"Cadenza!" Steele barked, and ten seconds later, the doctor came trotting down the stairs, eyeing Nightwatcher suspiciously.

"Who's she?" Cadenza asked coldly, looking down at Nightwatcher.

"You can tell I'm a girl, Cadenza?" Nightwatcher said, interested. "Do you know who I really am?"

"No."

"Good," Nightwatcher said, turning back to Steele. "Let's go."

Doctor Steele led the way up to his office, and tossed back over his shoulder: "Ignore the screams, Nightwatcher. It's normal for this place."

"Thank you for the concern, Steele, but screaming patients is hardly one of my fears."

"Very few express that."

Nightwatcher ignored the comment and continued following the two doctors up the stairs, pausing only to stare down an abandoned corridor, where everything seemed to be falling apart. The floor was old, linoleum, and was ripped and torn up. Plaster hung down from the ceiling in great chunks, and the air smelled strongly of mold, dust, and decay. "What's down there?"

Cadenza answered first. "That's where we kept the truly insane patients, but we had to move them down to the cellar ward. We never wanted to fix that place up, anyway."

"Hmm," Nightwatcher said, not so sure she believed the story.

Once they reached Steele's office, Nightwatcher seated herself in a chair opposite the desk, brushing aside the manacles that were on the arms.

"Let me be a patient here," Nightwatcher said as soon as the doctors were seated.

"What do you mean?"

"I mean, let me be a patient here."

"Why?"

"So I can help you."

"Why would we need help?"

"Queen Odessa is growing stronger. She will soon take you down."

"We can take her."

Nightwatcher acted as if she had not heard. "I have already helped you with the queen. I am going to poison Odessa, but I need a special chemical from you. I will plant evidence that it was her daughter who poisoned her, the one who's destined for the throne, as a rush for power, to turn the other youngest sister against her. Then I'll tamper with the younger sister's memory, to get her on our side. She would be too powerful an enemy. There is no possible way that any of this can lead back to us."

"Is there any way the younger sister can remember correctly? And if she does, what about the Rules of Betrayal?"

"Then she will be broken, and the older sister will be gone by then. She will no longer be a threat."

"We will not be alive long enough to see this all happen," Cadenza snarled. "So why should we agree?"

"You will need to fake your own deaths, to shut down the asylum. But before that you must kill me, then bring back my spirit."

"And how is faking our own deaths making us immortal?"

"The chemical you have that I need, if it is mixed with the right things, can create a drink that makes you immortal. Or, at least, you can't die from old age. I have a feeling that Odessa and the rest of the royal family drink this when they become a certain age, but it would be too risky to steal it from them," Nightwatcher explained.

"So, the royal family is taken care of. What now?"

"Have you heard of the prophecy of the Destined Ones?"

"Yes, of course. You seriously think they'll be a threat?"

"The first ones are the most dangerous, actually."

"You mean the first generation, the ones that are prophesized to fail?"

"Yes."

"But we already know they are going to fail, so how are they a threat?"

"Because they will raise the ones that will take us down."

"So we need to take them out?"

"Yes."

"And you will be helping us with this?"

"No."

"No?"

"You heard me correctly, Steele. No."

"Why?"

"Because when it is time to kill them, I must be dead already. And I must appear on their side, give them false hope."

"Okay...you have a deal, Nightwatcher."

"Alright. And for that, I'll let you know who I am." Nightwatcher dropped her hood, letting the cloak fall to the floor.

Steele and Cadenza stared at her in amazement. "Why the name Nightwatcher?"

"It's my true last name. I'm taking on an easy alias, a last name that's seen very often."

"Oh...you mean--?"

"No, don't speak it. Only call me Nightwatcher, or my first name in front of other patients."

"And one more thing, Nightwatcher."

"Yes?"

"If the first ones are not killed? What then?"

"I have a connection with two of them. If you do not succeed in bringing the first ones down, I have an...influence, if you will, on two of the latter."

"Alright, Nightwatcher."

"Thank you, Steele, Cadenza. I'll be seeing you again soon."

Nightwatcher turned on her heel and strode out the door, out of the asylum, and back into the cold rain, putting her hood back up in the process.

Chapter 56: Fractured Memories – Kevin

Down, down, down
The spiraling descent of madness
All those fractured memories
Help me
Help me
Help me
Save me
Save me
Save me from all of those fractured memories...

-- Fractured Memories, written by patient Joshua White

Morgan had fallen unconscious by the time they had reached the room. However, at Trixie's examination, she didn't seem to be in any danger of dying.

"But what happened to her?" Corey asked again, huddled in a corner of the room, tears still cutting tracks through the light layer of dirt and dust on her face. She had been like this for the past hour or so, never making a move to wipe away the tears. Kevin had felt the tears slip down his cheeks too, but, like Corey, hadn't bothered to wipe them away. There was no one here that would care about seeing him cry.

"If I'm not mistaken, shock therapy," Trixie finally answered. Corey whimpered and buried her face in her hands, her head meeting her knees as her shoulders shook. Kevin just stared at her in disbelief, an annoying buzzing noise in his ears. He must of heard wrong. Morgan...had been given shock therapy? That couldn't be true...it couldn't be true...

"That can't be true. It can't possibly be true," he whispered, sinking down to the floor. Fleur cast him a worried look.

Why was he breaking over something like this? Trixie said

Morgan would be fine…she wouldn't lie. Yes, he would normally be upset if his sister was injured, but not like this. He wouldn't be on the floor, saying that what happened couldn't be true…so why was he?

Kevin wasn't aware of standing up and walking out of the room, of Fleur trying to grab him and stop him. All he knew is that they were done for; they would never leave Graystorm Asylum. *So you're giving up?* A voice that sounded remarkably like his sister's echoing in his head.

Normally, he would have denied this immediately, but he was so tired…so afraid…so wounded….

Yes. Yes, I am giving up.

That was the last sure thought in his head as he walked, almost as if guided by some spirit, down to the cellar ward, oblivious to all, and locked himself in a cell, curled up in a corner, and stared into nothingness.

Nightwatcher cheered silently. Yes! She had done it! She had finally broken the three Destined Ones! It had been easy to break Corey: all she had to do was send her through the Tapestry. Morgan had proved more difficult, and she hadn't come to a decision, until the doctors did it for her. They had tried to slither out of her grasp several times, but this time they had actually done something for her!

Nightwatcher slid away from the Nightmare Pool. She just had to retrieve the right memories…yes, these would do…and Kevin would be out of reach, across the Threshold of Madness, forever! Taking the memory, she let it slide out of the tube and into the pool. It spread out like ink snaking across a page, except it didn't form words, but fell into the memory. Nightwatcher turned and walked away. She had more to do. Bargaining within Okkultens, for one.

Gray. Gray plaster walls surrounded him. He was dizzy—
something wasn't right. Where was he? He opened his mouth to
speak, but someone—a woman—shushed him. His tongue felt
heavy and numb, and his eyes were unfocused. Then, without
warning, he lurched forward and vomited all over the gray floor.

Everything faded to black.

This time, he woke up strapped to a table and saw Doctor
Steele leer at him as he poised a metallic object just over his
forehead...a lobotomy...

The scene faded again.

He was at the Tapestry of Decay...it was glowing green...he
was begging, begging not to be taken through it again...but it
claimed him anyway...

Black. He was being led down a hallway, wearing a straight
jacket and a muzzle, though he didn't know why...he didn't know
anything   anymore...except   that   he   was
insane...insane...insane...

The word echoed in his empty mind, taunting him and
torturing him. He tried to scream: "I'm not crazy!" but he
couldn't because of the muzzle. He was being led into a dark
room...strapped to a chair...there was a flash of bright light, and
he felt himself fade away...

Finally, he could think clearly. He floated through the
building, searching for something. He wasn't sure what...until he
spotted the two kids wandering the building. One had red her,
the other a more dullish red-brown. They were brother and
sister, by the looks of it, and they were wandering around
Graystorm Asylum.

He tried to tell them to stop. They couldn't go any farther.
They would die...

He woke up again. The kids were lying on the table next to
the Tapestry of Decay. Of course...he couldn't have stopped
them...

This time, she was coming for him. She chased him through
the building, trying to find another personality to add on to her

many ones. But he slipped through her fingers again.

He saw three girls enter, and he tried his hardest to get them to go away. But it was to no use; they couldn't see or hear him. When he woke up, there were only two of them at the Tapestry. The other one must have escaped...

The next time, there was a lone woman at the Tapestry. He had missed her entrance...he then saw her shape shift into that woman on the table, and walk out of Graystorm. Where was she going?

She was chasing him again. "Come to me!" she screeched. "Come to me, now! Do you really want to spend forever like this? Being chased around?" she hissed, breathing hard.

"If that's what it takes to stay away from you and put a rock in your plans, yes!"

"So be it!" she hissed, and set off after him again.

He watched for the final time as three kids and an older woman marched into the asylum. Why were people still coming? Did she lure them here? Or were they really that stupid?

He watched them go through the files. He watched one girl be sent through the Tapestry and come out still herself, though a bit broken. He saw the other girl be put through horrible shock therapy, though not at her hands. Or was it her, just shape shifted to look like Cadenza? He didn't know.

Something tugged him outside of Graystorm, to the cemetery in the back, that very few ever knew about. Something pulled him toward his gravestone.

He stared at his name; so weathered it was almost impossible to read. But it was still there. He had long ago forgotten his name; it had not been important. But he saw it, and he remembered. He remembered well enough to toss away all the fractured memories...

"You lose," a female voice hissed. He stiffened, and whirled around. There she stood, before reaching out to grab him.

And just as everything faded to black for the last time, he tried to shout out his name...names were what she took away from you...she took away who you were.

"My name," he hissed as he struggled against her. All he could see were her eyes. "My name is...is..."

But he couldn't. She was too strong.

"Goodnight, Joshua White."

Chapter 57: Aiden and Corrine – Jessica

Away and away they ran, far away from the Okkultens and Waverly. As they ran, for some odd reason, Jessica pondered what Waverly's last name was. She did have one, right? If they ever saw the shape shifter again, she'd ask what it was. Last names aside, Jessica wasn't sure if the others felt the same way about Waverly betraying them. She was sure it hadn't been Okkulten instinct—Waverly knew that they would escape, and she was doing it to get them away from her. Why? Waverly didn't want them risking their lives for her—that was her job, as their guide and unofficial, unspoken bodyguard.

And without Waverly they were as good as lost.

Where were they heading next?

Every part of her body burning, Jessica called up to Joseph, "Hey! Where are we going? And when...can we...stop...running!"

Joseph didn't answer, but Cassidee replied: "What? Getting tired?" Her voice was snide, but her face was violet and her breathing was ragged. She had also dropped a few spaces from her second place a little while ago. Her voice then changed to sincere. "Me too. And I don't know, to either question."

Jessica wished they would stop soon. They had probably run at least two full miles at a near sprint, and her body was begging her to stop. Her lungs felt like knives had been thrown into them, not unlike her time at the Circus of Lost Souls when she had been the Ring Master's target practice. Her legs felt like melted jelly, if there was such a thing; and a stitch so painful she couldn't even describe the pain, except that it felt worse than a thousand knives stuck in her side. They were almost out of Okkulten territory; she could see the green grass and welcoming trees in about another quarter mile ahead.

"Can we stop at the trees?" Kyle asked, his long stride allowing him to be a bit slower and still keep up with Joseph.

The old man grunted, still zooming along on his little rocket-skateboard-cane contraption. Jessica realized he hadn't been experiencing the same extreme exhaustion that they had. Well, if they could all have canes like his, it would sure make things easier. All of their enemies would be left in the dust at the press of a button!

It felt like forever, but they finally reached the trees, and Joseph let them slow down a tiny bit, but wouldn't let them stop until they were a good ways in. *I probably just near-sprinted three miles!* Jessica exclaimed in her head as they finally slowed to a walk. Not stopping, Jessica clutched at the stitch in her chest and side, breathing long and deep to ease it out of her. Her throat burned for water, so she removed her bag from around her hip and took out a bottle of water. She longed to drink it dry, but she knew better, and let a few drops of water fall down her throat before lowering the bottle.

She remembered back when they were training, after a long run through the woods, when she had just stopped walking and sat down. Cassidee, in a rare moment of kindness, pulled her to her feet and said: "Never sit down right away. You have to keep the blood circulating. The blood vessels in your legs expand, meaning that more blood moves through them. If you stop exercising abruptly, that blood pools in your lower body, which can lead to dizziness or fainting."

Jessica remembered that as she forced herself to stumble on some more, taking small sips of water as she went. Slowly, her breathing eased, and while she still felt incredibly tired, she didn't feel the need to lie down and never get up again.

Now they were probably about a mile into the woods, and Kyle insisted that they make camp somewhere soon, eat, and sleep, even though it was only midday. No one argued, however.

"Where are we going next?" Jessica asked Joseph as they found a wooded clearing that would be perfect for the camp.

"To the village of Harlimoore. It's not too far from where Alex and Jonathan are supposed to be."

"Right," Jessica panted. In all the excitement of their last adventures, she had forgotten why they were really out there—to find Queen Sarissa's long-lost brother and sister.

"How far away?" Cassidee asked, wiping some sweat off her face with the back of her hand.

"About five miles. It will only take a few hours."

Jessica glanced at the sky. Even though it was midday, by the time they set off on foot again the sky would be darkening. "Should we make the journey to Harlimoore first, before we rest?" Jessica asked. "We shouldn't be traveling in the dark this close to Okkulten territory," she elaborated, responding to the curious looks that her question had elicited. Slowly, everyone nodded in understanding and agreement.

"Um...good. Alright, let's keep walking."

Even though, through the next few miles, her legs threatened to buckle, she kept walking. The sun slowly started to make its final descent of the day. She had been right to keep walking. The woods never seemed to change no matter how far they walked. As they traveled on, Jessica began to ponder what was going on at Graystorm Asylum. Were they out already, anxiously awaiting their return back at the castle with Queen Sarissa and Hailey? Or were they still inside that place of madness, unable to get out? Or...were they dead? Jessica forbid herself to think of that. They had to be alive...right? Otherwise the prophecy couldn't be carried out.

That made her thoughts stray somewhere else. The prophecy...ever since finding out about the Destined Ones, she had never heard the prophecy. "Hey, Joseph?" Jessica called up front, brushing a sweat-soaked strand of hair back behind her ear. "What was the original prophecy?"

Joseph stopped for a second, rigid, then picked up his regular ambling gait. "You'd have to ask Hailey," he said, almost too loudly. "She's the one who received the prophecy, you know."

"So...you don't know a single thing about it, then?" Cassidee asked curiously.

"About what?" Joseph retorted, too enquiringly.

"The prophecy," Kyle said patiently.

"No, I don't. I told you you'd have to ask Hailey!" he snapped.

"But you must know *something* about it," Cassidee persisted.

"You're mistaken," he said furiously, gnashing his teeth together in agitation. Jessica noticed that he looked scared, however, and he hurriedly turned around to continue on their walk.

"I don't think we are," Kyle said.

"Yeah, Joseph. Why are you scared?" Jessica finished.

"Scared? I'm not scared!" the old man replied indignantly. "The prophecy is a...delicate subject with me."

"Why? Do you not approve of us?" Cassidee said, glaring at him.

"No, that's not it at all! If only you knew...but I have been forbidden to tell you by Queen Sarissa herself! Now quit pestering me about that stupid prophecy!"

"Why doesn't she want us to be told about it? It's about us, why shouldn't we know what it says?" Kyle retorted. Jessica shot him a warning glance. *Be careful.*

"She only wants you to know at the right time," Joseph grumbled. "And it isn't time yet."

"But what if we die? We ought to know what we died for!" Cassidee exclaimed.

"You won't die! And you do know what you're doing. It was all explained when you first arrived."

"But it wasn't much of an explanation, was it? Come on, Joseph, just tell us!" Cassidee pleaded.

"No," he said stubbornly. "Now do what's good for you and leave this subject alone."

No matter how many questions they asked, how much they pestered him, their guide would not give in. Eventually, Jessica, Kyle, and Cassidee simultaneously agreed that this wasn't getting them anywhere, and they stopped talking altogether.

Finally, after what seemed like forever, a village was

spotted over the crest of a hill. It looked peaceful, serene, like they didn't live only a few mere miles away from Okkulten territory.

As they walked down into the village, Jessica noticed heads turned to stare at her. She looked down at her feet as she walked, suddenly self-conscious. The clothes the people wore were old and faded, with holes torn in them. Most of their hair was done up in a plain ponytail or was cut short to the scalp. Scars were prominent on most faces, like these people had been in many battles. Their eyes were all the same color: green. They were the same pale green, like a faded moss color, and they looked fairly strange. No one seemed to weigh over one hundred and ninety pounds, and the people were either young adults (twenties to thirties) or over sixty. The houses seemed in good condition, with thick thatched roofs. The wooden signs that hung from posts creaked on rusted iron hinges as they lazily moved back and forth with the small stir of a wind.

"Welcome to Harlimoore," Joseph whispered to them. "The only town that is thoroughly loyal to Queen Sarissa."

Really? Jessica thought, amazed at Joseph's statement. She had thought that there would be more people who followed Sarissa loyally.

Joseph led them to a sturdy looking inn by the name of 'The Lauruna Inn'. *Strange name,* Jessica thought as they entered the three-story hotel. Inside, a completely bald man in his early twenties stood behind a wooden counter. He wore wire-rimmed glasses that threatened to slip down the bridge of his straight nose. Other than that, the lobby of the Lauruna Inn was deserted.

Except for two people in the corner, Jessica noticed, who were hiding behind a newspaper. As Joseph checked them in, Jessica stared at the people curiously. She could not see any clear detail that might identify the people, but their presence felt familiar.

Suddenly, a woman spoke from behind the paper. "Hello,

Jess."

Jessica's face suddenly broke into a huge grin as the paper was lowered. Behind the paper was a woman with long black hair, identical to Jessica's, with the same green eyes of the rest of the town. Next to her was another woman with very short black hair, who looked very much like the other woman. Grins were present on both of their faces.

"Aiden, Corrine! What are you doing here?" Jessica exclaimed, running up to her cousins to hug them. She hadn't seen them in forever...so she didn't even mind it when they called her by that disliked nickname.

"Well...it's a long story," Corrine said as she let Jessica go.

Cassidee and the others turned around. "Uh, Jessica, who are they?" Cassidee asked, looking the twins up and down.

"These are my cousins I told you about, Aiden and Corrine." At their blank looks, she elaborated. "Remember, the first time I told you not to call me 'Jess'? I told you that they call me that," she said, jabbing her thumb at her cousins.

"Well, there's nothing else to tell about them, except that they didn't inherit the rest of our family's brains—" Aiden punched Jessica's shoulder when Corrine hit her back, causing her to stumble forward.

"Care to say that again?" Corrine muttered. Jessica shook her head. "That'll count as an apology for now, but we'll be expecting a real one later."

"Well, what are you doing here in the Empire?" Jessica asked.

"Give us that apology, say that we did inherit our family's brains, which we did, and we'll tell you."

"I'm sorry. You two are smart," Jessica replied, not daring to look up. She had always taken a lot of grief from her cousins, and couldn't help trying to bully them back.

"That's better. And as for why we're in the Empire...well, that's a long story."

Chapter 58: Blue – Fleur

Fleur was in the dark. Kevin had wandered off sometime ago, and she didn't know where he'd gone. Her heart told her to go, try and find him, but her brain refused to follow that order. All she could do was sit at the foot of Morgan's bed and stare at the opposite wall, become lost in its dull gray depths. Corey was still huddled up in a corner, crying quietly. Morgan was unconscious. And Trixie was gone.

Wait...Trixie was gone?

Fleur found herself on her feet and walking to the door. She peered out into the even darker corridor, strands of her blonde hair dangling in front of her face. Brushing them aside with trembling fingers, she could not see Trixie anywhere. Had she gone to find Kevin? Or was she going to hurt him?

Fleur felt herself flinch. She didn't trust Trixie, but her excuse wasn't solid. She just didn't feel that something was right about Trixie. Morgan and Kevin were right; she *had* been in Graystorm for years upon years... but there was something sinister about Trixie. When Corey had collapsed on the stairs going down to the cellar ward, Fleur was sure she had seen a flash of acidic green in Trixie's eyes. And Trixie spoke of darkness falling not with fear, but with pleasure, like it was her favorite time of day and not something that should be feared. Something so frightening that she loved it for exactly that reason.

Fleur sighed. Thinking back, maybe calling Trixie 'evil' was an overstatement. Then, something else popped into her mind. A single name. Nightwatcher.

When she had first come to Graystorm, Fleur had found a transcript from the doctors about a conversation concerning a woman named 'Nightwatcher'. This was, of course, before she had met Trixie. But she had reviewed the papers when they were in Doctor Steele's office. Everything fit with Trixie. She had arrived at Graystorm only a few days after Nightwatcher came for her meeting, and they had died on the same day, the same way. Unless, of course, it was just a coincidence. Lots of patients died from shock therapy on the same day. Fleur sighed again. It wasn't getting easier. If Trixie really was Nightwatcher, she covered up her tracks pretty well.

Like a murderer, Fleur thought inwardly. She shook her head. Trixie had been trying to help them…why was she so narrow-minded?

Fleur stepped out into the hallway, looking left and right again. The shadows covered just about everything, and she imagined how easy it would be for Steele or Cadenza to be hiding in one; how easy it would be for them to silence her with a quick needle and drag her away.

But as she walked down the hallway to her left, it wasn't one of the doctors that ran out of the shadows. It was Crystal. Her curly black hair was soaked and unnaturally straight, falling to her waist. Her brown eyes were dark and scared. The gray patient gown that normally hung off her body clung to it, showing her dangerously thin frame, and tears ran down her already-wet face. Fleur could hear the sound of Crystal's wet feet hitting the wooden floor. She didn't need Crystal to tell her where she'd been—she could figure it out.

"Who, Crystal? Who's down there?"

"Asana."

Fear coursed through Fleur's body. Asana? Why Asana? "Let's go."

Crystal led Fleur through the halls. She hadn't been down there in some time…what was Asana doing there? Unless, of course, it was the doctors…

"Hurry, Crystal!"

They entered the stairs that would have led to the Tapestry of Decay, had they gone up. However, Crystal led the way down.

Fleur could barely see. She could only rely on hearing Crystal's wet footsteps to guide her. Until, of course, she couldn't hear them anymore.

The sudden silence was ominous, especially in the darkness of this place. "Crystal?" Fleur whispered. As if in answer, she heard a loud splash and a scream come from the door a few feet in front of her.

Now knowing where she was, Fleur rushed out of the stairwell and into a big, under-ground room that had slightly better light.

None of the overhead florescent lights were on, but the rippling blue water shimmered on the dark ceiling, giving everything an eerier look. The sound of water lapping at the edges of the pool echoed in the cavernous room, and as Fleur stepped across the threshold, her feet were making audible sounds on the wet tile. She could see no one in the room, not Crystal, not Asana, and not Trixie.

"Crystal?" Fleur called out hesitantly. No reply. "Asana?" The water was the only reply. "Anyone?" This call was a whisper, barely heard even in the echoing room.

Fleur felt something change. Her feet felt wet, and when she looked down, she saw that her shoes had vanished, and so had the rest of her clothes, to be replaced by the thin, gray patient gown that hung off of the other's bodies. Fleur turned to find the staircase gone, replaced by a mirror. Transfixed by what she saw, she stepped closer, no longer caring that her feet hitting the water made a loud sound. Her skin was sallow, and her eyes seemed overly big. Her blonde hair looked liked it had been drowned and hung limply over her shoulders.

Hearing what sounded like a footstep behind her, Fleur spun around, almost slipping on the wet tile. But no one was present. She started walking toward the pool again. Kneeling down at the blue-and-white tiled edge, she stared into its depths. She could clearly see the bottom, and there wasn't anyone there---

"Fleur!"

Fleur's head whipped up, looking around the room wildly. Someone had screamed her name in a plea for help. "Asana?" she called out, still not seeing her.

There was a loud splash, not unlike the one she had first heard on the stairwell.

Fleur raced back to the pool and fell to her knees, gripping the tiled edge to stop herself from falling in. Now, she could see Asana, out in the middle of the pool, her red hair billowing out around her head as she struggled with the chains binding her hands together.

Just as Fleur was about to dive in to get her friend, Asana was yanked above the surface of the water by a black claw and up to the ceiling. Water hit the surface of the pool from Asana's dangling figure, several feet above it. Fleur heard her give a sob, her eyes closed. "Please, don't!" Asana cried out. "Please don't do it! I'll tell you anything, please just don't—"

Asana was released, and she fell back into the pool with a scream that echoed around the cavernous room. Something invisible kept her pinned under, unable to fight her way to the surface. Fleur seemed to be held in place as Asana was snatched back up, choking and sputtering, her chest heaving as she tried to force the water she had swallowed out of her lungs. This time she didn't cry out as she was forced under again. Fleur felt like she was witnessing one of those cruel games where someone kept repeatedly dunking a person before they could properly breathe again.

Fleur scanned the room for whoever was operating the claw. She could spot no one.

As Asana was lifted harshly from the water again, she gasped: "Fleur! Can't you...make it...stop? STOP IT!" she shrieked as the claw tightened around her chest, making it difficult to force the water out. *"Stop it, please make it stop—"* Her bare feet kicked at the air helplessly as she hit the water again.

Fleur regained her voice. "Quit it! Stop doing that to her! What do you want from her?!" she yelled into the darkness. Her body still immobile, her cry was to no avail. Asana came back up, crying openly.

"*I'm sorry! I'm sorry!*" she sobbed. "*Just don't do this anymore, Nightwatcher. I'll do whatever you say, just don't continue this PLEASE!*" Her last word was a heart wrenching, pleading scream as she fought against the tightening claw. Suddenly, the claw was gone, but Asana was still suspended in midair. The shackles binding her wrists vanished, and Asana sobbed with relief. "*Thank you, thank you, thank you—*"

Something glimmered in the air, seizing Asana's arms and breaking them with a simple twist, before letting her fall into the water again with a final scream.

Fleur was able to move again. Without giving it a second thought, she dove into the water, swimming straight to the center. Asana was suspended in the middle of the water, face down, her arms twisted strangely, her red hair billowed out, blocking a clear view of her face.

Fleur dove under her and was startled to see Asana's face. It was calm, relaxed, and blue. Her eyes and mouth were closed with no appearance of pain or the slightest trace of dislike. Fleur pushed up on her friend's body until she reached the surface. Taking in a pure lungful of air, Fleur turned Asana over. "Asana!" she cried. "Asana, wake up! You can't be dead again, you're already dead! Wake up, Trixie said you couldn't die, wake up, wake up, wake up—"

Her plea was cut off as she was yanked beneath the surface of the water by some invisible force. Fleur tried and tried to reach the surface, but she couldn't. No matter how hard she swam, the surface still twinkled high above her. Suddenly, Fleur felt herself rocket to the surface of the water, and frantically began treading water again. It took her a second to realize that Asana's limp body was gone.

Trembling with fear, sadness, and fatigue, Fleur swam doggedly to the edge of the pool and dragged herself out, rolling over onto her back as she heaved her legs out of the water. She panted, trying to get control of herself again. Her heart seemed to have climbed rapidly into her throat, and she tried to force it back down. Fleur rolled over onto her side and retched into the water, her breathing finally beginning to slow as her throat burned.

Her clothes changed back to normal. They seemed dry, even though the rest of her body was soaking. Fleur unsteadily got to her feet, every part of her body shaking. Tears spilled rapidly from her eyes as she remembered Asana's final scream as her arms broke, sending her into the water for the final time. Why? Why had this happened? The pool torture usually only happened on 'severe cases'. Asana had been pleading to Nightwatcher; Fleur had heard her say so. Why had Nightwatcher been angry with calm, friendly Asana, who could never tell a lie? What needed to be forgiven?

Fleur started back toward the staircase, but a familiar voice stopped her. "Don't go anywhere, Fleur, you're not done here."

Fleur spun on the spot, her tennis shoes finally getting some traction on the slick floor. Had her ears deceived her? They must have, because there was no way that she could be Nightwatcher...

Letting her hood drop to reveal her face, Nightwatcher stepped forward, making Fleur freeze, her mouth hanging open with astonishment at her identity. By the time Fleur had regained her senses, Nightwatcher was only a few inches away, and it was too late to run.

"It's impossible...you're with the others...you can't be Nightwatcher...you can't be..."

Nightwatcher laughed. "But I am. And I'm sorry I have to do this Fleur," she simpered, her face giving away that she was anything but sorry, "but I have to."

Waverly plunged her hand into Fleur's chest as if it was made of water, and drew out a silvery substance as the now soulless victim crumpled to the floor.

Chapter 59: Surveillance - Corey

"Corey...Corey...wake up...she's gone, Corey...Fleur's gone...Kevin's gone...wake up Corey, I know you're in there..."

Corey blinked open her eyes with some difficulty, since she had fallen asleep crying. She woke up to see a frail-looking Morgan only two inches away from her face.

She scrambled backward, startled by the girl's proximity. Morgan gave a small, half-smile. "Sorry, but I knew that'd wake you up." She stood up slowly, then offered her hand to Corey. Gripping the other girl's wrist, Morgan pulled her up to her feet.

"When'd you wake up?" Corey asked, looking at Morgan. Her hair looked a bit wild, and her face was somehow dirty, with tracks that tears had cut through it. Her jacket was discarded on the bed, along with her shirt. Her tank top was pulled up to her ribs, while a bandage was wrapped around her stomach, no blood visible. There were a few rips in her jeans, and her tennis shoes were laying underneath the bed, discarded, leaving Morgan in just her white socks.

"Oh, about an hour ago. Kevin and Fleur are missing," she repeated, a hint of worry in her voice.

"Did you see any of them leave?"

Morgan sighed, almost as if she was exasperated with her. "Do you think they'd still be missing?"

"No." Corey suddenly realized how stupid her question had been. If Morgan had seen one of them leave, she would have done anything possible to get them to stay behind unless it was for a very good reason.

"What's the bandage for?" Corey asked, changing the subject. To answer, Morgan turned around, revealing that blood-stained bandage in the back. Corey clapped a hand over her mouth. "What happened, Morgan?"

Morgan winced slightly, as if remembering. "Well, it has to do with a knife...I honestly don't know how it happened...it's like that part of my memory was erased..." She stared off into space, wondering what had happened and what had caused her to lose her memory, finally deciding that the doctors had injected her with something to cause this amnesia.

"Well...I only know of one way we can find out where they've gone," Morgan continued.

"Oh, yeah? What's that?" Corey asked disbelievingly.

"Surveillance cameras," Morgan said with a grin.

About twenty minutes later, Corey still couldn't believe that they'd found Doctor Cadenza's office, entered, and accessed the footage without any disturbance.

"How'd you know it was in Cadenza's office?" Corey asked Morgan.

"We'd searched Steele's office, right? And there was no security footage in there."

"But why Cadenza's office? Why not, oh, I don't know, the security surveillance room?"

"The doctors don't have a security detail anymore. They do it all themselves. And there's no one else here, so it had to be in one of their offices."

"And you didn't see it in Steele's?"

"Did you?" Morgan retorted.

"No."

"There you have it, then."

Morgan just shook her head and looked back to Cadenza's computer as Corey moved through the archive footage. Finally, she spotted Fleur standing outside their room, about forty-five minutes ago.

With Corey flipping through the cameras to keep up, they saw what happened to Fleur as she followed Crystal to the stairs, and down to the pool.

"Graystorm has a pool?!" Morgan exclaimed. "Mom must have known it was there, why didn't she tell us? And why would Graystorm even have a pool?"

"In some select asylums, they used it as a form of water

torture," Corey explained. "The patient would be in a claw that is attached to the ceiling, above the pool, with their arms and sometimes their legs tied together, so they couldn't swim. Then, the claw would drop them, they'd sink under the surface of the water, and just when they thought they'd drown, the claw yanked them back up, and tightened so much around them that they couldn't choke up the water they'd swallowed, and they'd do it again and again—"

"Stop!" Morgan cried. "It's happening on screen, so can't you just shut up for once, Corey?!"

Corey turned back the screen, more than a little wounded. "Sorry. You just asked," she muttered

They watched in silence as the incident with Asana played out, saw as Fleur dove in to get her, and a brief burst of static later she was above the surface of the pool, Asana's body nowhere to be found. Morgan's mom climbed out slowly, shaking, and stood up weakly. A cloaked figure appeared behind her, and dropped its hood. Corey and Morgan just watched as the cloaked figure's hand went into Fleur's chest and withdrew her soul. And when Waverly turned and faced the camera, smiling, Morgan stumbled backward, hit the wall, and slid down until she was sitting on the hard wooden floor.

Corey hastily shut off the footage and leaned back in Cadenza's chair, her thoughts racing. Why was Waverly in Graystorm? How could she be? And why steal Fleur's soul?

Corey clicked out of the surveillance tapes and clicked on Finder. When it popped up, she went to Documents and started searching through the folders. There were no files deemed helpful, so she turned to the file cabinets and started yanking on the doors, and when that didn't work, looking for the keys.

"Ugh. Morgan, are you okay?"

Morgan nodded. She seemed close to tears, but Corey understood completely. If she wasn't searching for all of this information, she'd be in the same position.

"Can you help me search for the keys? If you're up to it?"

Corey asked.

Morgan nodded. "No reason why I shouldn't make myself useful," she whispered, and stood up, running her hands over the walls.

Corey uncovered Cadenza's desk, sorting through the papers and picking things up. Nothing. She checked the desk for hidden compartments and drawers, but nothing was to be found. Everything was tight and secure, like it had just been built.

Standing up, Corey walked over to a painting on the far wall, where a picture of Cadenza herself sat tall with emotionless pride, Steele standing behind her, a hand resting on the top of her chair, eyes cold, his back rigid and excessively straight. Neither was smiling. Neither wanted that portrait to be painted. So, Corey questioned, why keep it?

Corey lifted it off the wall easily and set it on the ground. She noticed two things: there was a safe on the wall behind the painting, and a letter and key were taped to the back of the painting. At that moment, a piece of wall succumbed to Morgan's push of hand, and she withdrew a small metal box.

Corey removed the letter and key from the painting, handing the key to Morgan. Unfolding the piece of paper, Corey began to read.

Never again will we succumb to the pain.
I will not think lightly of it if it is broken.
Good job if you succeed, not many do here.
Her rules are hard and unfair.
To succumb to madness is to become as bad as they are.
Why are we even here?
And again and again and again
To ask, I ask, I cannot get an answer.
Control it all, they cannot take over.
Her hold is too tight; we can no longer carry out our plan.
Every single day I hope something will change.
Red. It is already too late?

It is.

Corey could not make sense of Cadenza's poem. The beginning, up to the third line, sounded like everything was going as planned. The fourth line to the ninth line sounded like control was slipping out of the doctor's grasp, and the last four lines confirmed the fact that they no longer had any power in Graystorm Asylum. Corey put the piece of paper in her jeans pocket, along with the letter from Doctor Steele's office.

"Morgan, what'd you find?"

"Two pictures!" she shouted, hurrying over, taking two things from the box. The first picture was a faded photograph of Trixie, standing against the doorway, and was dated the day she died. Her skin was ashen, her eyes looked lost and distant, sunken into her skull. Cuts and bruises were on her face, arms, and legs. Her hair was longer than it was now and was scraggly and oily. The patient gown she wore hung off her limp frame, falling down farther than it was currently.

The second picture also dated the same day, showed Trixie just like she was as her ghost. She was standing in the same place, and something seemed off about the whole thing. Why take two pictures? And why had the doctors cleaned Trixie up so much and given her a shorter patient gown? What was the point, if they were doing that the day she died?

Something else in the picture caught Corey's attention. She grabbed a ruler from Cadenza's desk and placed it next to Trixie on the first photograph, then the second one.

"Morgan," Corey said. "Trixie was killed the day this photograph was taken." She pointed to the second picture.

"Why? How do you know she didn't have some sort of makeover or something?"

"Because of this." Corey jabbed her finger at the doorway in the second picture. "She's taller in this picture, because the length of the doorway from the top of her head to the ceiling is smaller than it was in the first photograph. And she's clearly not standing on anything." Morgan noticed that she was right.

"Okay, but why would the doctors mislabel a picture, unless they did it on purpose?"

"I don't know," Corey said slowly, looking at the pictures. "I want to see Trixie's file again. Maybe it will tell us something we didn't notice before."

"Okay, but I don't really want to go back to Doctor Steele's office," Morgan answered.

"There's no need," Corey replied, and on the computer screen, Trixie's file popped up. Only this time, it was different.

"Lots of things have changed on here...it says that she used to have a criminal record, saying that she was a lunatic murdering people under the name 'Nightwatcher'. The charges were dropped, however, and were transferred to one Persephone N. Desimara. It says here, on a side note, that Persephone was an Okkulten, and it makes a special note about Waverly!"

"But why?"

"They're both Okkultens...but maybe the doctors thought that sort of thing runs in the family? Oh, I hate talking like this about Waverly, I really trusted her."

Morgan wasn't listening anymore. She was crying silently, finally having too much on her mind. She didn't know where her brother was; she had just seen her mother's soul be stolen, not to mention by a person they had all learned to trust.

Something else caught Corey's attention. It was the real reason why Trixie had been committed. "Morgan!" she exclaimed. "Trixie, she was committed for MPD!" At Morgan's blank look, she elaborated. "Multiple Personality Disorder. It means 'in which somebody appears to have two or more distinct personalities that are present at different times and dominate behavior.' It means that, in short, she saw people that weren't even there, but they were just branches of her personality."

"So...that's a bad thing, right?"

"Yes! It can also be very dangerous, especially if a person becomes obsessed with becoming other people, if they realize what they have. This only happened in the last half-century, I heard. They dabble in all sorts of black magic...a lot of Okkultens have been locked up for letting their shape-shifting get out of hand."

"What if Trixie was actually Okkulten?!" Morgan exclaimed, the idea suddenly upon her.

"That's not what I was thinking, actually. Maybe it's Waverly with the MPD."

"And Trixie was just Trixie?"

"No, I'm saying that, quite possibly, Trixie never existed at all."

Chapter 60: Shadow Forest – Aiden and Corrine

The sky immediately cleared, but I knew that we had failed. Don't ask what, because Queen Sarissa ordered us not to tell you. Anyway, Aiden and I fled the scene, not even trying to say goodbye to our comrades—we'd see them again, we were sure.

We both ran deeper into the Shadow Forest, not daring to look over our shoulders. Surely you know why—no? You don't? Well, the Shadow Forest is the only thing that stands between Harlimoore and the Asilde Mountains, which is the nearest door leading out of the Empire. And no one dares go through the Shadow Forest because of what lurks there. Well, no one knows what, that's the problem, Jess. Journal entries, written by famous explorers, have been found. They met their end in the forest, and even they couldn't tell what followed them around and eventually sucked the life out of them. Well, perhaps I shouldn't say 'sucked'. I mean, well, what do I mean, Aiden?

She means that, um…well, the bodies were never found. So we don't know *what* caused them to die.

There was Jordan, remember Jordan?

How could I forget Jordan, Corrine?

I don't know, but he gives the only slightest inkling of what might have happened to the others.

You know this is hard for me.

Do you want me to tell the story?

No, we both should.

Well, you first. Tell them who Jordan was.

Okay, Corrine… Jordan was my boyfriend. You, Jess, know that I rarely saw guys because I got along with them on a platonic level. Well, it started out that way with Jordan, but it changed. Things happened that drove us even closer together. It's classified—don't ask. So, we—Corrine, Jordan, and I—left the scene of our failure and fled into the Shadow Forest. We had known that we were going to fail—the...um...never mind.

Anyway, as we ran deeper into the forest, we started to notice things. It was a dark forest already, with plenty of shadows, but these shadows seemed...different. They reached for us. And I'm sure I caught a glimpse of an eye peering out of the darkness as we ran. Something else was in the forest with us, and I didn't know what it was. But I knew we had to get to Harlimoore...to let them know that we had failed.

You see, Harlimoore isn't just any town. Lauruna Inn and, the whole village of Harlimoore, is where Queen Sarissa and her family grew up.

Her mother, Odessa, didn't become Queen until she was quite older. She lived in poverty for most of her life and had two of her four children before ascending to the throne. Those two children were Sarissa and Chandra, born exactly one year apart, but apart from that were as different as darkness and light, as they proved, quite incidentally. Alex and her twin, Jonathan, would come after Odessa had come to the throne. And I can't tell you why—yes, right on the nose, Cassidee. It's *classified*.

Lauruna is Sarissa's last name. It's her entire family's name, since Odessa married Shannon Lauruna.

So...where were we, Aiden? Oh, yes, we were running through the forest. And when I say running, I mean tearing-across-the-ground-and-leaving-a-trail-of-fire-behind-you running. I mean, I've never run that fast before. Not in training...not anywhere. Suddenly, Aiden stopped, making me screech to a halt. She spun around and ran back, and I noticed that she was crying. Yes, Jess, Aiden was crying.

I don't deny it.

I never said you did. When I spun around, I noticed that Jordan was gone, and Aiden must have been running after him. I don't know how she knew he wasn't there—

And neither do I, to this day—

So, I had no choice but to follow her. Aiden noticed some

blood on the ground and freaked out, thinking it might be Jordan's.

So I ran deeper and deeper into the woods—

I called for her to come back, and then followed because she wasn't answering—

And I saw him getting dragged away into the darkness, and Corrine had to drag me away from there, before whatever it was got us, too.

It almost did, remember?

Yes, yes, it was horrible, we only just got away…

And we exited the forest, arriving here at Harlimoore. We announced our defeat, and Jordan's capture.

Then, the mayor told us to stay here, at Harlimoore—

We had directions from Sarissa that this would become our new outpost, you see—

If anything dodgy came through here to go to the Asilde mountains, we'd know—

And we'd stop them before they could escape. 'Cause, you see, it's not only the Nightmares that wish to do the Outside harm…

And we've been here for thirteen years, waiting for you all to show up.

Yes, we knew that you'd come here, don't ask why—I know you're getting tired of hearing that, but it will all be explained in good time. Now, where're Morgan, Kevin, and Corey? Not to mention Fleur, we thought she'd be here… And Waverly, what happened to her? We thought for sure she'd be with you.

We told you our story…now it's time for you to tell us yours.

Chapter 61: Looking Glass – Morgan and Kevin

There was pain...a lot of pain...in my lower back. It wasn't a cramp or anything—it was actual pain, like someone had stabbed me.

Wait...

I reached one hand behind my back weakly and felt my fingers dabble in my own blood. I looked at them carefully, making sure that it wasn't paint. They slid in and out of focus, and I let out a small cry of pain. No...definitely not paint.

What happened?

I was on the ground, back facing the ceiling, and I could barely twist my neck to see who my attacker was. However, I twisted my torso instead, nearly screaming full-out this time. Why did it hurt so much? Why was everything sliding in and out of focus? Why couldn't I remember?

The knife in my hand had blood on the end of it, dripping onto the hardwood. My entire body was shaking. I felt like I had just eaten too much candy...it was like a sugar rush. My grip on the knife was weak.

I looked down at my victim. She lay, spread eagled, on her stomach, trying to catch a glimpse of me without hurting her lower back, which was soaked with blood.

I laughed.

I kicked him in the stomach, and he was sent to the floor, still giggling like a crazy psycho. He didn't even react to the pain. My head spun. I needed to find a bandage for my back. But what to do with him? What if he attacked my mom, or Corey?

Where did he even come from? Who was he?

She was suddenly gone, and I was on my side, still

chuckling as I sat up and started to rock back and forth, before laughing out loud like a madman. My knife was missing. I didn't care. I could always find another one. And somewhere, inside my brain, someone screamed with rage.

I paid him no attention.

The picture trembled in my hands. Where had it come from? I don't remember picking it up, or even seeing it before. Hot tears slipped down my face as I started to rock back and forth, crying silently. I recognized my attacker in the picture.

Was it true? Had my own twin really stabbed me in the back with a knife?

Paige watched sadly. She knew how Morgan felt. She had once heard a song, and it sang:

It's sliding in and out of focus
Changing everything
Bits and pieces here and there
Not a complete picture
I'm seeing the world through a shattered looking glass.
Shattered, shattered, shattered…

Chapter 62: Fear – Hailey

"Why didn't you tell them, Sarissa? You could have saved them!"

"Hailey, can you just shut up for one minute! Do you think I'm proud of what I did?" Sarissa near-yelled, despair rising in her voice.

"No, Sar, of course not! But still...wouldn't it have been easier to tell them?" Hailey questioned.

"I told you my answer already, Hailey, and it's too late now anyway. Nightwatcher has taken control of Graystorm, and there's nothing more we can do to help them."

"We can't let the innocent die!"

"The doctors were never innocent."

"But they don't want to kill Morgan, Kevin, Corey, and Fleur! She's making them!"

"How do you know they're not acting of their own free will?"

"I've been watching the pool more often than you have, Sarissa. I've heard them talking where Nightwatcher can't see them. All they want is to be left alone."

"Are you sure?"

"Sarissa, the doctors have actual feelings. They might have turned themselves to demons of shadow and crystal, but feelings are still present. They wish to stick to the deal they made with us, shortly after Fleur's misadventure there."

"It wasn't a misadventure, Hailey. It was just another part of their failure," her sister replied wearily.

"Two innocent girls lost their lives in there! And you toss it aside as 'just another part of their failure?!'" Hailey snapped.

"Damn, Hailey, I don't like talking about this!"

"You brought up this subject in the first place!" Hailey reminded her sister harshly.

"Do you think I'm happy that Crystal and Asana died? Do you seriously think that?"

"No, but you seem like you're ready to let Fleur die, too, like you're expecting them to all fail."

"Prophecies have been wrong before," Sarissa murmured quietly.

"You wish them to die, then?!"

"Hailey, dammit, that's not what I said!"

"You as good as said it," her sister growled.

"Why did you even come to see me in the first place?" Sarissa sighed, exasperated.

"I came to tell you that it's changing out there."

"Can't you be more specific?"

"It's changing on the outside! Those three kids who disappeared in Delaney Manor, it's all coming back! He'll come back, it'll be the end of us—" Hailey began in a panic.

"Unless this was what the Destined Ones were meant to do," Sarissa interrupted. "But, did we act too soon?"

"You mean, 'did we kill our last chance to defeat the Darkness?'"

"Yes," Sarissa whispered quietly.

"I hope not, Sar. But, really...do you think this all could have been avoided if you just told them? Come on, Sarissa, were you scared? Were you too scared to admit the truth to them?"

"Yes, Hailey, I am afraid."

"Afraid of what?"

"Failing where we should have succeeded."

"You do not understand, do you? These are kids who have absolutely *no idea* about what they are facing. They think that if they complete their missions, that they have succeeded and that they can just go home," Hailey said sternly. "You have been lying to them this entire time, because you just don't want to die! Did you ever, *ever*, think about the outcome of this? If they succeed, Chandra will fail, and if she comes back—"

"Hailey, she won't come back! I won't let her!"

"You are! You are afraid of dying! If you truly wanted this to all end well, then you know that you will have to die, because we need Chandra to truly end this!" Hailey shouted. She was

quickly losing her temper at her sister, who was becoming just as angry. *"You are sending these kids on pointless missions where they'll die—"*

"THEY WON'T DIE, HAILEY!" Sarissa roared, stopping Hailey's speech, tears leaking out of her eyes. *"THEY WON'T DIE, THEY CAN'T, THEY WON'T—"*

"You are blinded!" Hailey yelled, marching for the door of her sister's room. *"You are blinded by your own fear of death, so much that you don't care if everyone else dies, let alone six helpless kids—"*

"They aren't helpless, damn, you know that!"

"They might as well be, because they are facing things that you could barely get away from!" Hailey's chest was heaving, and her throat was sore, but she had to get her point across, before it was too late. *"Everyone else has sacrificed everything for you, and you haven't done anything for them!"*

"I have sacrificed plenty!"

"Like what? What have you laid down on the line to help them reach their goal?"

Sarissa's face was beet red, and she was shaking as she sank down onto her bed. Her steely glare was fading to more of a delusional gaze.

"You haven't done anything for them! You expect them to go out there and save your neck again and again and again while you just sit here, pondering what will happen and if you'll die because of it." Hailey took a deep breath. She only had two more things to say to her sister.

"YOU. NEVER. CARED. Never, about anyone! No one but yourself! So, how scared are you, Sarissa? How scared are you now?"

Tears fell down Sarissa's face. For a moment, she didn't answer, then sobbed out: "Terrified, Hailey. Terrified that I'll die—"

Hailey had reached the breaking point. She said, in a deadly calm voice, "You are despicable." She wrenched open the door and walked outside, not daring to look behind her as her sister faced the truth.

Chapter 63: Solitary Confinement – Kevin

I'm back. I'm...me again. Or am I? Is this another trick? I hope not. But, I'd like to remember how I got out of this cage. Maybe I shouldn't be here, however. Maybe he'll strike the second I leave, and kill Morgan this time. I don't want Morgan to die. I don't want any of them to die. And now, I can't trust myself. Will I, ever again?

I cannot see my surroundings, so I must sit in this corner and think during this period of solitary confinement. My own thoughts might drive me mad...is that what the doctors are hoping for? Are they hoping that I become as crazed as they are? Perhaps I am...perhaps because he came out, the evil side, my sanity is slowly starting to deteriorate.

I have never thought this...formally in a long time. Perhaps it is my own touch of madness that I am so calm. After all, some Lunatics aren't running around, eyes rolling around in their sockets, holding a knife above their head with shaking arms as they laugh maniacally. Okay...that was me an hour ago. But I think I regained control.

"Kevin! Time to come out!" someone barks at me. I cower unexpectedly. Who knows I'm down here? The doctors, that's all. But it isn't Steele or Cadenza who's calling me...

Trixie appears around the corner of the stairs. "Kevin! There you are! It's time to come back up! Morgan and Corey are looking for you, and uh...there's some bad news about Fleur."

She has my attention. I scramble forward but find that I cannot reach the bars. My foot is chained to the wall. I open my mouth, but no sound comes out. Something, deep inside my brain tells me to remain there, in the cell and continue to think until I have this all figured out. But I am missing so many pieces of the puzzle, I would be in here forever. I must ask Trixie a question, however, but I must not speak. I don't know why, but I know that if I do, Morgan and the others will die.

Bring me the files of everyone who ever came to Graystorm. The doctors, everyone, I scratch into the dirt.

Trixie glances down at it. "That is a lot of reading, Kevin. Come with me and we can both look through them."

I must not leave.

"Okay, then, have it your way. Go insane. Everyone does down here, in the end. I'll bring you the files, but Kevin, be warned," she said as she headed toward the stairs. "The truth will not help you this time."

I am halfway through all the files. The photos are scattered on the floor, and I am making a time-line of sorts of Graystorm's history since it was first instituted. I have been down here for several hours, maybe even an entire day, but I have so much time to think. My head has been hurting for the past fifty files. It has not helped. He is laughing, back there, at my futile attempt to find the truth, and solve the mystery of Graystorm Asylum.

Look through all of these documents and recounting what I have seen does not line up. There are gaping holes were there should be facts. Time stamps are missing from several photographs. Words have been crossed out and are illegible. But there is one thing that must be true: there is another player in this sick, twisted game they play here. But who?

Then, I reach what is probably the most important file; located at the very bottom of the last stack that Trixie has brought me. It is a conversation between Cadenza, Steele, and a woman they have titled 'Nightwatcher'. Her real name is blocked out, and I have no way of telling what is underneath it. I cannot remember the name Nightwatcher appearing in any of the other files, but I know that now I have found my third player. But, who is she? There are no photographs, only the chunks of time where (apparently) nothing was happening.

I pick up two articles, one from a newspaper and another is an online article from the very website Morgan and I searched when seeking the truth before we ever knew about the Empire. As I read them again, the pieces begin to fall into place. The hangings...the twelve patients didn't hang themselves, and neither did Doctor Emerson. It wasn't the doctors; there was proof of that. Nightwatcher must have done it. The missing chunks of time were unearthed as I reassembled the pictures, lining up the time stamps so that it was clumped into groups of twenty-four. There was one month in each cluster of photographs, and it was assembled in such a way that the earliest AM stamps were on the outside border, and the PM stamps were in the middle, down to 11:59:59 AM on the last day of each month.

I stared at them. And stared. And stared. Trixie did not come back down. It suddenly leapt out of the pictures. A single name. I hurriedly flipped the photographs over, and found the missing, scratched out words and missing chunks of time. Nightwatcher, the 'monster of Graystorm Asylum' was being watched, and she didn't even know it. But I had to let the others know, before she killed them. She was here, in Graystorm.

Who knew that solitary confinement could be so good for a person?

Chapter 64: Phantasmagoria – Corey

There it went.

Corey's last connection to Graystorm was out the window.

If Trixie never existed as an actual person, then why was I here? Why did I have these strange, scary nightmares that had finally started haunting my living life? Trixie had been my explanation, the link to it all.

Now it was gone.

A lump rose in her throat and she struggled to not cry out in the complicity of it all. Had this all been a mistake? Should she not be here? *I had come here to find the answer to my dreams, and possibly stop them, not fight for some stupid empire that didn't want to cave in, with all their silly prophecies and all of that. Let the others believe it, if they are gullible enough to do so. Those people are cowards, and they don't need kids to protect them.*

Right? What can we kids do to save these people that are so powerful, they could wipe out our existence with a swipe of their hand? They needed our help to destroy a damn passageway? Seriously? They could do it from the castle themselves, not to mention Hailey could conjure up an image of where Alex and Jonathan were. Did they really need them to risk their lives for something so minor, something that was probably a breeze for them?

Unless, those were just covers for something they couldn't do.

What if there was no passageway? What if the doctors weren't a threat? What if Sarissa didn't want them to destroy something, but someone? Someone who was so powerful that Sarissa couldn't destroy that person. So powerful that the person found a way to keep living beyond the grave, to stop anyone from finishing her off, once and for all.

Corey grabbed Cadenza's poem that she had taken from the office and immediately looked at the first letters.

Never again will we succumb to the pain.
I will not think lightly of it if it is broken.
Good job if you succeed, not many do here.
Her rules are hard and unfair.
To succumb to madness is to become as bad as they are.
Why are we even here?
And again and again and again
To ask, I ask, I cannot get an answer.
Control it all, they cannot take over.
Her hold is too tight; we can no longer carry out our plan.
Every single day I hope something will change.
Red. It is already too late?

Nightwatcher.

Except who was Nightwatcher?

Oh, *damn.*

She had to tell Morgan.

Except, where was Morgan? She wasn't in the room...

"Morgan!" Corey shouted, her voice echoing abnormally loudly in the hallway as she stuck her head outside the room.

No answer, of course.

Then where was Kevin, she had to find Kevin and tell him what he probably knew already...

Corey found herself running down the hall, down stairs, to the bottom floor where the party had been set up and abandoned. Suddenly dizzy, she sank to the floor and sat down.

Everything seemed blurry. And then...the light came on, flooding the floor with beautiful warm light that she hadn't seen in what felt like forever. Who had gotten it working again?

People she hadn't noticed before were also sitting around the table, dining on the stale cake. "Don't eat that, it's not good for you!" Corey tried to call to them, but she might as well hadn't spoken, because they showed no sign of hearing her.

She ran up to a person with short blonde hair and tapped her finger on her shoulder hurriedly. When the woman turned around, she said: "Don't eat that cake, it's gone bad you could get—"

The woman's hand slammed over her mouth, causing Corey to go silent. "Forget about Nightwatcher. Leave it alone. Let yourself go insane, got that? You'll never take her down." Corey found herself nodding and all of that information started to replace everything else inside her brain. "Good," the woman whispered. The cold hand came off Corey's mouth and she stumbled backward, hitting the wall and sinking down the floor. The light overhead went out, plunging them into complete darkness.

Corey heard a small laugh echo in the room. "You really thought you could unravel the mystery of Graystorm Asylum and figure out the real reason Sarissa sent you here? You're just as pathetic as they are."

"You are here because you are insane. Why would anyone else come here? Agree?"

Corey found herself nodding again.

"Good. Now...enjoy the party."

The green light flickered on overhead, revealing the butchered guests of the party, lying on the floor. Corey couldn't scream. She could barley register the scene before her. Taking a tentative step in their direction, she noticed one girl had her eyes still open, still glazed over. It was the girl with the blonde hair.

"Say goodnight, Corey," the corpse whispered, and when she screamed, the world turned into dust.

Chapter 65: Crimson Hourglass – Kyle

It took them much longer than Aiden and Corrine to tell their story, as it was much more in depth, and there was the fact that Jessica and Cassidee kept cutting each other off, trying to correct the story even when there was no error. Finally, though, enough was enough.

"Would you two just be quiet?!" Kyle snapped when Jessica and Cassidee engaged in yet another correction argument—this time, over the attack on *Pays de épouvantail*.

Jessica stopped mid-sentence and glared at him. Cassidee smirked but fell silent as well. "You tell the story then," she said unhappily.

He closed his eyes and took a deep breath. Why were those two at odds all the time? The story would never get finished if this kept up. So, he finished the story, and Jessica and Cassidee stopped butting in, although they kept glaring at each other as if daring the other one to interrupt.

"You guys have been through a ton of stuff," Aiden said solemnly. "None of it pleasant. You must be bone tired, why don't you go on up to bed…"

"Thanks, Aiden, Corrine," Jessica said sleepily as she walked up the stairs. The group hadn't shown it, but the many weeks of traveling had worn them all down to a point where they could sleep for a month.

"I hope everything's going well at Graystorm," Cassidee said thoughtfully as they trudged upstairs. Kyle thought about the asylum. He hadn't thought about Morgan, Fleur, Kevin, and Corey much after they'd gone their separate ways, but he knew that Graystorm was a frightening place with more of a mental, psychological horror than what they were facing while out looking for Alex and Jonathan. He hoped that they were safe, alive, and sane. He wished that it wasn't too much to wish for.

As Cassidee and Jessica went into the room they were sharing, Cassidee made an offhand comment about Aiden and

Corrine. "I'm surprised you're related to them," Cassidee said with an air of surprise. "I mean, how can someone like you be related to people like them?"

"What do you mean, Cassidee?" Jessica asked, her eyes growing dark.

"How can two such kind people be related to you? Are you sure they're in your family?"

Kyle grabbed Jessica's arms suddenly and pinned them to her back as she struggled to break free and hit the smaller girl, who just smirked and walked into the bedroom.

"Let me at her, come on Kyle, let me go—"

"No."

"So you're on her side?"

"No. I'll talk to her. What's up with all the hate between you two?"

"No idea. She started it." Jessica was panting with the effort of trying to wrench her arms away from him. "Her shoulder still hurts right? I want to see how loud she swears when I punch it."

"And then we'll see how black your eye is." Jessica looked at him disbelievingly. "Trust me, she can hit hard."

Jessica raised an eyebrow. "You know from experience?"

"Yeah...long story. It was when we first met."

"I want to hear this story."

"It's for later."

Jessica stopped struggling for a moment and looked up at him. "What's your real story? You know, why you're a Destined One?"

Kyle felt—and looked—surprised. "I thought I told you all," he said nervously. *Oh please, oh please, don't let her pick up on the fact that I—*

"You just skated over all of the stuff. What's your real story? What's your connection to the Empire?"

"Long story," he forced himself to say, starting to feel sick.

She gave him a long, hard look, all anger at Cassidee

forgotten, before finally speaking. "You can't keep saying that forever."

She turned and walked away into the bedroom, Kyle not even having realized that he had released her arms. "Cassidee?" he called into the room, and she emerged, looking like she had just gotten ready to fall asleep.

"What?" she asked sharply, hands on her hips. "This better be important, I need a good night's sleep, soon—"

"Why do you treat Jessica like you do?"

Cassidee looked shocked at the question. "Because she's a pompous brat."

"No, she's not."

The small girl raised an eyebrow. "Oh? She sure comes off as one."

"Maybe, but only around you."

"Why would she do that?"

"Because she thinks that you're a cocky smart-alecky person who doesn't take anything seriously."

Cassidee paused, considering this information. "Okay. So can I go to sleep now?"

"No."

"Why not? You got your answer." As she turned around to head back in, he grabbed her shoulder. She spun around. "Let me go."

"No."

"Is that your only answer?"

"Quit being a brat, okay? You might think that she deserves it, but she doesn't. And we don't need any feuds between you two for the rest of the trip."

"I'll be kind to her, for you. And only you, got it? Only because we're friends."

"Try and be her friend."

"You're asking too much. Good night, Kyle," she said, before brushing his hand off her shoulder and going back into her room, closing the door in his face.

He wanted to ask why he was asking too much, but he knew that it would be pointless. When Cassidee didn't want to talk, she wouldn't talk. Perhaps she would be more sensible in the morning. *Quit kidding yourself,* he chided himself. *You know Cassidee too well to believe that.*

It was morning too soon. Breakfast passed by in a silent blur, and before he knew it, Aiden and Corrine were showing them around town.

"So you said you're looking for Alex and Jonathan? Didn't Sarissa tell you that they were here the entire time, and were waiting for her next instructions for what to do with the Crimson Hourglass?"

"What?" The question came from all of them, genuine surprise on their faces. What was the Crimson Hourglass? And did this mean what Kyle thought it meant?

"So..." Jessica said, taking the initiative, "Alex and Jonathan aren't missing with their memories erased?"

Aiden and Corrine exchanged skeptical looks. "What do you mean? Where'd you hear that?"

"That's what Sarissa told us, she said for us to return them to the castle—"

"What? She wants them back at the castle?" said Aiden, her eyes wide.

"But they're not safe there," Corrine said, sounding thunderstruck.

"What do you mean?"

"What do you mean, what do you mean?"

"But this doesn't make any sense!"

"Finally we agree on something!" Aiden said excitedly to Jessica, who had spoken with a great agitation in her voice. "Come on, we'll show the hourglass to you—"

"—And show you Alex and Jonathan. Maybe they can make sense of Sarissa's message," Corrine finished.

They walked a ways until they were on the very outskirts

of town, where a lone shop stood. "In here," Aiden said, holding the door open.

Corrine bellowed inside: "Hey! Alex! Jonathan! You've got visitors!"

The shop was dark and musty inside, with no furniture or decorations. Aiden pushed open a door that led down to a basement, and the group descended the stone steps, which looked pretty clean and cobweb free, despite the upper floor.

They entered what looked like a laboratory, that had two beds, a couch, three computers, a table holding an assortment of food and papers that were all jumbled together, and a tall, magnificent gold hourglass that had blood-red sand. There were two people in the room: one person was a tall, young-looking man with glasses and dark red-brown hair that was tied back in a short ponytail, and the other was an even taller, probably-over-six-foot woman with a red-brown bob of hair. Both wore stained white lab coats over faded t-shirts and torn jeans.

"Aiden, Corrine," said Alex, nodding at them. "Who are these people?"

"Are they the Destined Ones?" Jonathan asked, pushing his tortoiseshell glasses farther up the bridge of his nose.

"Half of them," Aiden said. "Alex, Jonathan, this is Jessica Knight, Cassidee Scott, Kyle Hill, and their guide, Joseph Elphinstone."

"Nice to meet you," the twins said at the same time.

"Where's the other half of you?" Alex asked, picking an apple up off the table, wiping it on her coat, and taking a large bite. Kyle was reminded of Cassidee and her slightly rude table manners as Alex spoke through the mouthful of Granny Smith.

"Corey, Morgan, and Kevin are at Graystorm Asylum," Jessica said, not looking Alex in the eye.

"Hmm. I don't fancy being there," Jonathan muttered with concern, snatching the apple from Alex with a cross look and taking a bite of it himself. "Not a good place." He tossed the remains of the apple over his shoulder into the trashcan that was almost overflowing. "Why aren't you with them?"

"We came here to find you, restore your memory, and take you back to the castle," Cassidee said bluntly. Jonathan stopped mid-chew, and Alex spat out what was left of her apple into the trashcan. They said at the same time, with the same amount of shocking disbelief in their voice, "What?!"

"That's what we were wondering," Jessica said quietly, still looking at her feet.

Alex broke into a grin suddenly. "This is a joke, isn't it? It's all a joke?"

"No. Otherwise, we'd be with the others, helping them fight insanity."

Alex was frowning again. "Good point." She nudged her twin in the ribs with her elbow. "What do you think, Jonathan?"

He shrugged. "I do not know. But perhaps we can ask the hourglass..."

"It answers questions?" Jessica said disbelievingly, an eyebrow raised. "It's just an hourglass, isn't it?"

"Oh, no it's not," Alex said, placing her hand on it. "Otherwise, we wouldn't be charged with the proud duty of protecting it."

"It's the key to the past, present, and future."

"So it's like a Magic 8 ball?" Jessica asked, only to amend her statement at the twins' confused looks. "Never mind."

"Hmm...if it is comparable, yes then, I suppose so," said Jonathan. He too put a hand on the smooth glass that separated them from the red sand, which was completely on the bottom.

Alex seized part of the golden metal that surrounded it, and pulled it, so that the hourglass began to spin in a circle. "Come closer," she said, beckoning them.

As they neared, the area around them began to change, mutating until they were in a castle room. Sarissa paced nervously, her dress flapping around her ankles, and Hailey was sitting on some stone steps, staring into oblivion.

"What's going—?"

"Shh!" Aiden said, cutting off Jessica's question.

Sarissa finally stopped pacing and looked up. "The gap is growing stronger each day, Hailey. Do you think they'll make it there in time?"

"They have."

"So, they are there already?"

"Yes."

"Oh, good." Sarissa paused for a second. "I wanted so badly to tell them the real reason they were going, but I couldn't, not without threatening the safety of every single person in the Empire!"

"You were right to give them a false mission that would have them wind up in the same place. If they got to the Asilde Mountains, they wouldn't be able to get anywhere closer to the border."

"Ugh. Then why does it feel so wrong? I feel like I should have prepared them better! The powers of the Shadow Forest are about to break free, and if they aren't stopped, this could be Delaney Manor all over again, and the downfall of Justine—"

"Sarissa, stop," Hailey said. "You're right. It could turn out to be both of those things, and the probabilities of that are high. However, I have a feeling they'll be okay. History will not repeat itself, Sar."

"But those who don't learn from the past are doomed to repeat it, Hailey," Sarissa said, wringing her hands. "And what if we didn't learn? What if the Siege of the Asilde Mountains is going to happen again? What if—" her breath suddenly caught in her throat "—what if the *hourglass malfunctions*? Hailey, if that happens—if that happens—"

"Then they might as well be doomed," her sister said quietly. "You were right, Sar. We didn't learn. And we just condemned our only chance to defeat the Delaney curse, once and for all."

Alex tugged on Kyle's arm, telling him to step back, and when he did, the image wavered until they were back in the underground room, the hourglass still and motionless, all the red sand at the bottom. They all stared at it, more questions filling their brains than they had the entire mission.

Chapter 66: Creeper – Morgan

Morgan needed to find the doctors. It was critically important. Nightwatcher had taken over Graystorm, and she had to find out who Nightwatcher was.

Leaving Corey in her room, Morgan sprinted down the hall to Steele's office. He wasn't there. She turned around and raced down the stairs, toward the abandoned gym. Still, no one. It clicked into place in her brain, quite suddenly. The Tapestry. She had to go to the Tapestry of Decay.

Morgan turned on her heel, and rocketed back up the stairs and to the stairwell that led to the Tapestry. But...she didn't know how to get in. She had to say something in Latin...

Lightning—real lightning, this time—cracked outside and rain pounded the windows of the asylum. She ran up the stone steps, and kept running for what felt like forever until she reached a door at the top. Realizing that she had passed the door to the Tapestry, Morgan turned to go until she heard voices.

"Why can't we stop her, Cadenza? We've tried getting rid of her other personalities, but she just adds another one," Doctor Steele said on the other side of the door.

Then, something strange happened. The door wavered, like it was an illusion, and suddenly Morgan was seeing through it like she was looking into a pool. Steele was sitting on the floor of the bell tower, his head in his hands. Cadenza looked as defeated as Steele. She was still standing, but the evil look was gone from her eyes, replaced by a somber gaze that made her acid green eyes look dull.

In all respects, looking at them now, they were just normal doctors.

Normal *people*.

"We crossed the line we never should have crossed," Cadenza mumbled, staring out at the fierce gale that was whipping her blonde hair around her face.

"No one should," Steele said sadly. He lifted his head from

his hands, and Morgan saw a wavering image of someone who wasn't made of shadow. "It's all our fault. We never should have let her push us that far."

"Yeah, well, we were young and stupid. We wanted to take down Sarissa. But now that we've had so many years living under Nightwatcher's rule, what if we hadn't? What if we had just closed down Graystorm and lived for good in the Empire? None of this would have happened. Sarissa wouldn't have sent Fleur and those three poor kids here, where they'll lose their lives and before that, their sanity. They'll just become more reflections of her personality, more pieces in this chess game she continues to expand," Cadenza said.

"We can't fight anymore. And if we try and kill ourselves, she'll be here before it can end for us. We're trapped," Steele said. The doctors fell into silence.

Morgan backed away from the door. She still didn't know who Nightwatcher was, but she had learned a lot. Now she needed to find Corey and Kevin and tell them what she'd seen.

Morgan reached the hallway and was running back to the room where they'd been staying when suddenly she noticed a figure standing there. A figure with piled blonde hair and a familiar stained, faded pink shirt...

"Macy!" Morgan exclaimed.

"There you are!" Macy exclaimed, spinning on the spot and seeing Morgan. "I was gettin' worried, you all hadn't come back yet from this creepy place—hey, where are the other three?"

"I don't know—isn't there someone in that room?" Morgan asked, motioning to the entryway of the room Macy was standing in front of.

"Oh yes, there is! The poor dear's all tied up, too."

"Kevin!" The name burst out of Morgan's mouth and suddenly she was inside the room, trying to untie the rope that held his wrists together. Then just as quickly she was being pushed away from him, forcing her out of the room, as she yanked the duct tape from his mouth, and he was shouting something but she couldn't tell what.

"Corey?" Morgan asked as the turned around and saw the familiar figure standing behind Macy. Macy spun around too, but then said, "Child, that isn't Corey."

"What?" Taking a step closer, Morgan realized that it wasn't. She did recognize the figure, however.

"Trixie! I've been looking everywhere for you!" she cried, then cursed silently at herself. Trixie didn't exist. It was Waverly, really. And they shouldn't be looking for Waverly—or Trixie, it didn't matter.

Suddenly, Corey ran into the room and skidded on the floor like it was made of soap. "Morgan, it's not Waverly, Trixie exists, Morgan—" But something shoved her backward into the room where Kevin was trapped, and she could speak no more, despite trying to escape by ramming her shoulder into the invisible shield.

All of this swirled around in Morgan's brain, trying to process what Corey had said. "Trixie is real?" she repeated. Corey gave a frantic nod and then mouthed something else, but Morgan never figured out how to read lips.

Morgan turned back to Trixie. "You're real?"

A thin, strange smile appeared on her face. "Yes. I've always been real," she said softly. Morgan stepped sideways so that she could see Macy's face, too, which was flabbergasted. "Oh, that's good," Morgan said, filled to the brim with warm relief. "Now, you can help us get out of here."

"Wha--? You know this girl? Well, we need to get out of here, grab your brother and friend and let's go—" Macy began, but she never finished.

It happened so fast Morgan wasn't sure it had. All she noticed was the gleam of a blade and the crimson stain spreading across Macy's chest as the knife stabbed her heart. Morgan heard a scream so loud she was surprised to discover it was her own scream, but the yell was so harsh that it felt like her throat would tear.

When she lifted her eyes to Trixie, she saw the young woman holding the bloodstained knife in her hand, knuckles white, the thin smile still on her face. "Trixie..." Morgan gasped as she felt her knees buckle. "What? Why...?"

Suddenly, when she looked back at Corey and Kevin, who were both mouthing the same thing, she understood.

"*Nightwatcher*," she whispered.

Chapter 67: Soul Stealer – Corey

Poor, poor Morgan.

Corey felt tears burn her eyes. If only she could have warned her in time, then maybe the shock of seeing Macy dead at Trixie's feet wouldn't be as great. But now was no time to be crying.

Whatever force field that was holding her and Kevin in the room vanished, and Corey helped him stand up. They ran out into the hallway and stood behind Morgan, whose chest was heaving. Fresh blood was staining the bandages wrapped around her back. Her eyes were filled with confusion, hurt and, perhaps most abundantly, fear. Her hands, hanging limply by her sides, shook with horrible tremors. They had all thought that she had reached her breaking point with the shock therapy, and then Kevin's stabbing. Apparently, this was just another hammer swing brought down onto her head.

Trixie watched them with a wary expression, as if looking to see if they would attack her. Corey didn't know why, but something held her back. She knew that if any one of them charged Trixie right now, her knife would end up in their heart, just like Macy.

Trixie smiled faintly. "I'm guessing you want me to explain everything?" Her voice was calm, collected, like they were having an everyday conversation. This, added to her smile, blood-stained clothes, the dead body, and knife, made her look truly insane, which is what Corey should have noticed long ago...

There was neither assent nor complaint, so she went on. "It's a long story. A long, tiresome one. But thankfully, you already know most of it.

"It started when I was fifteen. I was your regular girl, going to school everyday and doing all my homework and hanging out with friends. The only exception was that I was rather bookish. I loved reading fantasy and horror and watching all of the movies where a mystical world is hidden inside your own. My infatuation with it grew into an obsession, an obsession I could no longer control. I started finding signs and clues that led me to believe that we housed a mythical world on our own planet. I became friendless and withdrawn. My grades slipped. My parents were getting more worried by the day: what was happening to their perfect daughter? Yes, they had always applauded my imagination and my love to read, but they were convinced that this was going too far. They couldn't see what I could.

"Finally, when I was seventeen, I found a portal. I entered the Empire, and stayed there for a month on my own, just traveling, no longer caring about my family. But, they followed me."

"Your family followed you?" Corey asked, interrupting Trixie's story. She was met with a piercing gaze that silenced her immediately.

"Yes, they followed me. They were in shock. They couldn't believe that what I had been searching for was real. So, they begged me to forgive them and let me take them home, and it would all be over and done with. But I couldn't agree with that. They wanted me to leave the Empire, the place I had been obsessed with finding.

"It started out as an argument, then an uncontrollable feud. I killed my parents, buried their bodies, and started off across the Empire, searching for what, I didn't know, but I would find something soon.

"That something turned out to be the Barren Lands, where the Okkultens live. Desdemona wasn't their queen yet, and they were few in number. But, I felt as though I belonged, which I hadn't felt for two years. It was a good feeling.

"The Okkultens told me that there used to be more of them, but they ventured into the Outside disguised as humans and were carted off to an insane asylum called Graystorm.

"Of course, I wanted to rescue them, because I felt like these creatures were my brothers and sisters. But they forbade me to go. They didn't want me to be captured, too. So I obliged. I watched them every single day, changing forms back and forth in the blink of an eye.

"I began to covet that power to change forms at will. I didn't like my body or my spirit anymore. I wanted to be someone else entirely. I was sick of being Trixie Jefferson, the seventeen-year-old girl who had murdered her parents after finding out she couldn't stay in a mythical world she had hunted for obsessively for a year. So, as compensation for not being able to give me their powers, the Okkultens gave me a new name: Nightwatcher.

"I liked it. They called me that name because I always stayed up late at night, watching the Barren Lands. They called me their 'guardian of the night'. But, it grew tiring, just to sit and watch every night. So, I started to explore. I began to find people and suitable places where I could conduct experiments. My new name was fine, but I wanted to leave the tiring body of Trixie Jefferson behind and find a new form that was more suitable for the name Nightwatcher.

"I returned to the Outside at night and the string of long, grisly, unsolved murders and disappearances that baffled the police began. I stole from multiple laboratories and experimented inside their halls, no longer returning to my Okkulten friends when moonlight waned and daylight approached. I was too busy. And yet, I kept missing something, some form of technology or some ingredient that prevented my experiments from succeeding.

"Then, the war started. The Okkultens were searching for me and blamed my disappearance on the queen, Odessa. The tensions were high between all of them, and then another name popped up again: Graystorm, along with Steele and Cadenza. I vaguely remembered the name Graystorm Asylum, and then I realized what I had to do.

"I had to make sure I was correct, though, and after some intensive research, I confirmed my suspicions. Graystorm was the testing site of a special kind of drug called Visdelues. It used to only make people really sick, but the doctors realized that there could be a greater use for it. Perhaps, to stop aging, create insanity, raise the dead, or even cause someone to change beings.

"So I waited for the war to die down, because Queen Odessa was obviously going to win. Her troops were too strong and solid. And then, I ventured to Graystorm and met with Doctor Steele and Cadenza for the first time. I promised them that I could take care of Odessa for them, and the rest of the royal family, as long as they allowed me to become a patient, and use the Visdelues they had. I told them that they would have to kill me at some point. And they agreed, because it would look too suspicious if I, a nobody, kept living forever. They took it themselves, and then used the Visdelues to wake me from my grave. But later on, they started working on something that I never heard about until it was too late: Jenika.

"They took an ordinary girl and turned her into the Okkulten queen. They used the Visdelues to change her human DNA into that of a super-Okkulten's. The Visdelues, combined with the Okkulten DNA, caused her to change her appearance, develop new powers, and lose all of the memories that made her Jenika. It was exactly the new kind of start that *I* wanted, and it should have been mine!"

Trixie was pacing now, in mad circles, twirling the knife in her hands like she was about to throw it at one of them. As her anger boiled up, everything about her grew darker, like she was turning to shadow.

"But no. I was already dead, and the Visdelues wouldn't work on someone who was *dead*! So, I had to aim for the next best thing. I channeled all my energy into becoming a soul stealer. I could steal a person's soul and possess that person, or else just control them by inserting a little bit of my soul into them. Sometimes, I let them keep their soul if they were dead, but the tiny part of my soul that let me control them kept them pinned to Graystorm.

"The Crystal Heart helped me achieve this. It was a rare

artifact, stolen long ago from the first Queen's armory by a man made of shadows. From it, he formed his partner in crime, a woman formed from shadow crystal. Together, they created plans for the Heart but never put them into action, never realizing what it could really do..."

"So the stories, about Doctor Steele being made of shadows and Cadenza of crystal are true?" Corey asked, butting in.

"Partially. They are descendants of the two thieves, so Steele can still morph into shadow and only Cadenza can truly control the Crystal Heart. But they are both human, or at least, 98.701%.

"Anyway, with Cadenza's assistance, I was able to wrangle the souls into doing my bidding. If I was to use a human body, however, I needed the Tapestry of Decay.

"The doctors were unwilling to let me enter, but caved eventually. It, like the Crystal Heart, was immensely powerful and not used correctly. So, I learned how to master it myself and sent the doctors through it as tests to see if it would work. It did, but only enough to make sure they followed my orders. However, they've been eluding my grasp lately and they need another trip through the Tapestry. I suspect the reason it hasn't fully worked on them is because they aren't fully human. A little control is better than none, I suppose. But lately, it hasn't been enough. The Tapestry, if used on a complete human, leaves it with some of my soul placed in it, if I haven't decided to possess that person. If I do decide to possess, however, their soul stays in the Tapestry while mine goes into their body. Trust me, it took a lot of tinkering and experimenting to be able to do this. But it was completed in time, before you 'destined saviors' arrived.

"I had heard about the Destined Brats long ago, around a camp fire at the Barren Lands. At Graystorm, I could finally build up an army against you little wretches, and I've been doing so ever since Paige and Bailey Harkrider stepped inside. I used to have a lot more people on my side, but Asana, Crystal, Paige, and Bailey were the only ones that were left when you arrived.

The doctors had started rebelling by then, and they were finding a way to rid the souls of me and chase them off to the other side, where I could never call them back. Asana thought that it was me handling her in the water contraption, but that was all Steele, blending into the shadows.

"And that woman from the town that lent you her room for the night? I possessed her too, though only briefly, to get a glimpse of you before you entered Graystorm."

"But what about Waverly? Is she still alive? She's not even here!" Morgan argued, her voice coming back to her.

"I wanted to trick your mother so she would drop her guard and I could steal her soul. I bargained with the Okkultens through my Nightmare Pool, and eventually I was able to reach through the water and suck her soul out of her chest. I returned it once the job was done, not because I wanted to, but because once you promise an Okkulten something, you can never break that promise."

Trixie let out a maniacal laugh. "I fooled you all! I manipulated you and used you, bending you to my will. And it doesn't matter now that you know who I am, because I still have something above you! No, wait, make that two things. One of them is your mother's soul," she said with an excited edge to her voice. "The other…is far more complicated to get back."

"What do you mean?" the three Destined Ones said at the same time.

Trixie looked at them with an excited expression. "Remember what I said about the Tapestry, that whoever went through it has a piece of my soul in them?"

They nodded, and then Morgan clapped a hand to her mouth. Her eyes were wide. Kevin's eyes grew larger too, then suddenly he was angry and called Trixie a pretty bad name, at which she only smirked.

Corey's brain felt like it was running through mud. But, she managed to piece it together, and when she realized the truth, she noticed that she wasn't really all that surprised. She looked up at Trixie with a dull expression on her face.

"What's the other thing I have above you?" Nightwatcher asked, grinning.

Corey answered with a plain voice, not giving away a trace of how scared she was feeling at the moment.

"Me."

Chapter 68: History Will Repeat - Cassidee

"'The hourglass malfunctions?' What does that mean?" Cassidee asked, the first one to break the silence. She looked questioningly at Alex and Jonathan, who looked just as puzzled.

"I...don't know. I don't know," Alex repeated. Her green eyes were wide. "I didn't know that it *could* malfunction."

Jonathan shook his head in agreement. "How would it, anyway? All you do is spin it, really."

"And the glass doesn't break—"

"—So the sand can't spill."

"Could you become trapped in a period of time?" Jessica asked, studying the hourglass carefully.

"What do you mean?"

"I mean, could you get stuck in the past? I'm not sure how, but if just stepping back out of the picture didn't work, how would you get back to your own time?"

Alex was now running her hands over the hourglass, as if checking for cracks. "Hmm. Possibly. We don't know a lot about this thing, even though we've been guarding it for nearly five years. We rarely use it."

"I don't think it's about getting stuck in the past," Cassidee interrupted. "Sarissa said that 'history will repeat itself.' That doesn't mean we'll be going to the Siege of the Asilde Mountains, whatever that was. It means that the Siege will be coming to us, again."

"But how does that involve the hourglass? I don't get it," Jonathan said, sitting down on the couch and running his fingers through his hair. He rested his chin in his hands and stared avidly at the hourglass, as if hoping it would tell him what this was all about.

"Well, can you first explain what the Siege of the Asilde Mountains is?" Kyle asked. "Then maybe we can understand this better."

"The Siege of the Asilde Mountains was one of the bloodiest battles of the Empire's history," Alex began. "It happened ten years ago. The Shadow Forest and the Okkultens banded together and completely cut off any connection between the Outside and Harlimoore. No one noticed for a few days, but when patrols guarding the portal started vanishing and never returning, we realized what was happening."

"So we sent out our militia," Jonathan said. "They didn't find any sign of an Okkulten or Shadow Forest Demon, so they must have been hiding. They wanted us to find what was causing the Siege. And what we found was the Gap."

"Gap?" Kyle asked.

"Yes. It's the only known border between the Empire and the demons of the Infernal Home."

"Infernal Home?"

"It's like Hell or the Underworld, whichever you prefer."

"It's where all monsters come from."

"And while we already had monsters in the Empire, the worst were in Infernal Home and we had no desire for them to get loose. Some of the worst ones are down there: Lilith, The Serpent King, Medusa, Princess Mallory—"

"What was that last one?" Jessica cut in.

"Princess Mallory," Alex explained. "She lived back when the Empire was still young, she was in line to be queen, but she practiced tons of black magic and was creating dark creatures left and right. She was waging war on the land and was ready to take it to the Outside and control everyone there. So, our army at the time barely managed to send her to the Infernal Home before her attack began."

"Anyway," Jonathan said, going back to the explanation of the Infernal Home. "You get the idea of what resides there. And the real trouble began when, perhaps the worst creature of all, escaped the Infernal Home through the Gap. The Necromancer."

"People started getting slaughtered in their sleep, and then their bodies were no where to be found. All we saw was blood on the sheets. And when we started fighting back, we saw our dead people fighting with the other army. It was an army of the dead."

"Harlimoore couldn't fight back," Jonathan said. "If we tried, we would be killed instantly. The Necromancer was taking his time, slowly going through all of us trying to gain total control. He never got that total control, thanks to Queen Justine Emerson."

"I feel like I've heard her name before," Jessica said, trying to page through her memory to find out who Justine was and where she'd heard of her.

"She's known by many titles. 'The Exiled Queen', 'The Ruler of the Southern Empire', and 'The Peaceful Destroyer' are her most popular titles," Alex explained.

"Oh! When I first came to the Empire, Waverly explained about her, but not much. She said that Sarissa ruled all of the Empire, except for the southern bit, ruled by Justine, the Exiled Queen. Hold on, aren't we *in* the Southern Empire?"

Alex and Jonathan exchanged a look. "Yes..." Jonathan said slowly.

"Then where's Justine? It doesn't look like there are too many places to live around here."

"Justine is dead. She died in the Siege after saving us all," Aiden said quietly from the doorway. Cassidee had forgotten and she and Corrine were just standing there.

"What? Then who controls the Southern Empire?"

"Sarissa, obviously. Why she didn't have Waverly tell you the truth, I don't know."

"How did she die?"

"Well...the Siege was getting really bad. As soon as the Necromancer gained control of Harlimoore, he was going to strike the Outside. I don't know why he did it this way; he could have struck the Outside quite easily without us noticing for a day or so.

"Anyway, Justine was suddenly just there one day. She just

came out of nowhere, really. We don't know how she got past the Shadow Forest, Okkultens, and the Necromancer. But she did. And the next thing we knew, the Necromancer was gone, the Gap had closed, the Shadow Forest had retreated, and the Okkultens were back in their land. But it came at a price. Justine was dead."

"It took all of her energy to banish the Necromancer to Delaney Manor as something that was weak and powerless, unable to escape except for an incantation that she made sure was never seen by any mortal."

"The Siege was over, but there were only a handful of people left, and a dead queen in their village. So they buried Justine in a nice grave, the best they could, and we slowly became stronger. We knew that if the Siege ever happened again, we wouldn't have another savior like Justine. We increased patrols and kept a 24/7 watch on the Gap, which was just a tiny dot in midair, like a speck of dust. But over time, its grown, and we don't know how to stop it. Do you think it has something to do with the hourglass? And that's what Sarissa meant by it malfunctioning?"

"Yeah, that's it exactly," cut in a voice from the doorway, sounding familiar but not belonging to Aiden or Corrine. Waverly stepped out of the shadows, sporting a few bruises and cuts but otherwise looking no worse for wear. The look on her face was dark and grim. "I have some news from Sarissa. It's about the others."

Chapter 69: The Cellar Ward & The Condemned – Kevin

Kevin grabbed his sister's wrist and yanked her up off the floor onto her feet, and Morgan grabbed Corey's wrist before they started running down the hall, trying to escape from Nightwatcher.

The hallway stretched on and on until it was surely an illusion, a trick Nightwatcher was playing on them. Morgan had let go of Corey's hand, but Kevin kept his right hand wrapped tightly around her wrist. His twin was clutching her lower back as she ran, and he knew that the pain from the stab wound must be killing her. He remembered how much his foot had hurt before Trixie had healed it—

Had she done something to his foot to hurt him? Or had she really helped it? He didn't know, but really, really hoped it was the latter, though that was almost so ridiculous it was laughable.

Foot aside, he felt a ton of remorse and regret rise inside him, and he heard Morgan hiss with pain through clenched teeth as she ran. He had stabbed his own twin in the back, literally. Thankfully, he hadn't done any serious damage that put her in a life-threatening situation—though, hadn't he done just that, now that they were running from Trixie? Wouldn't she be able to run faster if she wasn't in pain? And now they might all be killed because he had been brainwashed. It was a depressing thought, really.

He shook his head to clear his thoughts and just focused on seeing through the illusion of the endless hall. Because that's all it was, right? Just an illusion? There was a blank expanse of wall to the right, but if he was correct—

He yanked Morgan to the right as he turned and ran toward the wall. She gave a faint scream, sure that they were going to run right into concrete, but Kevin found himself tripping down a set of stairs. He heard Nightwatcher's scream of rage as they escaped her trap. He grinned, only to suddenly lose control of himself and fall down the stairs. Corey had collided with Morgan's back (he had heard the telltale growl of pain), and his twin had rammed into him, completely knocking away his newly regained balance.

The stairs underneath him were metal, and it hurt beyond words when he hit the rusted steel (especially his face—he must have quite a few bruises on his forehead by now). The three of them finally crashed at the bottom of the stairs trembling and shaking with exhaustion. It had been an extremely long day— but hadn't Trixie said that weeks had passed on the Outside since they had first entered Graystorm? Then again, that was Trixie's info. Maybe she had lied...

Corey was the first to stand up, and she looked around the room with large, frightened eyes. Her mouth hung open. "Oh no."

"What?" Kevin asked, nudging Morgan in the ribs so she would get off his back.

Morgan crawled off, grabbing the wall for support as she stood up. Kevin stood up and surveyed the room. Grimy white tile walls surrounded them, and beneath their feet there were cracked linoleum tiles, water seeping through it. Broken glass was scattered across the floor, glistening in the water. Rusted steel bars jutted a few feet in front of the back wall. Cages.

They were in the cellar ward.

"Where's this water come from?" Kevin asked, looking at the trickles of water that wove their way through the cracks in the floor.

"I think we're next to the pool," Morgan muttered. "Oh, my back. Corey, why are you so pale?"

"I was here, as Genesis, when I went through the Tapestry." Her already pale figure was sweating and trembling. "It was horrible. So...horrible. There were people in here, and..." She swallowed, and looked like she might vomit. She did not finish her sentence, but Morgan and Kevin got the idea.

"Where do we go? Trixie—I mean Nightwatcher—she'll be

here any minute now," Kevin asked, looking around the cellar ward as if a second stairwell might appear out of thin air if he looked in one place long enough.

"We'll have to either go into the pool, or stay here and risk it."

Suddenly, an idea—an impossible idea—clicked into Kevin's head. "Shadows!" he exclaimed. Corey and Morgan gave him appalled looks that both clearly said 'what are you yelling about?' "Doctor Steele! He's made of shadows, he might help us!"

Corey just shook her head. "That will never work."

But it felt like time itself had stopped. The water no longer ran through the cracks, and only Morgan, Kevin, and Corey could move. Everything had literally come to a halt. Corey had a look of disbelief on her face.

The shadows were sucked into the corner right in front of them, forming the shape of a man, while the excess curled atop his head like a sleeping black snake. His green eyes glinted in the dark with what Kevin guessed was supposed to be an edge of malevolence, intended to frighten, but his pale figure was sweating slightly and his frightening figure was wavering.

"Doctor Steele...can you help us?"

He looked startled by the pleading question, but at the same time he understood. They were fighting the same enemy, and this was their last chance...

He shook his head. "I can't help you."

"Yes you can! Come on! We're both fighting her, and I know you want her gone, I know you do," Kevin said, starting to feel angry and hopeless at the same time. Doctor Steele was the master of Graystorm Asylum, there had to be someway he could help them...

"Get your mother's soul back. And you need to break the connection between you and her. Use the Threshold of Madness." But before they could plead for him to continue, he had turned back to shadow and retreated.

"That's all? How do we get our mother's soul back? How do

we break the connection between Corey and Trixie? And what in the name of all things crazy is the Threshold of Madness?" Morgan blurted out.

Kevin glanced at the water in the cracks. It was beginning to move again. They only had a few precious moments before Nightwatcher found them—

"I know! I know what the Threshold of Madness is!" Corey said enthusiastically. "Steele told me about it, when I was Genesis. He said...he said..." Her face fell as she recalled his words. "I need to become insane. I need to lose my grip on everything in order to cross it."

"What?! No, you can't!" Morgan yelled.

"I have to. And I'll get Fleur's soul back, I promise. Just...hold her off."

Corey sank to her knees and buried her head in her hands. Kevin imagined her going through every frightening thing that had happened to them here, all the times she had almost died or lost her hold on everything. Now, she needed to let herself slip.

It looked painful. It only took thirty seconds as Corey summoned forth everything she could think of that would break her, snap her sanity clean in half—

Her shoulders started to shake. Tears of every emotion she had ever felt surged forward and down her face. All the feelings she had ever kept bottled up inside of her, all the times she forced those tears down because she *couldn't* break, came forward now because she *had to* break. It was a sacrifice of the worst kind.

Sick rocketed up her throat and she made no attempt to restrain it. It hit the linoleum floor and immediately seeped into the cracks. She coughed up a few specks of blood, her throat burning. She felt herself losing consciousness, drifting away...

Kevin was on his knees, and didn't remember them giving out. Morgan was in the same position he was, watching Corey with wide violet eyes, tears running down her face.

Corey gasped, her shoulders shaking, but she never looked

up. Then, she became quite still, and her hands fell from her face. Morgan crawled over immediately and pressed her fingers to Corey's wrist.

"Yes, there's a pulse..." she murmured, tears running down her face thick and fast, but now tears of gratitude.

Footsteps thudded down the stairs, and suddenly Trixie was there, knife in hand, her glare threatening to slice them apart, knife or no knife. Then she caught sight of Corey.

"Did she finally break, then?"

"Yes."

"Good. That's one I don't have to bother with." Nightwatcher turned to Corey and hissed something in Latin.

Corey felt herself being called. She rose up on unsteady feet, but was surprised to see that she didn't have a real body. She was just smoke, wisps of smoke...was she dead? No, she wasn't, hadn't Morgan just checked for a pulse? And wouldn't she be at the Threshold of Madness right now?

Then it clicked. Ah, yes. This was the part of Trixie inside of her.

She looked around. It was mostly black, and Trixie stood there in the darkness, arm held out to her, looking like smoke herself. Corey turned her head and saw other souls lining up behind her...just fragments really...but they didn't stay lined up. They swirled around her, never staying in one place, whispering to her:

"Beat her."

"Come on, fight it."

"We'll help you with the Threshold of Madness."

"We will bring the soul to you."

"You just hold her off here."

Corey felt her vapor-like body move toward Trixie. She nodded, and the Condemned vanished like the wisps of smoke they resembled.

Chapter 70: Threshold of Madness – Corey

The bridge she had seen when she was Genesis flashed in front of her eyes, its image becoming firmer until it didn't waver at all. She was really there.

Corey looked around. It was all black. She, herself, was painted gray like she was in an old black-and-white film. It was completely silent. A gentle wind blew around Corey's ankles, urging her on.

She eased herself forward, not sure what was coming next. All she could see was the bridge stretching in front of her. She looked around, now at the beginning of the bridge, which swung gently back and forth, hanging on rope. She stepped on tentatively, testing the weight of the bridge with her shoe.

As her foot touched the bridge, images flashed in front of her eyes, none of them lasting longer than a tenth of a second. Desdemona's face, leering at her like she was an inch away; spiders; a woman—herself—stepping into a lake with her arms held out; the glowing Tapestry of Decay; a spinning Crystal Heart, blackness swelling at its center; Macy's startled face as the knife hit her heart—

Corey immediately lifted her foot off of the bridge. It had only been a blink, but she had seen some of the things that had frightened her the most. She looked around, hoping that there was another way to do this. But there was no exit. Corey told herself to lose control again, and put her full weight on the bridge, closing her eyes.

The images blinked in front of her like a strobe light put up to maximum speed. Things that she had been scared of when she was little flashed in front of her eyes—clowns, her stuffed animals (she was never watching *Poltergeist* again), Death's scythe and the matching Halloween costumes with that scary mask—and then all of the images she had just seen, flashing so quickly that it looked like a movie edited oddly—

Inexplicable, un-namable noises crowded her ears and overloaded her senses. She told herself to keep putting one foot in front of the other, and forget everything else. Clear thoughts could not make it through her head. She was more scared than she had ever been before...it was like she was trapped in her own mind...

Suddenly, it was over. Silence filled the air again. All the images cleared from her mind, but even though her eyes were still closed, she saw only one thing happening...

She was walking farther and farther into a lake, wearing a dress of white, arms held out in front of her like she was a zombie. Her eyes were closed in the images, but she knew what she was doing. Corey felt the water pulling at her and soaking her...up to her waist...her ribcage...her armpits...her neck...

Corey's eyes snapped open, and so did hers in the water. The water was up to her chin, but she could see the other side. And when she took a confident stroke forward, abandoning her walk down into the watery depths, the image dissolved, and she found herself on the other side of the Threshold of Madness.

Chapter 71: Frenzy

"Fleur?" Corey whispered, kneeling down to look at the battered form at her feet. She had just crossed onto the other side of the Threshold of Madness when she saw the pale, skinny, small body, balled up into a tiny circle. Pale hair hung down the woman's back, and her frame was tiny and shaking.

Corey placed her gray hand on the soul's shoulder, and it rolled over. Fleur's terrified face stared up at her. "It's okay, Fleur, I'm taking you back." But where was Fleur's body? Still at the pool? How did she get back there? Turning around, Corey stared across the bridge, back where she came from. Could she survive a return trip?

Trixie motioned with her finger for Corey to step forward. She did, against her will. But the Condemned said they would help her...exchange their souls for hers...people she had never met, sacrificing themselves so she could complete hers.

She knew that Kevin and Morgan could not see her, judging by the confused looks on their faces, as Trixie seemingly beckoned empty air. Stepping forward, Corey felt her left arm extend out until it was fully in front of her, palm up. Trixie set the knife—still stained with Macy's blood—in her hand.

Corey expected it to fall through her fingers, which looked like they were made of smoke, but it didn't. Morgan gasped; Kevin stared at the floating knife in astonishment. Of course, they couldn't see her, and a knife hovering by itself in midair must be a shock. But Corey saw realization register on their faces—they knew that it was part of her soul holding the knife.

Corey felt her feet and body turn in the direction of Morgan and Kevin, arm with the knife in hand still fully extended. She moved their way. *No...Trixie...don't make me do this...not to my friends...*

The trip back across the Threshold of Madness was just as

painstaking as the first, but it felt slightly easier, perhaps because she had done the same thing before. Fleur was weightless in her arms, perhaps because they were both souls and they weighed almost nothing. Morgan and Kevin's mother was completely unconscious.

As she walked into the blackness again, on the other side of the bridge, she felt Fleur growing heavier in her arms like a dead weight. Corey did her best to keep the fully-grown woman supported. She arched her neck back, looking at the endless nothingness that stretched above her. She found it difficult to breathe—her chest tightened, and cramps spread rapidly across her arms and legs. She hoped this meant what she thought it meant—they were returning to their bodies.

Morgan swallowed hard as the knife neared her. She could imagine Corey slowly walking toward her and Kevin, forced to drive the knife into them, forced to watch herself cut up her friends—

Hurry up with mom, Corey.

Kevin was aware of Morgan grabbing his hand as the hovering knife neared them, right between the two of them. Who would its first target be? Kevin could practically hear Trixie going over it in her head: Morgan or Kevin? Which twin first?

All he could hear was his heart pounding in his chest. A cold sweat broke out on his skin, trailing down his face and neck and arms, mixing with Morgan's perspiration at their joined hands. He could feel her shaking. Tears slipped down his face. They had failed. Nightwatcher was going to win...

Fleur was back in her body, but Corey was still a soul. "What the—Corey? What happened?"

"You can see me?"

"Yes, yes, you look a little gray, though—"

"No time to explain, Fleur, but you were right about Trixie, we have to stop her from killing Morgan and Kevin—"

Fleur was already on her feet and dashing into the cellar ward.

Corey's head turned to the doorway that led to the pool. The knife trembled in her hand. Trixie was looking at the door too, along with Kevin and Morgan. What had their attention, they weren't sure. Was it a noise? Was it—could it finally be--?

"Don't you dare hurt my kids!" an irate Fleur yelled, running into the room.

"Mom, stop!" Morgan and Kevin yelled at the same time, and their mom obeyed just before she ran into the knife hovering between her and Trixie.

Fleur glared at Nightwatcher. "I knew it. I knew that it was you. But you put that doubt in my mind, and I let it grow until I thought myself wrong. I trusted you…and now you have my kids at knifepoint with their friend holding the weapon that could kill them both," she said, her voice shaking, almost spitting with rage.

"Yeah? And what's wrong with that? I'll have Corey kill Morgan and Kevin, then you, then herself—"

"Don't you dare say their names like that—in that casual way!" Fleur, no longer caring about the knife ran forward, about to attack Trixie. She had reached her breaking point.

Corey ran past Trixie as Fleur, apparently alone, burst into the cellar ward. She breezed past her other soul and to her body, which was still crouched on the floor. She yanked her other self around the waist and instead of their bodies colliding, they slid into each other and unified. Corey maintained her grip on the knife, but no longer felt the pull of Trixie's control.

Corey leaned backward, trying to keep the knife level, but it would never work, not without the knife slipping, and then everyone would notice—

But she got her distraction when Fleur ran forward toward

Trixie as if to tackle her. Corey yanked the knife down before Fleur ran herself through with it and fell backward into her body.

It felt like everything clicked into place, and suddenly she was propelling herself onto her feet and forward, fully in control of herself now, as she drove the knife all the way through Trixie's heart and out her back, the hilt buried in Nightwatcher's chest.

No blood bloomed across her shirt, though. Nightwatcher began to laugh as Corey's eyes widened while she tried to calculate what she did wrong.

Trixie grinned at the surprised girl and said: "I'm not alive."

Corey felt her face grow warm. She would have face-palmed, if they weren't in a life or death situation. Of course. She had been so ready to end this battle; she had forgotten that Trixie was no longer alive, and a knife couldn't hurt her.

So, what could?

"Go upstairs," she hissed at Kevin. "Go through the pool room and up the stairs. Find the Tapestry."

"What about you?"

"Go! Just go!"

Kevin grabbed Morgan's wrist and the two of them ran out into the pool room. Fleur looked at Corey for a split second with a questioning glance, and she was answered with a miniscule nod. Fleur ran after them, leaving Corey and Trixie alone in the room, Nightwatcher looking wary but not going after the three runners.

"The Tapestry can't beat me," Nightwatcher hissed, drawing the knife out of her chest and pressing the tip of it just above Corey's heart. "I've been through that thing before, and it doesn't effect me like it does you."

"I know. You made sure that you were immune to everything here, as long as you had a bit of control over something else. A person gave you the most control. But you said that you lost every soul you had on your side, and the doctors are

301

free also."

"But what about you? Aren't you still under my control?"

"No." Nightwatcher raised an eyebrow. "I was able to cross the Threshold of Madness without getting lost in everything it was throwing at me. And I came back across with another soul. I beat the one thing that no one else has. And when I united myself with the rest of my soul, I triumphed over that part of you that was inside of me. You no longer have any control."

Corey turned and ran past Trixie, shoving her out of the way. Nightwatcher stumbled, almost dropping her knife. By the time she had righted herself, Corey was already up the stairs.

"How do we get in? I forgot!" Kevin shouted at Morgan as they ascended the steps to the Tapestry.

"I...have...no...idea," she panted, clutching her back again.

"Oh, come on! Doctor Steele, just let us in!"

To his surprise, the door immediately formed and opened. "Wow," Morgan muttered, running inside.

The Tapestry hung on the wall, looking as frayed as ever. It glowed an electric green.

"What do we do now?"

Instead of running to the Tapestry, though, Corey ran till she reached the very center of Graystorm Asylum, where the Crystal Heart was kept. Cadenza was in the room, watching the Heart with interest.

"Cadenza!" Corey barked as she entered. The doctor spun around, about to yell something, but Corey cut her off. "I need your help. Can you move the Heart?"

Cadenza looked like she was fighting a battle of wills. She looked like she wanted to try and kill Corey right then, but after she opened and closed her mouth several times, she finally choked out: "Is this about defeating her?"

Knowing that she meant Nightwatcher, Corey nodded. "You need to take the Heart to the Tapestry. Can you do that?"

Cadenza blinked, then nodded. "Go up there. It will only take me a minute."

Corey turned and ran out of the room. She hoped that Steele had let Kevin and Morgan in...

Morgan waited by the Tapestry with Kevin and their mom, wondering what in the world was going on and what Corey's plan was. The door burst open, but it was Cadenza who appeared in the room, holding the Crystal Heart. Corey, who quickly shut the door and turned to Cadenza, ignoring the shocked others, followed her. "Can the Heart absorb the energy of the Tapestry?"

"Yes, but why?"

"Never mind why, just do it, she'll be here any second!"

Corey hurried over to the other three and sat down next to them, her breathing heavy. "I really, *really* hope this works."

"What're you planning to do?" Fleur asked. "What is Cadenza doing here? How can we help?"

"There's nothing anyone can do anymore! We just need to hope and pray that this plan will actually work!"

Cadenza had turned the Heart to face the Tapestry, and the glowing green light of the object seemed to be edging toward the Heart. It was slowly being sucked to its center, where it stayed, slowly growing bigger and bigger and the Tapestry, dimmer and dimmer.

Nightwatcher opened the door to the Tapestry of Decay and ran inside, looking for her prey with wild eyes. She would not let them escape again.

Cadenza pressed the palm of her hand against the back of the Crystal Heart, and the green energy of the Tapestry shot out of it, hitting Trixie's chest just as she realized what was happening. The crystal was rapidly spreading over her, encasing her.

She screamed with rage or pain—Corey couldn't tell which; maybe it was both. Trixie caught Corey's eye and pointed at her, about to yell something, but then the crystal covered her head, leaving her immobile.

The green energy from the Tapestry pulsed inside of the new crystal case for a moment, and then the fissures began to appear, spreading all over—

"Run," Cadenza said simply.

Fleur, Corey, Morgan, and Kevin fled the Tapestry of Decay and ran down the stairs, across the hall, and down another stairwell until they were at the front doors of the asylum. They heard the explosion as the Nightwatcher's soul shattered, along with all of the power of Graystorm Asylum—

They were outside in a heartbeat, running away from the crumbling asylum faster than any of them had run before. It was finally over, and they weren't stopping until they reached the Empire again.

Chapter 72: Fade to Black

"What about the others? Are they okay?" Cassidee practically yelled, running toward Waverly.

"They're fine. They're on the Outside," she replied, her face giving away nothing.

Cassidee gripped the Okkulten's shoulders. "Are you sure? Why do you look so somber, then?"

Waverly brushed away Cassidee's hands. "I told you, they're fine. Sarissa said for you to go home."

"What?" everyone else in the room said simultaneously.

Jessica and Kyle had run up to Waverly as well and were looking at her with a curious expression on their faces. Joseph just looked at her and shook his head.

"She said for us...to go home?" Jessica repeated slowly.

"Yes."

"As in, back to the castle?" Kyle butted in.

"No. She means for you to go home. Back to where you came from."

"What?! Why?" Cassidee blurted. "After everything we've done for her, we aren't allowed to see Morgan and Kevin and Fleur or at least get an explanation about some of the things that are going on here?"

"I'm just passing on the message. She also said that there was something she and Hailey had to figure out."

"Yeah, and we can help her!" Jessica said indignantly. "We're the Destined Ones—we need to know what we're running into! I'm sick of being in the dark all the time, literally and figuratively."

"Me too," Cassidee said.

Kyle nodded his agreement. "It isn't fair that we're saving everyone from something we don't even know about. We aren't soldiers, and Sarissa isn't our Commander. You can't just drive us blindly into a line of fire."

"Hey!" Waverly shouted. "That wasn't my decision. I'm just

passing on a message!"

"And how'd you get to the castle and back here in only a day?" Jessica asked, acting as though she had not heard Waverly.

"I didn't. I got a message from Hailey after I escaped the Okkultens."

"How'd you get a message from her?"

"She sent me a dream. She can do that, but it uses a lot of her strength and takes all of her concentration to do it. She wasn't able to explain anything to me—just that I needed to tell you guys to go on home."

"Did she tell you anything else?"

"Yes. She said that you fought valiantly, but it isn't safe for you to go back to the castle. You'll need to go to the Asilde Mountains, where you can go home."

"And what about Morgan, Kevin, Fleur, and Corey? Do they know not to come back?"

"They'll find out, it's just not safe, the castle's under attack by some dark, malevolent force—"

"Where's it coming from? We need to go help!" Cassidee insisted.

"No, you can't help! You only destroy darkness at its root—"

"Then where's it coming from? We can go destroy it!"

Waverly ran her fingers through her hair and sank down onto the couch, looking flustered. "It's not that simple."

"Then explain! Tell us what's really going on! And we're not leaving until you do!"

"No. I'll explain everything that I know, but only when the other three are present. They need to know the truth too."

They were on the Outside again, in a small town called Asilde. The reunion was full of tears and exclamations, both of the groups happy that the other one was safe and all alive. Their stories were exchanged in a small pub that was almost empty. Morgan had been given medication for her back, Cassidee had her arm in a sling, and they all listened with rapt attention as Corey explained in full detail what happened at Graystorm Asylum, including how the Doctors had finally died and gotten the freedom they had wanted. Then Cassidee voiced their own story with an edge of excitement to her voice, despite how scary it had all been.

Through it all, Waverly was silent.

All the food was gone by the end of the story exchange. Brains were overloaded with information and everyone was feeling tired and sluggish. But they all wanted to know the truth.

"So, Waverly," Corey said, taking a sip of water. "Tell us everything."

Waverly looked at her with a stern eye. "You think the truth will free you?"

"We don't care what it does, we want to know everything. You lied to us before, and again and again, but now we need the truth. We deserve it," Cassidee said angrily.

Waverly ran her fingers through her hair again and sighed. She looked utterly defeated. "I know you do." And she began her story.

"A long time ago, Hailey received a prophecy stating that six people would save the Empire from the Darkness. Somehow, the information leaked out and spread around the Empire. Chandra betrayed Sarissa and the rest of the Lauruna family, and formed the Nightmares. Odessa was dead, and everything was in an uproar.

"Then, when you guys arrived, Sarissa knew that she would need to give you fake missions that would still get you where you needed to go. It's not that she didn't trust you—it's just that she wasn't sure if the castle was being bugged. She knew that you would figure it out eventually."

"Well, 'eventually' might have been too late!" Jessica exclaimed. "What if we had failed?"

"That was what Sarissa finally realized, only a week ago. She fell apart, thinking that she might have thrown away her last chance to save the Empire."

"But save it from what? It wasn't anything on our missions, was it?"

"No. She didn't read the signs correctly. You were supposed to save the Empire from the Necromancer, bringer of the Darkness."

"But I thought he was in Delaney Manor?" Morgan cut in, remembering Cassidee's story.

"Yes, but he needs to be defeated, once and for all. He murdered the last of the Delaney family and is steadily growing stronger. He'll break free himself unless you stop him."

"But we're only kids! A powerful, magical queen could barely defeat him and we're supposed to?!" Kevin said incredulously.

Waverly just shook her head. "I know how insane that seems, but three of you defeated a diabolical circus of great magical strength and the other three destroyed the monster of Graystorm Asylum. Imagine the power you would have if you worked together."

"So this was like a test run? Seeing if we were the right ones to save the Empire?"

"No! That's not it at all!" Waverly jumped to her feet and banged her fist on the table. "You aren't listening, any of you! What you did wasn't a test. It was a mistake."

"Oh, and that's supposed to make us feel better? We went out there and risked our lives because Sarissa *read the signs wrong*? We could have died, but we didn't, and now you're telling us that we aren't listening!" Jessica yelled, on her feet. She was seething with rage. "What if we don't want to listen anymore? What if you're just lying to us again? Because you know, they're getting worse and worse each time you try to deceive us!"

"This isn't like that! You asked for the truth, and you're getting it!"

Jessica breathed hard for a moment through her nose, and then angrily sat down in her chair, almost knocking her glass of water over. "Go on then," she said roughly, angrily gesturing at Waverly to continue.

"The real prophecy said this: *The first generation to fail, the next to succeed. They will save the Empire from the Darkness, they are destined so. The stars tell their story, marked out long ago. They will trial and suffer, they will pay a price. But they will save everyone.*"

"What the hell does that mean? 'The first generation?' Is that how you knew to find us?" Kevin said after a moment of almost palpable silence.

Waverly nodded. "The first generation was the first six Destined Ones. Fleur Smith, Aiden Knight, Corrine Knight, Joseph Alan Elphinstone, Jordan Hill, and myself, Waverly Desimara."

"Waverly? Aren't you fourteen? Who's Jordan? And Kyle—why does he have your last name?" Corey asked.

"I'm actually thirty in Okkulten years, but don't change the subject," Waverly said.

Jessica told Corey, Morgan, and Kevin about Jordan, and then looked to Kyle for the answer to the last question. "Well?"

He shifted uncomfortably in his seat. "He was my cousin."

Everyone's jaw dropped, except for Waverly's.

"So you knew about the Empire?" Cassidee asked after another tense moment of silence.

"No—well, not everything. I'd heard about Desdemona and Graystorm and some about Delaney Manor. I had never heard the prophecy, and I didn't know what I was destined to do. I would have told you, honestly, if anything I could say would help."

"But you've know for all these years..." Cassidee said slowly. "And what about my nightmares? You couldn't have told me about them, what they were about?" Kyle just shook his head.

"It's not that simple."

"Would you quit saying that?! I'm sick of hearing that, it just wastes words when we could be hearing the truth!"

"Let Waverly explain the rest."

"Fine." Cassidee turned her back to her friend and glared at Waverly with narrowed powder blue eyes. "But one question: Corey and I aren't related to anyone on that list. Explain how you knew to come to us."

"Joseph is the great-uncle in your family that no one talks about, because he was supposed to be crazy and then disappeared when he was a teenager," Waverly said briskly. "Anyway, we failed at the Siege of the Asilde Mountains, like the prophecy said. The Necromancer was banished to Delaney Manor, and has been growing stronger ever since."

"And that's where we come in?" Morgan asked again. Waverly nodded.

"That's all I know."

"So...what do we do next?"

"Huh?"

"I mean, 'what do we do next?'" Morgan repeated. "We need to fulfill this prophecy, don't we, and get back to our normal lives?"

"Your lives will never be normal after this."

"So? At least we don't have to be constantly living in fear. We can either defeat the Darkness, or we can let you all die. We don't care."

"It's not just us that will die. Everyone on the Outside will perish too. Make up your mind, then. I don't care right now, either. So go on home."

"Wait...how do we explain everything to our parents?"

"Sarissa modified their memory, like she said in the beginning. You guys were never gone. It will all be normal for them."

"But...when is this going to end?"

"I don't know," Waverly said, shaking her head. "But I can send you guys home, and you can rest. I'll let you gather your bearings, your wits, and then it will be time to return to the battlefield."

Jessica and the others exchanged looks. Together, they already felt stronger. The truth wasn't better than the lies, but it was something. "All right, Waverly," Jessica said. "But just know something." Waverly nodded and leaned closer. "We aren't doing this for the Empire anymore. We're doing this because we feel like it's the right thing to do, and we need to save our family, and our friends on the Outside. The only thing we're doing for you is finishing this mess that you started. We aren't returning on anyone's orders. We'll regroup when we want to. And you aren't splitting us up again. We'll get our information ourselves. We're smart enough, believe it or not. And once we defeat the Darkness, the Necromancer, you'll leave us to live in peace. Got that?" Waverly nodded. "Good. Pass that on to Sarissa, okay?"

Jessica stood up and faced the others. "Come on guys—let's go home."

Epilogue: Warning

"Chandra's here, Sarissa."

"What, Hailey?" Sarissa asked, looking up from her desk in the grand hall.

"Chandra's here."

"What do you mean, 'Chandra's here'"? Sarissa asked again. *Chandra can't be here,* she thought frantically. *If she's here, that means…*

"I mean, 'Chandra's here.'"

"You mean, 'here' as in 'here in the castle?'" Sarissa persisted, hoping there might be a way to dissuade the truth.

"What else would I mean, dimwit?"

"Hailey!"

"Sorry, Sar, couldn't resist."

"So…is she really here?" Sarissa asked, drawing in a deep breath.

"For the final time, Sar, yes!"

"Okay! No need to snap. But, how do you know?"

"She's in the doorway."

Sarissa whirled around to see her sister standing in the doorway, her black hair blowing around her thin frame, a crackle of electricity around her.

"You finally noticed me," she murmured, not looking up.

"Chandra—but—how…?"

"Sarissa, easy, I'm not here for you. I'm here for Hailey."

Chandra stepped forward, striding across the hall, her cloak flapping around her ankles. She lifted her hand into the air, as if gripping something. Hailey rose too, clawing at her throat, and she was pressed against the wall as Chandra kept walking toward her.

"Chandra! Stop!" Sarissa rushed forward, and was about to move her hand to produce some sort of spell, when Chandra's hand flew out first, knocking Sarissa off her feet and into the wall.

"I won't hurt you, Hailey," Chandra said calmly, her voice placid but shaking a little. "Not unless I have to."

Hailey groaned and struggled against Chandra's grip, who now actually had her hand around the seer's neck.

"See for me."

Sarissa stood up, not daring to believe what she had just heard Chandra say. Nothing about Chandra's voice was sarcastic, babyish, or the slightest malevolent. It was calm, steady, like she was holding a normal conversation.

"Huh?" Hailey managed to say.

"See for me."

Chandra's grip tightened.

Sarissa could only watch.

"It's...in...the...doorway..." Hailey croaked, now seeing past Chandra, into the doorway through which she had just arrived.

"Who's there, Sarissa?" Chandra asked, not daring to take her blue eyes off Hailey.

Sarissa looked at the dark doorway. "No one," she said shakily. "Chandra," she called, turning to her sister. "What is this about?"

Chandra ignored her. "Who is it, Hailey?"

"I...I..." Hailey tried to shake her head.

"Is it Justine?" Chandra asked.

"N...no..." Hailey could barely take in the breath for words, but not because of Chandra's grip. Something fierce was in the doorway. It wasn't moving. She couldn't tell who it was.

"Is it Belladonna?" Sarissa asked, her eyes still locked on the doorway.

Hailey couldn't speak now, she just shook her head.

"Then...who..." Chandra couldn't speak now, either. Darkness was spreading over the hall, and everything was turning cold. Chandra turned her head, looking for anyone in the dark, but there was only Sarissa, her eyes on the doorway.

"I can't see anyone," Sarissa whispered. She felt its presence. It was dangerous. It wanted blood. "But it's here." She whipped around to face Chandra. "Did you bring it with you?"

"Shh!" Chandra snapped. She turned her attention to Hailey, who was struggling to speak.

"Who is it, Hailey? Tell us, dammit, who?!"

"It's...it's..." Hailey croaked out. Chandra was shaking violently.

"Chandra," Sarissa whispered.

"It's...right...behind...you."

Chandra dropped Hailey and spun around, a ball of black electricity forming in her hand.

The darkness that had consumed the hall had suddenly vanished, being sucked into the doorway. It was still oddly cold, though.

"Hailey...Chandra...look," Sarissa stammered, her ice blue eyes fixated on the doorway.

Chandra stared at it, and her eyes grew wide. The shadows had formed the shape of a man, but it wasn't Doctor Steele. The specter was still completely shadow.

He reached out an arm, pointing at Chandra, before vanishing into thin air.

Warmth and sunlight filled the hall again.

It was as if the man of shadows had never existed.

"Gone...?" Hailey whispered.

Chandra looked around the room. "I think so."

Behind their turned backs, the shadows formed a sinister face.

The face grinned.

How good it was to be back.

About the Author

Leigh Kenyon is a 14-year-old teenage girl who loves horses, writing, reading, and anything that is scary or has to do with ghosts, demons, and haunted buildings. She lives in Florida with her parents, a dog, and four cats who enjoy interrupting her writing time.

She has published one book prior to this--The Zebra Riders, which is of a different tone and is available on Amazon.com.

www.ingramcontent.com/pod-product-compliance
Lightning Source LLC
Chambersburg PA
CBHW052031260626
47163CB00005B/133